Dreams of Fire

Maple Hill Chronicles 1

By Elizabeth R. Alix

Pullman, Washington
USA

Printing History: First Edition, October 2015

Edited by Jacqueline Beam

Cover illustration and layout by Victorine Lieske, http://bluevalleyauthorservices.com/

ISBN-0578171228

Supported by Palouse Digital Press, Pullman, WA USA: palousedigitalpress.com

To Austin, my first, best reader.

Chapter 1

"YOU'RE nothing without me," Geoffrey said with the amused, pitying expression that he'd worn for the last year. White-faced, holding back tears, Marianne Singleton silently threw her clothes and personal possessions into boxes. He pretended to watch a ballgame on TV, while she struggled to and from the elevator multiple times, hauling her stuff out of their fancy apartment. The doorman was the only kind person, watching her things and holding the doors for her while she loaded the car. She'd run that day, and she was still running. She shook her head to escape the memory.

The mid August heat of the Hudson Valley shimmered off the roof of the house, and humidity made the air heavy. Sweating, she emerged from her car and slammed the door. She stood at the edge of the weedy front yard, noting the peeling paint and general air of neglect.

How disappointing, was her first thought. When Mrs. Thomas said it needed a little work, I wasn't expecting something from *Sad Homes and Empty Lots*. I hope the inside isn't as shabby as the outside. All the same, she amended, maybe it'll be the perfect disguise, and Geoffrey won't look for me here.

The realtor was supposed to meet her at eleven to give her a key, but there was no one here. Marianne wondered briefly if she'd mistaken the day or the place, but a quick check of her note said she was in the right place. Sweat trickled down the small of her back as she stood there. Rolling down the windows of her mother's car, "the Flea"—her car now, she supposed—she gave poor Oscar some air before carefully working her way past the peeling picket fence and along the overgrown path to the front door. The movers were on their way up the Thruway now. What if the lady from Gloria's Valley Homes and Properties didn't get here in time? Marianne could just picture her furniture heaped on the weeds in the yard or left in the street of the cul-de-sac.

1

As she fumbled in her pocket for her cell phone to see if she could find the realtor's number from her previous calls, a car came down the street and stopped in front of the house.

It was a sleek silver Lexus. She tensed, and her heart started to beat a little faster. Geoffrey had a silver Lexus.

The car rolled right up to the curb by the house, but to her relief, a plump, middle-aged woman in a well-tailored, fire engine red linen suit got out and hustled up the walk.

"I'm sorry to be late!" she huffed, trying to hitch a smile on her face in spite of her sweatiness. "Mrs. Thomas told me you were coming today only yesterday."

"Oh," Marianne said in some confusion, "I told her last week I'd take it. I thought…"

"Mrs. Thomas, bless her heart, is a little forgetful," she said cheerfully. "She's had a some trouble renting this place." The woman fumbled in a capacious handbag and came up with a key on an old piece of string with a worn paper tag.

"Really?"

"No matter, it's a great little place. You'll love it!" After a few moments of fiddling with the key, she managed to turn it. The realtor threw her a hundred watt smile. "The lock works. It's just a little tricky. It turns just fine when you find the sweet spot. You'll figure it out."

A plaintive yowl came from her car. Marianne said, "Just a sec. I think my cat is overheating." She dashed back down the steps and waded through the vegetation again. "Sorry, Oscar. Let's get you inside. I sure hope it's cooler."

Struggling with the carrier through the long grass back to the front steps, she made it up through the open door into the shade of the house. Sadly it was not much cooler inside. If anything, the air was stale and smelled of old house: musty, dusty, and somehow, like old people. She'd had a neighbor in the city whose apartment smelled like Ben-Gay, Eau de Toilette, and cabbage. This place held the stillness of long emptiness. "Miss….?" Marianne called. Her voice fell flat in the gloom and heat. It was as if the woman had vanished.

A sound from the back of the house indicated that the realtor had gone into another room. Marianne put the cat carrier down on the hardwood floor and Oscar yowled and rattled the cage door in complaint. "Sorry, mister. I'll let you out in a minute."

Marianne followed the sounds to the kitchen and met the realtor bustling back in her direction. "I was just making sure the electricity was turned on. You'll have to run the water a little to clear the pipes and you might want to open some windows."

"When was the last tenant here?" Marianne asked in dismay, noting the dust and particularly deep silence of an unoccupied house.

"Oh, about August I guess." The woman said vaguely, rummaging in her bag.

"Just a couple of weeks then?"

"No, last August," the agent said quickly and handed her the key. "Here's the key. Mrs. Thomas said you would be paying reduced rent in return for cleaning up and painting and getting the yard in order."

"Yes, she mentioned something like that. I can't really afford the full rent…" The place had been empty for a year? That explained the dust and the yard.

"That's just fine. If you have any questions, you can call the office," the realtor said sweetly. "We have a handyman who does basic maintenance and repairs. If you need more, let me know, and I'll refer you. You have the number? Good. I have to get on to the next appointment. You can swing by our office on Main Street and drop the rent check later today." She waved a hand over her shoulder.

"What's your name? I'm sorry I didn't catch it." Marianne stood on the front steps watching the realtor head back to her car.

"SueAnn Talmadge. Just call the office, if you need anything!" The car door was already shutting, and the Lexus nosed out of the cul-de-sac with a sleek purr.

That was weird. She'd left with almost indecent haste. She must be very busy, thought Marianne, or she didn't want me asking any more questions. Well, one didn't examine the horse's mouth when one needed a gift like this so desperately. The house and yard needed some serious TLC, so the deal of doing work in exchange for reduced rent might not be the bargain she'd thought it would be. Grandma Selene said her friend needed the favor as much as Marianne needed to get out of the city, so she'd just have to take it.

The metal door to the carrier shook loudly as Oscar yowled again. "Sorry, Oscar! Okay, mister. Here you go." She squeezed the catch on the door, and the big, orange and white tabby pushed his way out into her waiting hands. She stroked his fur and rubbed his chin as he enthusiastically bumped his head on her hands.

"Well, Oscar, this is our new home. The shelter booklet said you shouldn't go out yet. So maybe when the movers come, you can go in the bathroom or something."

Oscar gave her a look that said, "We'll see about that" and strolled off to explore the room waving his crook-tipped tail. Marianne watched him fondly for a moment as he sniffed the floor and padded around the empty room.

"I'll go and get your stuff." She went back out to the car to retrieve the litter box, bags of litter and cat toys, food, dishes, and miscellany and brought them inside. He had almost as much stuff as she did, she thought with amusement.

She headed down the little hallway to the back of the house and found a bathroom halfway down on the right. A quick look showed that there would be room behind the door for the box so she filled it with litter and put it there for now. Later she'd have to find a better place, so she didn't end up with kitty litter toes after every shower. Running the bathroom sink tap, she waited for the spurting, slightly brown water to run clear before filling a dish with water and putting it under the pedestal sink near the litter box. The toilet looked clean, so she relieved herself as well.

Her cell phone rang in the silence, making her jump a little. She glanced at the number and answered, "Hi, Mom. I just got here."

"Oh good, the car got you there in one piece. I was a little worried. How is the house?"

"The car was no trouble at all. Thank you for letting me use it indefinitely. The house seems really nice. I don't think anyone has lived here for the last year, though. I'm so glad it was available."

"Your grandmother will be pleased this worked out for you. Be sure you call her and thank her."

"I will, Mom! The movers are going to be here any minute so I've got to go. Thanks for calling."

"I'm just glad you're away from the city and that awful man."

"Me too, Mom." She hung up, sighing at her mother's choice of words. When Marianne had gotten married, her mother had been so excited for her. Because she seemed to be marrying up in the world, her mom had overlooked some of Geoffrey's faults for a long time. Though, to be fair, she had been very supportive of Marianne for the last year.

Maternal reassurance completed, Marianne returned to the front door to start her tour of the new house. She kicked off her sensible sandals and flexed her toes as she pushed back her wavy brown hair, its curls going wild in the humid heat. Extracting a rubber band from her pocket, she quickly made her hair into a ponytail, pulling it through only halfway on the last turn to get it up off her shoulders. Her shorts and white tee shirt clung to her curvy frame, and she pulled at the fabric to release it from her damp skin. She took a deep breath, let it out, and took a long critical look at her new surroundings.

The living room was the first room to the right inside the front door. The walls were a faded pink Marianne hoped she'd be allowed to repaint. At least they weren't peeling, but it was like being inside a Band-aid box. August sunlight filtered through the dusty front windows onto a dull hardwood floor. Maybe with some work, the wood would clean up. The proportions of the room were decent, and there was a fireplace on the center of the south wall with a beautiful ornamental mantle piece and trim around it. A set of floor to ceiling built-in bookcases flanked either side. She smiled as she imagined her books and knick-knacks filling the shelves. She could picture her grandmother's rosebud china tea set and a vase with a sprig of flowers in pride of place on the mantelpiece.

To the left of the front door a narrow staircase led up to a second floor. She decided to explore that later. The stairs to the basement were behind a door next to the stairs going up. She chose to save that dark musty space for later too. A funny little pantry or walkthrough closet with rows of narrow shelves painted a dark gray-green color came next. There were a few dusty jars webbed together with spider artwork. Grandma Selene had a canning room like this in her old house. It would make a great place to store things.

The kitchen was decorated in hearty red and yellow paint, bordered by a strip of faded wallpaper with a repeating design of an old fashioned coffee pot, and sugar and flour containers up near the ceiling. It was 'vintage,' she told herself, and good enough for now. She really hoped Mrs. Thomas would let her repaint as part of their arrangement. At least the fridge was humming and cold inside. There was an electric stove, and an ancient dishwasher squatted under the counter. She leaned over the double white enameled sink to see out the window and spotted the huge old maple tree behind the detached garage.

The swinging door with the little round porthole window in it reminded her of the house where she'd grown up, and she smiled. She remembered being five and swinging the door endlessly, listening to the music of the hinges, until Dad had come along and shooed her outside. The noise must have driven him crazy, she thought nostalgically, but he just sent me outside to play instead of yelling. It was one of her few memories of him. He'd died of pneumonia not so long after.

She pushed past the door into a square dining room papered in dull blue and white stripes. It had a look of faded grandeur in its modest proportions, and she could imagine dinner parties with people in fancy cocktail dresses. Her antique wooden table with the carved legs would fit in here with one leaf in it and still leave room for her sideboard-cabinet. Sunlight came in through two small windows on either side of a door onto the driveway.

Another door opened onto the central hallway from the dining room with the bathroom across the hall. She stepped in again to really look at it. The tile was gray-blue and white around the tub/shower and up the walls to waist height. The plain white plastic shower curtain would have to be replaced with something more interesting when she had a chance. One inch white tiles on the floor were outlined in dark brownish-black grime under the radiator and along the walls and made her think of old New York apartments from the twenties. A wooden medicine cabinet hung over the sink with a beveled mirror, streaky where the silver was peeling. Her toffee brown eyes gazed at her wan reflection, and she made herself smile for encouragement.

The back of the house featured two bedrooms down a squeaky, wooden hallway. Although they were painted in drab colors, cement grey and institutional green, they were spacious, and she picked out the bigger of the two on the left for her own. She walked around listening to the echoes of her footsteps and felt a momentary tightening of her throat. Someone had been sad here in this cement gray room. She walked through the dark green room and felt less sad, but she didn't like the light from the windows as much. It would serve better as an office. Mrs. Thomas had to let her repaint.

She was suddenly conscious of the empty house around her, and the hair on the back of her neck and arms prickled a little. She felt a little frisson of apprehension. There were almost no noises coming from outside. In New York City she'd always been aware of the activity of people behind every floor, ceiling, and wall. It was like living in an anthill, but comforting. She'd forgotten that in the country there was a lot more empty space. Mostly she liked that, but in this house it felt eerie, shabby, and sad somehow, like the previous people had cried a lot or been unhappy. She wondered who had lived there before her, and why Mrs. Thomas had had trouble renting it out.

She tried to shake the mood. The place was going to need a lot of work, a new coat of paint on everything for starters. The windows all needed cleaning, each one accompanied by the solid iron bulk of a radiator underneath. The floors all needed refinishing. She sighed again and shook herself a little, trying to imagine how it would look in fresh colors with her furniture in different arrangements. It was a good thing she was not one of those people who wilted in the heat. Summer was her favorite time of year.

She made a circuit through the house again, this time opening the windows wherever she could to let the fresh air of the day into the house. The heavy feel faded as the sounds of insects buzzing in the flowers wafted inside with a rich, warm summery smell. The aroma brought back happy memories of visiting Grandma Selene and Grandpa Clare in the summers as a kid. They were only a couple of towns over in Vandenberg and Marianne remembered driving through Maple Hill on the way to other places. Maple Hill was also home to the best ice cream shop in the world as far as she was concerned. Now that she lived here she could go to Jonathan Sweets' ice cream parlor any time! She grinned and put it on her list for later after the movers were done.

Oscar finished his tour of the downstairs about the time she did, and she watched his crooked tail disappear up the stairs to the second floor. She looked at her cell phone. The movers should be here soon, so she couldn't leave. She could bring the rest of her stuff in from the car, though. She was just about to go out the front door when she hear a frightened meow, and Oscar came racing down the stairs, an orange and white blur. He bolted for the carrier in the middle of the floor and disappeared inside.

"What happened to you?" Marianne murmured as she knelt down and peered inside. Oscar was bushed up as big as he could be, looking twice his normal size. She reached in and stroked his fur, murmuring soothing noises until he relaxed enough to let her gather him up into her arms. His heart beat a frantic tattoo against her hand. "Goodness! What did you meet upstairs? Is my big, tough guy, city cat afraid of the country? It's okay. We'll clean up in here and make it our home. We'll chase out all the birds and squirrels in the attic, and you won't have to be scared anymore," she cooed lovingly.

Oscar had come from the animal shelter after her divorce. Geoffrey wouldn't have liked him, but she had always wanted a cat. She remembered with a smile how he'd calmly sat and stared at her while she looked at all the other cats in the white cement room. Finally, when she'd looked at him, he'd put his paw between the cage bars and given her a look that said, " What took you so long? Get me out of here!"

And that was that.

She cradled him until his fur settled back down, and she put him back into the carrier and shut the door. Carrying it to the bathroom, she put the cage in the bathtub for now, opened the metal door to give him free rein, and closed the bathroom door behind her.

Chapter 2

RUARI Allen closed and locked the doors of his workshop reluctantly. It was a little before nine o'clock, and he was due at work on the dot. He wished he had enough orders to keep him working at his bench all day. He got up at five usually to take advantage of the coolness of the day and spent a few blissful hours shaping and caressing wood into furniture and a variety of objects. He'd inherited his grandfather's talent for woodworking and learned as much as he could at the old man's knee. He just wished he could make a living at it.

Right now he was in the middle of making one of the sculptures that came into his head occasionally. They happened a couple of times a year and were so compelling that he had to drop what he was doing and focus on them until they had worked themselves out of his system. If he didn't, his commissioned work suffered or ended up with elements of the sculpture in them that his client hadn't requested. Better to follow his subconscious muse and let it have its way.

Sighing, he climbed into his old white truck and headed to Gloria's Valley Homes and Properties. Fixing mechanicals and doing odd jobs for the manager paid the bills at least, even if it didn't make him happy. Fortunately he had only himself to look after. Still single at thirty-four, it was a bone of contention with his parents. He'd managed to convince them he wasn't gay. He simply hadn't found the right woman to settle down with. His younger sister Erin got along better with them than he did, though she wasn't married and "producing" yet either. Better that she was living at home with them than him.

It had been another long and boring summer fixing things, and he wondered if his life was going to go on like this indefinitely. It was not a happy prospect. He'd lived in Maple Hill all his life, and though he loved its familiarity, it was confining. He was in a rut and didn't know how to get out of it.

He pulled into a space in front of the converted family home on

Main Street that now bore the flowery sign for Gloria's and stepped inside. His boss, SueAnn Talmadge, was already bustling around and looked at him with an irritated glance. Her tailored red linen suit practically glowed with energy. She must drink high test, full caf coffee from the moment she got out of bed, he thought. Or maybe she had an untreated manic condition.

Thrusting a printout at him she said, "You're late. It must be nice to be able to sleep in without a care in the world. I've been here since seven. Here's the punch list for the day. Keep the billing straight, will you? You've been sloppy, and it's a bitch to straighten out."

Bitch. Right. He thought it but didn't voice it. She wasn't likely to find another handyman as good as he was, so in spite of her complaints, she paid him a living wage. All the same, he didn't usually rock the boat. Looking at the sheet, he saw it was another day of annoying repairs and paint jobs and sighed quietly.

"The Thomas place on Violet is being rented finally so make sure you stop by and turn the electricity on first thing and bring the key back. The tenant moves in at eleven today, and I need to let her in," SueAnn said briskly.

The Thomas place on Violet? He thought. That's been empty awhile. He vaguely remembered a brief occupation by a lady from the city a year or so ago. She hadn't stayed long. He remembered having to go fix something there but couldn't for the moment remember what it was. That bugged him. Usually he remembered places by the things he'd had to paint or fix.

"What are you waiting for? Get going!" SueAnn urged him out the door.

"Keep your shirt on, Talmadge," he murmured resignedly. "I'm on it."

Kelly threw her arm over Sarah as they lay under the sheet together and whispered, " 'Morning, I love you."

"Mmmm," Sarah replied sleepily.

"I'm going running before it gets too hot. See you at breakfast." She kissed her partner's cheek before slipping out of bed.

"Love you too," Sarah mumbled and rolled over. She could never understand Kelly's energy so early in the morning. Seven-thirty was early enough for her. None of this five a.m. stuff.

Two hours later Sarah woke again to the sounds of Kelly clattering in the kitchen below. She'd had a vague, disturbing dream, the details of which were rapidly fading. She was familiar with most of Maple Hill's inhabitants, either from growing up here or through the law firm where she worked, and sometimes had premonitions about them. Often they weren't very clear, though, which was frustrating. This time there was an impression of a woman running away from someone through a field of little purple flowers. That could fit pretty much half the population of Maple Hill. She sighed and figured she'd just have to wait and see what developed.

Her thoughts turned reluctantly to the big meeting this afternoon at work. Smith, Walgust and Brown, the biggest law firm in town, often handled the Ballister family's affairs. The Ballisters were arranging to purchase a historic piece of property. She wasn't looking forward to it much since the Ballisters treated her at arm's length rather than as the solid, respectable lawyer she was. In spite of that, she was always professional and bent over backwards to do her homework and prepare each document and case thoroughly.

She'd grown up in Maple Hill, gone away to law school, and come back a competent professional. But somehow, it was hard to change people's minds about her. Being openly gay was becoming less of a problem even in the small Hudson Valley town, but her ability to converse with the dead was just too weird for most people. Even though it had proved useful on more than one occasion. People often focused on the wrong things, she shook her head sadly. Mercifully, the partners who ran the firm trusted her and respected her judgment, or else she'd never be able to keep her job.

The doorbell sounded a Big Ben chime, and Marianne hurried to the front door. Two burly men were standing on the stoop, their maroon moving van with "Burgdorf's Moving Service" in black and gold fancy lettering was parked at the end of the cul-de-sac.

"Hi! You found the place okay?" She said with a shy smile.

"Yes, ma'am," the taller of the two rumbled in reply. His maroon shirt had the name "Joe" stitched on the left breast.

Geoffrey would never have stooped to fraternize with blue-collar working class types, but she sympathized with their jobs and always talked comfortably with them when he wasn't looking. It had been a source of annoyance for him. She smiled again more broadly. "It's pretty close to lunch time. Do you want to eat something before you unload? It's a little cooler inside, and there's a bathroom if you need it."

Joe hesitated a moment then said, "That would be very nice." Without a word the other man, "Bobby," returned to the truck and brought back a couple of paper bags and thermoses. Marianne invited them in and went out to her own car to grab her own lunch.

The movers were sitting on the floor in the living room with their backs to the north wall, consuming large shapeless sandwiches. Marianne smiled at them politely and sat down on the floor as well to eat her lunch. They ate in awkward silence for a little before Marianne said, "Did you have any trouble getting up here?"

Joe answered, "Nope. GPS got us here fine. No traffic on the Thruway to speak of." He ate a few more bites and surveyed the living room. "Nice looking house," he said noncommittally.

"Thanks. It seems very nice," she replied.

"It's not yours?"

"Well, I'm fixing it up a bit for a friend of the family in exchange for rent."

He looked around again, chewing thoughtfully. Marianne surreptitiously observed the men. Joe was somewhere between thirty and fifty and had a touch of the Old World about his features,

14

someplace Slavic maybe, she thought. She could imagine him growing up with a stern Polish or Ukrainian grandmamma and smiled at the fleeting image of a big, strong, doughy woman, arms crossed over a faded flower print dress and floury apron. Joe's arms were bulky and solid, looking like he could bench press three hundred pounds without breaking a sweat.

Bobby was younger, maybe in his thirties, and was possibly of Irish descent, given the vivid red stubble over the crown of his head and freckles across his face. His arms looked less bulky than his partner's, so she guessed he was the wiry type. They both looked like they'd grown up in the moving business and moved a lot of stuff in their lives.

"You going to be here long?" Joe asked between bites.

"I don't know. Maybe until I find something better." She'd learned to banter a little with tradesmen over the years, but this seemed unusually personal.

He considered this, his features impassive. Bobby, who had been silent all this time, nudged him slightly. Finally, Joe shrugged a little. "You mind if we give you some free advice?"

Marianne raised her eyebrows and said, "Okay. I guess not."

"We been in this business a long time, seen a lot of places. We've developed a feeling about things. Mostly they don't feel like anything. Sometimes, though, they don't feel…right. You look like a nice lady, and we'd hate to leave without saying anything. But, this place doesn't have a good feel to it."

With his pronouncement, Marianne felt her stomach drop a little. It was uncanny having him voice her own uncertainty. "Really? How bad do you think it is?" She asked in dismay.

He shook his head. "Not *Poltergeist* bad. Just doesn't have a good vibe."

"Like people cried here a lot," she said quietly.

They both nodded.

She sighed unhappily, "Well, unfortunately, I don't have a lot of choices. I can't really go back to the city and can't afford a lot of rent right now."

"So, you still want us to unload your furniture?"

"Yeah," she said with another sigh. "Thanks for the advice. Let's hope it's not too bad. Maybe some fresh paint and cleaning will do wonders." She tried to sound cheerful and optimistic. Joe shrugged again and let it go.

The men finished their lunch and went out to the truck again. Marianne's temporary relief at leaving the city gave way to misgivings. Surely they could be wrong, she hoped. Besides, what choice did she have? Geoffrey had signed the divorce papers in June, and although he'd stayed with his mistress, he'd taken to following her around. He pestered her by email and text. She'd put up with this for six weeks and finally got sick of it. He never threatened her exactly, but it was so unnerving the way he seemed to be spying on her. Leaving the city seemed the only way out. This favor for a friend was perfect in many ways. Her name wasn't on any papers, either as a buyer or a full-fledged renter, and Grandma's friend seemed to need a tenant.

The front doors were propped open, and the early afternoon was spent moving her possessions from the truck to the house. Marianne gave the movers each an extra hundred from her limited cash supply to stay and help her set things up. The heaviest piece by far was her old upright piano. She'd inherited it from her mother when she'd moved a couple of years ago to a retirement community. Geoffrey had complained at the time that it was old and ugly and not worth much and begrudged the space it took up in their apartment. It was one of the few times she'd insisted they keep something he didn't approve of. She loved the old thing and had memories of taking piano lessons in grade school and practicing on it. She'd had some vague idea of getting out some of the easy-play piano books stored in the bench and starting again. Well, now that she was in her own house she could do that without her ex's disapproving eye on her. At least she'd had it tuned back in December before everything in her life went crazy. She hoped it had kept its tune during the move.

The piano fit best in the living room on the west wall, and the boxes slowly accumulated around it. After an hour, the house was full of boxes and furniture, and the truck was empty. Joe and Bob set up the bedroom furniture and moved the couch a couple of times, so she could see it in different places. She left it under the front windows after a particularly hard look from Joe and guessed they were out of patience. Their shirts were plastered to their backs and underarms and in a deep vee down their chests while sweat dripped off their brows.

On the last trip in Bobby handed her a clipboard with dog-eared papers jutting out untidily. "Here's the receipt, Miss Singleton. Just sign here and here. You can write a check for the balance."

She dug around in her purse and found her checkbook. "Thanks again," she said. "Have a safe drive back to the city." Bobby gave her a sympathetic look. "Good luck, miss." When they left she felt like her only allies had gone.

Her ears buzzed with the sudden silence of the post move frenzy. She stood in the living room surrounded by carefully labeled boxes and suddenly didn't want to deal with unpacking just yet. It was 3:30 and time for ice cream. Letting Oscar out of the bathroom, she told him she was going into town. She had to fiddle with the key in the front door to get it to turn but finally managed it.

The sidewalk led back to town past four houses on each side. These houses were set well back from the road like hers and shaded by huge, old maple and oak trees. It was peaceful summertime, and she relaxed.

A faint stirring like a wisp of smoke awoke after a long slumber. Neither alive nor completely dead, it drifted through the house trying to pull itself together. A woman had come into the house, young and newly vulnerable. She was in danger. Must warn her...

An orange tabby cat watched its progress with lashing tail and slitted eyes.

Chapter 3

VIOLET Lane intersected with another residential road, Primrose Street, and Marianne turned left and headed a block up to Main Street. The town of Maple Hill was small enough that many businesses were on Main Street or within a block of Main. It looked much the same as she remembered from her childhood trips. There was a decent sized co-op grocery with organic and bulk foods, a post office, a hairdresser, the bank, a couple of cafes, two B and B's and a motel-inn, a department store, a new age goddess store with a colorful display of jewelry and semi precious stones, and a hardware store, among others. Moderate street and pedestrian traffic enjoyed the sunny day.

Before she it slipped her mind, she walked down to Gloria's Valley Homes and Properties. It was in an old two-story family home with a white picket fence and a neatly trimmed lawn that looked like a green carpet. The receptionist was busy on the phone, so Marianne took a moment to enjoy the air conditioning and cool off. She sat and wrote out a check for the security deposit and first month's rent. A man somewhere in his thirties, wearing a dark green polo shirt, emerged from a back room. There was something open and honest about his strong cheekbones and square jaw. His straight sandy brown hair was a little too long and strayed into his eyes. Clearly, he was sweaty and harassed, a slight frown creasing his forehead.

Oh my, Marianne thought, as her stomach did an unexpected flip.

He didn't look past the reception desk that separated the public and business spaces. Instead he grabbed a cluster of papers, murmured a fleeting, "Thanks," and disappeared back through the door. Marianne supposed he was another salesperson for Gloria's.

The phone clicked back into its cradle and the woman at the desk said with a polite smile, "Hello, can I help you?

Marianne stopped staring, swallowed and said, "Yes." She handed her the rent check, made sure the receptionist knew what it was for and

18

left.

She indulged in a brief fantasy of the cute guy looking up over the receptionist's desk, seeing her and smiling like he thought she was pretty. She sighed and thought, that'll never happen.

Jonathan Sweet's shop was across and down a ways from the co-op, and the tables with umbrellas set out front on the sidewalk were crowded with people. It was Thursday, so she supposed that the city people were beginning to come up for the weekend. Maple Hill was not as posh as Rhinebeck or as populous as Poughkeepsie further north, but it got its share of weekenders.

A cluster of local teenagers blocked the ice cream case, giving Marianne some time to adjust her eyes to the interior. It was mostly as she remembered: white painted walls covered with vintage posters, signs, and pictures of Gibson Girls with dark hair piled on their heads and impossibly pinched waists, eating ice cream. Dark wood paneling covered the lower three feet of the walls. There were perhaps a dozen small tables with round-seated wood chairs on a red and white square linoleum floor. The cold case contained fifteen flavors of hard ice cream made locally and now included a handful of sugar free and yogurt varieties for people who wanted to pretend ice cream wasn't fattening. Marianne never ate faux-cream herself!

The chatting and laughing teens departed, and she took advantage of the lull to approach the case and look over the flavors. Ah, yes, they still made her favorite, coffee Oreo, and she ordered a double scoop in a dish. The scooper was a young woman with ice cream smears up to her elbows. When Marianne was little, the owner, Jonathan, still came in. She remembered him as a dark, curly haired man with a passion for ice cream and a ready smile.

She ate inside appreciating the air conditioning and savoring each bite of coffee Oreo. It was every bit as good as she'd remembered it. Life wasn't so bad if you could have delicious ice cream. Currently her ex didn't know where she was and wouldn't for a long time. Okay, the house felt a little old and sad and needed paint and some repairs, but it was otherwise very low rent. She didn't know anyone in the city who paid so little. She would have to check with Mrs. Thomas, but she bet she could choose her own color scheme and make the place homey and comfortable in no time. It was a good thing her research position was slow in the summer. She might just be able to repaint most rooms before school started, and the requests for research began to come in again. She might even be able to give some thought to designing her own class. NYU and Columbia, not to mention other places, did more and more online courses, and she might be able to convince one of them to take her on.

She finished the last bites and headed out the door. She wanted to see what paint colors were available at the hardware store and to get some groceries before she went home. Brown's Hardware was just up the street on this side according to the sign hanging over the sidewalk. A little bell hanging on a string on the inside handle jingled as she entered. She didn't remember coming in here much as a little girl. Sometimes her Grandpa Clare had needed something and would come here to get it. All she remembered was a jumble of things and endless, dark, gloomy aisles with squeaky floors.

Now, the interior was better lit, though the floors still creaked at every step, and the floor to ceiling shelves held a variety of merchandise common and obscure. There were a number of patrons, mostly men in work clothes, including a man examining a wall of small plastic wrapped packages in the electricals aisle. Everyone seemed to know what he was looking for.

"May I help you, miss?" A young man behind a large wooden counter asked.

"I'm here for house paint. What do you have?"

"Let me show you," he said as he led her to one side of the store. When she couldn't specify a color, he handed her a few palettes of compatible colors and asked what she needed.

"I'll just take the color samples for now, " she said hastily, feeling a little overwhelmed. "I'll need some time to think about them."

"We're open Monday through Friday nine to six and Saturdays till three," the young man informed her.

"Thanks, I'll come back before then." She retreated onto the hot sidewalk again and slowly made her way back toward the co-op. Paint cost so much, and there were so many things she was going to need. She would have to bring the car back to carry it all. Geoffrey's settlement with her had been reasonably generous, but she was going to have to nurse it carefully to be sure she didn't blow through it. He'd been so horrible during the whole divorce process. She hadn't wanted anything from him, only to get away and be done with him. But her lawyer appealed to a more practical part of her and had insisted she take a decent sum to live on. There would come a time when she had to be completely self-sustaining, but she needed time to regroup and get there.

She stepped into the cool shade of the local co-op market and got milk, eggs, some bread, and a couple of cans of cat food for Oscar. The Maple Hill Community Co-op had been a staple of the community since she was about ten. It boasted all the usual whole foods, bulk foods, international, and fair trade products but also had added a meat counter, local flowers and produce in season, and a deli with a nice assortment of foods made on the premises. As she wandered the aisles looking at products and reading labels, she heard the PA system click on, and a male voice, heavy with ennui and steeped in profound weariness, say with a deep sigh gusting across the mic, "Scott, you have a call on line one. It's *hhher*." And the mic clicked off.

Startled, Marianne looked around to see what people's reactions were. There were a few other startled looks and several smiles. She happened to be near the deli and saw the two women behind the counter stifling their laughter.

A few minutes later the PA mic switched on again, and a cool British voice reminiscent of James Bond in his Roger Moore phase said, "Good evening, shoppers, and welcome to the Community Co-operative. There is a sale on hair and body care products on aisle eight and don't forget to get some dinner for the missus. Have a delightful evening."

Marianne smiled at the thought of James Bond reduced to PA announcements at a co-op and headed to the deli counter. It was a good idea to get something here and not have to cook tonight. The two women were grinning broadly as a small line of customers queued up. She got a container of curried chicken salad and Mediterranean green salad with lots of vegetables, olives, and feta and headed out again into the heat.

Outside the co-op, Marianne decided to call her grandmother

before heading home. She sat in a convenient wire chair and dialed.

"Hi, Grandma, it's me, Marianne."

Grandmother Selene's warm voice with its trace of upper crust British curled into her ear and made her smile. "Hello, dear. Did you get to Maple Hill all right?"

"Yes. The house is lovely. I think it will be perfect. Thank you so much for finding it for me."

"You're welcome, dear. Lily will be glad to know it suits you. It's so nice to know you live only twenty minutes away! You must come visit when you have a chance."

"I will, Grandma. You'll have to come over when I get settled and see the place."

"I'm sure it will look lovely. It's been such a long time since I was last in that house."

"You've been here before?" Marianne was surprised.

"Yes, a long, long time ago. It was quite an elegant home inside and out."

"It needs quite a bit of work to become 'elegant' again. I would love to come visit you."

"If you come tomorrow, you'll just catch me. I'm going to be away for a few days visiting an old friend."

"I'll come tomorrow for sure. My place won't be ready for visitors for a while. But maybe I'll have a housewarming party."

"That would be splendid! See you tomorrow, dear."

Marianne hung up, still smiling. Grandma had the ability to make her feel warm and loved whenever she talked to her. She sighed. It was time to go home and face some boxes before bedtime.

The walk down Primrose and Violet was shady and cooler now with late sunlight streaming through the trees, and she paused at her gate to look at her new house. The shadows hid the need for a paint job and softened the overgrown vegetation. She could picture it with roses and clematis and warm light glowing out of the windows. Maybe next year. Robins sang their evening songs, and the air smelled rich and fragrant with earthy green garden smells. It was a beautiful, peaceful place, and Marianne was determined to make things work out somehow.

The house was dim when she entered, and she put down the two grocery bags to grope for a light switch. The overhead in the living room cast a wan light over a small mountain of boxes. "Oscar! I'm home!" she called.

She went down the left hand hallway through the pantry and into the kitchen, switching on lights as she went. Plunking the bags on the counter, she called him again. It was strange. Usually he came running when she got home. Maybe he was just nervous about being in a new place. "Oscar kitty, where are you?" She peered into the bedroom and the office, leaving a blazing trail of light behind her. Finally she found him in the bathroom, snoozing in his carrier in the tub.

"Hey, mister! There you are. Not a very homey place with all these boxes, is it? Let's eat some dinner then we can unpack some things before bed, okay?" She knelt down and stroked his head and scratched him under the chin right where he liked it. She began to feel a little vibrato purr under her fingers.

Marianne put away her purchases, leaving out the salads. Oscar came trotting into the kitchen promptly at the sound of the lid being pulled off the cat food. She joined him, sitting on the kitchen floor. From that perspective, she contemplated color schemes from the three sample palettes laid out on the floor around her. The ceilings were high. She was going to have to borrow a ladder from someone. Maybe a neighbor would be willing to lend her one? Perhaps she could introduce herself tomorrow evening after people got home from work.

She wanted to unpack and get rid of these boxes, but if she was going to paint, that wasn't a good idea. The floor in here was pretty dirty, and there was dust everywhere. Maybe clean everything first, then paint, then unpack. It was a really good thing she didn't have pressing deadlines at the moment.

She polished off both salads and gathered Oscar into her arms for some quality kitty time. He sat in her lap, twelve pounds of solid tabby, purring loudly and rubbing his head on her hands. When she put her hands down, he butted his head against her chin. After a bit, she urged him off her lap and cleaned up their respective dishes.

Wandering down the hall to her bedroom, she looked at the stacks of boxes piled everywhere, the unmade bed, and closet doors ajar. It wasn't particularly inviting, so she found the boxes with sheets and blankets and towels and set about making the bed and making the bathroom homier. The evening sun streamed in the western window and added to the heat inside. There was no air conditioning in the house, only central heating, she recalled. Curtains might help. She earnestly hoped the house cooled down overnight.

With the bed made and the boxes pushed against the walls so she could get around without tripping, the room looked a little better. Tomorrow she would deal with putting the rest of the house in order.

There had been no time to hook up cable or Internet service, so she was temporarily out of entertainment. But she found her bedside clock/radio and brought it into the living room. She spun the tuner to a classic rock station and turned it up to fill the heavy silence as she pushed some more boxes around in the living room. She'd wanted to put the sofa in front of the fireplace but realized that might not work. Whoever had designed the house had made a straight path between the front door and the hallway right past the fireplace. She supposed that she could set the sofa back from the pathway and still use it but couldn't see how it would work yet. She stood with her back to the fireplace and tried to imagine how things would look.

It was nearly full dark outside now, and only the light from the overhead fixture lit the room, making shadows everywhere. The silence was broken only by the forlorn, small sound of the little radio. She was used to the constant noise of traffic outside as well as the muffled voices, footsteps, bumps and bangs of other people living in the building around her. The quiet was disconcerting and got on her nerves. She really hadn't thought about this when she'd imagined living in the country.

She suddenly remembered Oscar's fright upstairs and the unexplored basement below her feet. She was in a little island of light between two unknown, foreboding floors. Her belly did a few anxious flip-flops. What if the basement and attic were full of old junk? She'd have to spend hours cleaning it out. Much worse, what if there was a body hidden under all of it? Sometimes the house felt creepy enough to have a dead, shriveled corpse in the rafters. She shivered.

"Oh, this is stupid! I don't want to be afraid in my own house!" She got up and went to the kitchen for some more ice cream. She took the whole pint back to the sofa and tucked her feet up on the cushions. Oscar jumped up and joined her.

"There you are. Want some?" She offered him some ice cream, which he sniffed and disdained. "Cherry vanilla not your flavor, huh?" He seemed perfectly at ease for now. She stroked his beautiful fur till he curled up next to her and began washing himself. At least Geoffrey was no longer there to make her feel bad about eating the whole pint. She wasn't fat, but he always treated her as if she would blow up if she ate cookies and ice cream. His family was inclined to overeating and heaviness, not hers. Her mom was not fat, and her dad hadn't been when he was alive.

Marianne stared moodily at the mess in the living room and steadily emptied the pint container one bite at a time. Their marriage hadn't been perfect, but it had worked. They'd met in college when their futures had been bright, his in business and hers in historic research. He was so handsome and charismatic. She'd been amazed that he'd wanted to spend time with her. She hadn't thought of herself as particularly pretty, but he'd made her feel special. They'd truly enjoyed each other's company, and when he asked her to marry him, she'd been overjoyed. They'd moved to the city and made a life together each having promising careers and spending their free time seeing shows and taking trips into the country for romantic getaways. The first couple of years had been a little tight financially. For some reason Geoffrey's parents had insisted he do everything on his own. When things were too tight, her mom's discreet financial help had filled the gap.

For a long while, she'd been content, and she'd attributed her lack of joy to a tough work schedule or local politics or the war in the Middle East, rather than something closer to home. Marianne had dutifully played her part, making a million meals, washing a million clothes, and gradually spending less and less time with him having any kind of fun. Geoffrey took care of all their finances and gradually took over their social lives as his career at the retail company had soared, and he'd needed to entertain or travel or stay late. Eventually, he'd made six figures at his company, but his habit of self-promotion turned into outright denigration of her. She'd lost herself along the way, becoming subsumed by his needs.

The only thing he'd let her do entirely for herself was to take classes at Columbia and earn her doctorate. He must have figured it added to his prestige, she thought resentfully. After that, when she wanted something, he'd frown and talk her out of it, calmly and reasonably. Eventually, she quit trying.

When she was a little girl, she'd sometimes had dreams that came true. The earliest one she could remember was in third grade. She'd woken up one morning feeling elated after a dream but couldn't recall the details. Later that day, her teacher told her that her artwork was to be featured on the winter concert program cover. When she was twelve, she dreamt her Grandmother Selene was crying at a funeral. She dreamt about the funeral twice more over the next week and then her mom told her that Grandpa Clare had died of a heart attack. Her own father had died of pneumonia when she was little, and she barely remembered him. Mercifully, she hadn't had any anticipatory dreams about losing him. It was hard enough that she'd grown up without him.

Her dreams scared her at first, but over time she learned to tell the difference between those that were random and those that were likely to be harbingers of events to come or things that were happening somewhere else. Those kinds repeated themselves until she got the message. Sometimes she wondered if the true dreams were messages from her own subconscious about things observed but ignored. Maybe her dreams were similar to the way a camera records bits of background that go unnoticed until a closer viewing of the actual picture. In reality, most of her dreams hadn't come true. As she grew older, they grew fewer and farther apart.

Two years ago she had a series of unusual dreams. They implied that Geoffrey had destroyed a colleague's work in order to get promoted. Unhappy but unwilling to rock the boat, Marianne did her best to dismiss them. Eventually they went away, and she helped him celebrate his promotion with a fancy dinner at an exclusive restaurant in the city.

Then, last year a new set of vivid nighttime visions plagued her. She dreamt repeatedly that she was lying in bed next to Geoffrey, but there was another person lying between them, facing away from her. Upon awakening, she'd find only Geoffrey. The vision recurred until one night Geoffrey's body was intertwined with the interloper's. Marianne's dream self shook the shoulder of the person between them. The stranger's head rotated on her neck to face Marianne, grinning with kiss-swollen lips. Marianne screamed and flung herself backwards.

She awoke with a jerk, her heart pounding. She must have made a noise because Geoffrey was staring at her in the semi darkness, sleepy and irritated at being woken. "What's the matter?"

Shaken she asked, "Who is she? Who are you sleeping with?"

"What? What are you talking about?" He sat up straighter.

"I dreamt you were with someone else," she insisted. "Who is it?"

A look of panic crossed his handsome features momentarily, and he said, "No one, baby. Only you. You having funny dreams again? You did that in college, and the shrink said they were the product of an overactive imagination. You're just stressed."

The reminder of that unpleasant experience in college woke her the rest of the way with a jolt and stopped her tongue. In their senior year at college she'd made the mistake of telling him she had dreamt he was conspiring with a professor to overlook blatant plagiarism on his undergrad thesis and emerge with an A in the class, to boot. He'd looked scared and then dragged her to student counseling. After one session in which Geoffrey had talked a lot, and the young counselor had tried to convince her she was making things up to get attention, she'd never mentioned her ability to dream true again. Rumors at the end of the semester hinted that she'd been right.

Last year, though, the nightmare had upset her so much she'd just blurted it out, although she wished she hadn't said anything. She might not have had to live through six months of hell.

A month later, during Geoffrey's office Christmas party, she'd seen him fondling Sandra, his buxom coworker, in his darkened office. He'd tried to deny it, but Marianne had gotten mad and not given in. He became more and more bullying, first reading her electronic and postal mail then trying to buy her back with expensive gifts. Any time she tried to stand up to him, he'd get furiously angry, intimidating her, and she'd back down, cry, and apologize. For a while she just wanted things to return to the old way when he loved her. He insisted she not mention his indiscretion to anyone they knew, which seemed crazy to her since everyone seemed to know already. At last she could stand it no longer and demanded a divorce.

In the end, he agreed to a generous settlement, so he wouldn't look bad to his boss and the rest of the company. He hinted to everyone that it was Marianne's desire to grow and move on, not his indiscretion that drove the proceedings. Privately, he continued to intimidate her or buy her silence with sudden gifts.

She moved out of their posh apartment on the Upper West Side and into a much cheaper place. When the ink on the divorce papers was dry, she thought it was over and done. Within a week he began turning up at their old haunts, sometimes with Sandra, sometimes alone. It began to feel like he was following her everywhere, mocking her with his new relationship and his success. She stopped going to the familiar places and sought out new ones, but he'd turn up there too after a few days. The dreams started again with a shadowy figure relentlessly pursuing her no matter where she went and waking her with a growing sense of fear.

When an old client turned her down for a new contract for vague reasons, she suspected somehow Geoffrey had been involved. He was going to harass her until she gave up or cracked up. Her mom had been sympathetic and finally told her she was going to have to get a restraining order against Geoffrey to get him off her back. The enormity of having to go that far just seemed too much. As an alternative, her mother had suggested visiting her Grandma Selene for a while just to get some breathing room. Grandma had told her about this place in Maple Hill and made arrangements with her old friend, Lily Thomas. Flight seemed better than more battles with her ex and an uncertain outcome.

A tear slid down her cheek, followed by a sob and more tears. Face crumpling helplessly, she shook as her chest heaved with every moan. Drawing her knees up to her chest, she wrapped her arms around them and rocked back and forth. "Just leave me alone," she sobbed over and over. She cried until she didn't have any more. Finally, she sniffed and wiped her face and took some deep, shuddering breaths. Oscar insinuated himself into her lap, purring and rhythmically kneading her stomach with his big paws. Her hands moved automatically to stroke his soft fur and rub his chin where he liked it best.

Suddenly, she was exhausted. She felt drained and blank. The whole day came crashing down on her, and she picked up Oscar and carried him to the bedroom where she dumped him on the bed. He gave her an aggrieved meow and then settled down. After brief ablutions, she crawled under the sheet in the darkness, and let her tired eyes stare at the unfamiliar pattern of streetlights on her walls, listening to the lack of street noise until she fell asleep.

She was surrounded by flames. As she stood in the living room, she watched the curtains become a terrifying wall of flickering orange and yellow, fall off their hooks, and collapse onto her sofa, which began to smoke and smolder. Everything seemed larger than life, bigger than normal. The upholstery of the sofa browned, then blackened as the fire greedily tore into it. She turned in horror to escape down the hall but found that flames had somehow rolled out of the fireplace, towering over her head. The hallway beyond was unreachable across the wall of orange. Inhaling mouthfuls of thick, smoky air, she began coughing and choking. The heat was like a blast furnace, and the stench of smoke was overpowering. Her fear turned to blind panic. The front door to the right of the flaming curtains was her only avenue, and she ran. Her hand touched the scorching metal handle, and she screamed as she tore at the door trying to open it. Behind her the fire roared and fell upon her.

Chapter 4

SHE woke bolt upright in bed, her breath coming in harsh gasps, her heart pounding, fit to burst. A heavy, hot weight trapped her under the sheet, and she pushed it harshly away from her, still in the grip of the nightmare. There was a heavy thud as Oscar leapt awkwardly for the floor. A pressure filled her ears with a distant buzzing noise. She thought she could smell a faint scent of acrid smoke. As she awakened further, her fear receded along with the buzzing in her ears. The room was cool and dark, her nightie twisted around her, damp with sweat.

"Sorry, Oscar," she croaked. "You can come back now." She had no bedside lamp yet and was strangely reluctant to put her feet on the unseen floor to turn on the overhead. Instead, she lay back down, feeling a slight breeze waft in. The memory of smoke was gone.

What the hell was that? Am I true-dreaming that the house is going to burn down?? She panicked for a few moments, feeling like she was being turned away from every safe haven. Taking some deep breaths, she tried to calm herself and think more rationally.

The vivid dream seemed almost like a memory of a fire, as if someone had told her a story about a fire, and she'd then dreamt about it. But she couldn't recall a single conversation about a house fire. If this was a prediction, it remained to be seen whether the nightmare would repeat itself. She fervently hoped it wouldn't.

Reluctant to close her eyes again lest the vivid images return, she lay between the sheets unable to sleep. When Oscar jumped back up and curled against her hip, she was able drift into uneasy slumber with his company.

Marianne woke some hours later to Oscar tickling her face with his whiskers. It was an adorable, albeit annoying, habit of his. She rubbed his chin and snuggled with him for a few minutes, feeling him purr on her chest, but an already warm breeze was coming in the window, spoiling the nighttime cool of the house. Though she did not feel rested, she roused herself from bed anyway and went around closing windows to preserve the cool inside. By the light of day, the house seemed ordinary and certainly had no fire damage or smell of smoke.

After a lukewarm shower, she put her wavy, dark hair up in a ponytail, slipped on a fresh shirt with yesterday's shorts and got breakfast. A call to Mrs. Thomas was on the top of her list today since she couldn't really unpack until she'd painted. She also planned to get the utilities—mainly the Internet—up and running, and explore the rest of her new place. She saved the trip to Grandma's for a treat in the afternoon.

Retrieving her cell phone from the bedroom—she slept with it under her pillow ever since Geoffrey had started stalking her, she found Mrs. Thomas' number. It was after eight a.m. on a Friday and should be okay to call.

After many rings Marianne was ready to give up, but finally the phone picked up.

"Hello?" Mrs. Thomas sounded old and a little shaky.

"Mrs. Thomas? Hello, this is Marianne Singleton, Selene Singleton's granddaughter?"

There was a pause before she said, "Oh yes. Selene said you wanted to rent my house over in Maple Hill. That would be fine. I don't think I have any renters right now…"

"Yes, Mrs. Thomas, I know. Remember we talked last week about my living here for a while? I can't really pay you a lot of rent, but I'd be happy to fix things up in exchange for some of the rent." She sat upright on the edge of the couch as if Mrs. Thomas could see her.

"Oh?" There was a pause and Marianne was about to fill the void when Mrs. Thomas added, "Yes, I remember we talked about that. I'm sorry—sometimes it takes me a while to remember things. I haven't been able to do much with that house, and it would be nice to have things fixed up."

"Thank you, so much. I just wanted to let you know I'm here at the house, and I got in yesterday."

"Oh good, good. Is everything in order? Are you having a hard time?" She sounded a little anxious.

"What? No, the electric is on, and the water is fine. Listen, I wondered if you would let me paint the inside? It doesn't look like it's been repainted in a long time, and I'd be happy to do it. I promise I'll pick decent colors. I can show you the palette, if you want to approve it." She looked around the sad pink living room and crossed her fingers.

"Oh, no, I trust you. It'll look splendid with fresh paint."

Relieved she said, "Thank you! I'll get started right away. When I'm done you can come by and see it."

"That would be very nice. Are you sure everything is all right? He's not giving you a hard time?" She sounded worried.

"Who are you talking about? Gloria's Realty? The neighbors? SueAnn Talmadge seemed nice if a bit rushed, and I haven't met the neighbors yet."

"Well, if you're sure, then maybe you'll do all right there. I have to go. Miss Lisa is at the door to take me to bingo at the senior center."

"Okay. Nice to talk to you, Mrs. Thomas. 'Bye." The connection ended. Mrs. Thomas seemed a bit vague but nice enough.

She made a call to the local cable-Internet company and arranged for her hook up. Mid August was a slow time, so they promised to send someone out on Saturday for an extra fee. After that she walked around the house with the color palettes in hand thinking about paint until she'd decided on a simple scheme.

Backing the car out of the driveway, she drove back to Main Street. It was still early, but the tourists were clearly out and about, taking up parking spaces everywhere. She managed to get one within a half block of the Brown's hardware store and considered herself lucky. A couple of hundred dollars later, Marianne bought several gallons of high quality primer, paint, and other supplies and loaded the car with the help of the salesperson.

She was sweating freely by the time she'd unloaded the car into the living room of the house. Today was going to be as hot as yesterday. Luckily the house retained the coolness of overnight and was still comfortable. The two rooms at the back of the house were the least crowded, and she decided to start there. She'd never painted while she was married. Geoffrey would have had a fit. He always hired menial jobs out and seemed to take pleasure in being able to gripe about how poorly it was going.

After her divorce, Marianne moved to her own place and ended up painting over the last renter's color choices—black and red and silver—and learned quite a lot. So, she set up in the office and got to work. The faded and scuffed institutional green would be replaced by an off white with a touch of brown. She plugged in the little clock radio, turned on the classic rock station, and spent the morning preparing the room. A wooden kitchen chair served as a step stool for now. Oscar came and went as he pleased.

It was strange that Mrs. Thomas had said the neighbors were difficult. Marianne hoped she would get along with them fine. She'd begun to meet people in her last apartment building and had gotten along even with the more eccentric ones.

After she'd been at it for a while, smiling as she listened to Oscar racing up and down the corridor, she heard him come tearing into the room. Moments later she felt like someone was looking into the room from the door and turned to see. No one was there. Out of the corner of her eye, she caught sight of Oscar crouched and lashing his tail, staring at the door warily. The radio chose that moment to break up in static, crackling and hissing. She got down off the chair and turned it off. Her ears buzzed and hummed in the silence.

"Is someone there?" She called out. The Internet installer was due tomorrow. Could someone else have strolled in without her hearing? She couldn't see down the hall from here, so she went to look. No one was there, though she passed through a chilly zone near the door as if the A/C was on. The hair on the back of her neck prickled. The house didn't have a cooling system.

Okay, she told herself, that's weird. She returned to the office and saw that Oscar was no longer staring fixedly at the doorway. He had relaxed and decided on a nap amid the folds of the tarp. The sense of coldness was dissipating, and she went back to work, spackling dings and nail holes in the plaster while the radio played tunes from the eighties. She would have to let it dry before she could put the primer on.

After lunch she moved into her bedroom and began repairing holes in the flat, oatmeal colored walls. By the time she was done, the room looked like an abstract painting. 'Bird Poop on Sidewalk,' she thought, grinning.

The office was ready to paint, and she sang along to classic rock tunes as she slowly turned the room a neutral flat white. She'd gotten most of the way around the room and was back at the doorway when the radio crackled loudly again, and she felt a shock of intense emotion. She cringed and shivered in the suddenly cool air, and she was reminded forcibly of Geoffrey in an ugly mood. I guess he'd hate this color and hate that I'm working like a day laborer, she thought shakily, trying to explain her sudden fear.

Another part of her countered, where did that come from? He's not here. He is no longer part of my life. I don't care what he thinks. I do my own work, and I get to paint my own colors. The hell with him.

She dipped the roller in time to the suddenly clear Queen lyrics, "We will, we will rock you…" and obliterated the last of the green. Singing loudly helped drive away the unpleasant feeling of being watched. The raw umber tinted white would look great in this room, and she couldn't wait to top coat it. With the humidity, it was going to take the rest of the day and all night to dry properly. Given the strong smell of paint, she was going to have to sleep in the living room.

Her arms ached with the effort of moving the roller up and down, and she gratefully took a break. She grabbed her purse and a couple of paper bags from the co-op, told Oscar she was going out, and locked the door behind her.

In the silence and stillness of the house someone observed the fresh paint and blotches on the walls and grew angry. He had lain quiescent for a time absorbed by memories of a lifetime, but now someone was living in his house again. Her things clashed with his house and did not belong there. That was not to be tolerated. Once something was yours, you never let it go. This one was alone and would be easy to dominate or frighten off. Everyone had a weakness. He just had to find hers.

The verdant green of the maple and oak trees lining the Violet Lane filtered the hot August sunlight and made a cool tunnel on the way up to Primrose. Her immediate neighbors lived in a blue, two-story, raised ranch style house with a well kept lawn bordered by beautifully tended flower gardens. Maybe she could stop by that evening and introduce herself and prevail upon them to lend her a ladder. Further toward Primrose there were other well-tended lawns, making hers the only one that looked ragged and unkempt. Maybe someone would have a lawn mower to lend or have a teen or 'tween who wanted to earn a little extra.

Main Street was more crowded than it had been that morning, and she stepped into a bustling co-op market. Fresh fruit and veggies and something to cook for dinner were on her list.

The PA switched on and a nasal New York twang declared, "Scott? Scott? There's a spill on aisle three. It's the Hansen kid again. Bring the haz-mat team: it's reeeally sticky."

Marianne couldn't help chuckling. Whoever did the announcements had a good sense of humor. She got her produce and a small steak and was browsing the things in the supplements and herbal remedies aisle when the PA clicked on again. This time her ears pricked in anticipation.

A breathless, vapid valley girl voice said in positively orgasmic tones, "Ohmigawd! The deli just put out a plate of their like toh-tally amaaazing bak-lahva for samples! If you, like, want any, you'd better hurry and get some before they are, like, toh-tally vacuumed up!" Click.

Marianne glanced toward the deli counter to see the customers smiling and reaching for a plate on the top of the meat case. The two employees behind the counter were laughing and cutting up more. She smiled and finished shopping. While at the checkout there was one more announcement, this time in the voice of deepest ennui, "Floral, you have a call on line two." A heavy sigh wafted across the microphone, "Ffffloral, line two."

Marianne chuckled appreciatively. The statuesque, blonde woman in front of her turned and smiled at her in a friendly way. Emboldened Marianne said, "The announcements here are great!"

The blonde nodded, and Marianne noticed two lavender locks framing her face. "Yup. Arlo is a riot!"

"That's one person? It sounded like three different people."

"Yeah, he's local talent," she said proudly, then added, "Are you new to Maple Hill?"

Marianne nodded.

"It's nice to meet you." She stuck her hand out. "I'm Kelly Walker. I own Hair Magic, if you ever need a new hair dresser."

Marianne shook her strong, tanned hand and said, "Thanks. I'll keep that in mind."

It was Kelly's turn at the register, and she began putting up her groceries and an assortment of odd things including candles, incense, and some tiny bottles of essential oils.

Marianne left with her purchases and debated going back to Jonathan Sweets' for more ice cream but decided that she'd better not make a habit of eating there every afternoon, or she'd regret it. Reluctantly, she turned back toward the house.

The smell of paint was still powerful, and she opened the windows to air the room out. The house had warmed up during the day, so there wasn't a lot of overnight cool left anyway. Oscar had retreated to the sofa in the living room away from the hot squares of sunlight on the floor in back of the house. Stretching luxuriously, he jumped to the floor with a soft thud of his big paws.

It was time to explore the basement and see what was down there. She hadn't seen any laundry facilities, but thought Mrs. Thomas had mentioned them over the phone during their initial conversation.

"Hey, Oscar," she called, "let's go see what's in the basement." He strolled over to her and rubbed against her legs a few times before accompanying her to the cellar door.

She flipped on the light. The stairs were illuminated where the basement ceiling ended near her feet. They were wooden and worn with a narrow metal handrail on either side that looked like pieces of old pipe. The whole contraption wobbled as she descended halfway to a small landing that turned and led the rest of the way down. Oscar slunk cautiously down the stairs behind her and began exploring the cellar.

Basements were always a little creepy to her: dark and mysterious and vaguely ominous. The basement of her old apartment building had been full of clanks and thumps but was much better lit. This one was silent and somehow oppressive. She felt the underground cool on her bare skin, with an accompanying smell of rust and old water and damp cement. There were only a couple of bare bulbs down the center. The stone foundations outlined the footprint of the house above. Tiny, age-fogged windows let in very little light. The one in the middle of the south wall was bigger than the others. This one was angled outward at the bottom and opened onto a wooden sided stall the size of a walk-in closet. She wondered what that was and made a note to ask Mrs. Thomas next time.

Her sandals tapping across the cement floor, she walked cautiously to a white washer and dryer, both brand new front loaders. They sat in the gloom, looking modern and out of place halfway between the stairs and the wooden bin. Beyond the bin the shadow was deeper, big enough to hide something at least the size of a table. She made a mental note to come down later and replace the burned out bulb on that side. Vague images of things lurking and scurrying out of sight crept into her mind. She shivered.

The huge silent bulk of the furnace sat in the middle of the basement like a sleeping dragon, taking up an inordinate amount of space. A network of pipes emerged from it and ran along the underside of the ceiling through the supporting boards of the floor above, and Marianne could imagine hot water circulating like blood to each of the radiators. She'd lived in apartments with radiators before and remembered all the pinging and clanking and knocking sounds they made. No doubt a symphony of noises awaited her when the weather got cold.

Her chilled skin goosebumped, and she was more than ready to be back upstairs. As she turned to go up the stairs, the hairs on the back of her neck rose. She peered beyond the wooden bin and wasn't sure if there was a deeper shadow there or not. A bubble of fear welled up in her chest.

"Hey, Oscar, let's go upstairs okay?" Her voice sounded thin to her ears, and she suppressed the urge to bolt up the rickety stairs. She forced herself to walk up calmly. It was so silly to be afraid of a basement! She told herself. Geoffrey would have laughed at her. Still, she had never liked basements. This one definitely had a major creep factor to it. It was going to be hard to do laundry if she was afraid to go down and use the machines!

"Oscar?" she called one more time. "C'mon, Oscar. Kitty, kitty." There was a sudden scramble of paws on cement, and the orange tabby streaked up the stairs looking twice his normal size. As soon as he passed the door, she slammed it shut, her own heart beating faster. There was a bolt style lock on the door, and she slid it into the lock position without hesitation.

She found Oscar under the sofa in the living room backed up against the wall. Something had definitely scared him. She lay on her stomach and talked soothingly to him until she'd coaxed him out and into her arms. They sat on the couch together until he relaxed and began licking his fur back into place.

Oscar's behavior was unnerving. Maybe it was just being in a new place. Marianne hoped they would both get used to living here. They were stuck here for the duration and would have to make the best of it. If worst came to worst, she could find a laundromat in town rather than go into the basement again.

When she'd returned, he'd followed her. Her fear of the dark and silent basement radiated in waves off of her. Women were so weak and easily handled. He was sure he could have her running to his beck and call in time, and that would begin to make things right again.

Chapter 5

IT WAS mid afternoon already, and since she had promised to visit Grandma Selene in the little town of Vandenberg, she got into the Flea and made her way through town. She drove out into the hot, green countryside and zenned her way up into the hills overlooking the river. It had been some time since she'd been there last, and that time, her mom had done the driving. Geoffrey had not been keen to leave the city much in the last five years and hadn't accompanied her. With the windows rolled down, there was a breeze in the car, but it only moved the hot air around. Marianne wished the car had A/C.

Grandma Selene and Grandpa Clare moved to the Hudson Valley when they retired, and Marianne had visited them nearly every summer during her childhood. Vandenberg was spread out and mostly rural with a small post office, a bar, a sleepy gas station and not a lot more to speak of. Maple Hill was a big town by comparison. Since her last visit, Marianne noticed a lot more grand homes tucked away in the trees as she wound up the hill. The fancy entrances spoke of money from the city and getaway homes in upstate New York. Once upon a time, they'd all been farms. She felt a bit sad that development had changed her childhood territory but reflected that at least large expanses of identical tract homes had not been built.

She passed another small, rural cemetery along the way. Her Grandpa Clare was buried there, and she thought she'd like to pay him a visit in the next few weeks. Maybe Grandma Selene would like to go.

At last she bumped down the familiar driveway bordered by trees and set back from the road. The big white house appeared around the last corner, and she pulled into the parking area near the big old black Cadillac. She got out and breathed deeply, enjoying the slightly cooler air under the trees and up the hill from town. A two-seater, wicker swinging chair with its comfortable, rose patterned cushions hung from the porch roof beams, dominating the space, and the inner door was open to allow the cooler air in.

She got to the top of the steps just as Grandma Selene arrived at the front door.

"Marianne! How lovely to see you! Come in, come in before the mosquitoes find you." Traces of a British accent tinged her words.

Marianne entered, allowing the screen door to bang closed behind her. She embraced her beloved grandmother warmly. Selene was taller than Marianne by a few inches and moved with grace despite her age. Her iron gray hair was still thick and wavy and pulled back into a tidy bun held with a silver pin, and she was dressed fashionably as always. In spite of her nearly ninety years, she hugged Marianne with the strength of a younger woman.

"Let me have a look at you." Selene stood back and gazed critically at her granddaughter's pale face framed by dark wavy hair. She said with concern, "You look peaked, dear. Has that wretched man been harassing you again?"

Marianne shrugged and gave a half smile. "I think I made a clean getaway. No one knows I'm up here except you and Mom. So, I'm really hoping he won't think to look here and won't find me for a long time, if ever."

"Well, we can hope," Selene replied doubtfully. "Would you like to have some iced tea? I just made some."

"I'd love that," Marianne said gratefully.

"Stay here, and I'll get it."

Marianne breathed a deep sigh and relaxed a little. The wide vertical wood paneling was warm and comfortingly familiar. Landscapes, ships, and painted family portraits adorned the walls like old friends all around the room. She sat in her favorite spot on the blue and cream couch in front of the fireplace and listened to the sounds of glassware and liquid.

A few minutes later Grandma Selene emerged with a tray of cookies, a pitcher with ice cubes suspended in perfect amber liquid, sugar cubes, and two glasses. Marianne stood and took the tray, so she could place it on the table. Bending with heavy trays was on her grandmother's list of no-nos.

They held their ritual of pouring tea for each other and choosing cookies. It was a ceremony they'd been doing for each other since Marianne was four, and she loved all the well-worn movements and murmured words. It made her feel that everything was right with the world.

At last Marianne sat back and said, "Thank you so much, Grandma, for finding a place for me to live. I thought I might camp out in your guest room for a couple of weeks at most, and instead, you found me a whole house!"

Selene sipped her tea. "I'm glad you like it. Lily has been beside herself worrying about that empty house for the last year, so I'm glad you will be taking care of it for her. How is it?"

"It's in decent shape, just dusty and old feeling. Mrs. Thomas gave me permission to paint the inside, thank goodness, so that's what I'm doing now. My stuff is still in boxes in the meantime, but I'll get unpacked eventually and have you over."

"I'd like that very much. Are you doing everything yourself?"

Marianne nodded. "I don't mind. I don't have any research projects right now, though I'm hoping to contact a friend in the history department at NYU and see if they need anyone to teach a class this fall or in January."

Grandma Selene smiled warmly. "Oh, that sounds like fun! You always enjoyed tutoring when you had a chance."

They talked for another hour until Grandma said regretfully, "I have to finish packing, Lovie. I promised my friend Margaret a month ago that I'd visit her, and she's not been in good health so I daren't put it off. I'll be gone for a few days, but I promise to call you when I get back and see how you're settling in. It's wonderful to catch up with you, and I'm so glad you're right down the road."

They hugged each other and Marianne headed back down the

drive in the late evening shadows. Belatedly, she realized she had not mentioned the strange feelings of being watched.

Ruari Allen wearily slammed the door of his white truck and started the engine. It had been another long day of mindless repairs to things he'd fixed many times before. At least he wasn't on the housekeeping staff. Sometimes renters left behind the most godawful messes. His personal favorite had been the story about melted popsicles, soda, and beer coating the inside of a freezer. It had coalesced into a dense, gooey layer that had taken a couple of hours to remove. He'd sympathized heartily with Michaela and her cleaning crew.

Nevertheless, Talmadge nagged him to fit extra appointments into every available space, and as the only handyman for Gloria's, he had to take every one. When the business was smaller he could manage, but it had grown to thirty properties. He was going to have to get some help or quit. This summer he'd taken to not returning to the office for anything unless he had no choice. But she called him relentlessly on his cell phone anyway. In spite of that, he'd gotten done half an hour earlier than he'd expected and felt a glimmer of hope that he could do a little work in his studio before bed.

He inserted his key into the padlock on the old door and slid it across, revealing the woodshop with its machinery waiting quietly for him. The clean scent of wood shavings wafted out into the humid summer evening and cleared his head. He caught the scents of maple and pine, the sharp undercurrent of cedar, and the fruity aroma of cherry. As he walked through the shop, each project came to his hands like trusting animals in a barn. He stroked each one briefly and made his way to a table that held a mysterious object under a cloth amid a myriad of shavings. Carving and sanding tools lay where he'd put them down last night.

He pulled the cloth aside and gazed at the as yet rudely formed piece underneath. There were hints that it would be about a foot high and rounded, maybe oval, but it had not revealed itself to him enough yet to tell what it was. He picked it up and perched on the metal stool nearby and held it in his hands waiting for it to speak to him. After a time he picked up a tool and began to work on it.

The smoky wisp drifted and curled insubstantially through the house. Although it was doomed to stay here eternally, that didn't mean it had to let this new woman become trapped as well. It wasn't safe for her to stay. The danger was coming soon, a vortex inexorably drawing closer.

The silence of the empty house pressed on Marianne's ears again. The sad, anxious vibe stole over her, and she debated returning to the co-op for a late dinner. But, she reminded herself, I have dinner makings here, and I'm going to have to be frugal till I get the next project.

The smell of steak and onions was an effective antidote, and she made a salad to go with it. Oscar ate another can of kitty tuna while she ate standing by the counter. She surveyed the wallpaper up near the ceiling and tried to imagine cobalt blue in its place. The appliances were white, and the cabinets were light colored wood. Once she scrubbed everything down and painted, it would look nice, she thought. The linoleum on the floor was old and worn in places, but she could clean it, at least. Maybe Mrs. Thomas could spring for some new flooring? It was worth asking.

As she cleaned up the silence and loneliness of the house around her grew. Feeling unaccountably anxious, she grabbed her purse, and walked to Main Street where she wandered up and down just to be near people and movement and life. Her steps took her eventually to Jonathan Sweet's, and she got a dish of ice cream, lemon blueberry this time. As she sat by the window staring at the people on the street, she realized this was her new home. She wondered how she was going to meet people. Her research job was, by its nature, fairly solitary. She hoped for nice neighbors and remembered the cryptic remark Mrs. Thomas had made about them giving her a hard time. Maybe one of the other people on the block was eccentric or had extreme political or religious views? She was determined to meet her neighbors starting tomorrow. If that didn't work, she would have to find a hobby or get involved with something locally.

That night, Marianne dreamt she was walking through her new house, though it seemed to have more rooms or more space than she remembered. She heard heated voices, a man's and a woman's, somewhere up ahead. She couldn't distinguish the words, though it was clear he was very angry about something. The woman's voice was muted and pleading. There was a sharp sound of flesh being struck, and Marianne hurried down the now very long hallway to help. A woman came out of the back bedroom holding her face and looking away as she rushed past Marianne. A man's backlit silhouette filled the doorway, radiating anger and satisfaction. He was in his prime and full of his own power.

She approached him to say something like, "That was mean!" but he grabbed her arm hard, pulling her angrily toward the other bedroom. As he thrust her into the room, he said harshly, "Look what you've done!"

The room contained bookcases full of leather bound volumes overseeing an imposing desk of dark wood and a green leather wing back chair. A brass table lamp with a green glass cover illuminated the papers on the desk. The furnishings belonged in a tasteful gentleman's club from the early twentieth century, surrounded by moss green walls and expensive flooring. Instead these walls were glaring white, making the furniture seem out of place and overdone.

"You have no right to paint my house! This is my house not yours," he said angrily. "Put it back the way it was!"

Marianne surfaced from the dream, becoming aware of the dark bedroom with the unfamiliar lights on the walls and Oscar's warm bulk next to her. That was important. I've got to remember that, she thought muzzily as she sank into sleep again. Through successive dreams she kept trying to tell people about the angry man and the sad woman and the out of place furniture. When she woke in the morning, she recalled the dream enough to jot it down in her notebook.

Chapter 6

RUARI roused himself from his bed groggily and put the coffee on. He'd fallen asleep in his clothes, lying on top of his comforter again. His muse had only let him go reluctantly after he'd cut himself several times from tiredness. He thought of her as a tough old broad, but the outcome was nearly always worth it. He looked at his hands and saw the fresh gouge marks and dried blood. While the coffee perked, he carefully washed his hands, putting ointment and band-aids on. After he'd splashed some cream and sugar into a huge mug of coffee, he made his way down the steps to the workshop.

He was so lucky to have found this old garage/shed with the little room upstairs. It had come up on the realtor's sheet a couple of years ago, and he'd grabbed it before anyone else could. It hadn't been terribly expensive since it needed many repairs, but it was the perfect combination of living and working space for him. He needed the wood stove in winter, but the space was all his. He'd gradually made repairs and improvements.

Warm mug in hand, he went down to the table where he'd been working. The cover lay over his work, and for a moment he wondered what he'd find. He'd spent hours with the piece last night, but his muse took him to another realm when he carved. Sometimes he was only half aware of what his hands were doing. He drew the cover off and stood looking at it.

He could see the roughed out features of a face emerging from the red cherry wood. It was between the folds of something heavy, cloth maybe, and the vague shape of a hand seemed to be pushing aside the cloth on one side. He had the feeling the face was feminine and wondered if his muse was creating a portrait or an avatar. He picked up the piece and rolled it gently between his scarred hands and examined the back. It was roughly shaped, rounded like a pod or a seed. He set it down again, knowing that he was too tired to work for now.

Reverently, he placed the cloth over it again.

After breakfast Marianne took a walk up the block trying to determine if any of the neighbors were home. Next door there was a car in the drive, and the inner front door was open. She walked up the flagstone path and rang the doorbell next to the glass of the storm door. A middle-aged man with thinning, dark hair and a fleshy paunch under his T-shirt came to the door.

"Hello! Hi, I'm your new neighbor, next door," she called out cheerfully with her friendliest smile.

The crease between his heavy dark brows gave him a faintly annoyed expression, but his voice was pleasant enough. "Hi, nice to meet you. I'm John Cavarelli." He opened the door and invited her into the foyer. The cool air was a relief from the heat of outside. He thrust out his hand, and she shook it firmly.

"I'm Marianne Singleton. It's nice to meet you. I moved in to number 25 yesterday. I'm renting from Mrs. Thomas," she explained.

He nodded, "Welcome to the neighborhood. My wife, Maria, is out doing some errands. She'll be pleased to meet you. Our son, Mikey, is out at basketball practice." His New York accent made her feel right at home.

Marianne said, "This is a really nice neighborhood. I'm looking forward to living here. It's very quiet and peaceful compared to the city."

He nodded again. "You plan on cleaning up the yard? Gloria's never bothers to mow the lawn." He sounded unhappy about his beautiful property being next to such a dump.

She said apologetically, "Yes, I hope to tame it down and clean up the flower beds. Maybe you know of someone I could hire to mow for me? I don't have a mower yet." She looked hopeful.

"I might. Mikey is old enough to mow lawns. I'll ask him."

"Thank you, I'd appreciate that. I'm starting with painting the inside. I wondered if you had a ladder I could borrow?"

"Yeah, sure. What size you need? I've got a six-foot and a twelve-foot. Or do you just need a step stool?"

He took her to the tidy garage, and she selected the six-foot ladder. He offered to carry it over for her.

"Thank you," Marianne said gratefully after he leaned it against the wall in the living room. "I look forward to meeting your wife and son."

"Sure. Come by tomorrow," he said as he left.

Marianne spent the rest of the day putting the final coat of paint on the office and getting the primer on her own bedroom walls. She had a momentary flash of the angry man in her strange dream but told herself firmly, "My house, my colors."

Mid-afternoon the Big Ben door chime rang, and she came off the ladder to answer it. The cable Internet installer messed around with the junction box outside and then hooked up her TV in the living room. He also set up equipment for the Internet in the extra bedroom with a wireless router, so she could access it anywhere in the house. She named her router "History101" and sighed happily, feeling connected to the world again.

Hoping for a message from a fellow historian, she took a break and checked her email. As she scrolled through the accumulation, the pit of her stomach dropped. Hidden in the pile of messages like maggots in a jelly donut, there were no less than three emails from Geoffrey, telling her he'd found something of hers left behind at their apartment. He wanted to meet with her to return it, or she could come and pick it up. Even though they were only emails, electrons on a screen, she still felt sick to her stomach that her ex had invaded her space. Wanting to delete them off her machine, to make him go away, she forced herself to file them away in case she needed evidence for a restraining order. She refused to email him back, though a part of her wailed, "Leave me alone!" If he had anything left of hers, she didn't want it.

To make matters worse, there were no emails from her colleagues.

After the cable guy left, Marianne felt out of sorts and headed up to town again. Saturday was even busier than Friday had been with tourists and locals out and about in spite of the heat. She walked around exploring the side streets, relieved to have people around her. Surreptitiously, she kept an eye out for Geoffrey's silver Lexus, and her heart gave a little jump at the sight of every silver car until she told herself to get a grip. As far as Marianne knew, he didn't know where to find her. Those emails were only fishing for her, and she wasn't going to rise to the bait like a trout. She took a deep breath and put her anxious thoughts aside.

Maple Hill's Main Street was really about six blocks long if you included the historic stone building at one end. It had a plaque declaring it an historic structure and now housed part of the town library. She looked forward to checking it out next week, maybe as a break from painting. The post office was across the street in an early twentieth century brick and wood building.

There was one other old brick and wood building with an antique marquee on the front declaring the name of a recent movie. "Avery Theater" was spelled out in decorative plaster above it. The painted parts were weathered and chipping. Many of the marquee bulbs were broken or missing. The whole building had an air of grandeur gone to seed, like a movie star showing her age badly. Marianne couldn't remember seeing any movies there when she was little, but she thought it would be fun to see a movie there sometime.

The side streets off Main had shops and businesses for about a block to either side, segueing into residences after that. She even found Hair Magic, the beauty salon, down a side street, closed for business on alternate Saturdays.

Marianne returned to the house sweaty but happier. The clutter of boxes in the band-aid pink living room was a depressing sight. She had just gotten most of her stuff out of boxes after the divorce when she'd had to pack everything hastily and move again. This would be the next room to paint after the bedrooms, she vowed. Then she'd be able to unpack.

Across the room the old upright piano sat half hidden by boxes. She was glad to have hauled it all the way here. Her mother had played beautifully, and Marianne loved to listen. She'd wanted to play the saxophone, but her mother had insisted on the piano for starters. Needless to say she never did learn to play the saxophone. She recalled practicing grudgingly for what seemed like hours. Now, it would be fun to see how much she remembered. Exercise books, some easy Bach and Schumann, as well as some Disney books were soon piled up on the top of the upright.

Well, Geoffrey was not here to make her feel guilty or awkward about playing, so she sat down and opened a plain yellow covered book full of Bach pieces. She vaguely remembered playing the first one with all the pencil notes dated April 1986 (she'd been eleven) that Mrs. Yates had written.

After some minutes of struggling to play with both hands together and remembering how to read music at the same time, she gave up and put one of the simple exercise books on top of it and tried again. She surprised herself by spending more than an hour pleasantly absorbed in working her way through the first bit of the exercise book and dredging up her rusty memories. Finally, she tried the Bach again and managed to read the melody line well enough to raise the tune off the page and into her ear.

She stretched, pleased with herself and went off to the kitchen for dinner. After eating she sat with her laptop and surfed the Internet for a while, visiting some of her favorite websites both for history and for fun. At last she turned out the light and lay down on the mattress in the living room to sleep.

Please, no nightmares tonight, she thought. I really want to sleep. Oscar hopped up and lay on the bed with her, and she stroked his side till she dozed off.

Some hours later she dreamt of her mother, and when she emerged, she heard faint, familiar music playing. For a few moments she thought she was still dreaming about her mother playing, and then she realized the piano music was the Pachelbel Canon. The sound was ethereal and ghostly in the dark as if the pianist didn't want to disturb her but couldn't help playing. Her scalp prickled as she pictured someone sitting on the bench, playing only a few feet away. Who was there? The player felt more sad than angry. Marianne's heart beat hollowly, and she felt suddenly vulnerable and very alone. Oscar's sleepy warm weight lay next to her, and she touched his fur like a talisman. She took comfort from the realization that Oscar wasn't upset.

The piece ended, and the pianist didn't resume. The silence afterward was very deep. She didn't dare open her eyes for fear of what she might see. After a while she wondered if she'd dreamt or imagined it. Oscar shifted slightly in his sleep, turning his chin upward and stretching out his front paws. Her heart slowed into a gentle rhythm, and she wove in and out of sleep again.

Playing was the only thing that kept the fear at bay. It had been so long since she'd played. Drained but exhilarated from her encounter with the piano, the smoky wisp drifted away quietly.

Chapter 7

MARIANNE woke early when the sun came in the front windows. She felt groggy and tired. Her nighttime encounter seemed very far away, and she seriously wondered if she'd dreamt the whole interlude. The piano was perfectly normal looking with the key cover down. The piano books on the pull out music rest above the keyboard were open where she'd left them. She sighed with relief and was sure she'd dreamt it.

It was really hard to get a full night's sleep in this house, she thought as she made tea and ate some cereal. It's like I have another whole day after I go to bed. I hope this doesn't go on indefinitely, or I'm going to be a zombie.

She was just getting ready to paint her own bedroom a summery periwinkle blue when the door chime sounded. Curious, she went to the front and opened the door. Mr. Cavarelli, a woman about ten years older than Marianne, and a boy of about twelve stood on the front step. The woman held a paper plate of cookies under plastic wrap.

"Oh, hello!" Marianne said as she opened the outer door. "Please come in! Sorry about the mess."

John Cavarelli introduced his wife, Maria, and their son, Mikey.

Maria, with glossy black hair and strong Italian features, handed her the plate with a huge smile showing gorgeous white teeth and said, "Welcome to the neighborhood! John said you stopped by on Friday. You just moved in?" Her speech was a charming mix of Italian and Brooklynese and made Marianne like her at once.

"Thank you, they look delicious! Yes, I just moved here on Thursday from the city. "

"How's the ladder working out?" John asked. His somewhat gruff speech had a slight Italian lilt to it as it reflected off his wife's voice.

"Great! Thank you for the loan. I hope you don't mind my getting a little paint on it? I'll show you what I've been doing, if you want to see." She led them through the kitchen, depositing the cookies on the counter, and then through the dining room to the back bedrooms. They admired her work.

"This place really needed a coat of new paint. It was pretty… old fashioned looking," Maria said tactfully. "I'm impressed you're doing all your own work."

"Well, it's not perfect…" Marianne said modestly.

"No, no, honey," she assured her, "it's a good way to get to know a new place and make it your own. If you hire out, you never know your house as well." She waved her hand dismissively for emphasis.

They made their way to the front door again. Mikey had been silent the whole time, a shadow trailing behind his parents. He was wearing a shirt with a basketball player making a jumpshot on the front and looked like he couldn't wait to be elsewhere.

Mr. Cavarelli said, "We talked the other day about mowing your lawn, and Mikey here could do it." He squeezed the boy's shoulder. Mikey had the resigned expression of a kid who's been asked to do the new neighbor a favor by his father.

Marianne smiled sympathetically and said, "Mikey, would you be interested in earning a little extra cash by mowing my lawn? As you can see, it really needs it."

Mikey shrugged politely and unenthusiastically. "Sure, Miss Singleton."

"What are your rates?" She glanced at the Cavarellis as she asked the boy.

Mikey looked up at his parents and said hopefully, "Does eight dollars an hour plus gas seem okay to you?"

Again, she eyed Cavarelli senior who nodded slightly. "That seems okay," she said. "As you know the lawn hasn't been touched in months, so you'll have to work at it till it gets in shape. Are you up for some extra weeding and organizing?"

Mikey looked a little pained but nodded when his father squeezed his shoulder again. "When can you start?" She asked with a smile.

Mikey shrugged. "I guess I could start this afternoon if you want."

"Really? Okay! I hope you can use your own mower 'cause I don't have one." John Cavarelli nodded. "Alright, let me get some more painting done, and I'll come over around one o'clock and we can figure out where to start."

The Cavarellis left, and she went back to work with a smile. They seemed really nice. She turned on the little radio and rolled periwinkle blue top-coat on her bedroom while listening to Car Talk. She loved the relationship advice, and pictured Tom and Ray telling her she'd done the right thing to dump the chump.

After lunch she walked next door. Maria answered and invited her in while yelling over her shoulder, "Mikey! Miss Singleton is here."

Mikey emerged, pulling a well-loved baseball cap over his dark hair.

"Thanks for doing this," she said as they walked together back over to number 25.

"You're welcome," he said dutifully.

"No, really. I used to live in the city. We don't have private lawns and gardens there. I don't know the first thing about lawn care, so it's nice to have someone who knows what they're doing." She thought he stood a little straighter. "By the way, what do you like to be called?"

He considered. "Mikey is okay, but I think I'm getting a little old for that. How about Michael?"

"Okay, Michael it is. What would you do to get this yard in shape?

I mean, I have some ideas, but what do you think?"

He looked appraisingly around the yard, its long grass and overgrown gardens, and thought for a minute. "Well, mowing it a bunch will help but there's a lot of weeding. Some of your plants look pretty good, but there's a bunch of dead ones too."

She was impressed that he was so observant. "You guys have a pretty nice yard," she ventured.

"Yeah, my dad's pretty proud of it. I have to do weeding and mowing at our place sometimes, so I kind of know what to do."

"Well, if you want some paid work, I've got plenty." He looked pleased at the prospect and went home to fetch a lawn mower.

"Keep track of your hours, and I'll pay you as you go," Marianne said and returned inside. The paint smell at the back of the house meant another night on the mattress in the living room, but doing it all at once was the only way to go. She looked at the newly blue bedroom with pleasure. Ice white trim would set it off nicely. She'd chosen a complimentary dark brown paint for the trim in the spare room and spent the rest of the afternoon painting the trim around the two windows, the closet, and the baseboard. The intoxicating smell of freshly mown grass drifted in the windows with the beat of the mower engine.

Around three she put the lid back on the quart can and left it on the ladder and went outside to admire Michael's progress and invite him in for lemonade. She paid him $20 for his labor and a tank of gas. He promised to return Tuesday, " 'cause I have basketball practice on Monday, and I'm trying to get good enough for the school team."

Later Marianne was in the kitchen contemplating dinner when she heard a pop and a heavy thunk accompanied by a liquid sound from the back room. She hastened back to see what the odd noise was and gasped as she entered the spare room. The lid of the quart can had somehow exploded off, fallen from the ladder, and splattered the newly painted white wall with a huge fountain of dark brown paint.

She swore loudly and spent the next fifteen minutes scraping as much paint off the tarp into the can as she could salvage, tamping the lid on again firmly and leaving it on the floor. She wondered if the lid could have spontaneously popped off due to heat and pressure buildup inside the can. It was pretty warm, inside and out. All the while she imagined someone feeling very pleased with himself, which only served to annoy her more. She then took an old T-shirt and wiped the brown paint off her pristine white wall as best she could. There was a stain where the brown had been, and she would have to paint the wall with primer again tomorrow. She cleaned up her hands at the kitchen sink and decided she was too tired to cook for herself.

The co-op deli counter had plenty of options, and the place was emptier than it had been all weekend. She picked up several salads and a cool drink and sat outside at a table on the sidewalk to think and eat.

Something very strange was going on at her new house. The weird dreams, the eerie basement, the sensation that someone was watching her, the piano playing in the middle of the night, and Oscar being scared of something.

They all added up to a very scary idea. Is my house haunted? She wondered. If so, Mrs. Thomas' non-sequiter "is he giving you a hard time?" would make much more sense. That would explain a lot of things. The more she thought about it, the more unnerved she became. The idea of a spectral person watching her at all times gave her the willies. That was way worse than having Geoffrey stalk her. At least she could see Geoffrey and get away from him. She picked at her salads, suddenly without much appetite.

Her rational historian's mind tried to intervene. It was still possible that she was just scaring herself for no reason. She was definitely still upset from Geoffrey's unwanted emails earlier. But if it was true that her house was haunted, maybe she could figure out who it was. If she could give the ghost a name, maybe it would be less scary. Whoever it was didn't like her painting but did like her piano. Maybe a temperamental pianist had lived there? Maybe she could convince him or her to go away and leave her be. But what if it wasn't the ghost of a person? What if it was a demon or a poltergeist? That was an even more terrifying thought. She needed to talk to someone who wouldn't scoff or tell her she was losing her mind.

I wonder if I could tell Grandma Selene? She snorted at that idea and pressed the plastic fork against the table top, watching it bend. And what would I tell my proper English grandmamma? 'Hey, your friend's house is haunted, and that's why she can't keep her renters?' Grandma Selene had always been supportive, but she'd never indicated that ghosts were part of her worldview. Besides, she'd said she was going away for a few days, and she was too old fashioned to carry a cell phone.

She couldn't call her mom with this either. They'd been close when she was younger, but the years with Geoffrey had driven a wedge between Marianne and everyone she'd known. She hadn't had a heart to heart conversation with her mom in years. Now that she was on her own again, it was definitely time to reconnect. She just didn't think this would be the best topic. For now she didn't want to worry her mom since she was so glad she was safely away from her stalking ex-husband. The plastic fork unexpectedly snapped in two, jangling her further. She looked around her guiltily, but no one had noticed.

There really isn't anyone I can turn to, she thought with a sick feeling in the pit of her stomach. I've run out of places I can go, short of driving away randomly. I have to find a way to make this place work. Maybe I'm just imagining things.

Pressing the lids back on her half finished food, she left the sidewalk table and headed back towards the house. Walking back through the humid evening shadows, a measure of peace stole into her mind soothing her agitation. It really was a beautiful little town, and she wanted to be able to call it home more than anything at this moment. Driving off into the sunset to some random destination was not something she wanted to do at all.

Oscar met her at the door with a plaintive meow, and she opened a new can of food for him and cleaned the litter box. The house felt ordinary. Her appetite returned enough for her to finish dinner. She surfed the 'net for weather and the news on her laptop and learned that thunderstorms were predicted for the Hudson Valley tomorrow. Perhaps the heat and humidity would cool off for a few days.

Feeling pensive, Marianne sat at the piano for a while and did fingering exercises and worked her way haltingly through some more of

Bach's pieces for Anna Magdalena. She turned out the light and fell asleep on the mattress, feeling much better.

Marianne dreamt of fire again: all consuming, terrifying fire that burned everything in its path from furniture to curtains, to walls and floors. Smoke filled the air making it hard to breathe. Someone was screaming, trapped in the basement, unable to get out. Someone she loved. She searched for a way to reach the cellar door, but veils of smoke and flame cut her off. Increasingly desperate, she prepared to hurl herself through the flames to get to the stairs.

She jerked awake as her dream self jumped. Panting, heart pounding in her chest, it took several disoriented seconds to understand where she was and realize that she was in darkness and silence. The dream had been so real; it was almost as if she'd been teleported from the inferno to her quiet room. She had been convinced someone was trapped in the basement. Just a dream, she thought, trembling slightly with relief.

She lay back weakly on her damp sheets. Her skin cooled in the slight breeze from the window, and Oscar's heavy, warm weight pressed against her leg.

Rats, another night of crappy sleep, she thought in frustration. She couldn't go on living like this with interrupted sleep at night and jangled nerves during the day. She needed to talk to someone who would listen to her, or she'd go mad.

It took her a long time to fall asleep again, in spite of Oscar's reassuring presence.

Chapter 8

GEOFFREY Chubb put down the phone and glanced out the office door. Everyone was busy out there even on a Friday, and he had a few minutes before his next meeting. Toggling between windows on his computer screen, he brought up his email. There was no news from Perry yet. They were drinking buddies, and Perry worked downtown for an architectural firm close to NYU. Geoffrey had asked him last night to keep an eye out for Marianne because she'd been unusually effective in evading him for the last several days, and Geoffrey was annoyed. Perry had located her once before.

He sent off a carefully worded email to Perry asking him to keep looking. He wanted to be sure no one could tell what he was doing. Not that it was illegal or anything, just that it wasn't work related. Then he had an idea and skimmed through his address book. Yes, he still had the phone and address for one of her old professors. She might have told Wentwroth where she was. He'd have to think about how to word a message if she didn't' surface in a day or two.

He'd sent her a couple of emails saying she'd left her stuff at his house in hopes of eliciting a response. She'd always risen to the bait in the past, and he'd had fun meeting with her only to tell her he'd thrown it away already and no longer had it. She'd teared up, and he'd enjoyed pretending to be sympathetic.

He flipped to the retail business newsfeed he subscribed to and idly read the entries. Doing some homework before this meeting would probably be a good idea. It was hard to concentrate, though. He bounced his knee up and down, making the expensive leather shoe squeak slightly. The word 'settlement' came up in an item about a lawsuit with a manufacturer, and that reminded him of his own. The divorce settlement still irked him. Her lawyer had demanded far more from him than he'd thought was reasonable, and his own lawyer had told him just to take the deal. Who would have thought Marianne would hire such a sharp woman? When he complained, Mother told him she'd known all along Marianne was a gold digger after the Chubb family fortune.

Agitated, he flipped to his desktop and brought up a solitaire game. His knee resumed its ferocious vibration. His mother had never thought very much of Marianne or her family. The Chubbs were wealthier and moved in more elevated circles than the Singletons. His marriage to his college sweetheart had been a youthful decision. Mother had questioned his impulse at the time but let him have his way. Marianne had been pretty and completely devoted to him, which had been a heady feeling. They'd done some fun things together, but she'd become tiresome over the years. He really should have ditched her long ago and traded up. But the company partners were all married with kids and seemed to value the whole family thing, so he'd been reluctant to get divorced. For some reason they also seemed to like her. When he met Sandra two years ago, he'd enjoyed flirting with her before reveling in a full-blown affair. It had been easy to hide it from Marianne because she always took him at his word.

His desktop image was of him and Sandra together on a boat earlier that summer. Sandra was so much better! She was gorgeous, had better T and A, and was ambitious like him. She was a much better fit for him in so many ways, he grinned privately as his foot stilled. He could see himself as a partner at the company in a few years, if he kept working this hard. Even if he had to make his own opportunities.

He turned back to the retail newsfeed and tried to focus, but his thoughts kept drifting.

His good mood soured as he thought of his last promotion. That was the other reason he couldn't quite let Marianne go yet. Tormenting her was satisfying payback for the ridiculous settlement. But there was the matter of what she might know about him.

She was so timid and completely ordinary on one hand, but then she also had this weird side. She claimed to know things about him because she 'dreamt' about them. Completely absurd, of course, because who does that? Yet she'd known about his affair with Sandra somehow. Obviously, she was hiding her sources. Someone in his office or one of his friend's wives had ratted him out. It had reminded him of that time in college when she said she'd 'dreamt' he was plagiarizing a term paper and colluding with his professor to get an A in spite of his poor class performance. He had done that, but how could she have known? He and the prof had been very careful. Geoffrey had been able to suppress her suspicions and convince her she was merely stressed out, but it had always left him wondering just a little. He unconsciously jiggled his knee again.

In business school he'd helped himself along a few times, just when he needed it. She'd never said anything about that, but a part of him always wondered. At the time he assumed she'd wised up and was willing to let it go since his success benefited her too. He still wasn't convinced she knew about his indiscretions. Since then he speculated that she had sources who told her things about him, even though he'd been careful to monitor and steer her connections. At this point he didn't think there was anyone who would tell her what he did on the side. Yet she'd known about Sandra somehow.

He needed to keep tabs on her. Just in case she decided to use her information against him.

There was a tap at the door. He looked up to see his secretary, Diana, standing with a sheaf of papers. She was a pretty blonde and seemed appropriately in awe of him. "Mr. Chubb?" She said diffidently. "Your meeting's in five minutes. I have the information you asked for here." She held out the folders.

He straightened his tie and tugged his jacket into place as he stood. "Thank you, Diana. Could you get me a coffee too? You know how I like it."

She handed him the papers as he stepped through the doorway, and he brushed her tight ass with one hand as she turned to get his beverage.

Yes, it was good to be a marketing strategist on his way up the ladder.

Marianne woke to the tabby's whiskers tickling her cheeks, and his fishy breath in her nostrils. Rolling over with a groan, she tried to ignore him, but he persisted until she got up. Sore muscles from yesterday's work and lack of sleep made her feel pretty awful. She dragged herself through a shower and ate breakfast.

Even though the periwinkle blue paint in her room was dry, she wasn't sure she had the energy. If she could just get the rooms done, she could unpack and feel more like she lived here. Walking into the office, she discovered that the lid on the quart of brown had somehow come off again, and there were new insulting splatters of paint on the wall. They were already dry. Taking a closer look, she felt the hair rise on the back of her neck, and her heart start to beat faster. The organic splatters had been deliberately dragged sideways like finger paint across the wall. It was not an accident. Someone or something had made the mess, and that person or entity was in the house with her.

Suppressing the urge to scream, she backed away from the wall and retreated to the living room where she paced, arms wrapped around her torso.

Okay, my house really *is* haunted! She thought furiously. It's not just nightmares and me scaring myself. Some angry ghost or spirit lives here and doesn't like me. Is he still here? She looked around the room wildly, half expecting to see an apparition.

Just then Oscar strolled into the room, waving his crooked tail. He jumped up on the sofa, supremely unconcerned, and butted her elbow until she unwound enough to rub his head. She took a shaky breath and collected her panicked thoughts like scared sheep.

If Oscar isn't worried, maybe that means I don't have to be. She caressed his soft fur and calmed down. What am I going to do? I have nowhere else to go. I have to make this work.

She took another deep breath and channeled her practical PhD historian self. I've faced a difficult doctoral committee, surely I can do this. First things first: I can't be repainting that room endlessly.

An idea struck her, and she hauled all the paint cans from both rooms, tamped their lids down firmly, and put them on the step outside the dining room door.

Take that, Angry Guy, she thought defiantly. Then, rolling up her sleeves mentally, she got out the primer and slowly repainted the affected wall for a third time. Oscar watched her from the top of the pile of boxes.

"You're king of the boxes, Oscar," she said tiredly when she was done, ruffling his fur and rubbing his chin. "I think this would look really nice if I could just finish painting. I need a break, mister, so I'm going to town for a bit."

The air felt particularly muggy and oppressive with the threat of thunderstorms later in the day. Marianne walked up and down side streets trying to remember where she'd seen it, until the clean scent of green apple shampoo caught her attention. She followed the aroma until she saw the Hair Magic sign over the door. Gratefully, she stepped into the shadowy interior, hoping fervently they took walk-ins and had a space now.

The shop was cooler than the sidewalk by virtue of not being in direct sunlight. A small rectangle of light all the way in the back showed the alley door open to stray breezes. The comforting and delicious smell of green apple shampoo wafted through the air, making her think of her old stylist in the city. Vivid peach and granny apple green walls enclosed a working area with two sinks, two dryers, and two stations with a huge mirror reflecting the other half of the room.

The hairdresser stood with her full attention on an older woman sitting in the stylist's chair. Today, she had her thick, blonde-brown hair pulled back in a simple ponytail that dangled down between her shoulder blades. The pale violet colored locks had been corkscrew curled, framing her face. Her bare shoulders held up skinny tank top straps and sported surprisingly muscular arms and upper back. A full-length crinkle skirt of indigo blue draped over shapely hips. Her arms moved with surety as she combed and cut. The client, draped in a dark peach cape, sat and talked non-stop about people and events Marianne didn't know. They both glanced at her in the mirror, and the woman with the scissors said without turning, "Be with you in a few, hon."

There was no receptionist, so Marianne sat in the waiting area out of the relentless heat coming in the front window and picked up a magazine. Too keyed up to read much of anything, she looked more out of habit than anything else at pictures of famous people smiling or pouting.

The client eventually doffed the cape and came to the desk to pay, still talking almost non-stop. Marianne appreciated the attractive cut of the woman's iron-gray hair and began to hope she could relax and get a good haircut too. There was nothing like having her hair done to make her feel better about almost anything.

"What can I do for you, hon?" The stylist looked at her with a smile of recognition. "Oh, hey, you're the woman from the co-op aren't you?" She had a pleasant contralto voice.

"Yes, we met the other day and you said you did hair. Do you take walk-ins?"

"Sure." She flipped a page in her appointment book and said, "You're in luck. I have no one else right now. As long as it's just a wash and cut, I can take you right now. If you want color or a perm, you'll have to make an appointment for later."

"No, no. A wash and cut is all I need."

"What's your name?" Her pencil poised above the book, she raised a dark eyebrow.

"Marianne Singleton. I just moved here from the city," she added.

"I'm Kelly Walker. Welcome to Maple Hill. Nice to meet you again." Kelly stuck out her hand, and Marianne shook it. Kelly's hand was sinewy and her grip very firm. Marianne had to shake extra hard in return. She must have shown her surprise, because Kelly smiled and said, "I go rock climbing on my days off."

After Marianne was seated in the chair, Kelly fluffed the thick brown waves and commented, "You've got gorgeous hair. What are we going to do today?" She met Marianne's toffee brown gaze appraisingly with her own hazel green eyes in the mirror.

"It's gotten shaggy since my last cut." Marianne described what her previous hairdresser had done. Kelly nodded as she listened and asked a few questions then invited her back to the sink.

"So, you're new to Maple Hill. What brought you here?" Kelly asked conversationally as she turned on the water and tested it for temperature.

"I got divorced a couple of months ago and moved up here last week." Marianne began to relax as the pleasantly lukewarm water drenched her wavy locks, and Kelly's strong hands kneaded her scalp with shampoo. "My grandmother lives over in Vandenberg, and I used to visit her and my grandpa every summer so when a house came up here I took it. I have nice memories of coming here as a kid."

"Well, I hope you like it here," Kelly said sincerely as she rinsed Marianne's hair and began working in the conditioner.

"I'm really just settling in. So far it's great, though. I've lived in apartments most of my life, so I'm getting used to the idea of having a whole house to myself. It's a little strange. You probably know old houses make all kinds of odd noises and such."

Kelly did a final rinse and wrapped a towel around her head, and Marianne transferred herself back to the stylist's chair.

"Yeah, they do," Kelly laughed, showing white, slightly crooked teeth in her tanned face.

Marianne looked at Kelly in the mirror as she took the towel off and gently blotted the stray drips on Marianne's face and neck. Kelly's strong-boned, sunburned, and freckled visage looked down to earth, and Marianne decided to tell her everything. She wasn't sure if Kelly was a friend-to-be or a convenient confidante the way so many stylists seemed to be. She had no idea if Kelly would tell the next person in the chair all about her crazy last client, or if she'd keep her confidence. But Marianne really needed to talk to someone.

"Well, my house seems to make more than the usual share of strange noises," Marianne began with an apologetic laugh. "The basement is seriously creepy. It's completely clean, and I don't mind spiders or anything, but I really don't like being down there. The washer/dryer are down there, and I'm not sure I can stand to go down long enough to get my laundry done!" She continued to tell Kelly about her nightmares, feelings of being watched, and all the other weird events. She said far more than she'd anticipated, but it was such a relief to get it all out there.

"You probably think I'm completely pathetic. I'm not usually such a scaredy cat. Maybe I'm just frazzled by this whole move." Marianne laughed a little shakily at herself.

Kelly had been an excellent listener, cutting and combing with practiced motions at the same time. She'd paused when Marianne had told her about the paint splashes and again when the piano had played by itself in the middle of the night.

When Marianne had finished her story, Kelly put the comb and scissors aside, turned the chair away from the mirror so that she could look her client in the eyes, and said, "Hon, I don't think you're pathetic. You've had a rough year and moved away from everything you know to live in a totally new place. I don't know many people who are that brave."

Marianne embarrassed herself further when her face crumpled, and she burst into tears. Kelly got her a box of tissues and moved the trash closer until Marianne's outburst subsided. Marianne finally took a deep breath, scrubbed her face with both hands, and mumbled, "Thanks for listening and not telling me I'm an idiot. It's just that my ex has been following me around since the divorce, and I had to get out of the city just to get away from him. Now, I think my house is haunted."

"Hon, you've had a hell of a year, pardon my French," Kelly repeated firmly and turned Marianne back to face the mirror. She got the blow-dryer out and started drying and brushing Marianne's hair as she said, "I don't mean to pry, and you don't have to tell me if you don't want to, but where did you say you lived?"

"25 Violet Lane. It's a really sweet little house, and I love it and think I could live there but things keep happening that scare me."

Kelly stopped again and stared at her in the mirror with a carefully neutral look. "Violet? The little gray and white house at the end of the cul-de-sac?" Marianne nodded, and Kelly frowned and pursed her lips.

"How did you end up there?" Kelly asked casually.

"Mrs. Thomas owns it and needed a house-sitter. She's a friend of my grandmother's. She hasn't had much luck keeping renters, and after living there a few days, I can totally see why."

Kelly shook her head. "I don't know Mrs. Thomas, but the last woman who lived there was only there a couple of weeks before she locked it up tight and practically fled back where she came from. She stayed the last week at the B&B up on Main. Through the grapevine I heard some story about ghosts and nightmares and weird noises."

Marianne sat under the peach cape staring at her stunned reflection. It was one thing to have suspicions and another to have them validated by another person. She looked at Kelly's face in the mirror and realized she was dead serious.

She said apprehensively, "What am I going to do if I live in a haunted house? It's so eerie! I feel like I'm being watched sometimes and just feel anxious all the time. It's like I left one stalker for another."

"Well, you could try to ignore it," Kelly suggested tentatively, but Marianne looked so dubious Kelly reconsidered. "Let me make a few phone calls after you go, and I'll get back to you. Leave me your number. In the meantime, you could try talking to the spirit."

Marianne looked taken aback. "What would I say?"

Kelly shrugged again. "Whoever it is was probably a living person at one time. Maybe they just got stuck there for some reason. You could try telling them you don't like being scared and ask them to stop scaring you. You could say that the house is yours now and you can arrange it however you like. They have no right to throw a temper tantrum."

Marianne shook her head. "That sounds so strange."

Kelly shrugged. "It's better than running screaming from your house in the middle of the night."

Marianne considered this and let it go for now. She finally refocused and looked at her reflection properly. With her dark brown, wavy hair cut this way she thought she looked reminiscent of Karen Allen in *Raiders of the Lost Ark*, except with amber eyes instead of blue. She smiled and turned her head admiringly. Kelly held an oval mirror up so she could see the back, and Marianne nodded. "It looks great. Thank you so much for listening to me and for giving me such a great haircut. I feel pretty for the first time in a long time."

"You really have beautiful hair." Kelly smiled back, flashing strong white teeth in her lean, tanned face.

There was a distant rumble of thunder outside, and they looked out the front windows. The sun was fading steadily under increasing cloud cover. The air felt heavier than ever as it fled before the advancing storm.

"Uh oh, I'd better get home," Marianne said scrambling out of the chair and reaching for her purse. She paid Kelly and said, "I might make it before the rain if I hurry."

"It was nice to meet you, Marianne." Kelly's warm hazel eyes echoed her smile. "Good luck with your house. Be strong, girl, and I think you'll be okay."

"Thanks. I feel better already!" Marianne left the salon and walked quickly up the street toward home.

Chapter 9

As soon as Marianne left, Kelly looked at the clock on the wall and fished for her cell phone in her purse. Her next scheduled appointment was in fifteen minutes, and she had time for one call.

She pressed autodial and waited, twirling a purple lock with one finger, while the phone rang on the other end. On the third ring she heard, "Hey, Amazon, what's up?"

"Hey, Lawgirl, I just had a really interesting client." She paused momentously before saying, "She just moved into the Violet Lane house."

There was an answering pause before Sarah said quietly, "No shit."

"Yeah, no shit! It's been empty for a year, and the owner was desperate for someone to live there. Do you know a Mrs. Thomas?"

"I don't know, maybe. We get a lot of names through work. Is your client having problems?"

"Sounds like it." Kelly proceeded to tell her Marianne's story emphasizing the weird occurrences. She finished by saying, "She seems like a really nice person. I like her, and I don't know if she can handle things on her own. Would you be willing to come over with me some time and have a look around?"

There was a brief silence on the other end before Sarah said, "I could do that, I guess. Do you think she'll be okay with it?"

Kelly nodded. "I think she'd really appreciate it. If it doesn't work out, we can make some excuse and leave without too much trouble."

Sarah agreed and said, "When? Can she wait till the weekend?"

"I got the feeling: not so much. I don't start till noon tomorrow, so how 'bout then?"

Sarah considered. "Okay. I'll see if I can rearrange my schedule here and come in late. They owe me a little time."

"Thanks, Sweetie. You might like her, you never know," Kelly said with a wry grin.

Sarah snorted and said, "I've got a lunch break in a few minutes if you want to get something?"

"Sorry, Love," Kelly said regretfully, "I'm working through lunch today. But I can be home early if I don't get any late walk-ins."

"Okay, see you then," and Sarah hung up. Almost on cue the next client came in the door, and Kelly slipped her phone into her bag and greeted him with a smile.

Sarah put the handset back in the cradle thoughtfully. The uneasy, something's-coming feeling she'd had for the last few days settled into place like a compass needle finding north. She got up to stretch and water her plants to settle her mind before resuming work on preparing for the afternoon meeting.

As the self-proclaimed caretaker of Maple Hill's spirits, she monitored the interactions between the living and nonliving residents of the town, and she felt personally obligated to intervene if someone needed her. Whenever she had a feeling that something was going on, she was on heightened alert until she knew what it was, and it either resolved itself or she stepped in.

The spider plant on top of the filing cabinet had sent out another few sprigs on their long, droopy stems and needed trimming again. In the meantime, she watered it and gently steered it away from the avocado seed she was coaxing into life on the windowsill.

There were many skeptics among the living, some of whom considered her a downright fraud. If she had to talk to a known skeptic, it was usually because a deceased relative needed her to relay a message. Sarah did her best to be polite and nonthreatening, but sometimes the recipient took the news hard. She'd been accused of spying or lying more than once. Sometimes the opposite had happened, and the surviving relatives of a newly deceased person begged her to hold a séance so they could talk to the dearly departed. Sarah knew when a spirit was still present and when they were gone, and she had to break the news gently but firmly that she didn't do séances. The one thing she never did was take money in exchange for the use of her skill.

Her day job was very important to her. The law firm's partners, Dan Smith, Arnold Wolgust, and Hank Brown, were tolerant of her sideline partly because she never told them all that she did. She was also fortunate that each partner had a personal reason to believe in the paranormal. Dan had a grandmother who conversed with spirits. Arnold had a cousin who had an uncanny ability to sense structural damage no one else was able to detect. And Hank had never told her why he believed, but she gathered he'd had an unpleasant encounter with something supernatural. She'd utilized her talents on behalf of the firm a couple of times, and they'd recognized her value. Lucky for her, they were also the premier law firm in town and considered very respectable citizens. So, when gossip made its rounds, they firmly squashed it.

There had been a few so-called psychics over the years who had set up shop in Maple Hill. The first time Sarah had gone eager to find another person who could do what she did. Madame Z had been full of airy-fairy nonsense about crystal balls, séances, and card reading, and Sarah had been bitterly disappointed. When she realized that the phony psychic was also defrauding the people of Maple Hill, Sarah threatened to expose her. It didn't hurt that one of her spirit friends had put in an appearance and scared the bejeezus out of Madame Z during a fake séance. Since then, there had been a few others, but Sarah left them alone as long as they didn't fleece too many pockets and disturb too many souls.

Sarah finished watering the pots of herbs, basil, mint and lemon thyme she kept on a table by the window. They added a subtle fragrance to the room, and she found them soothing.

There were unpleasant members of the nonliving population as well: bullies and entities that downright scared her. She'd dealt with an angry poltergeist once when she was much younger, and it had taken everything she had not to run screaming like her client. Then, there were the occasional shadow beings who passed through Maple Hill, and all she could do was monitor them and put up wards around the most vulnerable places. She didn't know what or who they were, but they gave her the willies. She could handle most things by herself, but sometimes she needed help. Kelly was her rock, even if she couldn't see or hear anything in the spirit world. Sarah also had a few allies on both sides of the veil and drew on them as a last resort.

She would definitely try and get to the bottom of the unrest she'd sensed lately when she and Kelly visited the Violent Lane house tomorrow. With any luck, Marianne Singleton would not be an unpleasant skeptic.

The breeze billowed through the open window, rattling the blinds. Sarah lowered the old fashioned sash window and settled herself at the desk again. A thunderstorm would be welcome. She turned her attention back to the briefing she'd been writing before Kelly's call.

The smoky wisp felt the electric crackle of the coming storm and strained to draw energy from it. The newcomer had to be warned, and dreams weren't clear enough. She had to be kept out of the basement at all costs.

Marianne walked quickly down the sidewalk as the breeze picked up, lifting the dust fitfully from the pavement. The café owner outside the co-op was closing the umbrellas over the heavy metal tables, and people were moving purposefully toward cover.

She felt better than she had in days with a good haircut. Pouring her heart out to the hairdresser had also been cathartic. Kelly had been really nice. Admittedly, it was her job to be nice to her clients, but it felt like she'd been sincere when she'd told her she was brave. Marianne couldn't remember anyone ever telling her that before. Well, if she was brave maybe she could deal with this haunted house. She hoped that Kelly was worthy of the confidence and didn't blab Marianne's troubles all over town. It sounded like the last woman to live in the house had been freaked out by weird occurrences too and left in a big hurry.

The first huge drops of rain were beginning to fall as she turned the corner to her own street. She started to jog, but before she'd run more than a few yards the heavens opened up with a flash of lightning and a delayed peal of thunder. She was drenched by the time she reached her front door and fumbled with the keys.

Once inside she pushed her sneakers off and dripped her way down the hall to the bathroom to towel off. Oscar followed her. When she'd dried herself enough to not leave footprints everywhere, she got new clothes and hung up the wet things over the shower curtain rod. Her beautiful new hairdo was completely plastered to her skull, and she did her best to towel it dry. Oh well, she thought as she looked in the bathroom mirror, so much for looking like a young Karen Allen.

The lightning and thunder came closer and closer together as the storm approached. The light outside had turned into early twilight grey in spite of it being early afternoon. Marianne flipped on a few lights and turned on the radio, but every time there was a flash of lightning, the static made such a hideous noise that she turned it off almost immediately. Cool, moist air blew in through the western bedroom windows, and she raced in to shut them soundly before the rain could wet the floor any further. The wall in the office still looked white, and there appeared to be no new disasters.

She made tea for herself in the kitchen and put out a fresh can of cat food for Oscar. Given the spooky thunderstorm atmosphere, she half expected more ghostly happenings. It would be better to keep busy than idly anticipating something dreadful. So, she got a bucket and sponge and decided to clean the kitchen cabinets thoroughly.

The storm outside passed while she worked, but the wind and rain continued to lash the windows. She was just sponging mouse poop out of one of the lower cabinets when the hair on the back of her neck prickled, and she had the distinct sensation of someone standing in the doorway behind her. Goosebumps crept over her skin, and she felt a bubble of apprehension rise in her chest. She turned slowly hoping against hope to see Oscar and thought she caught a shadow in the doorway to the pantry, but when she looked, it wasn't there, nor was

Oscar. The unnamable anxiety was back.

Oh, damn, she thought. Kelly said I was brave. Time to be brave.

"Hello?" Her voice sounded tremulous in her own ears, so she cleared her throat and tried again. "Hello? I don't know who you are, but you're scaring me and I really wish you wouldn't." She got off her knees on the kitchen floor and went through the dining room door. She had the powerful feeling that someone was standing in the living room. Catching sight of Oscar in the dining room, she picked him up unceremoniously. His warm, soft weight was comforting as she carried him with her back through the kitchen and little canning room-pantry and past the basement door. As she passed the door there was a particularly strong gust of wind and something crashed outside. She jumped a mile and clutched Oscar to her. He meowed loudly in protest, and she eased up, apologizing and stroking his fur more to soothe herself. She felt like the basement door was radiating something like static or electricity that raised the hairs on her skin as she passed. She made sure it was locked.

Marianne paused in the doorway to the living room, standing between the foot of the stairs and a small closet. Oscar squirmed in her grip, but she didn't want to put him down. Instead she murmured to him and kissed the top of his head. The longer she stood there, the more she felt like someone was standing just out of sight around the corner by the fireplace, and if she stepped forward and turned her head to the left, she'd see them. Her heart pounded in her chest, and she felt a cold dread.

Be brave, Marianne, she told herself. The air felt heavy with the gravity of a person standing on the floor out of sight only a few feet away. The room felt cold as a freezer. She had to know or her heart would explode from fear, so she stepped forward and looked. As she did, she squeaked in a small voice, "Please stop scaring me." She stepped into the living room with Oscar as a shield in her arms and made her head turn left. Out of the corner of her eye she thought she saw a shadowy apparition by the fireplace, but when she looked full on, there was nothing there. "Please stop scaring me," she said again more firmly and felt an easing of the pressure of anxiety. The room gradually warmed up.

She took a deep breath and felt her heart slow down from its furious pounding. There was nothing there now, and as the moments passed, she felt more relieved and sure that she was alone again. "Thank you," she whispered to the empty room as she put the squirming Oscar down. He paused long enough to shake himself before dashing off down the hall.

The storm petered out and the air coming in the front windows felt fresher and less humid than it had earlier. She steadied herself as she opened all the windows again and aired the house out. The clouds passed and shafts of sunlight turned into full afternoon sun shining on a sparkling world outside.

She went outside and got wet all over again from the waist down as she walked through her storm-tossed yard. Her fear was gone, but she felt drained from the experience. Kelly had confirmed that she had a haunted house. Marianne didn't think she could live day after day being afraid of her own house. She could understand why the previous tenant had fled, but, tempting as it might be, she couldn't leave. There was nowhere else for her to go. If she returned to the city, eventually Geoffrey would find her again. And he would laugh himself sick if he heard she'd left her new house because it was haunted. That alone made her determined to stay and deal somehow.

She explored the garage and found some old gardening tools, a rake with a loose handle and some stiff shears, and decided to make a start on putting the flowerbeds in order. Michael's mowing job was rough but had begun to outline the yard. The garden borders were a mess. She went inside and filled a mason jar with water, so that when she found flowers she could put them immediately in water. The sun was hot on her back, but because the air was now cool, it was no longer a punishment to be outside. As the afternoon progressed, the post rainstorm colors only got richer and more beautiful outside and turned into the perfect late summer afternoon.

By 5:00 she was pleasantly sweaty and tired, and the walkway between the house and the drive and most of the patio out back had been cleared of weeds. It was looking much better already. Of course, now there was a huge pile of weeds and sticks. Maybe there was curbside yard waste? Hunger drove her inside for an early dinner.

Arranging the flowers she'd found while working, she put them in the middle of the dining room table on a woven straw mat. Even the weedy flowers were beautiful today, a mix of dandelions, fuzzy, caterpillar-shaped grass seed heads, and yarrow. She could see other colors peeking through the overgrown flowerbeds, and she planned to put a big bunch in each room. She ate the last of the co-op food from the deli and wrote out a list of groceries to get tomorrow. She didn't feel a trace of anxiety any more and felt empowered by speaking out earlier. Maybe that would be enough.

After dinner she finished wiping down the kitchen, feeling good about having a place for her dishes and pots and pans. She had enough energy to begin unpacking her kitchen stuff and made her way through several boxes. The dishes seemed to have newsprint smudges on them, so she loaded up the ancient dishwasher and turned it on. Instead of beginning the cycle, all she could hear was the sound of the motor. She opened the door and tried to reset it, but nothing happened. She sighed and made a mental note to call Gloria's Valley Homes and Properties tomorrow and get someone out to fix it.

She spent half an hour washing everything by hand and laying them out on tea towels on the counter to air dry. It was 8:30, and she went into the bedroom to appreciate the new color on the walls again. If she could get the trim done, it might dry over night and be done tomorrow, so she could move in and unpack. She got out her brushes, retrieved the quart of ice white from the side stoop, and got to work.

By the time she was done with the trim, her eyes were burning with tiredness. No one had looked in on her the whole time, and Oscar had kept her company without so much as a flickered ear toward the door. Maybe the request to stop scaring her had been heeded. She stood at the door and looked at the room with a big smile. It was really sweet: periwinkle blue-purple with bright white trim around the doors, windows, and at the baseboard. She folded the tarp and removed the painting gear, finishing by tamping the lid on the cans and putting them outside on the stoop. No need to press her luck.

She got ready for bed and lay down on the mattress in the living room hopefully for the last night. Although she was beginning to feel a little foolish for overreacting during the storm, she said aloud, "Please don't send me bad dreams. I really need to sleep tonight," just in case.

The wisp hovered anxiously, wanting to press her warning, but the vitality of the storm had passed, and she was exhausted from her earlier attempt. The new woman had been so afraid of her that the wisp couldn't bear it and had released the binding energy and let herself dissipate. Now, she drifted to the piano and brushed her insubstantial fingers over the keys.

Chapter 10

MARIANNE slept dreamlessly for the first time since moving in and woke when the early sun peeked through the front windows. In spite of the rest, she felt groggy and wished she could stay asleep. Rolling over, she tried to hide in the shadow of the couch, but Oscar had already determined she was awake and sat staring at her, tickling and sniffing her face from two inches away. He was relentless once he knew she was awake, so she groaned and got up.

She was eating a bowl of cereal when the doorbell chimed. Who was that? She wondered. Maybe Michael was back and eager for more yard work. She opened the door and saw two women on the doorstep. They were an unlikely pair.

Kelly looked tan and fit in a black and lime green athletic tank top and sport skirt that showed her well-muscled legs. Her blonde hair with the lavender streaks was French braided along both sides of her head and into a central braid down her back. Behind her stood a shorter woman with shoulder length, reddish-brown hair, glasses, and a conservative, white flowered button-up shirt with a khaki skirt and navy blue linen jacket. Her face was solemn with a hawkish Roman nose and dark eyes in a squarish face. Kelly was smiling, but her companion did not look so friendly.

"Hi! I hope you don't mind my stopping by. I tried your phone number but got no answer. I hope this isn't a bad time?" Kelly's voice sounded more concerned as she took in Marianne's wan face and messy hair.

"Uh, no. I think my phone went dead over night," Marianne replied, smiling hesitantly. "Please come in." She stood aside to let Kelly and her companion in.

"Marianne, this is my friend, Sarah." The other woman looked at her with an opaque expression and nodded briefly before turning away

81

to look at Marianne's living room.

Marianne was at a loss. At least, she thought, I have an excuse for the house being a wreck.

Kelly shrugged apologetically at Marianne as if her friend's behavior was normal and said, "Did you make it home before the rain?"

Marianne shook her head ruefully and said, "Your beautiful work was totally wrecked, sorry."

Kelly smiled and said, "It happens. I told you I'd make some phone calls when you left yesterday. Well, Sarah knows about houses with...problems...and she agreed to come by with me. I hope that's okay with you?"

"Yeah. Would you like something to drink? I just unpacked my glasses and can offer you water." Marianne glanced at Sarah who was skirting around the piles of boxes looking at things with an appraising air as if she were inspecting for cleanliness. Marianne imagined her visitor with white gloves running a finger over the top of the piano.

Kelly followed her into the kitchen, leaving Sarah behind.

"Don't mind Sarah," Kelly said conspiratorially. "She hardly likes anyone. Sometimes I'm not even sure she likes me, and we've been friends since elementary school. She just needs to walk around in all your rooms. Basement and attic, too, if you don't mind."

"That's fine." Marianne filled three glasses from the tap and handed one to Kelly who drank it. "What's she doing?"

Kelly shrugged again, an elegant rippling of her muscled back. "Getting a feel for the place. See what you're dealing with. So, how was the storm yesterday?"

Marianne sipped her water and grimaced. "Honestly, kind of freaky. I could have sworn there was someone else in the house besides me and Oscar. But I did what you said and asked them to stop scaring me, and the feeling went away. So I guess it worked."

Sarah wandered through holding something in her hand that glinted with crystal and silver. "Will you show me the attic and the basement, if you don't mind?" she said distractedly, clearly paying more attention to something else.

Mystified, Marianne led the way to the basement door and, hesitating only a little, she unlocked it and led the way down. She felt much braver with the two other women at her back.

The cellar was dim and cool and smelled slightly moist after yesterday's rain. Patches of sunlight slanted through the southern windows past the washer and dryer and onto the dusty cement floor. Two lightbulbs lit the area on this side of the wooden bin, accentuating the darkness of the missing bulb on the other side. Marianne couldn't help feeling uneasy, in spite of the company.

Sarah walked around the whole basement even the dark parts without a trace of hesitation. From the other side of the wooden divider, she said matter-of-factly, "Bulb out. You're going to want to replace that." She stood, dangling a little crystal over her palm and murmuring something Marianne couldn't hear.

"Yes. I have it on my list to do," Marianne replied, watching Sarah's movements with curiosity.

"Do you have any bulbs? We could do it now," Kelly inserted smoothly.

Marianne frowned, thinking, and said, "I don't have any new ones, but I could steal one out of a lamp upstairs and use that."

They went up the creaky wooden stairs together, once again leaving Sarah behind. Marianne was beginning to wonder if the other woman thought she was just a pathetic, scared little girl who was afraid to be alone in her own house, and there was, in fact, nothing to be worried about.

They pulled a bulb from a side lamp in the living room and went back down stairs in time to meet Sarah coming back up. She saw the bulb and said briskly, "Good plan. Best to make light downstairs as soon as possible. Attic?"

"The stairs up are next to the front door. Go on up. I'll be right there," Marianne answered, nonplussed and feeling distinctly behind the times.

She glanced at Kelly who shrugged and said sotto voce, "Don't mind her. It's not you. That's just the way she is. She does know what she's doing, though. Don't worry."

They finished their mission quickly. With the extra light, the basement seemed much less scary. Marianne turned the lights off and shut the door firmly before leading Kelly upstairs. On the way Marianne thought to ask Kelly what the strange wooden bin or closet was, and Kelly explained it was part of the old coal bin. A truck used to drive to each house, open a hatch where the oversized window now was, lower a metal chute, and deliver coal directly to the basement. Then it would be shoveled into the old coal fired furnace. Since the replacement of the ancient heater, the coal bin was no longer needed.

"This is a really nice house," Kelly finished. "I'm guessing it was built in the 'teens or 'twenties, right?"

"I really don't know much about it. I haven't done any research on it yet. So I'm not sure…" They turned the corner and stepped onto the sunny upstairs landing. Sarah was standing near the little door to the attic side. She caught the little crystal pendant in her hand and slung the silver chain over her head. "Okay. We can go back down now," she said with finality.

Marianne and Kelly pivoted and headed back down the stairs with Sarah behind them. Marianne was thoroughly confused. How was this tour helping her?

Standing in her living room, Marianne turned to her visitors with her arms crossed, facing Sarah's stern countenance. "So am I just crazy? Am I just being stupid?"

Sarah's face softened a little, and she pushed her glasses up her nose as she said more gently, "Tell me what happened to you since you moved in."

Marianne pushed the mattress away from the couch and gestured to the women to sit. Oscar jumped up and strolled along the back of the sofa behind them without the slightest hesitation. Marianne relaxed a little. If he liked them, they must be all right. After they'd seated themselves, she began.

A little uncertainly at first, her words spilled out as her reservations evaporated. "Well, I've had nightmares or bad dreams every night since I got here, except for last night. They're not like the usual nonsense dreams. They seem very specific. There's one about fire--I've had that one twice--and one about a man and a woman. He was very angry about something and hit her. Then he grabbed me—it was so real I could feel his hand on my wrist! He shouted at me about painting the office white. I woke up after that. Then one night someone played my piano. I'm not actually sure if that was a dream or if it really happened."

Sarah was idly rolling her pendant between her fingers and looked intrigued. "Have you had dreams that were like this before? Not about those specific things but the same sense of realness."

"Not exactly," she hesitated, unsure whether to tell a perfect stranger her recent sad life history or not, but then plunged ahead. "I sometimes dream about things that come true or that are true, but I have no other means of knowing about them except through my dreams. Does that make any sense?" she tilted her head to one side, and Sarah nodded.

She spoke slowly, trying to articulate her thoughts. "I don't feel like I'm predicting the future. It's more like my subconscious is telling me about things I missed during the day or is putting clues together and telling me in dreams. I used to be married but got divorced in June after finding out my husband was having an affair with a woman at work. I kept dreaming we were in bed, but someone was lying between us. I finally noticed that he was too familiar with a particular woman at work and guessed what was up."

Marianne added, shaking her head, "But the dreams I've had since I've been here are not like that. They are about things I've never seen and people I don't know. I don't really understand that."

Sarah looked at Marianne like she was a unicorn that had turned up in her yard, and she didn't want to scare her away. She rested her hands on her knees and said gently, "I think someone is trying to communicate with you using dreams. Two someones to be exact. When I walked around I could sense that there are two people here besides you."

"Two?" One ghost was bad enough, but two? Marianne sank down onto the mattress with its rumpled sheets.

Sarah nodded. "A man and a woman. He seems to be the one who is angry about the repainting you are doing. She is the piano player and probably the one who is afraid of fire. She seems to be more anxious than anything else. I'm not sure if they were in the house at the same time, or if they were here separately."

"That explains so much," Marianne murmured, wonderingly.

"She's never wrong," Kelly said with pride.

Sarah's brown eyes flicked toward Kelly gratefully then turned to Marianne calmly like she was telling Marianne about having termites not ghosts. At least she wasn't telling me to pack up and leave now, Marianne thought. "So what do I do?" she said, hugging her knees.

Kelly rose from the sofa with her glass and headed back toward the kitchen.

Sarah's hand returned to twisting the little crystal and said, "The man is angry. He's a dark spirit, and I think he's used to getting his way. However, it's possible that if you stand up to him and tell him you live here now, he may leave you alone."

She continued, "I don't think the woman wants to hurt you. I think she is very unhappy and is trying to find help. You seem to be able to sense her, and she is trying to tell you what's wrong through your dreams. Do you want to help her?"

"How do you know this?" Marianne said incredulously.

Sarah shrugged. "I can't explain how I know. I just do. It's similar to how you can tell the shape of something if you feel it with your hands. I can tell when spirits are present and can often tell what they are feeling."

"That's amazing," Marianne said, folding her legs Indian style.

Sarah said dryly, "It's really more of a curse than a gift. Anyway, there seem to be some particularly troubled places. The basement, the attic, and the living room are the strongest for the woman, and the white bedroom seems to be the man's focus. Try to think of these as clues to unraveling a mystery rather than being fearful of them."

Marianne shivered. She felt unhappy at this news. "I'll try. Do you think we can help them? If we do, will they go away and leave the house—and me--alone?"

Sarah raised her eyebrows and shrugged. "Depends on why they're unhappy. If you can figure it out, and help them resolve their issues, then they might move on to a happier place. You'd have the house to yourself."

"What can I do?" Marianne felt resigned. If this were the only way to get her house back, then she'd have to do it. "I'm not a therapist. I'm an historian."

Sarah sat back on the couch and crossed her legs. She resembled one of Marianne's history professors assigning her a project. "Excellent. Do some research. Try and figure out who they could be. There's a good chance they are people who used to live here. Maybe the current owner knows the history of the house and can give you some names. Go to the library and look them up in the county or town historical records. See what you can find out. Call me when you have some information, and we'll go from there." Sarah reached into her khaki skirt pocket, pulled out a business card, and handed it to Marianne.

Marianne took it and glanced at it: Smith, Wolgust and Brown, Attorneys at Law, Trusts and Estates, Family Law. Sarah Landsman, Attorney. Aloud she said with some surprise, "You work at a law office?" Somehow she'd expected "Psychic at-large. Crystal ball, palm and tarot readings."

Sarah nodded, as Kelly returned and chimed in with a wry smile,

"Yeah and 'Smith, Wolgust and Brown' are okay with her clairvoyant activities as long as they don't draw much attention. So, don't mention this to too many people."

Marianne looked at Sarah whose expression was once again shuttered and replied, "That's not hard. I don't know anyone here except you guys. But, I promise I won't tell your secret."

"It's not really a secret," Sarah relented. "I just don't talk about it a lot. People who need what I do find me."

"Okay. In the meantime what do I do? I guess I can deal if there are spirits with unresolved issues living here with me. I suppose it's a little like any other roommate, right? I certainly have my own issues," she laughed weakly. "The whole nightmare thing is really keeping me from sleeping, though."

"She's trying to tell you something," Sarah said, fiddling with her necklace again. "You could regard it as a way to understand her problem. Or you could tell her you understand it has to do with fire and please to let you sleep without nightmares. With the man, maybe standing up to him and being firm will work. You'll just have to try it."

Marianne remembered how she'd told the shadow to stop scaring her and how the feeling of the presence had disappeared. She was resolved to make the effort. "Okay, I'll try. I found the library when I was out exploring, so I'll go as soon as I can."

"That's the spirit. I said you were brave," Kelly said encouragingly.

"Can I call you if something really weird happens…?" She let her sentence trail off hopefully.

Sarah nodded, and Kelly replied, "Sure. I work most days except Sunday and Tuesday mornings. If you need to reach me, leave a message, and I'll get back to you as soon as I can." She told Marianne her cell number who put it directly into her own cell phone.

Sarah took her card back and wrote her cell number on the reverse. "Call and leave a message, if something new happens. I'll try and get back to you as soon as I can. Otherwise, hang in there. Do your homework and call me when you find something out." Sarah patted her arm awkwardly, got up and headed for the front door.

Kelly shot Marianne a grin behind Sarah's back and mouthed, "She likes you!" and headed out the door after the chestnut haired woman.

Marianne closed the door behind them and looked at the business card again. How unusual: Sarah was a clairvoyant lawyer and Kelly was a rock-climbing hairdresser. How could Kelly tell Sarah liked her? Sarah seemed like one of those people who was better with tech and things than with people. Or maybe in this case, she was better with dead people? Marianne found herself smiling in spite of her tiredness and hoped she'd begun to make friends in her new life. She'd had only a handful of acquaintances in her solitary research life, and Geoffrey had slowly isolated her from the few she'd made since college. It would be really nice to make some new friends.

She returned to the kitchen to clean up and was reminded about the nonfunctioning dishwasher. She put in a call to Gloria's and left a message describing the problem. Then she set about getting her bedroom in order. Sarah had said the ghostly man was upset with her painting over the dark green in the next room. At least he didn't seem particularly upset about the room she'd chosen as her bedroom. Oscar helped keep the packing paper in line by rustling through it and pretending there were mice or other critters in it. She made steady progress emptying boxes and putting things away. Eventually she was able to drag her mattress back down the hall and up onto the wooden bed frame.

The pile of empty boxes in the hallway grew, and after some thought she decided to stow them upstairs for now. She'd deal with them later. She peered up the stairs as far as the first landing. There was no sound from up there. She'd only glimpsed the space upstairs this morning for the first time. It seemed to have a small room and a mini bathroom under the slanted roof of the eaves.

"Hey, Oscar, big guy, let's go upstairs." She coaxed the cat to the stairs and tried to convince him to go ahead of her. Perverse feline that he was, he stood and waved his crooked tail around, and then sauntered off to the couch. "Traitor," she muttered and grabbed a couple of boxes by their flaps and made the trip upstairs alone. She made as much noise as she could, trying to feel braver.

The second floor was only partially finished. There was a dusty little bedroom and bath facing each other under the eaves with a charming dormer window in each. At the top of the stairs, there was a round window on the east side, and at the end of a short hall, there was a short, narrow door about five feet tall closing off the remaining attic space. Marianne guessed that the finished space occupied maybe half of the length of the house. Sarah had said the attic was one of the foci of spirit activity. That was an eerie thought, and even though warm sunlight poured in the windows, she didn't feel like lingering.

The little bedroom was carpeted in neutral tones with plain white cotton curtains at the north-facing dormer window. It would make a great spare bedroom someday. For now she began tossing boxes on its floor. Noisily hauling packing materials, she made the trip up and down a dozen more times. Eventually, the boxes could be folded and stored in the attic, and the really damaged ones could probably be recycled.

Her stomach growled plaintively. A glance at her cell phone told her that it was lunchtime. It was a good time for a break, so she grabbed her purse and headed into town with her shopping list.

Finally able to materialize enough to touch things, she delighted in the cool and familiar feel of the ivory keys. To her great pleasure, she found she could play without becoming exhausted this time. Keep the fear at bay. It also kept him at bay, she realized. Even though he held her here, he was more distant when she played the piano.

Chapter 11

MICHAEL was shooting baskets on his driveway when she returned from town. Catching the ball, he intercepted her on the sidewalk.

"Miss Singleton! I'm ready to do some more mowing."

"I remember. Come on over." Marianne found his enthusiasm infectious and got out the trimming tools to do some yard work as well.

He re-mowed the section he'd done over the weekend, trimming the grass down to a more standard lawn length. Then he took a first pass at the next section of long and weedy grass behind the house while Marianne worked on trimming back the wild growth of the front garden beds. She saved the best zinnias and Black Eyed Susans for the inside bouquets. They reminded her of the flower gardens her mom had around the house where Marianne had grown up, and she smiled. Setting to the cathartic work of pulling and clipping and digging, she began to uncover old bed boundaries outlined by an embedded brick border. After wrestling with the mower for an hour Michael stopped, streaming with sweat. They drank cold water and cooled off in the shade for a while.

"How's basketball going?" she asked after the first few gulps of water.

He pulled off his ball cap and wiped his brow. "It's okay. I've been practicing all summer so I can try out for the school team."

"When are tryouts?"

"Soon—first week of school."

"Good luck to you then. I hope you make it!"

He drank some more water and looked at her curiously. "What do

91

you do?"

"I'm an historian. I do research for other people and on projects of my own. I hope to teach a history class down in the city some day."

He drained the last of his water and looked thoughtful. "Are you also a musician?" he asked.

"No, my mom made me learn to play piano as a kid, but I never really kept up with it. Why do you ask?" she replied, puzzled.

"I coulda sworn I heard someone playing piano at your house earlier, and I thought it was you. They were really good," he added admiringly.

Marianne felt a chill steal over her. "Are you sure it was at my house? Maybe it was a radio somewhere else?"

He adjusted his ball cap over his sweaty hair and said, "It sure didn't sound like a radio. It sounded like it was coming from over here." He shrugged and slid off the steps, leaving his water glass behind. "I was going to finish the back and then go home, okay?"

"Sure. Let me know when you go, and I'll pay you before you leave," Marianne said distractedly. She didn't think she'd be able to get over having ghostly roommates.

She finished outlining the front garden bed and then hauled the cuttings to the growing pile by the front fence. Oscar sat like a statue watching her work from the windowsill inside. His crooked tail bobbed up and down gently. She paid Michael in cash, and he headed home, pushing the mower ahead of him.

Marianne ate dinner early and then got online to see what she could learn about 25 Violet Lane. After all the upset of moving and the weird, unsettling occurrences, it was such a relief to dive into the familiar zone of research. It reminded her how much she loved the thrill of discovery, chasing down side avenues, and building a picture of past events in her mind. She'd been hooked on history ever since ninth grade when her favorite teacher, Mrs. Driscoll, revealed the complexities of world history. Granted, it had been a survey course, but Marianne loved every minute of it. It helped that Mrs. Driscoll had been smart, beautiful, and no nonsense. She had high expectations of her students and told wonderful stories, making history come alive. Marianne had stayed in touch over the years, letting her old teacher know when she'd graduated from college as a history major and then again when she got her PhD.

It took some digging, but she found the public records of properties in Maple Hill and learned that Mrs. Thomas had owned 25 Violet Lane for about thirty years. Prior to that there had been only a couple of owners. Maybe some of Mrs. Thomas' renters had issues? She jotted down a short list of names and questions she wanted to pursue and then made a list of phone calls she could make tomorrow. She learned there was a Maple Hill Historical Society with a collection of volumes in the local library and planned to hit them up as well.

Basic research done, Marianne searched for websites on haunted houses and came up with lots of sites advertising famous places, Halloween entertainment, and places in the Hudson Valley that were said to be haunted. Finally she typed, "I have a ghost in my house" and turned up more than a dozen helpful sites. She had no way to vet them for authenticity so, instead, she jotted down their advice to see how consistent they were. They all agreed that ghosts and hauntings were rare and that many weird events had ordinary explanations that might be made spookier by fear.

She had to agree with them there. The sense that someone had been in her house during the thunderstorm might have been an overactive imagination made worse by the dramatic weather outside. The sense of being watched was one of the signs of possible haunting but could also be her subconscious worries of being stalked. It was somewhat comforting that the Internet "experts" seemed to concur most ghosts didn't want to hurt anyone. Instead, they were either trying to communicate with the living or stuck in some kind of time loop where significant events played out over and over, like footsteps or shadowy figures passing by. All the same, she was torn between skepticism and apprehension. It was one thing to read about haunted places and another thing to live in one.

There were even a few sites that discussed ghostly communication via dreams. The signs for visitation dreams included vividness, a sense of reality, a message being conveyed, physical touch, intense emotion and focus. The fire dreams she'd had certainly fell into this category as did the one where the Angry Man grabbed her and shouted.

Finally, she watched a bunch of YouTube videos that claimed to catch ghostly activity on camera. Some of it seemed a little too polished, which made her suspect it had been fabricated, but there was a series of videos based out of one house, haunted by a woman who'd died in a fire that began to wig her out. Shivering, she shut her computer down and went to bed with Oscar firmly in her arms.

She dreamt that a man was shouting at her. His face was turned away as he gesticulated emphatically at a room piled high with garbage. Marianne kept trying to apologize, thinking Geoffrey was angry at her for some reason. Then he turned toward her, and it looked like her ex but with a bristling dark beard instead, his features contorted in rage. Startled, she stepped back but was caught short as the man reached out and grabbed her arm, squeezing her painfully. Her own anger flared, and she wrenched her arm out of his grasp and shouted back, "You're not Geoffrey! Let go of me!"

She woke with a start to the nighttime silence of the house. The faint smell of fresh paint and grass cuttings helped clear her head, and she lay in bed listening to the crickets chirp outside, and the bedside clock tick the seconds. Oscar was not next to her, but she thought she could hear him down the hall using the litter box. After a little while, he padded back into the room and leapt lightly onto the bed and settled down beside her again.

Angry Man was still upset with her. He seemed to have no problem grabbing her, and Marianne wondered who he'd been in life— someone accustomed to control and power. For all of Geoffrey's faults, he'd never struck her or yanked her around. He had sometimes yelled, but mostly he'd used words and tones that made her feel stupid or small. Really, when she thought about it, it was a wonder she'd stayed with him for so long. But, sometimes, he'd looked at her with a trace of the love they'd shared, and she had longed for those moments so much, the rest seemed worth enduring. In comparison, she didn't think Angry Man had ever loved another person.

She woke again later to the sound of her phone playing the ominous theme song from Jaws. Groping for the device, she saw that Geoffrey had left her a text message, reading, "I'll find you." Waking completely, she sat up in bed, feeling scared in the pit of her stomach. He was still looking for her. His words implied that he hadn't found her yet, and there was always the chance he wouldn't ever find her. She hadn't told anyone of her current location other than her mother and grandmother. None of her new acquaintances knew Geoffrey as far as she was aware. It was a horrible idea that one them could somehow betray her, one that she put firmly out of her mind. It would be just like Geoffrey to undermine her confidence that way, and she refused to play that game.

Flopping back on the sheets she thought, I really should change my phone number. That might be enough to keep him away. I just haven't wanted to admit that he's systematically stalking me and isn't going to leave me alone without a fight. She sighed. All the anxiety and fear made her feel exhausted. If he didn't stop, she'd get a new number, she promised herself.

She rose, showered, and ate, trying to get over her jangled nerves. It was a library day, and she gathered her usual research materials together in a backpack and got ready to go out. Following up on her dream and Sarah's advice, she went to the office and said firmly into the silence, "I'm sorry you don't like the new colors, and the boxes upstairs seem to be in your way, but I live here now, and you don't. You had your colors in your time, and I get to paint the house in the colors I want. I promise to clean up the boxes eventually." There was no answer, and she couldn't tell if Angry Man had heard her or how he felt about it.

She was finishing sweeping up the scattered kitty litter in the bathroom before she went out for the day when the doorbell rang. She had a little spike of adrenaline, wondering momentarily if Geoffrey was standing out there. She pushed that thought away.

Maybe she'd forgotten that Michael was coming? She opened the door to tell him she was going out and instead saw a stranger standing on the stoop. It was that guy from the other day at Gloria's. Marianne had been wrong about him being good looking. He was absolutely gorgeous. Up close she could see his pale gray eyes inset in a lightly tanned face with a sprinkle of freckles across the cheeks and nose. Straight, reddish-brown hair flopped endearingly over his broad forehead. He looked like he worked with his hands for a living and took things patiently in stride. The dark green polo shirt he wore set off his outdoor tan perfectly. Her heart skipped a beat, and she stood with her mouth open for entirely too long.

His smile lit up his grey eyes. "Hi, I'm here about the dishwasher?" He had a pleasant tenor voice that seemed a little rusty. He cleared his throat.

"The dishwasher?" She said stupidly. He was a handyman not a salesman?

"Yeah. I'm from Gloria's property management, and you left a message about the dishwasher not working. Didn't they call you?" He hefted a large metal toolbox in one hand. She finally saw the logo on the breast pocket.

She shook her head. "No. Please come in. Sorry. I forgot I'd called. Yes, it still isn't working, but I haven't tried again. I've just been washing things by hand." She realized she was babbling and stopped. He stepped past her into the living room, and she was aware of how tall he was, at least six foot, and a faint scent of soap, Ivory, she thought. She shut the front door, feeling her heart pounding unexpectedly in her chest. "The kitchen is through this way."

"Did you just move in?" He asked politely, indicating the box-filled living room.

"Yes, last week. I'm repainting, so everything is still in boxes until I'm done."

He nodded and set the box down on the floor next to the appliance. "What is it doing?" He indicated the dishwasher.

She described what she'd done, and the noises it had and hadn't made, and he opened the door, knelt down, and began peering at things.

"Thank you for coming," she said. Duh, it was his job, she thought with a mental face-palm. Tanned, muscular arms and broad shoulders stretched the dark green polo he wore in a pleasant manner. She remembered Kelly's muscular back for a moment and thought fleetingly, I seriously need to work out or something.

"I work for Gloria's part-time," he was saying. "I'm really a carpenter. I make furniture. I'm trying to get my own business off the ground, but I don't make enough to live on yet, so I do handyman stuff to pay the bills." Deftly, he took the dish racks out and, leaning inside, began fiddling with the central mechanism. "Would you mind holding this?" He handed her a large flashlight.

"What kind of furniture do you make?" She asked as she aimed the beam inside over his shoulder. Oscar strolled through the kitchen, sniffed at the unfamiliar toolbox and peered at the dishwasher. Marianne smiled and shooed him away gently.

"All kinds really." His voice sounded a bit muffled from inside the insulated box. "I've made chairs and tables; lots of built-in bookcases like the ones you have; a few dressers and things with drawers. They take a lot of time to make so mostly I do work on commission."

"That's really neat. Most of my furniture is second hand or came from a do-it-yourself kit."

"There is an awful lot of kit furniture these days. That's why I think there's a market for handmade stuff."

"It's probably pretty expensive right?" She said ruefully, imagining a house full of beautiful handmade furniture. She leaned closer and tried to angle the beam of light better.

"Yeah. It always involves more time than most people are willing to pay for," he said honestly. "But there are buyers out there. I just have to find them. I think you're going to need some parts for this. It's an old model, but I think I can find them on the Internet."

He backed out of the dishwasher without warning, shoving her hand holding the flashlight into her face painfully. "Ow!" she said, massaging her mouth where the metal had hit.

97

He turned, and his eyes widened. "I'm so sorry! Are you all right?"

"I'm fine. My own fault for leaning too close and not paying attention," she said hastily, her face burning with embarrassment.

"I should have said something. Are you sure you're okay?" His look of concern hit her with the force of a blow. It was so nice to have someone care if she was okay or not. She felt her throat choke up a bit and hastily cleared it.

She smiled, feeling her lips swelling slightly. "Really, I'm fine. Here," she handed him the flashlight. "When do you think the parts will be in?"

He put his tools back and shut the lid, flipping the clasps with unconscious ease. "I'll look for them today and with any luck can get them shipped in a couple of days. So, next week, I hope?" He got out a small battered pad of paper and wrote down the model and serial number.

She followed him to the door, watching his big frame from behind and found herself wondering what he looked like without the shirt. Blushing furiously, she ducked her head as she opened the front door for him.

"Oh, here's my card, if something else goes wrong." He handed her a slightly bent tan-colored card. "You don't have to call the office first. You can call me directly."

She took it carefully and glanced at it. "Roo-ari Allen?"

"It's pronounced 'Rory'," he said with a smile.

"Nice to meet you," she replied, feeling fresh heat in her face. "I'm Marianne Singleton." Automatically she put out her hand to shake his and felt his hand envelop hers in a warm, strong grasp. An electric tingle seemed to run up her arm and, surprised, she gasped and let go as soon as she could.

He looked startled too but said, "Welcome to Maple Hill." Climbing into a battered white pickup, he stuck his hand out the window and waved as he completed the turn around the cul-de-sac and rumbled up the street.

She shut the door and leaned against it, grinning furiously. She looked at the card in her hand again and saw that it was from his carpentry business. "Ruari Allen Cabinet Maker Fine Furniture on Commission."

Too bad she didn't have a ton of money to blow on a whole set of handmade furniture. One piece at a time, she thought with a smile. He'd have to be here a lot. It could take months. She sighed and pocketed the card, realizing it would be foolish to blow her settlement on finely crafted furniture. She'd have to wait for things to break instead.

The truck motored around the cul-de-sac as Ruari steered on autopilot. He'd just met the most beautiful woman in the world. Her warm, toffee-colored eyes and shy, transcendent smile lifted his dull mood like the first snow after a dreary autumn. For a moment, he could feel the stirring of change in his soul, like a fresh wind. When she'd shaken his hand he'd felt a sizzle of something sing through his body. He couldn't recall meeting anyone else who'd made him react like that.

I wonder if she's single? Whoa, tiger, he thought. She's probably got someone special in her life. Well, I'll take care of the dishwasher and at least see her a second time. Maybe I can find out if she's single somehow.

He swerved abruptly to avoid a cat dashing across the road and slammed on the breaks to make the stop sign. Back to business, he thought, coming back to earth with a jarring thump. He looked at his list of stops for the rest of the day and groaned internally.

Chapter 12

WANDERING around her house with a goofy smile on her face, Marianne tried to gather her thoughts about her library visit. Meeting Ruari seemed to have temporarily short-circuited her ability to focus on research and mercifully made her forget her early morning nastygram. She forced herself to look at her notes and get back on track for the day. Oscar seemed content sunning himself on the couch, deeply involved in a cat bath. On the spur of the moment, she got out a selection of piano music and left it on the top of the upright next to a vase of flowers from the garden.

"I'm going out for a while today," she said to the empty living room. "If you want to play something, please help yourself." As before she couldn't tell if she'd been heard or not.

She locked the door behind her and headed up to town, her backpack sliding into place on her right shoulder like an old friend. The trees were such beautiful shades of deep summer green, and the smells of cut grass and earth filled her nostrils. She breathed in a happy sigh.

Ruari's face stole into her thoughts occasionally, making her smile.

The Maple Hill Library was located in an old fieldstone building at the north end of Main Street. The brass plaque on the outside said it was on the Register of Historic Places having been built in 1781 by a locally prominent citizen. There were actually three buildings connected to the library, the stone one and two much more modern cement and wood structures nearby. The stone one had library services and a smallish meeting room. The other two held the modest collections of books and periodicals, the small historical society and its collection of reference materials and a conference room/town hall meeting room.

Marianne went to the historic society room and checked in with the librarian. Mrs. Caldwell, a retiree of indeterminate age above sixty, with sharp eyes and artificially bronze colored hair, gave Marianne a nickel tour of the resources: old volumes of local history, family names, maps and periodicals and modern compendiums of cemeteries in the county, and local place name histories among other things. She seemed reluctant to allow anyone to handle her materials. She clearly took her role as guardian of local resources very seriously. Marianne did her best to seem professional and responsible.

Two pre millennial looking computer terminals hulked on a couple of desks in the corner, and Marianne wondered fleetingly if they even had Internet. Then she remembered the "WiFi" sign on the library window and figured they must have a landline for these ancient terminals. The whole room looked like it contained the sad, mismatched leftovers from an estate sale or three.

Marianne pulled out a heavy wooden chair and set out her research things. Her search last night on the Internet had turned up relatively little. Tax records indicated several previous owners and multiple tenants were noted in a fledgling landlord-tenant association registry. The first owners were a George and Anne Rutherford from 1925 to 1965, followed by a Markus Bordman until 1971. The house was then bought by Selwyn Thomas whom she assumed was Lily Thomas' husband. The Thomases registered an Adam Sullivan as their first tenant who lived there for five years, and then a Mr. and Mrs. Sundergard who occupied the house for about eight years. After that there was a string of other names both couples and singles who never seemed to stay longer than three years and usually less than two. The tenant registry ceased abruptly just before the millennium for unknown reasons.

Well, Marianne thought, the ghost problem might have originated before the string of short-term occupations and maybe explained the lack of retention. But it was better not to make any assumptions.

Mrs. Caldwell reluctantly disengaged from a cataloging project to show her the local newspaper, both on the shelf and those photographed and preserved on microfilm. Mercifully, it was a relatively short, weekly publication, only twelve pages. She started with the most recent issues and methodically began looking for mentions of any of the renter or owner names. She had trained herself to skim accurately and was fairly quick. Taking notes on things that caught her eye, she learned something about local politics, events, and people in the process.

By late afternoon she'd worked her way back in time to the 1970s. A few of the tenants' names turned up in passing either during or after their occupancy of the Violet Lane house. Adam Sullivan turned up in an article about the local chapter of the Electricians Union with a picture, and she frowned. The article reported on the awards and honors given to its members. In spite of his nice clothes, he had a kind of blank-eyed stare that made her think of rapists or killers in their mugshots. She wrote 'creepy' next to his name and made a note to investigate him further.

Later, the obituaries of the couple who'd first rented the house under the Thomases caught her eye. The Sundergards had died tragically in a car accident, leaving behind two children in their teens. Although they were no longer renting at the time of their deaths, Marianne wrote 'deceased—ghosts??' next to their names. Maybe their children lived locally, or Kelly and Sarah knew them through the grapevine.

As for the owners, Selwyn Thomas had been a local benefactor, contributing to the maintenance and partial restoration of a couple of historic sites including the library and the theater. He and his wife, Lily, had been in several community theater productions, and Lily had served on numerous boards locally. There had been no obvious mentions of mysterious or disturbing events related to the house itself.

Mrs. Caldwell came over to inform her sternly that the historical records center was closing at 4:30. Marianne stretched her aching back and returned her resources. On her way out, she made an appointment with the librarian to come back the next day to keep working. She would pursue her basic research on Markus Bordman and the Rutherfords tomorrow and see what turned up.

The muggy heat hit her like a wet slap when she stepped out of the climate controlled library atmosphere. She walked back toward her street, slowly adjusting to the temperature. Based on looks alone, Adam Sullivan fit the profile of the angry ghost at her house, she reflected. And the dead couple fit the profile of male and female ghosts. Selwyn Thomas' obituary in the late nineties had spoken glowingly of all of his accomplishments and contributions to the community. Mr. Thomas, the thespian, didn't seem the type to wig out over her paint job, and Mrs. Thomas hadn't struck her as someone who had been married to an abusive man, so she ruled out Selwyn. She sighed. There was always the possibility that people on her list but not in the paper were her ghosts. Historic research was all about finding pieces of a puzzle and fitting them together till they told the most likely story.

Marianne resolved to call Mrs. Thomas this evening and ask her about her renters and about the other people who had owned the house. Hell, she could ask her if she knew her house was haunted— and if she knew who it was!

After an early dinner she scrolled down her contact list for Mrs. Thomas' number and pressed send. The phone on the other end rang for what seemed like forever, and Marianne imagined a very old lady slowly making her way to the one phone in her house.

"Hello?" A quavery, elderly voice said.

"Mrs. Thomas? It's Marianne Singleton. I'm renting the Violet Lane house from you in Maple Hill?"

"Oh?" She seemed to think for a few minutes.

"I called you last week when I moved in," Marianne prompted.

"Oh, yes." Lily Thomas sounded stronger, more certain.

Marianne took a breath and plunged on, trying not to talk too fast and lose her listener. "Well, I wanted to let you know that I'm doing some painting. I've got the bedrooms in the back done. I also cleaned out the kitchen cupboards and found out the dishwasher doesn't work. The handyman from the agency came round today and said it needed new parts." She felt a distant thrill when she remembered meeting Ruari that morning.

"Oh, that's too bad." Marianne could picture her frowning. "Tell him to send me the bill. SueAnn Talmadge has my address. I'm glad you're painting. It hasn't been painted in a very long time."

"I would love for you to come and see it when I'm done," Marianne invited. "Oh, and the Cavarelli's boy next door is helping get the yard back in shape."

"Thank you, dear. I'd like to see it. You're certainly fulfilling your end of the bargain! Is everything going all right?" She said a little anxiously after a pause.

"Well, that's what I wanted to talk to you about. Mrs. Thomas, did you know…are you aware… I think your house is slightly haunted." Marianne temporized, unsure of the old woman's reaction.

"Slightly haunted?" She repeated, sounding a little guilty.

"Yes. I think there are some ghosts here." Marianne tried putting it another way.

"Yes, I believe there are," Mrs. Thomas stated, sounding unsurprised.

Marianne said incredulously, "You know?"

"Well, not everyone notices, so, I don't like to mention it."

"They're kind of hard not to notice!" Marianne couldn't help herself. "A really angry male ghost threw paint on my wall twice and shouts at me periodically. Then there is a woman who plays my piano when I'm not here. I've had bad dreams or outright nightmares nearly every night since I moved in." It was hard to keep the outrage out of her voice.

"Goodness! I'm sorry to hear that."

Marianne closed her eyes and counted to ten mentally before saying patiently, "Mrs. Thomas, do you have any idea who these ghosts are—or were?"

Mrs. Thomas was silent long enough for Marianne to wonder if she'd wandered away from the phone, but at last she said reluctantly, "Well, I can't be sure. It might be Anne and George. We bought the house from Mr. Bordman, Lucas? Mark? He was a very strange man, an insurance adjuster, you know. Our first tenant Arnold Sullivan was a very angry man. Selwyn always dealt with him, but he made me uncomfortable. I was glad when he left. I'm not sure what happened to him." She paused while she thought some more. "We rented to the Sundergards for a long time. They were a nice family, but they died, you know. They could be your ghosts."

Marianne made notes on her pad, jotting down Mrs. Thomas' imperfect recollection of the names. "Okay, is there anyone else you can think of?"

"No, not really. I think everyone else we rented to is either still alive or left town, and I don't know what happened to them."

"Thank you, Mrs. Thomas. Just so you know, I'm doing a little research on the house, trying to figure out who might still be here. I'm hoping to convince them to move on. I hope you're okay with that?" Marianne could just imagine Mrs. Thomas saying she rather liked them.

"Heavens no. I don't mind. It would certainly be easier to rent the place if they were gone! You won't hurt them, will you? I don't think they mean anyone any harm."

Marianne wasn't at all sure Angry Guy didn't mean her harm but let it pass. "No, I just hope to ask them to move on to heaven or the afterlife or wherever they would be happier."

"Well, if you're sure, that sounds all right."

Marianne rang off and sat staring at her notebook. She wanted to talk to Grandma Selene and wondered if her grandmother was back from her visit with friends. She pressed send on the right number in her cell address book and waited while it rang and rang. She left a brief message when the answering machine came on.

At least since she'd started her "homework," she'd felt a lot less scared about being in her own house. Having invisible, dead roommates was very strange. The piano playing wasn't so terrible, but the anger, anxiety and nightmares were not fun at all.

Her watch indicated that it was only 6:30. The afternoon sun was coming down the hall from the bedroom end of the house. There was plenty of daylight left, and it was too soon to go to bed. She toyed with the idea of getting the next room ready for painting. She had a tendency to get wrapped up in whatever research project she had going and forgetting everything else. Standing in her bedroom, she realized that she also had a pile of laundry that needed to get washed. In the interest of avoiding painting and keeping her daily life going, she collected everything she wanted to wash and put it in a basket.

She unlocked the basement door and flipped on the light below. Kelly said I was brave, so I can do this. Sarah said the woman's ghost was stronger in the basement, not the Angry Man's. I'm only going to be down there for a few minutes to get the laundry loaded, and then I'm coming right back up.

She picked up the basket and made her way downstairs and began loading the laundry. An untraceable anxiety stole over her, urging her out of the cellar. Something bad had happened down here, she was sure of it. Without thinking she glanced toward the area on the other side of the coal bin and threw clothing and towels into the basin faster. She had just turned the knob and heard the water start when she heard the basement door shut followed by a click. Then the lights went out.

Chapter 13

HER heart leaped in alarm as she ran for the stairs. Tripping on the treads in the dimness, she reached the top. Frantically groping for the doorknob, she turned it only to realize the bolt was locked. She felt for the bolt mechanism on this side and met only flat door. It was only lockable from one side, and she was on the wrong side. She felt for a light switch on this side of the door and found only gritty, peeling paint. There was only one switch, and it was on the other side.

Her fright blossomed into something just short of panic. She pounded on the door with her hands and shouted, thinking someone had come into the house and pulled the door shut behind her. She had the feeling that someone was just on the other side of the door, listening to her hammering. No one answered or unlocked the door after several frantic minutes.

The sound of the washer chugging away on the laundry down below served to calm her a little. She sat on the top step, eyes getting accustomed to the gloom. She realized there was indirect sunlight coming in through the coal bin window. Okay, I'm locked in my basement, she thought. How am I going to get out? She felt for her cell phone in her pocket, knowing it was a fifty-fifty chance she'd put it in there or left it in the living room where she'd made her call. She felt the little business card Ruari had given her but no comforting phone.

She sat at the top of the stairs in the darkness and thought, well, shit. Think, girl, think. How can I unlock the door from here? No one was likely to miss her for a few days, so she couldn't count on someone letting her out anytime soon. How had the door shut and the lock slid across? She knew she'd left the door open on purpose. Would Oscar have rubbed against it with his chin and caused it to close? If so, he couldn't have slid the lock.

Gradually, she became aware of a soft sobbing, a moaning sound in the basement below her. The hair stood up on the back of her neck and prickled along her arms, and her heart rate picked up. Down in the dark, someone was crying like her heart would break. Marianne sat and listened transfixed. She could picture a woman rocking back and forth, hugging herself as she wept softly, trying to stifle her sound. Marianne suddenly thought the crying woman had been locked in the basement too. And she was trying not to make too much noise, maybe to deprive her captor of the satisfaction of her distress

Somehow Marianne knew it was the Angry Man who'd done this to the other woman. And to her, too. Somehow knowing who it was transformed Marianne's fear into anger. He had to go. There was no way she was going to let his spirit stay.

First, she had to get out of the cellar. She went back down the steps and said uncertainly into the darkness, "Miss? I know he locked you in the basement. He just locked me in too. We're going to get out of here. Follow me."

She went to the coal bin, where the larger window let in dusty evening sunlight. Wanting to break it without hurting herself, she considered her options. The wicker laundry basket was not hard enough, and her sandals were rubber soled and not strong enough. She went back to the washer, opened the lid and pulled out a soaking shirt and wrapped it around her forearm. Returning to the coal bin window, she struck the glass tentatively at first. It took a few determined blows, but the window cracked and splintered. She stepped back hastily out of the way and cleared glass fragments away from the frame until she could climb out safely. She retrieved a sodden towel from the washer and laid it across the threshold so she could boost herself up and out.

She turned and called through the dark window, "Miss? Come on out. You don't have to stay down there anymore. You're free to go." *Did I lock my front door earlier or not?* She wondered.

She had not secured her front door, and relief washed through her. She walked back into the house and over to the cellar door. It was closed and locked, but she could see the screws that held the locking mechanism in place. She found a screwdriver and spent some time unscrewing the pieces of the lock on both the door and the frame then put them into a kitchen drawer. Well, getting locked in would never happen again, she thought with satisfaction. Oscar emerged from wherever he'd been and watched her activity with interest.

It was getting darker outside. If the angry ghost was willing to lock her in the basement, what else would he do if she stayed? Sarah's solemn face and blunt manner of speech came to mind, and Marianne hesitated. Marianne didn't want to be here by herself just now. Hadn't Kelly said that Sarah liked Marianne at the end of their visit? Locating her cell phone on the couch where she'd left it, she dialed Sarah's number.

"Hello?" Sarah's voice sounded curt.

"Hi, this is Marianne Singleton. You came to my house yesterday?"

"Oh hi, Marianne." Her voice thawed several degrees. "What's up?"

"Well," she took a deep breath, "I'm pretty sure the Angry Man's ghost just locked me in the basement. I got out by breaking a window and climbing out, and I took the locking mechanism off the door so it can't happen again. My question is, should I stay here overnight? If he's willing to lock me in, what else is he willing to do?" Her voice squeaked.

Sarah expelled a loud breath and said, "Wow. Okay, let me think. Tell me what happened exactly, including what you felt and heard."

Marianne proceeded to tell her everything she could remember.

"Can you feel him now?" Sarah asked intently.

Marianne put the phone down in her lap and closed her eyes for a few seconds, trying to "listen" with her emotional sensors. She picked up the phone again and said, "I don't think so. He kind of comes and goes. I told him this morning that this was my house, and he didn't live here any more, and I got to pick the colors for the walls. I also promised to clean up the boxes I put upstairs. Maybe he was mad about that?"

"You said you thought he'd locked the crying woman in the basement in the past. He sounds like a real sweetheart of a guy. Any leads on who they might have been?"

"I did some research today." Marianne gave her the abbreviated version of what she'd found. "I was going to look into several names tomorrow or the next day. I also called Mrs. Thomas, the lady who owns the house, and guess what? She knew there were ghosts here! She said she didn't want to bother me with that in case I didn't feel them on my own." Marianne relayed her conversation with Lily Thomas.

"I don't like the sound of Adam or Arnold Sullivan, whatever his name is, but you don't have any further information to go on, right?" Sarah commented.

"Nothing."

"It's hard to say how far an angry spirit will go to hassle the living. I've encountered some pretty nasty spirits and heard of others. It's possible that giving you bad dreams is the worst he can do since you took the lock off the door," Sarah said dubiously.

"That does not make me feel very safe!" Marianne exclaimed.

"Hold on." Sarah covered the mouthpiece, and Marianne heard her muffled voice say, "Kelly, could we have Marianne come over for the night? Yeah? Okay." She uncovered the phone and said, "You could stay here for the night, if you felt unsafe and needed a place to stay."

Marianne considered and then said, "I'd really appreciate that. I haven't been getting much sleep, and I don't think tonight will be any different."

"Okay. Kelly can come get you, if you like, or I can give you directions."

Marianne opted for the ride and hung up.

"Hey, Oscar." He'd curled up on the sofa next to her while she sat, and she told him she was going to be out for the night. She promised to come back first thing in the morning to feed him.

She was just finishing throwing some clothes into an overnight bag, scooping the litter box, and refreshing the cat's water when the doorbell rang.

Kelly, dressed in a long white crinkle skirt and a navy T-shirt, stood on the stoop, looking concerned. "Hey, you all right? Sarah said you had a scare."

"I'm okay, just weirded out. Let me grab my stuff. Do you think it'll be okay to leave Oscar here?"

"Sarah didn't say anything to me about evacuating everybody. So, he's probably okay by himself for a night," Kelly assured her.

Marianne locked the front door behind her and followed Kelly down to the old Volvo at the curb. "Oh, wait a minute! I had to break a window in the basement to get out. Should I just leave it?"

"Let me see." Kelly accompanied her around the side of the house and looked at the damage. "You really don't want raccoons or skunks in your basement, trust me. Let's see if you've got anything." She found an old piece of plywood in the garage that would do, dragged it back out to the window, and leaned it against the frame. "That should hold for tonight."

Kelly drove her through town and down one of the side streets to a part of town Marianne hadn't explored yet. It was several long blocks from Main and about a block beyond the last of the cheek-by-jowl houses of town, surrounded by old trees and a bit of lawn.

"Thanks," Marianne said with relief. "I really appreciate this. You guys are incredible to take a complete stranger into your house on a moment's notice."

Kelly glanced her way and said, "Honestly, Sarah's really glad to meet someone who's like her. Most people either can't sense spirits at all or think those who can are faking it, lying, or worse, nut cases. Even if they do have a paranormal experience, they don't want to believe it or somehow blame the messenger. All the same," she added dryly, "if someone is in trouble with something they can't explain, they somehow think Sarah can help them out."

Marianne was still stuck on "someone like her." Was she? She hadn't really encountered ghosts or spirits before that she was aware of.

All she had was the weird dreaming ability, which was sometimes so cryptic, it made no sense at all and wasn't very helpful. She wasn't sure if she was glad of the comparison or disturbed by it.

The women lived in a small white house set back from the road, surrounded by trees. The last of a deep blue sky showed the outlines of the treetops, and the porch light was glowing a homey yellow-white. Marianne was reminded of a Magritte painting she'd seen at the Museum of Modern Art in New York.

Sarah greeted them at the front door, her spectacles glinting in the porch light, and held it open while Marianne brought her bag inside. Sarah was dressed much more casually than Marianne had last seen her in a pair of roomy linen slacks with a draw string waist, a short-sleeved button up blouse with little blue and pink flowers on it, and her hair was loosely tucked behind her ears. She'd made peppermint tea, and the three women sat at the wooden kitchen table to drink it.

Marianne expressed her thanks again to her hosts. "I really appreciate your giving me a place to stay tonight." Both women murmured, "Not a problem." Then Marianne glanced at Sarah whose lack of a smile still seemed forbidding, and added a little hesitantly, "Kelly said on the way over that you were happy to meet someone like you. I'm not sure I am."

Sarah shot Kelly a frown, and Kelly replied with an insouciant one-shouldered shrug. Sarah then turned to their guest and said matter-of-factly, "You said you have dreams that the spirits in your house are telling you things. You can feel their presence when they are there." Sarah put her mug down and leaned forward, gazing at her intently. "You acknowledge that they might exist at all. Most people ignore them completely. I don't know how long you've been able to do this, but it makes you more like me than not."

Marianne looked troubled. "I told you I've had dreams that came true before." She told an abbreviated version of her story. Sarah and Kelly listened attentively, asking a few questions to clarify. "But I've never had dreams about ghosts before I moved to Violet Lane," Marianne finished.

"You have had a hell of a year, girl," Kelly said fervently, and

Sarah murmured an assent. "Let's hope your ex doesn't ever figure out where you've gone. Maybe your abilities with spirits are a latent talent?" She offered.

"Certainly possible." Sarah nodded. She hesitated then said, "I've been able to see and hear spirits when they wanted me to all my life."

Kelly raised her dark eyebrows in surprise, but Sarah took a sip of her tea and went on. "The first playmate I had was my grandmother who used to come visit me in my room when I was three and four years old. I didn't know until later that she had died shortly after I was born. My mother thought I was the easiest baby in the world." She smiled nostalgically at the memory. "She didn't know about the free 'daycare' her mother was supplying! Grandma was sad her daughter couldn't see or hear her anymore but was glad that I could. I had no idea that the nice lady who stayed with me wasn't alive! I did think it was strange that mom never responded to her, but Grandma made me keep her a secret so mom wouldn't freak out." She took another sip and said, "Kel, maybe Marianne would like some of those cookies you got the other day?" Kelly got up and rummaged in the cupboard. "When I got older I saw less of Grandma, but she always showed up if I was sad or angry. She gave me a lot of good advice. After l left for college I hardly saw her at all."

Sarah's expression sobered as she stared at the tabletop. "I also saw a lot of people while I was growing up who seemed pretty real to me, but I came to realize that they got ignored by everyone else because they were spirits not flesh and blood. They seemed to know I could see and hear them and sought me out if they had problems or needed to communicate with the living. After some bad experiences, I learned to be really careful how I passed their messages along. Mostly the dead have been more appreciative of me than the living have been," she finished sadly.

Kelly put a box of peanutbutter chocolate chip cookies from the co-op bakery on the table along with a handful of napkins and squeezed her partner's shoulder, saying, "I've been looking out for Sarah since we met in grade school. It bugged the crap out of me when other kids or the teachers made fun of her or hassled her for being weird. I got a reputation for pounding kids who picked on her, and after awhile they left her alone." Her expression was both fierce and affectionate. She reseated herself at the table and broke a cookie in half, offering her partner the bigger side.

"I'd wait for her to get out of detention, and we'd walk home together," Sarah said fondly, taking the sweet morsel and smiling warmly.

Marianne was aware of a deep connection between the two women and felt an ache in her chest. "It must be wonderful to have someone looking out for you. I used to think Geoffrey would do that for me, but after a while I realized he would not endanger his own career or reputation to do anything for me."

"Yeah. We'd go to the ends of the Earth for each other 'cause nobody else will," Kelly said, gazing at her companion. "You'll find someone who will love you, Marianne, don't worry," she said with absolute confidence.

Ruari's handsome face flashed across her mind, and Marianne smiled, "I hope so."

Kelly raised one eyebrow suspiciously. Clearly her well-developed sense for gossip was tingling. "Have you already found someone?"

Marianne blushed and shook her head quickly, filling her mouth with a sinfully rich bite of cookie instead.

Kelly looked like she wanted to pursue the matter, but Sarah interjected smoothly, "Leave the poor girl be, Amazon! How about you show Marianne the guest room? Some of us have to work tomorrow." She stood and gathered up the mugs and teapot.

Kelly led her up a flight of stairs to a small bedroom painted in a rosy-brown color. The windows were open to let the night air come in and alleviate the stuffiness.

"Sorry about the heat," Kelly said apologetically. "We don't have A/C. Bathroom's across the hall. We usually have breakfast around seven. I go for a run around five or six while it's still cool. Do you run? I'd be happy to have company." Kelly got a small fan going, trying to stir the air.

Marianne put her overnight bag on the counterpane of the guest bed. "I don't run. I'm afraid if I came with you, you'd spend more time waiting for me to catch my breath. Maybe I'll take it up now since I live in the country."

"I'll be happy to run with you some time," Kelly offered generously and padded back down the stairs.

Marianne could hear her in the kitchen, talking with Sarah. She looked at the fresh covers, turned down, the curtains lifting slightly in a breeze and thought, I don't think I ever knew anyone well enough, except Mom or Grandma Selene, to impose on them in an emergency. And yet two people I've barely met are willing to help me. For all the weirdness in my life, this is a definite improvement. I'll have to invite them to my house for dinner or something as a thank you. Footsteps on the stairs indicated her hosts were coming up for the night.

As she got ready for bed, she waited her turn for the bathroom. Maneuvering around each other in the small upstairs reminded her of being in college and sharing a suite with girl friends. Marianne turned out the light and said, "Goodnight, guys. And thank you."

"Goodnight, and don't worry about it. We'll get your ghost problem sorted out," came Sarah's voice next door.

I hope Oscar is okay without me, Marianne thought as she drifted off.

He was furious! The girl had dared to defy him. Not only had she broken his window to escape her righteous punishment, but she had removed the lock on the door. His wife would never have dared to destroy his property, and she had endured her punishment when she needed it. He was going to have to do something to impress upon this girl that this was his house, and he was in charge.

Ruari looked at the sculpture he'd been shaping over the last few days. Details were beginning to emerge. It was looking more and more like the face of a woman resting her head on the edge of a heavily curtained window or perhaps slumbering in a soft pod. He'd begun thinking of her as "Sleeping Lady." Her left hand was resting by her cheek perhaps holding the curtains aside.

A memory of Marianne's shy smile crept into his mind. And the memory of the fizz of electricity that had sizzled up his arm and exploded quietly in his brain. What an unexpected and wonderful meeting. He was looking forward to seeing her again. Maybe he could figure out a way to ask her out.

Smiling, he stared at the piece and rolled it from one hand to the other in his lap before picking up a tool and setting to work again. He slipped into the zone as fragments of wood curled away from the metal and fell to the floor around him in a growing pile.

Chapter 14

MARIANNE awoke in a sunlit room and experienced a few moments of disorientation until she remembered where she was. She stretched and sighed, feeling rested for the first time in days. A clatter downstairs told her the others were up, and reluctantly, she arose and made the bed neatly before dressing.

Sarah and Kelly were eating a light breakfast at the kitchen table. A pot of tea was under a quilted cozy, and a selection of cereals and fruit sat on the counter nearby. Marianne poured herself a cup, glad her new friends were fellow tea people. Geoffrey had been a diehard coffee guy and disdained tea as an effete British drink for wimps. She'd learned to make coffee for him and kept her tea habit to herself.

"What's your plan for today?" Sarah asked. She was back in conservative business attire, a tailored, beige linen suit with a white blouse and low heels. Her hair had been pulled back and rolled into a chignon held with a beautiful black and silver Celtic knot shaped clip. Kelly, in contrast, still wore her running clothes, and her own hair was pulled back and off her shoulders with a rubber band and big comb clip.

"Well, after last night I think I'd better find out everything I can about the names on my list. I'll see how far I get today. I don't want to lose momentum on painting either, though, or I'll never unpack! Maybe there will be time to work on the hallway."

Sarah swallowed her tea and nodded. "Research sounds good. Depending on what you find, maybe we can get the angry male ghost to leave you alone long enough to find a longer term solution."

"That would be great. I don't want to impose on you for too long."

"No worries," Sarah said with a warm smile that made Marianne feel more relaxed around the lawyer.

"You want me to come in and make sure everything is okay when I drop you off? My first client is at nine, and I have a little time," Kelly offered.

Marianne remembered the laundry sitting in the washer and the broken window. That was going to require a few phone calls...oh. She remembered the business card and suddenly felt it burning a hole in her pocket. She had a reason to call Ruari. After Kelly left. The heat in her pocket reached her face.

She looked up to meet Kelly's curious gaze. "Um, yes. I have laundry in the washer, and even though I took the lock off the basement door, I don't really want to go down there by myself. So, if you don't mind...?"

"Sure." Kelly looked like she was restraining herself from making further inquiries with great effort.

Half an hour later, they pulled up in front of 25 Violet Lane, and Marianne opened the front door, calling for Oscar as she went in. Kelly trailed in after her and closed the door. The big tabby came trotting down the hall meowing indignantly.

"Sorry, big guy," Marianne said. "Let's get you some food." Kelly stroked his soft orange and white fur while Marianne got a can open and threw away the old one.

"I hope you had a quiet night, Oscar," Kelly murmured while the big cat waved his crooked tail languidly.

They went down the basement steps together, and Kelly walked around to inspect the damage. It was darker with the board across the window, and she crunched carefully over the broken glass. Pushing the board away from the window to let in both light and fresh air, Kelly walked around making sure no animals had gotten inside. Marianne moved her laundry along and got the dryer going. Luckily, she only had one load.

"Looks okay to me," Kelly said. "No critters got in as far as I can tell."

"Good. Thanks a lot for checking it out."

Upstairs they walked through the whole house from room to room. Marianne couldn't see anything particularly out of place or sense anyone else there. But then usually she didn't feel anything until she'd been alone for a while.

"Do you feel anything?" She asked Kelly.

Kelly shook her head and shrugged. "I'm deaf as a post when it comes to that kind of stuff." Checking her watch, she added hastily, "Gotta go. See you tonight for dinner?"

Marianne's brow creased a little. "Hmm. Let's see how it goes at the library. Thanks for the invite." She was genuinely grateful for their generosity but didn't want to overstay her welcome.

Kelly departed in a swirl of energy, leaving the house quiet.

Marianne felt curiously shy about calling Ruari, so she showered and messed around for a bit. Finally, after she could delay no longer, she phoned the number on the card.

It rang a few times before he answered, "Ruari Allen."

She felt a flutter in her stomach and managed to get out, "Hi, this is Marianne Singleton. You came and looked at my dishwasher yesterday?"

"Yeah. I looked online for the parts and have them on order. They should be in by next week." He sounded like he was pleased to hear from her.

"Thanks. Um… I broke a window yesterday, sorry. Could you come and fix it?"

He sounded surprised. "Sure. What happened?"

"It's really stupid," she said in embarrassment. "I got locked in the basement by accident and had to break a window to get out."

121

"Oh, that's no good," he said with concern. "I'll come take a look at the lock and get measurements for the window. I could come by in an hour or so?"

"That would be fine."

"See you then," he rang off.

Now that her library trip was going to be delayed, Marianne decided to get the dings and dents in the hallway patched while she waited for Ruari. It seemed better than spending an hour or more being nervous. She put the little radio on and sang along to the tunes she knew. Oscar got his morning ya-yas out by racing up and down the hall and pouncing on bits of the canvas dropcloth that looked suspicious.

She was standing on the ladder up near the ceiling trying to fill in a crack that looked like it had been previously repaired, when she felt the air chill, and the hair on the back of her neck prickle. Oscar was sitting between the legs of the ladder with his tail curled around his front feet and staring intently down the hall toward the bedrooms. The radio crackled with a zizz of static before resuming. Marianne paused and looked back toward the bedrooms as well. She couldn't see anyone but had the sense that someone was watching her. She took a couple of breaths trying to sense whether the watcher's emotions were angry or upset or something else. Nothing came into her mind.

"Hi," she said aloud as if she could see a person there. "I'm just trying to patch up the ceiling and the walls before I paint them," she explained. "I hope you don't mind. As you can see, they need a little work, but I think it'll look nice when it's done. I was thinking of using the same off-white I used in the bedroom," she went on. "And then use the bright white for the trim around the doorways."

She didn't know what else to say and couldn't feel any reaction from the silent watcher, so she went back to spackling. Eventually, the feeling faded, and she breathed a sigh. Maybe that was the woman? Or the Angry Man doesn't mind the repairs and color scheme out here? Oscar had wandered off, probably to curl up and sleep somewhere.

Marianne had finished and was washing up her tools in the kitchen sink when the front door chimed. She wiped her hands on a dishtowel and walked unhurriedly to the front door to counter the ridiculous hammering of her heart.

There he was on her front step, toolbox in hand. His light gray eyes gazed past an untidy mop of straight, reddish-brown hair as he smiled. "Hi."

"Hi," Marianne smiled back, trying to act normal. She stepped aside as he came in.

"I'll take a look at that lock first, if you don't mind."

She walked to the basement door and said, "Actually, I removed it. I really didn't want to get locked in again."

"Well, that's one way to solve it," he said a little nonplussed. "Do you want me to put it back on? I can make sure it won't lock unless you want it to?"

She thought about the Angry Man and decided, "No, that's okay. I'd rather leave it off for now. I put the pieces in a kitchen drawer and saved everything so it can be put back someday. Just not right now."

"If you don't mind my asking, what happened?" He asked curiously. "I just can't imagine how the door would get locked."

She hesitated not wanting to appear like a crazy woman. "You probably wouldn't believe me if I told you."

He shrugged. "As a handyman I've seen some weird stuff. Try me. Maybe I can fix it."

She regarded his open expression and the hint of humor in his face and decided to take a chance. "Well, this sounds a little crazy, but there are a couple of ghosts that live here too," she said, looking at those beautiful gray eyes, her words speeding up, "and one of them is an angry, controlling man who doesn't like my choice of paint in his favorite room and doesn't like my telling him that he's not in charge anymore." She paused and took a deep breath to steady herself. "When I went down to the basement yesterday, he locked me in. So, I broke a window to get out, and when I got back up here, I took the lock off the door so he couldn't do it again," she finished and scanned his gaze for a reaction.

His eyebrows disappeared under his forelock, but he didn't laugh in her face. He finally said with an uncertain half smile, "I don't think I can fix that. The angry ghost thing, I mean."

Marianne held her figurative breath and said, "You believe me?"

"Well, it's the most...creative explanation I've ever heard for why something is broken. You said there are two ghosts. What—who is the other one?"

She regarded him steadily, willing him to understand, as she replied, "She's a woman who plays my piano in the middle of the night and sometimes when I'm not here."

He couldn't help himself; he laughed. "Really? That's pretty wild."

Marianne looked away, disappointed and regretted her honesty. "It is pretty hard to believe. Never mind. I'll show you the broken window." She led him down the creaky steps and showed him the window. Retrieving a dustpan and broom from upstairs, she cleaned up the shards while he took measurements and got the frame cleaned up for a replacement pane. Then the laundry buzzer indicated the cycle was done, and she pulled the dry clothes into the basket.

As he worked Ruari silently warred with himself. She was the most attractive woman he'd ever met but blaming ghosts for damage that she must have caused herself, even by accident, was not an excuse he'd ever heard before. She seemed serious, though. It would be really disappointing if she were a pathological liar. At the moment she radiated embarrassment, and he fished mentally for a conversation starter that might help reveal a little more about her, perhaps startling her into giving herself away.

Marianne was desperately trying to think of some topic of conversation that might return her to the moment before she'd told him about her haunted house. She couldn't think of anything casual to say. As she stood there awkwardly, Oscar cruised through, looked at Ruari speculatively and then rubbed against his legs. Ruari smiled and stroked Oscar's head and back.

"I never asked you what you did." He broke the silence first as he carefully removed pieces of glass from the window frame with a pair of pliers.

"I'm an historian--for hire," she said with some relief.

He looked at her quizzically over his shoulder, and she elaborated, "I have a doctorate in history, and I look things up for people. I sometimes write articles or summaries for a more general audience. I specialize in post Civil War America and dabble in Victorian England."

"Wow." He sounded genuinely impressed. "What made you move here, if I may ask?"

"That's a really long story," she said and added silently, that I'm really not going to tell you. "The short version is that I used to visit my grandparents in Vandenberg as a kid. When I needed to move out of the city, and this house was available, I took the chance to live in Maple Hill. I have fond memories of coming here in the summers as a child."

"How do you get your research done from here?"

"The Internet is often a place to start, I have my own books, and I can always get down to various libraries in New York for other resources."

He nodded. "Sounds like the best of both worlds—except for the ghosts, I mean," he added with a smile.

"Yeah," she said, embarrassed all over again. She opted to ignore the last bit. "I haven't been here long, so mostly I'm just hoping it will work out."

He'd finished his work and closed his toolbox. "Well, I'll have to order the glass from the hardware store. It should be cut and ready this afternoon, and I can come back and install it whenever you like."

"I was planning on going to the library today. I have some research I have to get done. Maybe tomorrow? I put a board across it last night to keep the animals out, so I guess I can just do that again?"

He nodded. "That will work for now, but it would be good to get the glass back in before it rains again. We're due for another thunderstorm in a couple of days."

"Tomorrow for sure then. Can you come in the morning?"

His lips quirked up politely. "I can be here by nine."

She grabbed the clean laundry and hastened up the stairs after him. After he left, she dumped the basket on her bed and got her research bag together.

Chapter 15

WALKING gloomily to the library, Marianne pondered the door she'd closed by being so forthright with Ruari. He clearly thinks I'm a nutcase. That relationship is probably not going anywhere now, she thought. Well, once all the repairs were finished, she probably wouldn't see much of him anyway. She didn't remember seeing a ring on his left hand, but he could easily have a girlfriend. A guy that nice and good-looking would surely have a girlfriend.

Quiet purpose permeated the library and helped her focus. Picking up where she left off the day before, Marianne spent the day leafing and then scrolling through back issues of the Maple Hill Register. She found no obituary for Adam Sullivan. He could have moved away, and if he died elsewhere, his death wouldn't necessarily be mentioned locally. She'd have to expand her search later. The bottom line was if he were still alive, he couldn't be her ghost no matter how creepy he was.

Her cell phone chimed, and she hastened to stop the noise. The caller ID said Dr. Wentwroth was calling. He was one of her professors from grad school. She had done a post doc project with him a couple of years ago but hadn't talked to him in almost a year. She stood up and said quietly, "Hello?" as she hurried out of the reference room.

"Marianne? This is Jim Wentwroth," his deep voice always reminded her of James Earl Jones.

"Dr. Wentwroth! How nice to hear from you!" There was a little alcove with chairs near the bathrooms, and she stopped there and perched on the arm of a chair.

"It's Jim, please. It's good to hear your voice too. How are you doing?" He sounded warm as always.

"Sorry, habit. I'm fine. I'm working on a little research project in

—" she hesitated and said, feeling a little guilty, "town. How are you?"

"I'm well." He sounded cautious. "I got a curious call from Geoffrey earlier today. Are you two still in touch?"

Her stomach dropped uncomfortably. "Um, no. The divorce papers went through a couple of months ago, and I try not to see him at all."

He sounded relieved. "Ah. Good. Then, I did the right thing. He called sounding very friendly, asking where he might find you, and I told him we hadn't spoken in a long while, and I didn't know where you were."

"I'm in—"

"No, no! Don't tell me. That way, if I'm captured, he can't torture me to tell," he chuckled, trying to make light of it, but her stomach fell further.

"Thank you, Jim. I appreciate it."

"Marianne, you were one of my best students and are a stellar person as well. Geoffrey never treated you with the seriousness and respect you deserved. When he called, I thought you should know. Wherever you are, you seem to be off his radar at least."

She'd blushed at his praise and murmured an automatic denial, before saying, "I hope I can stay that way."

"Let me know if I can be of any further assistance. I could tell him you've been spotted in Zanzibar, if you like," he offered.

She smiled in spite of herself. "Thanks. I'll let you know." She hung up and clutched her phone. Her ex was still trying to find her. Thank goodness for loyal friends, she thought. After a few minutes of fruitless speculation, she told herself, there's no use in stressing about it for now, and tucked the thoughts back into a box.

She returned to her table in the historical records room and tried to get back into her groove. It took some time, but the lure of history and an unsolved mystery drew her back in.

Markus Bordman's name turned up a few times linked to the insurance company he worked for and once for a Kiwanis Club event that he'd co-chaired. Mr. Bordman, the insurance adjuster, seemed more boring than angry. There had been no mention of a Mrs. Bordman. Also, Marianne hadn't come across his obituary, so he might still be alive. If she could find him, he might consent to an interview with her.

The lack of solid leads was getting discouraging. She moved on to the last set of names, Anne and George Rutherford, the first owners of the house. At last she found what she was looking for in a 1963 issue. Below a grainy picture of a woman with dark hair and thick 1940s glasses, Marianne read,

> Anne Elizabeth Rutherford (nee Eddy) died in her home on Sunday at the age of 63. She is survived by her husband George W. Rutherford of Maple Hill, NY. Born August 10, 1900 to Josephine and Samuel Eddy, Anne lived in the neighboring town of Schukill until the age of 5 when the family moved to Maple Hill. Anne attended Maple Hill Elementary, Junior and High schools where she earned top honors in her class. She was musically talented and from 1918-1920 attended the Institute of Musical Art, which later became the Julliard School. She withdrew before she earned a degree. Upon returning to Maple Hill, she became a beloved piano teacher for two generations of local students. It became a local honor to be invited to one of her piano concerts. She married George William Rutherford in 1925, and they lived in Maple Hill until her death from cancer. The Rutherfords have no children of their own, but she felt a strong connection to all of her students. The memorial service will be on Monday followed by the burial in Maple Hill Community Cemetery.

"Wow," Marianne whispered. "That explains a few things." She peered more closely at Anne Rutherford's picture and thought she looked solemn and a little sad. "I wonder…" she murmured to herself. Marianne asked the librarian to let her into the copy machine area. She made a copy of the obituary and asked her where the really early copies of the newspaper were located.

"The newspaper was founded in 1901, and we have microfilm of most of the issues here," Mrs. Caldwell replied with pinched lips. Marianne thought she looked like she'd eaten lemons for lunch.

"Would there have been news from more than one town reported in the Maple Hill paper?"

"Sometimes. You'll just have to see. Are you looking for something specific?" She seemed annoyed to have to help this visitor.

"I'm new to Maple Hill and don't know the area very well. Where is Schukill?"

The librarian frowned, tapping her pencil on the tabletop, and said, "I think Schukill may have been an early town or hamlet that lost its post office for some reason and became unincorporated. Its land would have been absorbed by more successful neighboring towns. Do you want maps of the area or early editions of the newspaper?"

"Maps first, please." She was able to find both towns in an 1899 survey. Schukill seemed to have been a little north of Maple Hill along a creek with a long Dutch name ending in –kill written in curly lettering she couldn't make out. There was a new survey for the area in 1915, and it seemed that Maple Hill and Schukill were roughly the same size. Both had businesses, homes, and churches. The long Dutch named creek seemed to have been renamed as the "Schukill Creek" which now divided them. After some further searching, she found a map dated 1921. Maple Hill was mentioned, but Schukill had mysteriously vanished.

So, something had happened between 1915 and 1921. Marianne thought about the dual effects of WWI and the 1919 flu epidemic that could certainly have robbed a small town of population and economic vitality. She went back to the 1915 map and looked closely at the tiny print indicating businesses and buildings.

She looked at the copy of the obituary and then went in search of the librarian. Mrs. Caldwell seemed upset at having to break off her own task. Marianne said, "I'm sorry to bother you again, but it seems the town I was looking for disappeared from the records around 1921. What would have happened to the buildings and such? There is a Maple Hill Cemetery mentioned. Do you know if it still exists? I was thinking of looking for a particular grave."

The librarian's lips thinned as she raised her penciled eyebrows and said, "Of course. That's probably now the Maple Hill Community Cemetery. Pardon me for asking, but are you a relative? I'm just curious why you are so interested."

Marianne replied in a companionable, you-know-how-it-is tone, "No, I'm not a relative. I think this woman," she indicated the obituary, "used to own the house I live in now, and I was curious. I'm an historian myself and wanted to learn about local history."

Mrs. Caldwell relaxed fractionally and nodded, "Well, it's possible that Maple Hill or Henryville absorbed Schukill. If it was originally along a road that survived, it probably would have just become part of one town or the other. The cemetery is not far outside of town along the main road, heading north. You can't miss it."

Marianne thanked her for her help and then went back to take some notes. She was just finishing making a copy of the 1915 map when the closing bell for the library sounded, and she looked at her watch in surprise. It was 5:00, and she suddenly realized she'd never had lunch. Her stomach growled reproachfully.

The faint notes of her favorite tune floated up from her purse, and she fished the phone out just before it went to voicemail. "Hello?"

"Hey, it's Kelly. Are you coming for dinner tonight? We're glad to have you. Besides Sarah is dying to know what you found out today." She sounded remarkably energetic after a full day's work.

"Okay. I need to go home long enough to feed Oscar and grab some clean clothes."

"I can meet you at your house, and we can walk home together. I've gotta stop at the co-op for a few things anyway."

"See you in twenty minutes."

She hustled back to the house in the late afternoon heat. After feeding Oscar, she got her overnight bag together. The hall looked unfriendly in the glare of the bulb, but the patching was dry. She could paint tomorrow. She was glad Kelly was coming soon. The sense of anxiety would have made it hard to sleep. Oscar seemed to be a little twitchy too, lashing his tail and pacing around. She was reluctant to crate him and take him with her, though, since he was not overly fond of the little carrier and seemed to be safe here even if she wasn't. Deciding to leave him a second night, she sat cuddling him in her lap while she waited for Kelly.

The blonde stylist didn't grill her on the walk back to Main, which surprised Marianne. Instead, she talked about her day, recounting a story involving a fussy customer who had come back to color her hair for the third time, clearly trying to match a shade only she could imagine.

They got a few things at the co-op. Marianne tried to contribute, but Kelly refused.

"Please let me give you a little something. It's the only way I can think of to thank you," Marianne insisted.

"Nope. We got this," Kelly said firmly.

Marianne groped for another way and had a flash of inspiration. "Do you guys like ice cream? We could go to Sweet's after dinner, my treat."

Kelly grinned. "You're on!"

Sarah and Kelly let her help with dinner, broiled fish and potatoes with lots of garlic, and Marianne made a salad to go with it. At the dinner table, Marianne recounted her library trip.

"It's interesting that Anne was musically talented enough to get into the early Julliard School but never finished," Kelly observed.

"Yeah. I don't know why she didn't finish," Marianne said. "Being a professional musician and a woman in that era was rare but not impossible. Maybe her parents couldn't afford to pay? Or maybe she'd met George Rutherford by then, and he married her before she could finish. It wasn't uncommon for a woman to give up college to marry."

"That's so wrong," Kelly said passionately. "It really ticks me off when women aren't allowed to pursue their goals and dreams as readily as men are. Especially if they are talented." She passed the potatoes across the table.

"Yes, but it was the norm for the time," Marianne pointed out, curious at Kelly's emphatic reaction.

"I know. I don't have to like it, though," Kelly said moodily.

Marianne looked at her curiously.

Sarah said matter-of-factly, ladling a small second helping of potatoes onto her plate, "Kelly and I had a past life regression done on us once. In one of her past lives she was a really talented artist, could draw and paint anything, and she gave it all up to get married because her parents insisted."

Marianne's eyebrows went up in disbelief, and she was suddenly reminded of that morning's conversation with a certain handyman. She drew them down again and thought, why should past lives be peculiar? They believe in them, so the least I can do is give them the benefit of the doubt. She tried to imagine the beautiful Kelly as an artist, working with paint on canvas. Marianne could more easily see her as the model. Instead she said aloud, "It's not the same, but you are an artist with people's hair."

Kelly shrugged. "I don't have an ounce of talent with a brush or pencil now. But you're right, I do like being creative with hair, and I like to take photos sometimes. Still, what a waste in that past lifetime just 'cause I was a woman. If I'd been a man, I would have been famous!"

Sarah nodded, "You probably would have been as famous as the men of your day!"

Marianne changed the subject back. "I wonder if I'm the first person to have a piano in the house after all those years? It might explain the ghostly piano playing. I hope she's not offended by my bad playing!" She laughed.

"If she taught piano all those years, I doubt she's bothered by your efforts. She probably appreciates that you're willing to practice!" Sarah chuckled wryly.

Marianne retrieved her notebook. "I was wondering if you knew anything about the other leads I had. Do the names Sundergard, Adam Sullivan, or Markus Bordman ring any bells?"

"Sundergard does. Kim and Jason were in high school with us. I had no idea they'd lived in your house," Kelly said with interest.

"Their parents died in a car accident not long after Jason graduated high school." Sarah remembered. "They were run off the road by a drunk driver out on Pig Hill Road. Kim was already in college, and Jason planned to go in the fall. They were really upset for a long time. Their parents stayed to make sure they would recover and then eventually moved on."

Marianne, still getting used to the idea of the dead occupying the same world as the living, said, "How did you know?"

Sarah gave her a sad, knowing look. "I went to the funeral and could see them sitting with Kim and Jason. During the reception, they asked me to tell their kids that they loved them and were sorry."

"Did you? Did Kim and Jason believe you?" Marianne asked softly.

Sarah shrugged. "I had a reputation by then as the weird girl who said she could talk to ghosts. Kim and Jason believed me, I think, but their uncle got mad at me and hustled them off. I'm pretty sure he thought I was exploiting their grief somehow."

"Do you get that a lot?" Marianne asked quietly.

Sarah shrugged resignedly. "It seems to come with the territory. People are often skeptical of things they can't perceive themselves."

Kelly stood to clear the table and announced, "Marianne offered to take us to Sweet's for ice cream!"

A broad smile transformed Sarah's face. Marianne was pleased she could make her look so happy.

They strolled down the sidewalk on the way back to town, listening to the birds as they roosted for the night. Marianne resumed her conversation. "I'll see if I can find out more about Anne's life tomorrow. I also need to find out more about the angry ghost. I don't feel great about staying in that house overnight till we can get him to go away."

"Definitely find out as much about him as you can. It will help us when we talk to him and may provide a key to asking him to move on," Sarah confirmed.

"Do you suppose I should try to find Anne's grave? There are a couple of places I can look."

She nodded. "Sure. I know the person who takes care of the Maple Hill Community Cemetery. I'll call him tomorrow and let him know you're coming."

"Thanks, I'd appreciate it."

Sarah shrugged. "John Irving understands about what I do, so he'll help you."

When they reached the more crowded Main Street, they turned to lighter subjects by unspoken agreement.

Jonathan Sweet's was full of Thursday customers. They stood in line waiting for the mix of locals and visitors to shuffle past the cases. Most of the inside tables were full. The three women talked about their favorite flavors as they waited their turn. Marianne was eyeing the coffee Oreo and mint chip and contemplating two indulgent scoops in a waffle cone when a familiar voice said, "Hey, Marianne!"

She looked up to see Ruari holding a dish of ice cream in one hand and wearing a friendly smile. Her gut responded with a pleasant lurch, and her answering smile lit up her face. She said shyly, "Hi." His glaze flickered to her companions as they turned to see who it was.

"Hi Kelly, Sarah." He nodded pleasantly as though he knew them but not well.

Marianne noticed that a shorter woman with coppery red hair cut in a spikey short 'do stood next to him. She looked at the trio of women and her lips tightened. She said a toneless "Hey" by way of greeting, punched Ruari lightly on the arm and muttered, "Let's go outside. It's too crowded in here."

"See you tomorrow," he said with another smile and followed the other woman out.

I knew he had a girlfriend, Marianne thought as her stomach plunged in disappointment.

"How do you know Ruari Allen?" Kelly asked, her face a mix of annoyance and curiosity.

Marianne felt the heat rise to her face and shrugged. "He's the handyman for my rental. He came to fix the dishwasher and the broken window."

Kelly's expression transformed into one of mischief as she said triumphantly, "You like him! I don't blame you--he's a total hottie!"

Marianne ducked her head, mortified, which only made Kelly laugh out loud.

Sarah elbowed her good-naturedly. "Quit picking on her, Amazon. You're up. What're you having?"

Kelly ordered, and Marianne got her coffee Oreo in a dish. She picked up the tab for all three as promised, and they retreated to the less crowded sidewalk. Marianne surreptitiously looked for Ruari and his date and saw them walking away on the far side of the street, clearly in conversation. The woman turned and grinned at him, punching him playfully on the arm again. He laughed in response, and they continued out of sight.

"How do you know Ruari Allen?" Marianne asked as they sat

down at a little wire table on the sidewalk.

Sarah answered neutrally, "We went to school with him and his sister."

"His sister? Was that--?"

"Yeah," said Kelly in disgust. Her face had clouded again. "He's okay, but Erin's a complete bitch. She was one of the girls who tormented Sarah all through elementary and middle school. At least she quit doing it openly after I had a few 'conversations' with her," she said with grim satisfaction. "Now she limits her commentary to a few snide remarks."

Sarah sighed. "It's amazing how junior high never leaves some people. Mostly I don't care anymore. I have established a good professional life, and my other talents don't usually come up."

Kelly scraped the bottom of her ice cream cup and grunted, "Huh. Word is that she was working at some fancy firm out west, and they fired her," she said with vindictive pleasure.

"Probably more due to the economic downturn than anything else," Sarah said mildly.

Marianne was still experiencing a sense of relief that the unknown woman was Ruari's sister not his date and only dimly registered their remarks. "So that wasn't his girlfriend?"

"Nope. As far as I know, he doesn't have one." Kelly sucked the last of her ice cream off the plastic spoon. She smiled slyly. "Not that lots of women haven't tried. From what I hear, he's dated but never settled down." She shrugged. "I'm pretty sure he's straight. You can try, girl, but don't get your hopes up."

Marianne said ruefully, "I'm pretty sure that's not going to happen. I took a chance and told him my haunted house story, and he just laughed at me. He was being polite, but he wasn't all that receptive."

"Well, Erin is one of the town's most vocal non-believers in that sort of thing. She's always considered Sarah a freak and a liar, at worst.

His parents are pretty straight laced too, so, if he grew up with that attitude, he wouldn't be inclined to believe you, would he?" Kelly observed. She saw the crestfallen look on Marianne's face and said more kindly, "Wait and see. You never know. When is he supposed to come back to your place?"

"Tomorrow morning to fix the window before it rains again."

"Well, I've got to work tomorrow," Sarah said, finishing the last bite. "Thanks for the treat. We love this place and don't get here that often."

Ruari and Erin walked back toward his workshop in the gathering twilight.

"So who's the new chick with Crazy Woman and The Fist?"

Ruari winced and said, "That's so rude."

"Yeah, well, The Fist used to beat me up all the time, so what of it?" She said aggressively.

"Only because you were so horrible to Sarah," he pointed out.

Erin snorted and waved her hand dismissively. "So, who's the new girl?" She asked again more insistently.

Ruari had to stay on his toes whenever he was with his sister. She changed subjects and moods blindingly fast sometimes, particularly when she was stressed. "She moved into one of Gloria's rental units, and I've been by to fix a couple of things."

Erin finished the first flavor and dug into the second. "Huh. I wonder if she knows Sarah is a total freak?"

Ruari shrugged but began to wonder about his conversation with Marianne earlier today. Maybe her ghost story was true, if she was hanging out with Sarah and Kelly? In spite of Erin's emphatic disregard for the supernatural, Ruari supposed stranger things had happened. It would be nice if she wasn't making things up to cover her own mistakes as renters sometimes did. She really was the most interesting and fine looking woman he'd met in a long time, and he wanted to get to know her better.

Erin elbowed him hard in the ribs, interrupting his reverie. "Ow! What?"

"I asked if you'd seen Pat Whalen recently," she repeated.

He yanked his attention back to his sister and frowned, "I saw him a couple of days ago at the town offices. Why?" They continued their conversation touching on people and places Erin had known in school.

Ruari unlocked the workshop door and slid it aside so he and Erin could enter. He flipped the lights on illuminating the open space, the tools and tables, and thick layer of wood shavings and sawdust on the floor. As always the scent of wood cleared his head.

"How can you live in this dump?" Erin asked as she tossed her empty ice cream cup in the trash by the door.

"How come you're living at home with Mom and Dad?" He shot back in self-defense.

She shot him a dirty look that fell short of 'The Look' Dad could level when he wanted. Ruari was profoundly glad he was not still living at home, and even though Erin got along with their parents much better than he did, he could still sympathize with her.

"I'm sorry, that was unfair," he said contritely. "Look, I don't need a fancy place. I just need a place where I can do my work."

She strolled between the half dozen projects, snooping the way only a younger sister would, poking at some things, picking up and putting down others. "What are you working on? Have you got any new commissions?" She asked.

He had picked up a broom and was half-heartedly sweeping woodchips and debris out of the main path between the door and the stairs to his one room apartment above. "Yeah, a couple, a bed frame

139

and a small side table."

She came across his hooded "muse project" and reached up to pull the cover off.

"Hey! Some privacy please!" Ruari objected, leaning the broom hastily against the railing and heading across the room.

"What is it?" She asked both curious and teasing.

"Just something I'm working on—an art piece. It's not done yet and I'd appreciate—"

Erin slid the cover off and picked up the half finished carving. She peered at it and turned it this way and that in the light. "Not bad, big brother," she said grudgingly. "It's a little weird, though. It's a person coming out of an egg right?"

Hastening across the room, he gently removed it from her hands and placed it back on the table. "Something like that. Like I said, it's not done yet. I'll show you when it's done." He laid the cover back over the work.

After a moment Erin said resentfully, "How come you got all the talent in the family?"

Ruari shook his head mentally trying to catch up with his sister's mercurial mood swings. "What do you mean?"

"I mean how come you got all the talent? I can't paint or draw or carve to save my life." She looked away. "Sometimes I wish..."

"Whoa, sis." He turned her to face him and read her mulish, frustrated expression. "You have plenty of talent. You understand numbers and math way better than I ever will. You can look at a spreadsheet, and it talks to you. It just looks like a big jumble of numbers to me."

"That's not talent," she said dismissively.

"I beg to differ," he retorted. Trying a different tack, he said, "Mom and Dad really respect your skill with numbers. Just because your boss didn't renew your contract in Arizona doesn't mean you aren't really good at what you do. Living with Mom and Dad is only temporary until you find another job."

She shrugged and looked at him with unaccustomed vulnerability. "Yeah. I just wish I could land something now. I got my 203rd rejection letter today, and it sucked big time."

He hugged her spontaneously and said, "Something will come up. Don't worry."

"Thanks." She hugged him back fiercely and then pushed out of his embrace and walked quickly to the door. She paused there and said dramatically, "Big brother, you are never going to keep a girlfriend if you live in this place. My advice to you is: get a real place." And she swept out the door. He watched her spiky hair bob away through the row of little windows in the sliding door. He shook his head half amused, half troubled by her parting shot.

Chapter 16

ANNE'S spirit drifted near the ceiling, passing over the electrical lines and causing them to crackle in her agitation. The inescapable fiery vortex was drawing closer. The memory of the all consuming flames and terrified screams prevented her from resting. She was desperate to get the woman away from the house before it was too late...

Marianne returned to her house the next morning, walking with Kelly as far as Hair Magic and continuing the rest of the way on her own. The sky was overcast, and the air heavy with the promise of rain. Oscar met her at the door with a vocal meow, and she got him fresh food and water.

While she waited for Ruari, she got out the painting things and spent some time getting primer on the walls and trim in the hallway. Hopefully it would dry by afternoon, and she could put on a color coat in the late afternoon maybe after a library trip.

Ruari arrived around 9:30 with a pane of glass in his truck all ready to install. She damped down her more primal responses, reminding herself that he probably thought she was crazy. Instead, she greeted him politely but without the breathless awkwardness of the previous times. His warm smile faded uncertainly, and the light in his gray eyes dimmed a little. Marianne felt a twinge of regret but led him around to the side of the house where he went to work fitting the glass and putting in glazing to seal it.

"Nice to see you last night," he ventured as he knelt on the walkway by the window, pressing glazing along the edges.

"Yes, did you enjoy your ice cream?" She asked neutrally.

He nodded. "How do you know Kelly and Sarah?"

"I met Kelly in line at the co-op, and she told me she worked at

Hair Magic. I needed a haircut, and we ended up talking. She and Sarah have been really nice to me, since I don't know anyone else here. I like them," she added with a hint of defiance.

"Do they…is Sarah helping you with your…house problem?"

Surprised, Marianne decided she had nothing to lose. "Yes. She seems to know a lot about spirits, and I'm grateful for her help."

He was quiet for a bit as he used a knife to smooth the glazing and shave off the excess. He rolled the soft putty in his hands, making a new snake shape to press along the next edge. "Most people here think Sarah is…odd, and they always have. But she's been able to help people who have had…problems, and a few have changed their minds."

"Sarah and Kelly told me last night your sister was not one of their fans."

He sighed. "Yeah. She's pretty opinionated and not too shy to share it with everyone else."

Marianne took a deep breath and said diffidently, "What do you think?"

He was silent for a bit before smiling and saying, "I guess I'm open to it."

"Well, that's something," she said with an answering smile.

"Miss Singleton! Miss Singleton are you here?" A young voice shouted from out front.

She raised her voice. "Michael, I'm back here!" Then she rose and went around the corner.

A breathless Michael stood on her walkway with his mower. "I thought I could do your lawn again before it rains. Would that be okay?"

"Sure. How's the basketball going?"

He grinned. "Pretty good. Tryouts are next week. If I get in, I have to get a uniform."

"Ah, hence the need for lawn mowing," Marianne said perceptively.

"Well, yeah." He grinned in embarrassment.

"No problem. It still needs it. If you have time, maybe you can start that last section in the back and at least give it a rough cut."

"Okay." Turning to the mower, he said admiringly, "By the way, I heard you playing earlier, and you are awesome!"

Marianne was momentarily puzzled. "I am?"

"Yeah, you're like a professional! Mostly I like the radio, but you make the classical stuff sound really nice," he said appreciatively.

"Uh, thank you." Realizing whom he'd heard, she was at a loss for what to say. Instead she looked at her watch, "Let's say you start at 9:50."

Feeling thoughtful, she went back around the corner of the house as the mower started. Ruari was shaving the excess glazing off the next side of the frame.

He looked up and said warmly, "You play piano, too? You're quite talented. Sounds like you have a fan."

She looked at him and shook her head. "I haven't played piano since I took lessons as a kid. And I was never very good."

He looked confused as his hands stopped their work.

She said by way of clarification, "That's not me playing. That's the lady ghost playing. Based on my research, I think she's someone who used to live here. She went to Julliard, by the way. That's why she sounds so good." She watched his expression go from confusion to disbelief to uncertainty.

"You're not just being modest? Or pulling my leg?" He asked suspiciously.

She shook her head with a wry smile. "I can barely do scales and pick my way through a really easy piece with both hands."

Marianne went back inside, leaving him to his thoughts. In for a penny, in for a pound, she thought. She would never have been so forthright with Geoffrey who would have scoffed her into silence. She didn't know Ruari much at all. He was either going to like her for everything, or not.

Sighing, she pulled her research bag together, hoping she could get to the library that day. She looked out the window and watched Michael's progress, pushing the mower over the uneven yard and guessed he would be only about an hour. It was pretty hot out and that discouraged much in the way of exercise.

There was a knock followed by Ruari pushing the door and stepping hesitantly inside. "Marianne? I'm done for now. The glaze has to cure before I can paint it."

She invited him inside and asked about the cost of the window repair. As she wrote a check out, he glanced speculatively at the silent piano. "I'll let you know when the dishwasher parts come in," he said and left.

Marianne felt let down. He must think I'm such a nutcase. She recalled the memory of their first electric touch and wished she could find a way to make him think of her differently. For some reason, that brought to mind the one liaison she'd had after the divorce was finalized and shook her head. It had been a hurried, fumbling, unsatisfying experience, and she'd regretted it almost immediately. At least she'd taken precautions at the time, and by mutual agreement they'd not kept in touch. Shallow, uncommitted relationships based on physical attraction were not what she wanted, though she knew plenty of men and women who bounced from one bed to the next. She longed for a partner she loved and who loved her as deeply. Celibacy was a better way to go until she found the right guy. And it looked like she was going to be celibate for the foreseeable future.

She checked her email and phone for messages hoping for news from her history clients while she waited for Michael to finish. Her stomach cramped with a little twist of fear when she saw she had a new text from Geoffrey. "I'm on to you and will be seeing you soon."

Even without Jim Wentwroth's help, her ex seemed to be slowly zeroing in on her location. She shivered in spite of the heat. What am I going to do if he turns up on my doorstep? She thought despairingly.

His text made it sound like he had begun searching for her outside the city already. That he would look for her in Maple Hill was not beyond the realm of his devious brain. He knew she didn't have many friends or relatives, so the number of places for him to pursue were limited. She didn't think he'd be so bold as to go to her mother's house looking for her. But he might think of Grandma Selene's house in Vandenberg. It was hardly a secret. She'd brought him up to Vandenberg and Maple Hill a few times to share her childhood places with him. She knew Grandma would never reveal Marianne's location, but he might somehow be encouraged to hang around either town. If he did, it was only a matter of time before he spotted her.

Why did he keep pursuing her? What was so urgent that he had to find her? She had no clues. I could spend weeks in turmoil worrying about this, she thought, and nothing might come of it. He'd love to know I'd been stewing in my own juices over him. Maybe that was part of his motivation. She took a deep breath and muttered to herself with more confidence than she really felt, "Screw you, Geoffrey. If you show up in my town, I'll deal with you somehow. This is my life now."

Putting her fears aside firmly, she scrolled through the rest of her messages and saw with pleasure that one of her old contacts at a New York University was interested in developing and running a history class with her on the influences of the Victorian era in America. That would play to her strengths very nicely.

She wanted to branch out the use of her history degree. Geoffrey's settlement had been very generous, but it wouldn't last forever. She'd toyed with the idea of developing a class, maybe for distance learners, so that she could do most of it online but didn't have the expertise to arrange it. This would be an excellent opportunity to do just that. She fired off an email excitedly, saying she was very interested.

Her mood restored, she got a glass of lemonade for her and one for Michael and stepped outside to catch his attention. Face streaming with sweat, he brought the mower to a halt. He accepted the glass gratefully and downed it in several panting gulps.

"Show me what you did. I'd like to see it," Marianne said when he'd recovered a bit. "Then I think you'd better quit before you pass out!"

Enthusiastically, he walked her around the yard and showed her everything he'd discovered. The grass had been allowed to grow for so long that it was very spiky underfoot in its newly cut state. However, she could see that new shoots were starting to emerge between the old stems and figured that the coming rain would probably help. There were brick borders around much of the edge of the yard, defining old flower and shrub beds. Marianne could envision the showcase yard it had once been and thought some trimming and judicious replanting might begin to restore it. *Maybe Mrs. Thomas will be interested in consulting,* she thought.

She paid Michael in cash for his hour of work and closed up the house before heading to the library. As she walked through town she couldn't keep herself from scanning the busy traffic for Geoffrey's silver Lexus or for his face in the crowd. The heaviness of the air was oppressive, and her shirt stuck to her back by the time she arrived. She earnestly hoped a thunderstorm would relieve the humidity rather than add to it. It was a relief to be inside. She set herself up at one of the solid, old tables before retrieving the spools of microfilm containing the earliest days of the Maple Hill Register at the dawn of the century.

Marianne lost herself in the early issues. The style of writing was different from the more recent sheets, more like storytelling than news. The front page was devoted to a mix of ads such as "Dr. Sugar's Miracle Headache Remover!" and "Farm Overalls $1.20 a pair" and articles that sought to educate and amaze the readers. They seemed to be about curious or odd subjects sometimes in exotic locales like "marriage customs among the Esquimaux of Labrador" or the development of the World's Fair Grounds. Pages two and three were devoted to more advertisements and local news such as meetings, births, deaths, and events. The paper was published only once a week. There seemed to be a dearth of farm and local events, but then she supposed farm news was found in a different outlet.

Eventually, she came across an article in late August of 1905 about a local residential fire in Schukill. The accompanying grainy black and white photo was of the smoking ruins of a house with nothing but the stone chimney still standing. She read the article with great attention.

Fire broke out midday at the home of Samuel and Josephine Eddy. Mr. Eddy is a local businessman and was at his office at the time. Mrs. Eddy was assisting at a church function at the time. Their two children, Anne, age 5, and Samuel Jr., age 3, were at home being cared for by Miss Abigail Leventhal, age 14. It is firmly believed after speaking with Miss Leventhal that the fire began accidentally when one of the irons was left on a sheet on the kitchen table. It has been a particularly dry summer, and the wooden frame house and its contents were tinder dry. Neighbors came immediately when they heard the cries and endeavored to put the fire out with a bucket brigade from the well. Neighbors responded to Anne's cries that her little brother was still inside, and one particularly brave fellow, Tom Kenny, ventured inside the blazing structure to rescue the boy. As he carried Samuel outside, both were overcome by smoke. The boy could not be revived and died at the scene, but Mr. Kenny is recovering. Mr. and Mrs. Eddy arrived as soon as they could. Miss Leventhal was hysterical and is recovering at home. The Eddy family home and belongings were destroyed. They are staying with relatives until arrangements can be made. Samuel Junior's funeral service will be on Sunday at the Episcopal Church. He will be buried in the Maple Hill Community Cemetery.

Shocked, Marianne reread the article several times and felt sad for Anne and her family. When fires happened today, she always imagined valiant firefighters and EMTs saving the family and putting out the fire in time. Yes, there were still deaths and loss of possessions but somehow not like this. They probably had to start all over again. And poor little Anne must have been profoundly affected for the rest of her life. That would certainly explain the fire dreams.

Marianne swallowed a lump in her own throat and sat back in her chair. Her imagination was entirely too vivid, she thought. Well, at least the paper hadn't said the little boy had burned to death; that would have been too horrible. And brave Mr. Kenny had survived presumably. She wondered what had happened to Miss Abigail Leventhal who had been hysterical at the fire. She must have been traumatized as well.

Marianne knew from previous research that life in the early 1900s was centered on drudgery for women. Well-to-do women had servants to do all the cooking, cleaning, and laundering, but if you were not well off or in the budding middle class, you got to do it all yourself—or hired a teenager who was all but an indentured servant. There was a reason time-saving machines had been so successful. Mrs. Eddy must have hired Abigail as her help around the house, leaving her free to be active in the church or elsewhere in the community, at least part time.

Marianne knew that young people at the turn of the century had been given a lot more responsibility and were considered adults a lot sooner than they were today. She'd read about farm kids as young as twelve being put in charge of driving the family wagon two or three days into town, buying supplies, and returning home. They relied on the kindness of strangers, as they slept in barns along the way and had to take their chances not to be cheated in monetary transactions. They also had to care for a team of horses and guard the valuable supplies all the way home. She shook her head. She couldn't imagine Michael or herself at that age, for that matter, being competent or confident enough to do that job.

Miss Abigail Leventhal was probably from a poor family, perhaps one of many children, and had been sent out in the world to make a living. Often such children had to send their meager wages home or worked for next to nothing. Their families were often relieved to have one less mouth to feed.

She looked at the article again. Abigail was doing the family ironing when the fire broke out. Ironing would have been an all day job in a stifling hot room. Yards of cloth shaped the ankle length skirts of the day, underlain by petticoats. Separate shirtwaist blouses were full sleeved and full breasted, making the women of the day resemble pigeons. Mr. Eddy probably wore white or vertical striped shirts over fitted trousers. In any case, Abigail would have done the washing in a laundry tub the day before and had to iron everything the following day. The article indicated that it had been a hot, dry summer, making the weekly ironing particularly awful. Marianne sympathized with the teenager of long ago and was glad of her own wash and wear wardrobe.

Abigail also seemed to be babysitting at the same time. Marianne had done some babysitting when she was a kid, and while some children had been decent to watch, others had been a real handful. The phrase "the fire began accidentally when one of the irons was left on a sheet on the kitchen table" stood out to her, and she imagined Anne and Samuel might have been in the distractingly rowdy category. She didn't know the details of how the iron had been left unattended but could understand how it had caused the fire.

After the death of little Sam, the Eddys would have had to bury him pretty quickly or risk putrefaction and disease in the late August heat. Burial customs of the day centered on the women of the family washing and dressing the body and readying it for burial. The men would have built the coffin and dug the grave. Anne would have been around for all of the preparations and would have had plenty of time to ruminate on the loss of her little brother. Marianne could easily imagine that Anne might have been in her own dark hole, thinking she'd caused her brother's death. Poor thing, no wonder she lingered in the Violet Lane house, warning people about fires and the basement!

Marianne made a copy of the article and put it with her notes and other copies she'd made. She noted with a frisson that the anniversary of the date of the fire was only a few days away. She scanned editions of the paper for several months after the fire to see if anything else was written up, but there was nothing further.

Resetting her mental filters, she started scrolling through microfilm of the Maple Hill Register from the 1960s and 1970s. Scanning for references to George Rutherford, she didn't register the low growl of thunder outside.

It turned out that George was a successful and well-respected lawyer both in town and within the county. He was connected to a larger family of Rutherfords who were also well known in business and community affairs across the county. George belonged to a local fraternal organization, started by prominent local businessmen. They emphasized philanthropy and held fund-raisers for worthy causes. Marianne did not doubt that it was also an opportunity for networking and being seen as generous and benevolent by the rest of the community. There was a photo of him and his buddies at the lodge's fortieth anniversary gala. No women, of course. Then, in a 1971 issue, Marianne found George's obituary. He'd died at the age of seventy-six.

According to the text, he was predeceased by his wife Anne Eddy Rutherford, survived by a brother and a sister and various nieces and nephews. He had been involved in various businesses, used to have concerts in his home where his wife would play piano, and would be missed by his friends. He was an upstanding citizen by all accounts.

That was interesting. Lily Thomas said she remembered him as a "difficult" man, and Marianne wondered what her definition of "difficult" was. Well, it wouldn't be the first time an upstanding citizen presented one face to his community and friends and was a real bastard at home. Marianne stared at George's photo and thought he seemed vaguely familiar. Something about the eyes, maybe. She racked her brain trying to place who he reminded her of and couldn't think of anyone off the top of her head. She printed out the obit and set it aside.

Anne Rutherford seemed like a good candidate for one of her ghostly roommates, but she hadn't been able to rule out Sullivan or Bordman yet for the other spirit. She did an Internet search on 'Sullivan' linking it with the search word 'electrician' and came up with several results. Noting that there were Adam Sullivans who lived as far away as Florida, Ohio, and Texas, she saw that one of them lived in Fishkill and jotted down that information. She found the address and phone of the local Electrician's Union for reference as well. Maybe there was someone who remembered him and could talk to her. Lastly, she did a search for Markus Bordman and found one living in Poughkeepsie. She got an address and phone number for him as well. She'd have to call Mr. Bordman and see if he was willing to talk to her about his stay at 25 Violet Lane.

A sharp crack of thunder outside followed by the lights flickering caused Marianne to flinch, and she logged off the terminal hastily. She put her materials away and headed for the front doors. It was pouring buckets outside the glass doors, and she stood in the entryway indecisively as she pondered her next move. It was 2:30 by her watch, and she was hungry for lunch. As usual her research zeal had carried her past mealtime. If the rain let up soon, she could make a dash for home and have something there. Depending on the weather, she could paint more or do her other research errand and see if she could find the Maple Hill Cemetery and pay it a visit.

After a twenty-minute tantrum, the thunderstorm stalked away over the hills toward the south, leaving cooler air sprinkled with light drizzle and lots of puddles. She walked back, mulling over the new discoveries and planning what to do next. Marianne arrived at home with wet feet, thinking she'd quite like to find the graves of the Eddy family. Grabbing an apple and hunk of cheese and some co-op bakery bread, she backed out of the drive and headed The Flea up to Main Street, where she turned left and headed north. Thinking about where the town or village of Schukill might have been, she set out to find it as well as look for the Maple Hill Community Cemetery.

Chapter 17

SHE drove north on Main Street until it crossed a little bridge. There were a few more houses and businesses and an Episcopal Church but more spread out here. After the last building, the road turned into County Road 301, winding through trees, fields, and hills. In about fifteen minutes, she came to Henryville, the next town over. Here she turned around and headed back toward Maple Hill. When she came to the bridge, she pulled over and got out. A small sign indicated that this was Schukill Creek. The bridge spanned a creek that was swollen with the recent rain and running over rounded stones some fifteen feet below the road.

Putting Maple Hill behind her again, she searched for the first road turning off 301. She explored west of the road, toward the Hudson, looking for rural cemeteries without success. Then she explored east of CR301, slightly uphill and came upon the Maple Hill Community Cemetery within a mile. There she drove past the entrance pillars made of rounded stones with a black iron gate. Ironwork letters in a graceful semicircle over the gate said "Maple Hill Cemetery," and a small sign to the right gave notice that the gate would close at dusk.

There was a small cottage made of the same rounded stones as the entrance pillars with a battered blue Ford pickup parked next to it. Marianne pulled up behind the truck and got out. She always felt a little shy about introducing herself to new research contacts but made herself knock on the front door anyway. Sarah said she'd notify her friends of Marianne's visit, so presumably, they would be amenable. Marianne knocked again, but no one appeared. Finally, she walked around the back of the cottage and found a shed with one door open. She called out "hello" but no one answered. Peering inside, she saw neatly stored tools for clipping, trimming, and pruning, and an old gas powered walking mower kept scrupulously clean, in spite of its age. There was space in the shed for something else, and the dark stains on the floor suggested another smallish vehicle.

The caretaker must be out and working, she thought. Maybe if I walk around I'll find him. She ambled slowly through neatly trimmed grass and evenly spaced markers. The stones closest to the caretaker's house and shed were from the 1970s and clearly legible. As she wound her way uphill, slowly looking at names and dates, she discovered there were rough groupings by date: 1940s and 1950s, 1960s and 1970s, 1980s-2000s. Closest to the tree line at the top of the hill were the most recent stones including a couple where the grass was only beginning to cover the dirt of the newest graves. At the top of the slope, there was a dirt road wide enough for a car and a half to pass where she turned to look back and catch her breath.

The landscape was breathtaking. The grassy lawn, dotted with white, sloped gracefully down to the road. The stone and iron fence and a line of old maple trees marked the beginning of the cemetery and protected it from casual access. Large maples and oaks clustered at intervals and created islands of shade, contributing to the park-like feel of the place. On the other side of the road, the land sloped further down and was lost in trees. The ribbon of the Hudson River glimmered and sparkled here and there obscured by the dense tree line. Dark green mountains purpling with distance bulked on the west side. The sky was now blue with fluffy white clouds after the storm. The air was somehow moist but mercifully, no longer sticky.

Marianne stood transfixed by the whole picture for a long moment, feeling peaceful and happy after the roller coaster of emotions this morning. For the first time, she was glad she'd moved here and could see this beautiful sight and know that she could come back any time and see it again and again. She looked down at the rows of headstones and thought how pleasant it would be to be buried here and spend eternity surrounded by this beautiful view. Thank heavens for John Loudon's brilliant reimagining of cemeteries as parks.

The distant hum of a small engine slowly came closer, and she reluctantly drew her vision back toward the approaching sound. A golf cart with a small flatbed containing an assortment of tools, tarps, and greenery was making its way up the dirt road toward her. She waited until it drew up a distance away, and the driver emerged. He was a tall, thin, dignified older gentleman with thinning white hair and the best Mark Twain mustache Marianne had ever seen. She smiled as he approached.

"Hello! What a beautiful day it turned out to be," Marianne said by way of greeting.

"Yes, indeed it did." He turned out to have a surprisingly deep, mellifluous voice. He was wearing faded canvas pants and a gray long-sleeved button up shirt with a short stand up collar open at the neck and looked altogether like he'd stepped out of an earlier age.

"Are you the caretaker here?" Marianne asked, enchanted. He nodded, and she added, "My name is Marianne Singleton, I'm a friend of Sarah's. She said she would call ahead for me?"

His beautifully groomed mustache waved gently up and down as he nodded again. "Yes, she said you might stop by. I'm John Irving." He held out his hand and shook hers solemnly.

"Irving, like the writer of *World According to Garp*?" She asked.

He shook his head and smiled, "No, like *The Legend of Sleepy Hollow*."

"Wow, really?" She was impressed.

"Only distantly related," he demurred.

"Still, that's so neat. Uh, did Sarah tell you why I was coming by?"

"Only that you were looking for a particular resident here. Have you found who you were looking for?"

"No, not yet. I'm looking for several actually." She paused and then decided to explain her situation more fully. "I moved into a house in town that seems to have the spirits of two former residents still in it. And after doing some research, I've narrowed it down to several possibilities; Anne and George Rutherford are among them. As far as I can tell she died in 1963 and was buried here. George Rutherford was buried in 1971 or so. I think the rest of her family is buried here as well. Her parents were Samuel and Josephine Eddy, and her little brother was Samuel Junior. He died when he was three years old around 1905. I don't know when her parents died, but it would have been after 1905. Do you know where any of them might be?"

"I don't know them in particular, but I can show you where to look roughly by year. Would you like a ride?" He gestured in a courtly manner to the golf cart/truck, and she grinned and nodded.

The cart's doors had been removed for ease of access, and she held onto the frame and braced her feet against the floor as the wheels bounced over the dirt road and off into uneven grass.

"How big is the cemetery?" She asked as he maneuvered skillfully between sections.

"We have five acres allotted to us by the county, but only about two and a half are occupied at present. There are approximately 8000 souls residing here. Our oldest residents are from the mid 1800s."

Marianne goggled. It didn't look like that many stones and monuments and said as much.

"Many grave sites hold more than one person, and we need less space after death." He pulled up to a row of relatively recent markers about a third of the way down. "This is the 1960s area. You'll just have to walk up and down until you spot the right one. I have to continue working, so I can't stay. If you look down toward the road, the early 1900s are about ten rows up from the fence." He indicated an area near some of the oldest trees farthest from the entrance.

"Thank you for showing me around," she said gratefully, adding, "You take really nice care of the place."

He dipped his head in acknowledgement. "Come back another time, and I'll show you around some more, if you want."

"Thank you. Maybe I will." Marianne felt genuinely comfortable around John Irving and thought it would indeed be worth a return trip. He departed in his mini truck with a clatter of rakes, shovels, and shears.

She turned and began walking up the row, reading names and dates and inscriptions. About ten minutes into her search, she came across a modern grey headstone with a flat top and slanted front side that said

George W. Rutherford 1895-1971
Anne Eddy Rutherford 1900-1963
May they rest in peace in the arms of their Lord

Marianne stared at the headstone trying to imagine the community piano teacher, who still haunted her house, resting here in peace. All she could picture was the sad-eyed woman in the obituary photo. Anne hadn't found peace yet.

She looked up and tried to fix the location of the gravestone in her mind relative to various landmarks and then set her sights on the older section. She neared the bottom of the hill and slipped beneath the shadows of the old trees. This part of the cemetery had a different feel from the open, sunny air of the upper slope. Here it was darker, and all of the gravestones were white stone but stained with something dark and streaky. They were a mix of three-inch thick, rectangular tablets with curved tops and more pillar-like stele inscribed on several sides. The graves were much closer together and more crowded feeling. The whole air was somehow darker and more intimidating, like wading through a forest of gravestones. Marianne had the feeling she was walking across people as they lay in their earthen beds with the grassy covers pulled up over their heads and felt like apologizing to the unseen sleepers. Instead, she trod respectfully up and down the rows looking at names and dates.

The oldest markers from the mid 1800s were closest to the road as John Irving had said. Many of them were nearly illegible, worn smooth by time and random damage. She worked her way back from the road, progressing through the decades slowly. When she got to the late 1890s, she turned in and began walking up and down slowly looking for Samuel Eddy Junior. She had to look closely at dates and after a while observed that many of the older people had full sized markers. A surprising number of them had reached respectable old ages in their seventies and eighties. Sometimes husbands and wives were listed on the same stone; sometimes they were on separate stones but next to each other. Children were sometimes listed on other faces of the stele-like monuments, suggesting they were buried with their parents in the same location. Other times young children had much smaller markers, hunkered sadly between bigger stones. A few of them had completely flat markers, flush with the ground and in danger of being obscured by grass.

She finally found a very small white tablet about a foot high and a foot wide with the words

Samuel Eddy Jr. Died 1905 3 years, 2 mos., 15 days

Next to it was a short, four-sided pillar with a pyramid shaped top. On the side facing the road was the inscription

Samuel Eddy 1877-1940

Josephine Eddy, his wife, 1883-1941

There they were, buried amongst their friends and neighbors. Marianne fixed their location in her mind relative to some trees and retreated to the edge of the dirt road that wound through the cemetery.

She stood and looked at the country road on the other side of the stone and iron fence and at the headstones in this corner of the graveyard. She tried to imagine the trees smaller, the county road unpaved and the rest of the cemetery all woods as it might have been a century ago. She pictured the horses decked out in their black ostrich plumes pulling the buggy from the hamlet of Schukill with Samuel and Josephine and the little coffin with Sam Junior in it. On a hot summer day, everyone would have been sweltering in their black mourning clothes. Little Anne might have gotten a ride with her family rather than walked, and the other mourners might have walked or taken their own buggies or wagons to the cemetery.

The pall bearers might have only been a couple of men carrying the small plain pine coffin between them as everyone walked solemnly to this corner of the graveyard. Their church pastor would have said a few words then, "ashes to ashes, dust to dust," before the small box was lowered into the ground. Anne might have been holding her mother's hand as she said goodbye to her baby brother with whom she'd played less than a week earlier. Then they all would have walked back to town and had a communal lunch courtesy of the church and sympathetic neighbors. How sad and bleak to have to leave your baby child, or your little brother, in a cemetery.

Marianne sighed and looked at her watch. It was nearly 5:30 and time to go home. Oscar would be hungry, and she was tired. Mr. Irving had returned to his shed and locked it up for the night. She knocked on the door to the cottage, and he came out.

"Did you find who you were looking for?" He asked politely in his smooth deep voice. She found herself appreciating his wonderful voice and awesome Mark Twain mustache all over again. He seemed like a person perfectly suited for his job in the local cemetery, lending it dignity and taking away any sense of creepiness at working among the dead all day.

"I did. I found all the people I was looking for. Now I just have to figure out what to do next."

"If you have Sarah helping you, you'll find the right thing," he said reassuringly.

Marianne hesitated slightly before asking, "Have you known Sarah long?"

"Ever since she was a girl. She grew up in Maple Hill and spent a fair amount of time out here." He looked at her with a searching gaze, and Marianne felt she was being sized up. He must have decided he could trust her because he cleared his throat and said, "Let me tell you a little story. I met Sarah when I was new here. She came to her aunt's funeral when she was five. The mourners were what you'd expect, solemn, bereaved. Sarah's father was particularly sad about the loss of his sister, who'd been relatively young. I showed them where the plot was, and the hearse drove up the hill. Sarah's little face was looking out the window of a following car, and I saw her face light up, and she started waving at someone. I couldn't see who she was looking at, but I followed them up the hill in case they needed anything. She was little enough that she was more or less forgotten while the graveside service was given. I watched her explore among the tombstones, stopping at some, passing others. She seemed to be listening and talking to herself as she went. At one point she looked up like someone had called her. She broke into a big smile and dashed off. She stopped near the tree line and stood holding her arm up as if she was holding hands with someone I couldn't see. It might have been her grandmother or even her aunt. Together they watched the ceremony until it was time to go."

He smiled gently and began unconsciously rubbing the frayed hem of one sleeve. "It took me a few years and some time with little Sarah to realize that she could see and converse with people who had crossed over. She has an affinity for helping people, both the living and the dead."

Marianne tried not to gape, feeling a slight chill, though the day was hot. "Wow. That's amazing." She shook herself and said, "She's a little forbidding, but she's been nice and very helpful to me, even though I'm new here. We met through Kelly from the hair cutting place," she added by way of explanation.

He nodded and smiled sadly. "Ah, yes. People haven't always been kind to her. Having a gift like hers is not very good for making friends. She's had to work hard to make people accept her for her other talents. Kelly has been a good friend to have."

"Sarah's a lawyer," Marianne said tentatively. "She must be pretty smart."

He nodded as rolled the soft threads in his weathered fingers. "That she is. And that's more of what she wants to be known for. Though somehow when people need her gift, they seem to find her."

Marianne nodded and decided not to probe any further, in spite of her curiosity. "Thank you for helping me out today. I may be back again."

"My pleasure. Please do." He extended his hand, and she shook it again. It was warm and strong.

Chapter 18

SHE drove back to Maple Hill thoughtfully. She was beginning to draw a clearer picture of what was going on with her "roommates" but needed some time for it to gel. It was like her more mainstream history projects. She did research, filling her mind with facts, images, and ideas until a pattern emerged. She just needed time to let it settle clearly. Her cell phone rang on the way, and dutifully, Marianne pulled over to the shoulder and answered it.

"Hey, Marianne! Can we expect you for dinner tonight?" It was Kelly.

"You know, I think I'd like to spend the night at my own place tonight. I spent the day doing research, and I don't think the angry ghost will actually hurt me. Scare, yes, hurt, no. So, I'd like to stay at the house tonight and see what happens. I'll call you if things get out of hand."

"Are you sure? We're glad to have you."

"Yeah. You guys need your space, too, and I don't want to overstay my welcome."

"Okay. Be sure to call if you need back up."

"I will." She continued home and pulled into the drive. The rain had left the grass very green and lush. It was already looking much better than it had when she'd arrived. Oscar greeted her at the door with a meow that clearly said, "Where's my fish?" Marianne fed them both and sat on the couch while she ate dinner. Oscar climbed into her lap and filled the space between her and the bowl of salad, until she laughed and scruffed his head, saying, "You make life so difficult!"

After supper, she opened the keyboard cover on the piano and played for a while. Working her way through more fingering exercises,

163

she was excited that her hands remembered more than she'd expected. She also was pleased that her hands were so much bigger than they had been when she'd played as a kid; she could reach an octave plus one now. When she got bored of "Dozen a Day," she got out the easy Bach pieces and worked through the first couple again. Even though it was slow, there were moments when the chords and melody sounded just right. Much to her surprise, it was 9:30 when she looked up again. She got out her most advanced music books, Beethoven, Grieg and Ragtime among others, and spread them out on the top of the piano. These had been the most difficult musically for her, but she bet Anne would find them easy.

Leaving the key cover open, she quietly addressed the empty air. "Mrs. Rutherford?"

Oscar, curled up on the sofa under the front window, flicked his ears. "Mrs. Rutherford, I learned that you loved to play the piano. I hear from the neighbor boy Michael that you have been playing already. He's quite a fan of yours. Please feel free to continue playing my piano any time you want. If you need music, these are the books I have, and you can play anything you want from them. I'm afraid they're pretty basic."

She paused and then said aloud, "Mrs. Rutherford, if there is anything you want to tell me about yourself, I'm going to be home tonight. You can contact me when I'm sleeping, I guess."

Marianne had no sense that anyone besides Oscar had heard her, and she rather hoped George would not take liberties with contacting her. After eating a little ice cream and cleaning up the kitchen, she went to bed.

She dreamt she was walking through the house. The layout was a strange mix of her old apartment and her new cottage decorated with familiar furniture—the sofa, table, piano, books, Geoffrey's high school sports trophies, and her favorite landscape painting on the wall. She wandered around the room feeling peaceful and wondering at the curious overlay but accepting it. Down the hall, she caught a glimpse of a little girl dressed in old-fashioned clothing, a stuffed animal clutched in her hand, giggling mischievously as she ran away down the hall. She could have been Michael's little sister, but she didn't think he had one. Marianne laughed and started to follow, but a woman's voice shouted at her loudly, "Get out! Get out now!"

As Marianne hesitated, the coffee table in front of her exploded into flames and was consumed before her eyes, all the magazines, old-fashioned iron and laundry turning white with flame. Fire leapt like wicked cats across the floor and raced up the legs of the other things in the room. A panicked child's screaming mingled with the growing noise of the fire, and she tried to move, to escape, but her legs felt like they were made of lead. The piano burned, emitting a tortured groan before turning into a smoldering cherry red image of itself and collapsing in a wall of flame. The shocking heat and terror engulfed her, and she screamed aloud.

She sat bolt upright in bed, sweating and panting, the echoes of a child's fear all but convincing her that she was burning up. The pungent smell of burning wood and clothing permeated the air. Gradually, the terror of the dream melted into quiet darkness. Her heart pounded for some minutes before slowing. She finally whispered, "Okay, Mrs. Rutherford. I know about the fire, but I don't understand the rest yet. Don't worry, I'll figure it out. How about you let me sleep now?"

The minutes passed, and her system calmed down. Oscar jumped up on the bed and rubbed against her arm before settling down with his furry bulk against her hip. Marianne drifted off again into sleep.

Anne drifted like a curl of fog. She'd never had much vigor even in life, but her students had always given her energy. After she'd passed into this strange limbo where she had consciousness to observe but little power to affect the people in the house, it had been a wonderful discovery to find that piano playing or a thunderstorm could empower her. Shaping Marianne's dream to show her a window on the past had been exhausting. Marianne was warned, and Anne hoped she would understand.

Anne had gotten to Marianne before he could. Somehow she blocked his ability to communicate, and it infuriated him. Even after she was gone, he found he could not enter Marianne's dream state for a time. The girl had stayed away since he'd locked her in the basement and not presented him with an opportunity to remind her this was his house. But Marianne's energy was remarkably similar to Anne's. They were becoming more and more alike. He could use that.

Marianne woke with Oscar's whiskers tickling her cheek as he breathed fishily in her face. His considerable weight pressed the pillow down, and her head rolled toward him. Sleepily, Marianne pushed him off the pillow and stroked him until he settled at her side, staring meaningfully at her. She fancied she could feel his gaze through her closed eyelids.

"Fine, I'll feed you," she mumbled after several futile minutes trying to drift off again while Oscar moved restlessly next to her.

He leapt off the bed with a soft thud and preceded her to the kitchen with a meow. Clearly, he felt it was a tough job moving his human out of bed and called to her down the hall as she stumbled after him. Not until she'd put the open can of food on the floor, did he relent.

She managed to drift off again for another hour before waking, feeling more alert than she had earlier. She mused about the fire dream as she showered and decided to write down as much as she could remember. She knew who one of her ghosts was, but she still had to identify the other. It was the weekend, so maybe she could contact Markus Bordman or Adam Sullivan.

After nine she got her notes out and dialed the number for Markus Bordman. It rang several times before a man's voice answered.

"Hello?"

"Hello, is this Markus Bordman? Hi, my name is Marianne Singleton, and I'm doing some research on Hudson Valley history."

"Yes? How can I help you?" He said cautiously.

"Well, I'm doing some research on some of the older homes in Maple Hill, particularly 25 Violet Lane. I got your name from a list of owners and your phone number off the Internet. I'm not sure if you are the Mr. Bordman who once owned 25 Violet Lane or not. Are you?"

There was a long pause at the other end of the line before he said very quietly, "Yes. I am. Look, what is this about? It's been years and years since I lived in Maple Hill."

He sounded on the verge of hanging up and Marianne hastened to reply, "I know. I'm sorry to bother you, but I wondered if you would talk to me about the house. I live here now and, honestly, it's a little weird. I just wondered if you'd had any strange experiences while living here. I would be glad to take you out for coffee, if you wanted to talk in person," she offered.

He hesitated before agreeing to meet her at an eatery on Route 9 in an hour. They exchanged brief descriptions of themselves so they could find each other. She thanked him and hung up.

Forty-five minutes later she was buying a pastry and a cup of green tea at a busy counter. She stationed herself at a small table with a good view of the door. She waited almost thirty minutes, watching the ebb and flow of people. She'd nearly given up, thinking he had chosen not to come, when a likely candidate entered. An older gentleman with the requisite porkpie hat, he stood scanning the room for a moment before he looked her way. She raised her hand tentatively, and he came over.

She rose to meet him and shook his hand firmly, saying, "Mr. Bordman? I'm Marianne Singleton. Thank you for coming. Can I buy you a coffee?"

They sat at the small table a little awkwardly, and Marianne appraised him as he put two sugars in his coffee. He was in his mid sixties with thinning gray-brown hair and a neat mustache and beard. His expression was closed and uncomfortable.

Marianne smiled, trying to put him at ease, and said, "Thank you again for agreeing to meet me."

"I almost changed my mind," he said candidly, sipping the hot beverage. "It was not a great time in my life and not something I want to think about much. But you said you were living there now so…" he gestured with an open hand, "I thought I should come."

"Well, let me tell you why I called." She told him about the sense of being watched, the unaccounted bursts of emotion, the paint, the piano playing, the cold spots, and her fire dreams. "I just wondered if you had ever felt any of those things or had other weird things happen while you lived there," she finished.

Markus Bordman grew more and more thoughtful as she spoke. He was silent for a few moments before he answered. "I did feel more anxious or sad when I was at home. At the time I attributed a lot of that to my own issues." He glanced at her and said a little defiantly, "I was wrestling with being gay and wondering if I could ever come out of the closet. I was really miserable." He paused and added softly, "I even thought about taking my own life a time or two. I always thought it was all me, but you're saying it might not have been?"

She nodded sympathetically and gestured for him to continue.

"Sometimes I thought I could hear a woman crying in the basement. That was not a happy place. I didn't go down there much. I wondered if I was going crazy."

"It wasn't you," Marianne said, trying to reassure him. "There *is* a woman who cries in the basement sometimes. I've heard her. The house is haunted, Mr. Bordman, and I'm trying to figure out when that started and who it might be."

"Please, call me Markus. You think it's haunted?" He considered this notion as she watched him reimagine his past. "That would explain some things. Who do you think it is?"

"I think it's Anne Rutherford. She and her husband were the first owners of the house and sold it to you. She was a gifted pianist and taught piano lessons in that house for decades. When she was little, she survived a house fire, but her little brother died. She died in 1963, and I'm pretty sure she's the one who haunted the house when you were there."

Amazement lit his face. "That would fit. How did you find all this out?"

She explained her research, concluding, "The thing is I think there is more than one ghost. Did you ever feel more than one person?"

He considered and said, shaking his head slowly, "No. I don't think so, but then I'm not totally sure. Why do you think...?"

She raised her eyebrows and said, "You'd be sure, believe me. I think the second person is a man who is angry and controlling. What was Mr. Rutherford like?"

He thought about it and said, "He was much older than me. I was in my early twenties but had just landed a very promising job, and he was selling his place. It was a little out of my league, but my parents were willing to help me out a bit, and the bank gave me a loan. Mr. Rutherford was very reserved, a little condescending. I think he'd lost his wife not long before, so I attributed his demeanor to our age differences and his loss." He shrugged. "We didn't have much contact. Do you have some reason to believe he is the second ghost?"

Marianne shook her head and frowned. "I'm not sure. He is one possibility, but I only have a few hints at his character." She smiled. "You were a possibility until I learned you're still alive."

He looked a little startled but nodded slightly in unspoken assent.

"I don't have a lot of other candidates." She was beginning to feel discouraged. She showed him the list of tenants up to the year 2000 when the registry had ceased. "Do any of these names ring a bell?" Marianne asked.

Markus looked over the list and pointed at the first name. "That's the only one. I work for a local insurance company. There was an Adam Sullivan who purchased insurance from us in the seventies. I remember him particularly because he lived at 25 Violet Lane after I did."

"What do you remember about him, if anything? I know you can't divulge finances for privacy reasons," she said hastily. "I'm not asking about that. I just wondered if you met him or could tell me

169

anything about him?"

"Well, we sold him accident insurance. If I remember correctly, he was an electrician and perhaps worried about job related injuries. He only came in a few times."

"What was he like?"

Markus grimaced. "He wasn't a very nice person. Bad vibe, you know? He seemed very tightly wound, kind of angry all the time. He had enough money to pay the premiums on a good policy but kept trying to badger me into lowering the rate. That wasn't something I could do, and he wasn't pleased about that." He sat quietly remembering the man. "He didn't seem to like women all that much. Any time one of the secretaries came through, he scowled a lot. There was one female agent in our office, and I remember thinking I was glad he wasn't her client."

Marianne nodded as she made some notes. "Well, there is an Adam Sullivan listed locally. I'm thinking about interviewing him to see what he remembers about living in the Violet Lane house," she said reluctantly, not at all happy about Markus' opinion of the man.

"Don't worry about it too much. That won't be him," he said with certainty. "We cancelled his policy only a few years after he'd taken it out. He died. I heard later it was a job related accident."

Marianne sat back, stunned at the revelation and it's implications.

Markus continued, "I guess he was right to be worried about accidents. People sometimes think buying insurance is like having a shield against the unexpected. It really doesn't work that way," he finished a little sadly.

Marianne said slowly, "Wow. If Adam Sullivan was as unpleasant as you say, he'd be a great candidate for the angry ghost in my house. When exactly was that?"

Markus looked at her, recognition dawning. "I see what you mean." He thought hard and said finally, "I think it was in the mid seventies. Well, at least you have an identity. I don't know what you would do about it." He looked apologetic. "I'm sorry I can't be more specific. It's been a really long time."

Marianne tapped her pen against her cheek. "That's okay. I'm not sure either, but I have a few resources, and I'm hoping to convince both spirits to move on. To heaven, or the afterlife, or wherever one goes after death."

Markus raised his cup to her in a salute and drained the last of his coffee. "More power to you. I wish you success."

Marianne sipped the last of her now cold tea and gathered her things together. "Thank you so much for your time, Markus. Can I give you my phone number? If you think of anything else, please call me." She jotted it down on a piece of paper and tore it out of her notebook.

He stood up and shook her hand again, saying with a genuine smile, "Thank you for calling me. I'm glad I came. It clears some things up about that part of my life."

She returned his handshake warmly and said, "I'm glad you came too. It was a pleasure to meet you."

Chapter 19

THE house was quiet and sunny when she turned in to her driveway. Oscar looked up from a nap on the couch and put his head back down as she came in the front door. Marianne put her research stuff away and decided to change gears and finish painting the hallway. She made it the same off-white color as the office and did the trim in brighter white. Putting her brain in neutral she let ideas, images and words from her conversation with Markus pop into her head as they occurred to her. Some she mulled over, others she let drift away.

As she rolled paint across the walls, a vague sense of anxiety and a dull hum accumulated in her ears, making her jittery and uneasy. Attributing her feelings to her unseen roommates, she ignored them and broke for a late lunch.

As she put the paint can out on the side door step, Michael approached her, cruising his bike around the cul-de-sac one-handed, the other arm draped over a basketball.

"Hi, Miss Singleton!" he called out.

"Hey, Michael! How are you?" She smiled in relief. She felt better out here, and it was good to see Michael's lively presence.

"Good. Do you need any more help with your yard? I have some time tomorrow."

Marianne looked at the yard in the early evening light. It looked better than it had when she'd arrived by virtue of having the lawn mowed. She'd done some work too, but so much more needed to be done.

"I have some things I need to do tomorrow," she replied. "How about you come later this week and do some weeding for me?"

He made a face. Clearly he preferred mowing to weeding.   A thought occurred to her. "Hey, Michael, do you have a little time now? I need to move some furniture around and could use a hand."

He turned the bike, and riding his momentum up the gravel drive with a crunch, he said, "Sure." Dumping the bike and ball, he followed her inside. With his help she was able to get the office in some semblance of order and things rearranged in her bedroom. After that, all she needed to do was unload boxes and put things away. Their activity dispelled her sense of unease.

"It looks really nice in here. You did a lot of work since I first saw it," he said, complimenting her. "Hey, I really like what you were playing earlier."

Marianne paused in her box breakdown. "Oh?" she said lightly. "What was that?"

"I don't know. It was all flowing like water or clouds or something."

Feeling a little guilty for accepting responsibility for Anne's talent, she looked at him speculatively and said, "Can you keep a secret?"

He looked intrigued and said enthusiastically, "Sure!"

"I mean it. It's a dead secret for now. Well," she amended, "if you have to tell your parents, you can, I guess."

Sobering, he said more seriously, "Sure. What is it?"

"I'm not the piano player. I mean, I learned as a kid but haven't played in many years. My playing is terrible." She paused and then said significantly, "The person you hear playing the piano is a ghost. I live in a haunted house."

Looking startled, he said incredulously, "You're serious?"

She nodded.

His face lit up, and he said excitedly, "Can I see it?"

"*Her*. The ghost is a woman, and I don't know. I've never really 'seen' her and the one time I heard her play was in the middle of the night, and I thought it was a dream."

"Wow! That is so cool!" He said half in envy, half in admiration.

In the face of his excitement, she almost regretted saying anything and cautioned him, "Please don't tell anyone beyond your family, okay?"

His face fell, but he nodded and said solemnly, "I swear I won't tell."

She shook his hand and said, "Okay. Will you help me haul the boxes upstairs before you go?"

They dragged a dozen or so boxes up the stairs and around the u-turn midway. Their noise broke the dusty stillness on the second floor momentarily. Marianne was glad she had company for this job. The little second floor always seemed eerily silent, like it was waiting for something.

Michael, impervious to any spookiness, bounced back down the stairs and shouted a goodbye as he dashed out the door. Marianne followed more slowly and went to join Oscar on the sofa. He had stayed out of the furniture moving earlier. Now he yawned and stretched elaborately and sat up. She stroked his fur and rubbed his chin and behind the ears until he purred.

After a little bit, she made their respective dinners. While hers cooked, she inspected her work in the hallway. It was dry to the touch, and she turned the light on to see the effect. It was a huge improvement, and she smiled. Mrs. Thomas was going to love it. After dinner she spent some time in the office and the bedroom, putting things away and organizing her space. Once or twice she felt like someone was watching her. Oscar was sitting up on the desk and staring watchfully at the door with his crooked tail twitching rhythmically. Marianne glanced automatically in that direction herself and felt someone's presence. It wasn't angry, so she thought it might be Anne Rutherford.

"Hello, Anne," she said conversationally. "I hope you don't mind the painting I've been doing. Someone doesn't like it, but I hope you do. You wouldn't know who the Angry Ghost is would you?"

There was no answer that she could discern, so she continued. "Today I talked to the man who lived here after you died and George sold the house. He seemed like a nice guy and told me that the person who lived here after him was a man named Adam Sullivan. He was an electrician, and Markus said he wasn't a very nice man at all. Is that who is living here besides you and me? Sometimes when I have the radio on, it gets all crackly and the lights flicker a little. Is that you or is that Adam, the electrician? Is he the one who locked me in the basement and yells at me in my dreams?"

A precariously balanced stack of papers at the edge of the desk slithered suddenly onto the ground making her start. "Is that a yes?" she asked softly. A few moments later Marianne felt the other presence fading into the empty room and strained her senses to 'hear' any other response. She didn't know how to interpret the fall of the papers. It could easily have been a coincidence of gravity and not a ghostly communication at all. Eventually she gave up, tidied the mess, and went into the living room to watch a rerun on TV. Oscar returned and curled up in her lap.

Before she went to bed, she opened all the windows to let the cooling night air into the house and ventilate the paint smell. Lingering in the office, she smiled, enjoying the look of the fresh paint and the order that was distilling from chaos. Her bedroom was similarly starting to look more lived in. She sighed. If she could resolve the unwanted roommate problem and remain undiscovered by her crazy ex, she could make a new life here.

In her dream, she was walking down a street in a place that was part New York City and part small town in the poorly lit twilight of dreamtime. Someone was following her, but she didn't know who it was. Looking for something that was always just around the next corner or on the next block, she walked and walked. Her tension grew as her sense of being followed increased. Whoever it was seemed to be getting closer. She turned down her own street and tried to run, though her steps felt no faster. She reached the Violet Lane house and hurried up the front steps. The door was locked, even though she could hear people inside. She pressed the doorbell and hammered on the door, trying to get in. There seemed to be a party with quite a few people who were all talking excitedly. When the door opened, she pushed her way inside.

She passed through the crowd of men and women in forties style clothing like a ghost in her own house. Thinking to get away from her pursuer, she went to the bedroom in the back of the house. There, she found a couple talking. The woman had dark, carefully curled hair that framed her pale face. Heavy, dark framed glasses did not hide the dark smudges under her eyes. She was wearing a one-shouldered evening gown. The man had a neatly trimmed beard and cold blue eyes. They ignored Marianne as if she were invisible.

He addressed the woman coolly, "You will play beautifully, my dear, as you always do."

A haunted look crossed her face, and she put her hand to her head saying, "I don't feel very well. I'd rather not. Can't we just tell them I'm not well?"

He said sternly, "We've been through this. You are fine, and you will play. They are all expecting you to play. You can't disappoint them."

She said with a hint of pleading, "Then let me take my pills. It helps with the pain."

He said, "You can have your medicine afterwards. You know your wits only get duller. Come now. Chin up. You will do this."

Marianne, standing in the doorway, couldn't help herself. She burst out, "Can't you see, she doesn't feel well? I'm sure everyone would understand if you just told them she was sick."

He turned and pierced Marianne with a glare. "You have no say in this matter. This is my house, and you don't belong here."

The dark haired woman behind him said, "Who is it?"

He said, "No one. Finish dressing, my dear. It is nearly seven o'clock." He pushed Marianne out of the room and grabbed her wrist.

His intense blue eyes bored into her. "In fact, *you* are not to disturb our guests. He will be here for you soon. You can wait down here."

Suddenly Marianne found herself at the top of the basement steps with the door shutting behind her, and the lights shutting off. Terrified, she turned and grabbed for the door handle, but the wood was smooth and blank. I'm trapped in the damn basement again, she thought. But I took the lock off! She heard the doorbell chime and felt a sense of dread. He's here. He's come for me! She stumbled down the steps in the darkness and felt her way across the now cluttered floor with her hands outstretched. She kept trying to open her eyes and see better but could get no more than a glimpse or two. She ran painfully into the boards of the coal bin, groped her way to the opening and climbed on top of the dirty pile of coals, trying to get to the window she'd already broken. The coals shifted beneath her causing her to lose traction. She scrabbled more and more desperately trying to reach the elusive window and freedom. Behind her she heard the door open again and a man's voice say with satisfaction, "She's down here, waiting for you."

Then she heard Geoffrey's voice say clearly, "Perfect."

Marianne clawed her way out of the nightmare, heart pounding. The cool, quiet darkness of her bedroom took some time to penetrate her anxiety. She took deep breaths and slowly let them out, trying to calm herself.

This kind of dream was new. Parts of her dream had felt almost like a window on the past, and other parts had the now familiar sense of true dreaming. She'd never had them mixed together before. She didn't like it at all.

One thing was clear: George Rutherford was a very controlling man. If that was a window on the past, he'd clearly made Anne's life miserable. Marianne remembered that Anne had died of cancer. She didn't know what kind, but Anne had it for a while before she died, and George valued her ability to play more than he considered her comfort. He also didn't appreciate Marianne's interference and had the ability to see and hear her when others did not.

Another worrying aspect of her dream was hearing Geoffrey's

voice. It was a very disturbing idea: dead George helping Geoffrey find her by locking her in the basement and holding her there. Could George somehow lock her in again for real? Could he actually hold the door shut and keep the window from breaking? Well, she didn't have to go down there ever again. Maybe George had another way to lock her in her own house? Or lock her out? Her heart began racing in anxiety again.

Night fears. These are night fears, she told herself over and over without success. I am seriously not going to sleep after that, she realized. Turning on her bedside light, she got out her research notebook and wrote down her dream as she remembered it. The only silver lining was that unless there was compelling new evidence that Adam Sullivan was a better candidate, George Rutherford was definitely her angry ghost. Then she got a book to read for as long as it took for daylight or sleep to come. Oscar put his paw over his eyes and tightened his curl next to her on the coverlet.

Chapter 20

BLEARY eyed, Marianne awoke a couple hours later around dawn. She had slept badly, her anxiety waking her regularly. Feeling hollow and shaky, she got up, showered, and ate some eggs and toast for breakfast. The shower was unexpectedly cold as if the hot water was out, and she sighed, mentally adding 'check the heater in the basement' to her to-do list. Fortunately, a decent breakfast always helped after a bad night. She drank herbal tea for comfort as she debated whether it was too early to call Sarah and Kelly on a Sunday.

The opening bars of her favorite tune rang. The ID said "Grandma S.," and she answered with alacrity.

"Grandma!" Marianne was so relieved to hear from her.

"Hello, Marianne. It's so good to hear your voice! I got home last night and saw your message. I hope it's not too early to call. Is everything all right?" Selene said anxiously.

Marianne laughed shakily and replied, "Yes and no. I had a really horrible nightmare last night and didn't sleep well at all. Other than that, things are mostly okay."

Selene sounded audibly relieved. "I'm glad. Tell me about your nightmare. It sounds like it was a doozy."

Marianne hesitated for a fraction of a second, and then decided to share her dream and some of the other eerie occurrences, trusting her grandmother would understand. She finished by saying, "The worst thing was I think Geoffrey was at the top of those stairs."

Selene listened attentively all the way through before she said, "I wondered if something was going on. I dreamed you were trapped in a dark room a few days ago and wanted to call you, but I'd left home without taking your cell number so I couldn't call sooner. Last night my dreams were troubled again, and I felt I should call you as soon as possible."

Marianne was stunned. "You dreamed about me being trapped? Grandma, I was locked in the basement here for real a couple of days ago! I got out on my own, but you dreamed it? Have you done this before?" She asked incredulously.

Grandma Selene had the grace to sound a little embarrassed. "Yes, dear. I sometimes have dreams that have come true or that told me about events far away before I learned of them the conventional way."

Marianne paused before she said, "Did you know I dream true?"

There was a pause and Grandma said contritely, "Yes, dear. I have known for a while that you have the same talent as I do. I'm so sorry I didn't say anything sooner. Please forgive me."

It was Marianne's turn to be silent a moment with her thoughts whirling.

Her grandmother said pleadingly, "If it makes any difference, I wasn't sure until a year or so ago when you told me about your dreams of Geoffrey's indiscretions. I hope you're not too angry with me…"

"No, I'm not mad at you, Grandma! I'm relieved! I didn't know where this came from, and now I know it's you. I sometimes wondered if I'd been cursed by a wicked witch at birth or something!" She took a deep steadying breath, feeling a little lightheaded. "It's nice to know I'm not alone. Thank you for telling me. Did you know Mrs. Thomas' house was haunted when you suggested I move here?" She asked suspiciously.

Grandma Selene was shocked. "No! I knew she had trouble renting it, of course, but I didn't know it was for that reason. Did she know?"

"Actually, yes, she did. I talked to her a few days ago, and she admitted that she was aware of it."

"Bloody hell!" Selene's cultured British voice muttered. "I'll be having a conversation with the old dear."

Marianne was startled. Her grandmother was usually so ladylike. It was very unusual for her to swear.

"Is it bad, Marianne?" Her grandmother said with concern.

"Well…" Marianne found herself relating more fully everything that had happened, including her research that indicated Mr. and Mrs. Rutherford were her ghosts.

When she was done, Grandma Selene said, "Well, it doesn't surprise me that your extra 'roommates' are the Rutherfords. I knew them when I was much younger. Poor Anne! George did not treat her well at all. I remember going to their house once for a concert. He was very proud of her talent, but he showed her off like a prized poodle. Later, when she got ill—you know she died of cancer?—he still insisted she play for his friends and lodge mates. George was a piece of work. His whole family was, really. His parents were very controlling and rather frightening as I recall. I was a little worried about Geoffrey, honestly, when you first got married. But he seemed to treat you well. At first anyway."

"What?!" Marianne yelped. "How does Geoffrey fit into this?"

"George Rutherford had a brother and a sister," Selene explained. "They were all born around the turn of the twentieth century. George's sister married into the Chubb family and had children in the 1930s right before the Second World War. Geoffrey's father is one of those children. He could be a right bastard at times. Geoffrey was their last child, and I'm afraid he was quite spoiled. I did hope he had escaped the genes for a controlling nature, but it seems he did not. I'm so sorry, Marianne."

Marianne was absolutely blown away. In one sense, this revelation made Geoffrey's behavior so much more understandable, still inexcusable, but at least understandable. On the other hand, it was horrifying to realize she was related to the cold, angry ghost of George, however distantly, by marriage.

"Why didn't you tell me this before?"

"Well, you didn't know the Rutherfords before," she said simply. "Family history didn't seem very relevant until now. Forgive me. Let me know if there is anything I can do to help you."

Marianne thought and finally said, "If I think of anything, Grandma, I'll call, I promise. I met some people here in Maple Hill who I think can help me. Do you know Sarah Landsman and Kelly Walker?"

"No, I don't."

"Well, Sarah is...someone who can see and hear spirits and has done all her life. She's helping me with this. She's the one who suggested I do research to identify the ghosts, since it might help her understand them and ask them to leave."

"Very good," Selene approved. "Well, if it lets poor Anne get some rest after the difficult life she led, then more power to you, dear. I'd like to meet your friend Sarah some time. She sounds like quite a woman. Give that dreadful George a kick for me, will you?"

Marianne smiled in spite of everything. "Okay, Grandma, I will. Thanks for calling me. If you have any other warning dreams, please call me, okay? I don't always understand the ones I get, and I'm a little slow on the uptake sometimes."

"I promise. No more secrets between us," and she rang off.

Marianne felt immensely better after talking to her grandmother. She ruminated about the revelations on George's character and Geoffrey's surprising relationship with him. Going to her office, she got out her notes and the copies she'd made from the library and stared at George's obituary photo. It stared back at her with Geoffrey's eyes. Well, that made things both easier and harder, and she would have to figure out what to do about the Rutherfords, both the living and the dead.

Cell phone time said 8:30. She opted to wait a little longer, put her dark hair into a ponytail, and spent some time cleaning the bathroom and kitchen. Putting her house in order helped clear her thoughts and settle her soul. She felt tinges of anxiety begin to gnaw at her but firmly pushed them aside, thinking how good it had been to hear her grandmother's voice. Finally around ten, she sat on the couch, put her bare feet up on the edge of the coffee table, and dialed Sarah.

"Marianne?" Sarah's voice answered.

"Hi, I hope it's not too early to call? I was wondering if I could come over and talk with you sometime today? I did a lot of research yesterday and the day before and got some additional information over night, if you know what I mean, and I'd really like your thoughts on the matter."

"Absolutely," Sarah said unreservedly. "We're home right now. Kelly's doing some cooking. You want to walk over, or do you need a ride?"

"I'll walk," Marianne said in relief, thinking it would do her good. "I'll see you in a bit."

She threw her research folder and notebook into her pack, grabbed her purse, and said goodbye to Oscar.

Geoffrey Chubb sat at his desk staring at his computer screen. Papers were scattered across the surface, his jacket was hanging over the back of his chair and his tie was loosened a bit. The papers made him look busy and important as he ostensibly prepared a market analysis for a product line. However, at the moment, he was staring unseeing at his computer screen, trying to recall an odd dream he'd had last night. He generally classified his nighttime visions as jumbled nonsense from his waking life. Last night, though, was different. All he could recall were a couple of fragments.

In the dream his Uncle George had invited him to a party. He had met Geoffrey at the door and invited him in, shaking his hand. It didn't seem important that his uncle had died when he was little.

"Geoffrey, I found something that belongs to you. She doesn't belong here." Uncle George ushered him to a door with a look of Santa giving out an especially wonderful present. "Go ahead. Open it.

Take her back. She belongs to you."

Geoffrey remembered feeling a mix of surprise and eagerness. He had reached for the door handle and pulled it open.

"She's down here, waiting for you."

With dawning realization that Marianne was below, Geoffrey said, "Perfect. Thank you, Uncle."

Such a strange dream. Interesting idea, though, he considered. I hadn't thought of Maple Hill, that stupid, little podunk town she was so proud of. I should check that out. He needed to find Marianne in case she got any ideas about calling his boss and telling him stories about Geoffrey's dubious behavior at the company. Geoffrey knew he would use that kind of information as leverage if he had it.

He looked quickly at his calendar and saw that he and Sandra were scheduled to go see a new exhibit at the Guggenheim. This was more important. Maybe he could convince Sandra that going to the Hudson Valley on an antiquing expedition would be more fun. He did a quick online search and found there were several antique stores in Maple Hill. He dashed off a quick email and put his plan into motion.

The air was still relatively clear after the recent thunderstorm, and she walked the several blocks without getting more than dewy with perspiration. The distant drone of several mowers gave way to smells of cut grass, green leaves and late flowers, and she breathed in deeply. By the time she reached their house, breakfast and the walk had steadied her a good deal.

"Hey, come on in. We just put the kettle on for tea, unless you want iced?" Sarah said with a smile when she opened the door.

Kelly gave her a quick hug, holding her food-covered hands away from Marianne's dark hair, before returning to the cluttered counter. Marianne sat at the kitchen table while Sarah made chamomile tea. Marianne sat at the wooden kitchen table and watched the two women move seamlessly around each other, relaxing into the good smells of the kitchen. Finally, Sarah sat down and poured three mugs, and

Marianne opened her bag and described her findings at the library, her trip to the cemetery, and her conversation with Markus Bordman. The table was littered with photocopies and her research journal by the time she was done. Marianne experienced a little jolt when she realized that today was the anniversary of the fire that had killed little Samuel Jr.

Sarah sipped, listened, and examined each item for herself. "You're very thorough," she complimented Marianne. "I really appreciate that. As a lawyer, thorough research is crucial. Not many people do that. Anne seems most likely to be your lady ghost. Poor woman; having such a trauma in her childhood. It sounds like she married the man she thought she needed."

Marianne looked at her quizzically.

"If George is the person your grandmother describes him as, then her family probably felt she was marrying up in the world," Sarah explained. "As for her, George was well-to-do and controlled every aspect of her life, and that meant she didn't have to. Maybe she thought he'd keep her safe. In addition, she may have felt responsible for the death of her little brother, and subtle punishment may have seemed justified to her."

Marianne sat back silently absorbing this. She felt some uncomfortable parallels with her own life and wondered if she'd done the same. She didn't have a trauma in her early life, but she had certainly married a man who had controlled much of her life for the last fifteen years. Had Geoffrey's treatment of her seemed justified somehow? She'd have to think about that.

Kelly turned around with a broad chopping knife in her hand and a fierce scowl on her face. "That doesn't make it right! What a dickhead. She didn't have to live her life under his thumb. She just let it happen! Didn't she have any friends at all?"

Marianne shrugged awkwardly. "I have no idea. If George ran her life, she might not have had any. She did teach piano lessons to a whole lot of children, though, so she had some light in her life. And, maybe when she played piano for their friends, she could lose herself for a little while." I didn't have a lot of friends to tell me my husband was treating me badly, Marianne thought. We just had his friends who probably didn't see anything wrong. It would have been nice to have met these two women years ago!

Sarah nodded. Muttering darkly, Kelly turned back and chopped some vegetables loudly.

"You said you interviewed the first owner after the Rutherfords yesterday?" Sarah asked.

Marianne nodded and poured herself another cup of tea. "He almost didn't come. He told me that he'd been especially unhappy in the house. He's gay and at the time was trying to decide if he should come out of the closet or not. He thought he was going crazy because he could hear Anne crying in the basement."

Sarah nodded sympathetically.

"He seemed a lot happier after we talked." Marianne related her discovery about Adam Sullivan and her suspicion that he might be the angry ghost. "But then my grandmother told me about George Rutherford. That and the incredibly vivid nightmare I had last night make me pretty sure it's him, not Adam." Marianne retold her dream, concluding with hearing Geoffrey's voice.

Kelly stopped her food prep and turned to listen to Marianne's dream. "Do you think he could lock you in the basement again somehow and lead your ex to your door?" She looked at her partner. "Can he do that as a spirit?"

Sarah considered, unconsciously rolling her little crystal necklace between her fingers. "Spirits can do some pretty weird shit. I don't think he could be in two places at once. There's no evidence that he has communicated with Geoffrey directly, unless he has reached him through dreams?" She looked at Marianne.

Marianne laughed mirthlessly. "That seems so unlikely, since Geoffrey spent so much time denying that was possible."

Sarah nodded and mused slowly, "If Geoffrey figures out on his own that you are living in Maple Hill and gets an address, it might be possible for George to key in on his presence in or near your house and somehow hold you there till Geoffrey arrives. I think George mostly wants you out of his house. If his nephew is the means to remove you, then I think he'd use that chance."

Marianne said explosively, "But we're divorced! He's with Sandra! Why would he want to bother with me?"

Sarah shrugged and said, "Tell me about your ex."

Marianne bit her lip and described their relationship up till the last year, trying to keep the details of the worst bits succinct. "After the divorce was finalized, I got a few emails from him telling me he had something of mine he wanted to return. I went the first time he sent me one, and he told me he'd thrown it away by accident. It was a photo I would have liked to have had back," she said sadly. "At this point, if he has anything else of mine, I don't care. I never want to see him again. He was pretty much stalking me for the last several months. It's why I left New York—to get away from him. Now I'm getting texts hinting that he knows where I am or that he's going to find me."

She gestured helplessly. "I don't understand why he's hassling me! He's got what he wants, a divorce. As far as I know he's still seeing Sandra, and they plan to get married. I don't understand why he needs to keep harassing me!"

Sarah observed, "Some people need to exert their control or influence over others to justify their own existence. Maybe he just likes tormenting you."

Marianne made an unhappy face. "That would be typical. How can I get him to just go away?" She asked softly.

Sarah reached across the table and took her hands. "You are going to have to stand up to the bully he is and show him your power."

Marianne looked at the table and said miserably, tears starting in her eyes, "Some days I think I could do that. After I get a nasty text from him, I'm not at all sure I could."

Sarah squeezed her hands comfortingly. "You are stronger than you think. You'll find a way."

Kelly wiped her hands on her apron and gave Marianne a big hug and a kiss on the cheek. "Remember what I told you when we first met? I think you're one of the bravest people I've ever met. You can do it, girl. When the time comes, you will kick his ass!"

Marianne hugged her back, feeling tears spill down her cheeks. "Thanks, that means a lot."

Sarah retrieved a tissue box from the counter, and putting it on the table near her guest, changed gears. "Does your ex know about your dreams, the true ones, I mean?"

Marianne wiped her eyes and blew her nose, gathering her thoughts. "When we were in college I dreamed about him cheating on a paper and mentioned it to him. He dragged me into counseling with him and all but convinced the counselor that I was imagining things due to stress. So I never talked about it again even when I dreamed things that came true.

"For instance, I dreamed of a person sleeping between us for months. When I confronted him with my suspicions of his affair, he denied it at first. He'd been careful to hide it from me, though I'm pretty sure his coworkers suspected. But I'd finally seen her face in a dream and said so."

Sarah looked at her intently. "Did he take you seriously?"

"He rarely took anything I did seriously unless it benefited him." She remembered the fleeting look on his face and said, "I think he was frightened just for a moment, but then he treated it as a joke."

Sarah said speculatively, "I've been doing family law and estate planning for nearly ten years. People do the most screwy, illegal things you can imagine from embezzlement to affairs to murder, thinking they will never get caught. Would Geoffrey do anything illegal now?"

Marianne started to say, "No, I don't think..." Then she remembered. "A couple of years ago Geoffrey got a big promotion that I thought was out of his reach. Around that time I had a series of dreams that suggested he'd trashed a co-worker's presentation to get ahead."

"Did you say anything to him about it at the time?"

Marianne opened her eyes wide. "Are you kidding? The last thing I wanted to do was rock the boat. No, I just suppressed it, and those dreams eventually went away."

Sarah nodded. "What if he thinks you know what he did, and that makes him afraid of you? What if he thought you could somehow spy on him through your dreams?"

Marianne's brows lifted as she protested, "But it doesn't work that way!"

"He doesn't know that. If he thought you knew he'd done something illegal, he might be worried you will expose him. He doesn't have to believe you're dreaming. He might just think someone told you."

Marianne threw up her hands in exasperation. "No one told me anything. I wish they had! Instead I just dreamed about it, but I don't have any proof."

Kelly looked over her shoulder as she stirred something on the stove. "Sometimes people imagine everyone else is guilty of the same things they are. If they're willing to bend the rules, they think others are willing to do the same and have a hard time believing they wouldn't. I've heard that one more than a few times, I can tell you."

Sarah nodded in agreement.

Marianne shook her head. "How can I convince him I don't know anything about him? If I tell him I don't, he'll just think I'm lying."

"Hopefully he'll never pursue you up here. But your dream suggests he might turn up here someday." Sarah ran the loop of the little crystal up and down the chain before she said, "What if you tell him in a general sort of way that you do know something about him?"

"What could I say?" Marianne replied. "Besides, I really don't want to give him a reason to hassle me more!"

Sarah pursed her lips. "Don't be specific. Just hint that you know

191

something and you won't tell as long as he leaves you alone. If he continues to hassle you—calling, emailing, stalking—you'll go to his boss."

"I don't know. I'll think about it." Marianne looked as unhappy as she felt.

Sarah patted her hand. "I'll keep thinking about it, too, and if I come up with anything better, I'll let you know. Besides a Restraining Order, I mean. We could go that route if you need to. That's just a piece of paper, though. It would be better if you could stand up to him and show him you can't be bullied anymore."

Marianne nodded dejectedly.

Sarah made another pot of tea. While she was at the counter, Kelly offered her a bite of something that smelled delicious. Sarah smiled and kissed her partner fondly before returning to the table.

Sarah cleared her throat and changed the subject. "Now, regarding angry George. You took away his ability to actually lock you in the basement, and you very effectively escaped him last time. So I don't think he can make that work again. But, he also made it clear he doesn't want you to interfere in his relationship with Anne. He may be part of the reason she is still lingering here. Her childhood trauma is probably part of it as well: she may still feel guilty about her brother's death. And George may be keeping her here, or she may be afraid of him and can't move on."

"That would be awful to have a sad life and still not be able to escape it even after you died," Marianne said emphatically.

Sarah refreshed her cup and added honey. "Tell me about it. That's often why people's spirits get stuck in limbo, neither here nor there."

"How can we get them both to move on? I don't mind having a piano-playing roommate, but George is really horrible, and I don't want to live with him."

Sarah raised her cup in salute. "Amen, sister. Maybe we can empower her to stand up to him. Maybe that would serve to banish him and free her up to pass over to the other side as well."

"How would you do that?" Marianne asked, mystified.

"I'm not sure yet." She clarified, "I usually burn sage and cedar and have a conversation with them and try to convince them to let go of this plane of existence and move on to the next world. But each case is different, so it varies."

Marianne was thoughtful and nodded slowly. "I'll let you know when I have a clearer idea of what the situation is. When can you come over? In general, I mean. You probably can't take off work to do this, right?"

"Unless it's a total emergency, weekends or evenings will have to be it. It's not easy to take sick days, particularly when we're busy at work. If I think I'm going to have a hard time, I'll have Kelly come along. She's my anchor sometimes."

"I think I'd like to be there," Marianne said tentatively.

"I expect you," Sarah responded promptly.

"Oh! Thank you," Marianne was both curious and a little nervous at the prospect.

Sarah laughed. "It's so nice to work with someone who believes me, and who is powerful in her own way."

Marianne flushed and shook her head. "I don't think I'm powerful at all."

"We'll be working on that," Sarah said with a wry grin. "First, we need to get you some sleep. I can give you some things that will offer protection from intrusive dreams from your 'roommates.'"

"That would be great," Marianne said gratefully.

"Do you need to sleep here tonight?"

"Maybe. I have some things I need to do at home today. Let me see how it goes. Can I call you later?" Sarah nodded. Marianne felt much better after talking things over and realized she was hungry again. The tantalizing smells coming from the stove only made her stomach growl more plaintively. Glancing at her phone, she realized it was after noon.

"I wondered if you guys wanted to go to the co-op for lunch? I know you're cooking and all, but...?" She asked them.

Sarah glanced at Kelly who gestured at the stove with her wooden spoon, "This is for dinner and the freezer. Give me a moment. I'm out of cumin and turmeric anyway."

The co-op was busy and full of both locals and people up from the city for the weekend. They each did a little shopping and met at the deli counter to get lunch. While they were there the PA mic clicked on.

A man's voice said in a heavy Scottish accent, "Scotty? The Enterprise wants to know if you're planning to return soon. They have a wee bit o' engine trouble they want you to look at. And, by the way, there's a spill in the bulk foods section, something involving beans and pasta."

While they were chuckling about the announcement, a harried looking young man with an awkward, gangly body hurried out of a back room with a broom and dustpan and trash bag, headed for aisle four.

Once they'd gotten food, they retreated by mutual consent to the sidewalk table area to get out of the press.

Still chuckling, Marianne said, "I can't believe that's just one person!"

Sarah replied, "That's Arlo Gordon. He hopes to do standup in New York someday."

"He's amazing," Marianne admired, shaking her head.

Kelly laughed. "The co-op agreed to let him do different voices and styles as long as he kept it clean and non-personal. It was meant as a way to get customers to come back."

"It totally works! I love shopping here. The co-op's already got a great selection of stuff, but the funny announcements are a big bonus. I hope he gets into a good club. Does he ever perform here?"

"He hasn't yet, but people have badgered him to do something at the community talent night," Kelly answered.

"Was that other guy 'Scotty'? I hope he doesn't mind..."

Sarah smiled. "Scott Fleishman helped dream it up. He wants to be an actor. Sometimes he gets a little annoyed, but mostly he's cool with it and hams it up."

Before they parted company, Sarah handed Marianne a paper bag. Marianne peeked inside, and the scent of some fresh herbs wafted up over a linen pouch and about a dozen smoothly rounded stones.

"Your best bet is going to be to ask George and Anne not to communicate with you by dream tonight. Be firm and clear. But just in case they don't hear you or are too insistent, these things should help block nightmares." Sarah told her to put the herbs under her pillow and to lay the stones around the bed and on the bedside table to ward off unwanted dreams. The stones would have to soak in the sun for the afternoon to 'charge.' Then she and Kelly headed home.

The time of burning was upon Anne, and Marianne had to leave for her own safety. She must be kept safe! Anne had failed to save her little brother, and he'd died. That must not happen again...

Chapter 21

MARIANNE headed home thoughtfully, the paper bag a reassuring weight in her arms. Her conversation had made her feel much better overall, but tired and thoughtful. She mulled things over as she strolled through the richly scented August afternoon. A picture was gathering in her head of all the bits and pieces. She just needed time to let it fall into place.

She contemplated finishing the work she needed to do in the dining room or doing some work in her office. Maybe Gillian, her history colleague had gotten back to her. Wandering down to the bedroom to get something, she realized she hadn't seen Oscar for a while. Going through each room, she looked for him with increasing anxiety.

"Oscar?" She called. Standing at the bottom of the stairs to go up she called upstairs a few times with no answer. Finally, she noticed that the door to the basement was ajar. Since she'd taken the lock off, it hadn't really closed properly. It was certainly possible that he'd gotten bored or curious and gone down into the basement. She approached the door and opened it reluctantly.

"Oscar, are you down there?" She called. Her voice fell flat in the dank silence below.

From out of the depths there came a pitiful yowl. He sounded like he was stuck in something and unable to get out. Her unease increased, and she did not want to go down there to look for him.

Oscar yowled sadly again, and pushing against her apprehension, Marianne slowly went down the stairs. "Oscar, where are you? Come on, mister, let's go back upstairs." She listened hard in the dense silence and thought she heard him back behind the furnace. She began to detect a faint sulfurous smell that set off warning bells in her head. Gas leak!

Abruptly she remembered that the shower water had been stone cold that morning and that there was something wrong with the hot water heater. It must be a gas heater, and the scent of gas in the air might mean a leak. She was not about to try to relight it. She would leave that to the professionals, but in the meantime, what if a spark set off an explosion? She knew somebody whose apartment had been severely damaged by a gas explosion, and the thought had always terrified her.

Fire in the basement could rip through the floor and torch the whole house if it got started. She had to get out now! But not without her cat.

"Oscar! Where are you?" The hair raising, primal smell of smoke began to penetrate her awareness, and she began to panic as she looked quickly around the bulky furnace sitting in the middle of the room. Catching a glimpse of the orange and white concentric rings of his fur, she reached down to grab him. He protested and scratched her arms in his distress and her haste. "Come on, baby, we got to get out of here." She turned and found there was more smoke in the air, obscuring the way out. She started to cough, each intake bringing more smoke into her lungs.

"No, no, no. Where is the door? Stairs were right here." She blundered forward feeling the heat behind her pushing her forward. Oscar twisted unhappily in her too tight grip. "Stay with me, baby! Don't go." The basement was too dark to see well, and she stumbled into something hard and slammed her head. Reeling dizzily and truly panicking, she heard the high-pitched screaming of a child lost in the smoky darkness. A woman shouted, "Get out! Get out!"

She couldn't find the stairs anywhere and banged her shoulder painfully against something splintery. Part of her thought, there's a window. Find the window.

Dimly, she could see daylight through the smoke and heat. The fearsome crackle of the fire was growing behind her, and she stumbled towards the light, the gravel of the driveway just inches away behind glass. She had to put Oscar down on the stone ledge in order to break the window. She had nothing safe to break the glass, and the fire was blazing behind her, consuming the floor above. She reached down and grabbed her sandal and pounded it against the glass. The stubborn pane, a mere eighth-inch thick, refused to break easily, and the rubber sole was too soft. She pounded harder, fearing both the fire and being sliced open. As the floor fell in behind her with an animal roar, she howled and slammed her hand through the glass. It shattered into jagged pieces that tore her flesh as she battered at it with the sandal, one-handed. The moment the hole was big enough, Oscar leaped through it and vanished. Marianne took deep lungfuls of clean air and sobbing, hoisted herself through the opening. She pulled herself painfully through the window and lay on the walkway coughing, panting, and sobbing hysterically.

The relative cool of the summer air revived and calmed her. Her hand throbbed and she looked in horror at the blood streaming down her left arm. Pressing her arm to her chest, she moved to get up and found that her palm hurt, and there were numerous sharp pains in her knees and shins. She moved away from the window and looked back, expecting to see smoke billowing out of the shattered hole, but there was nothing. The dark square of basement beyond the window was quiet and blank. There was no smell of smoke.

She pulled her phone out of her pocket with shaking hands and dialed Sarah. It seemed to take forever to scroll down to her name. Gotta put her on speed dial, she thought.

"Hello?"

"Hey, it's Marianne," she said in a low voice.

Something in her voice caused Sarah to say urgently, "What happened?"

"I think I just escaped a fire that happened more than a hundred years ago," Marianne said shakily.

"We'll be right there. Are you hurt?"

"Yeah. Yes. And I lost Oscar." She could feel her voice break. "Please come."

Marianne made her way to the dining room door stoop, sat and leaned against the railing, trembling, as the adrenaline ebbed. Some time passed before a car pulled up to the curb, and she heard voices come up the drive. Gentle hands pulled her to her feet and guided her inside, half swooning. Soft swearing accompanied her. She was laid on the sofa with her feet propped up and a blanket over her just in time to counter her shivering.

She faded in and out of consciousness, and she felt her wounds being cleaned and bandaged.

"I think there's glass in her knees. We're going to need to take her to the urgent care place."

Marianne revived a little and tried to sit up. Kelly's strong arms propped her up and put pillows behind her. "Hey take it easy. We've got you. Sarah, see if she's got some soda or something sweet."

"Oscar ran off. He's never been outside here," Marianne murmured.

"Don't worry. We'll put some food out for him, so he knows where to go. He'll be okay. You've got some cuts, and we think you need to go to the urgent care place. You might need stitches in your arm."

Sarah returned with a glass of cold tea, and Marianne gratefully took it and sipped. She made a face at the horrible sweetness of it but knew it was what she needed, so she drank a little more. The cobwebs began to clear, and she felt stronger.

"Okay," she agreed. "My purse is in here somewhere. "

The trip to Urgent Care took a few hours, in spite of there being few emergencies other than her. She took more than a dozen stitches in her forearm and palm and was told several times how lucky she was that she'd missed everything important. She sat through the glass shards being picked out of her knees by a patient nurse. When asked how she'd come to hurt herself she said she'd stupidly put her hand through a glass window and then fallen in her surprise. Sarah and Kelly backed her up solidly and took her back to their place.

Marianne sat gingerly on their rosebud patterned couch, wincing at all the little cuts and aches and pains. "Thank you guys so much for rescuing me yet again."

Sarah got a couple of glasses of cold water and some snacks from the kitchen and sat down with Kelly nearby. "You want to tell us what really happened to you?"

Marianne related what she had experienced, saying, "I realized that today is the anniversary of the fire that killed Anne's little brother. That must be why it happened. It was the weirdest sensation." She looked at them perplexed. "I was sure it was all going on for real at one level, and another part of me was trying to think more clearly. I'm not even sure what actually occurred since there was no fire or smoke damage. All I know is that I don't really want to sleep there tonight." She closed her eyes, feeling drained.

Sarah said thoughtfully, "It kind of sounds like Anne and you are in synch with each other. People are beings of energy at some level, and spirits are all energy. If a person and a spirit are on the same wavelength, they can resonate with each other sympathetically. I think somehow you got caught up in Anne's memories of the fire."

"That's the thing. She was never in the fire herself," Marianne protested. "It was her little brother who was trapped, not her."

Sarah shrugged. "I can't explain that. Still, I think somehow you and she resonate with each other."

While they had similar life experiences in some things, Marianne felt she was significantly different because she'd left her abusive husband.

"Maybe Anne likes you for that reason," Sarah suggested. "You are much feistier than she was. Hmmm," Sarah mused thoughtfully. "Maybe we can use that."

Marianne nodded. "I see what you're saying… I mean I don't know how to ask someone to move on, but I think I understand her. George, on the other hand…"

Kelly scowled, "Do you think he had a hand in anything this

afternoon?"

Marianne frowned and shook her head. "Maybe he lured Oscar downstairs or somehow kept him down there, making me go down after him. Other than that, it just seemed like Anne."

The shadows were lengthening outside, and the air was cooling off a little. A plaintive growl came from someone's stomach, and they all laughed.

"Me too!" Kelly said emphatically. She got up and went into the kitchen and began banging pots and pans around.

Sarah said, "If today's the anniversary of the fire, there's a pretty good chance that Anne will stop being so worried and trying to get you out of the house."

"Can I please stay here tonight?" Marianne asked in a small voice. "I don't think I could stand another round of fire dreams, or George yelling at me. If I didn't have a complex about basements before this, I sure have one now."

"Of course. We need to get your 'roommates' out as soon as possible," Sarah said firmly. "You need rest tonight, and I need to go to work tomorrow. We could do it tomorrow night, if you're up for it?"

Marianne nodded emphatically. "Tell me what I need to do."

Sarah wrote out a short list of things to get at the co-op and set the time for early evening while it was still light out. Marianne breathed a sigh of relief. She didn't fancy having to perform some sort of exorcism after dark. It was likely to be scary enough as it was.

Marianne slept long and deeply. She woke to her phone ringing persistently. Disoriented for a moment, she recalled where she was and winced as she reached for the phone.

"Hello?" She said sleepily.

"Hi, Marianne?"

She said in confusion, "Ruari?"

"I'm sorry. Is this a bad time? It's after nine; I assumed you'd be up."

"No, no. It's okay. I had no idea it was that late. What is it?"

"I was just calling to tell you the parts for your dishwasher are in, and I could install them today if you like."

"Uh, sure. When were you thinking?"

"I could come around eleven, if that works for you?"

"That'll work. Um, do you still have the measurements for the window you replaced last week? I broke it again, and you'll have to fix it again. Sorry." She winced at her inadequate words.

He hesitated before saying, "Okay. I'll see what I can do. It's supposed to rain later today."

She thanked him, and the phone clicked as she disconnected. He sat in his truck a moment longer. She was such a strange woman. She seemed so sincere but had such odd things happen around her. Perhaps she had a good explanation, and it was an accident of some kind. Maybe her "ghosts" were somehow responsible. He really did not know what to make of her ghost stories. They sounded suspiciously like excuses to him.

Sighing, he turned the key in the ignition of his truck and headed back to the hardware store.

Marianne lay in bed for a moment, feeling rested but rather flat after all the excitement. Her stomach had only flopped a little when she'd recognized his voice. She wondered if she'd gotten over him or lost interest somehow when she wasn't looking and felt a little sad about that. Eventually she rolled over, muttering, "Ouch, ouch," as she caught her bandaged right hand. It was overcast and relatively gloomy out, which explained how she'd slept in so long. Getting up produced more winces and stifled hisses as she hobbled to the bathroom and found some ibuprofen.

Kelly had thoughtfully left a T-shirt and shorts out for her to borrow as her own clothes were covered in blood. Wearing the clothes of an Amazonian goddess didn't work so well for Marianne's shorter, stockier frame, but she appreciated it anyway. Downstairs her hosts had left her a note on the breakfast table saying they'd gone to work and would meet her later. She ate a bowl of Kelly's homemade granola and some fruit and let herself out.

The walk home was a little slow, but she managed. Her bandages earned her a few odd looks, which she did her best to smile at and ignore. Fretting about Oscar's whereabouts all the way home occupied most of her thoughts.

Once she was home, she checked the side stoop. The shattered glass and reddish brown smears on the walkway gave her a start, and she had to swallow a momentary wave of disgust. Her knees and shins twinged as she looked at the window frame with the remaining glass shards in it. Edging around them, she looked for the can of cat food on the steps her rescuers had left out for Oscar. It was licked clean and lying on its side, so she was hopeful. She called his name a few times with no answer.

Heading inside, she dropped the plastic bag with her bloody clothes on the floor and dumped her purse on the couch. Oscar came bounding down the hallway and threw himself against her legs in his happiness to see her. She winced but laughed aloud in relief and bent down to pet him. It was too awkward to pick him up one-handed, so she sat on the couch and rubbed his fur all over as well as under the chin in his favorite spot.

"Oscar! I'm so glad to see you! I was afraid you'd run away after yesterday. How did you get back inside?" A glance at the basement door showed it was ajar. "Did you jump back in through the window? You smart boy!" He lay down next to her, purring ecstatically and loudly. While she cuddled with him happily, she checked all of his paws carefully for damage and found none.

When she rose to go to the bedroom, she winced painfully and hobbled stiffly down the hall. She had just finished changing into something more her size when the Big Ben chime of the doorbell rang.

She made her way down the hall again and opened the door. Ruari stood on the front step looking devastatingly handsome in Gloria's dark green polo shirt. His pleasant smile faded to a look of shock.

"Come in," she said with an apologetic half smile, favoring her bandaged arm.

"What happened to you?" He blurted, looking stricken.

Her toffee brown eyes gazed at him with a hundred-year-old stare and a wry smile. "If you really want to know, I'll tell you. Do you have time for a glass of iced tea?"

He followed her into the kitchen and set his toolbox down. She poured him a glass gingerly with her bandaged hand and got him sugar, ice, and a spoon. They sat at the dining room table. She began while he doctored his tea.

"Do you remember I told you I had a piano playing ghost named Anne? Well, when she was five, something really awful happened to her." She told him the story and segued into the reliving of the anniversary of the terrible fire.

He listened solemnly before saying confusedly, "So you're saying she possessed you?"

Marianne thought about it and shook her head. "No, not exactly. More like I got caught up in her memories, but you know what's weird? She was never in the fire herself. At least not according to the newspaper article. She was outside the whole time. There was a neighbor who went into the basement and brought little Samuel out. So I don't know why she relived it from the inside." She paused thoughtfully, beginning to make some new connections.

After a moment she shook herself with a rueful laugh. "Anyway, I can tell you that hundred-year-old panic is just as potent as today's panic. Her memories had me out that window faster than you can say jack rabbit."

"Is that how you got hurt?"

His grey-blue eyes held such concern, it made her heart jump and her throat constrict. She swallowed her sudden longing. "Yeah, lots of band-aids, gauze, and more than a dozen stitches' worth." She tried to sound offhand.

He moved as if to get up but stopped himself, saying awkwardly, "I'm sorry you got hurt and hope you feel better soon. How about I fix the window? I got another piece of glass before I came."

She levered herself up out of the chair gingerly, feeling her shins and knees stinging, and nodded. "That would be great."

He brought the pane around to the side of the house from his truck. She got a broom and dustpan to sweep up the shards. They worked in companionable silence. Oscar joined them, jumping up on the ledge of the coal bin window, twitching his crooked tail, and watching them from the inside as Ruari cleared the broken pieces, placed the new pane, and pressed more glazing around the edges.

She sat on the stoop to watch him work when she was done. "How's your carpentry going?"

"Pretty good. I'm almost done with the art piece I started a couple of weeks ago."

"What kind of wood are you using?"

He looked at her, surprised by her interest, and said, "Cherry. I have a pile of odd pieces left over from different projects and that seemed like the right kind. It's got a dark reddish brown color, a really beautiful grain, and smells sweet, like fruit. I like incorporating the colors and textures into the final piece."

"Kind of how the Paleolithic cave painters used the texture and shape of the cave walls to make their paintings more three dimensional?"

He laughed in delight at her analogy. "Yeah! Kind of like that."

She smiled, pleased that she'd pleased him. "When you're not woodworking, what else do you like to do?"

He considered. "I like to hike and walk in the woods, but I haven't had a lot of time to do that this summer."

"I used to walk in the woods around my grandparents' place in Vandenburg." She smiled. "I have a lot of fond memories of Grandpa Clare telling me about plants and birds."

"Well, if you ever want to walk again, I could give you some recommendations. I know some nice places."

"That would be nice."

His cell phone rang as he was finishing the glazing. SueAnn Talmadge's sharp voice was clear all the way to the steps. He grimaced. "There was more work than I anticipated at Violet Lane. Yes, I'll be late to the next job. Yes, I'll get there before three. Yes. Yes."

He looked at her regretfully. "Gotta keep moving. Sorry." He got up and went inside to work on the dishwasher next. Fortunately, the part cooperated and went in relatively easily.

Marianne watched him work. "I know you're running late. Could you restart the pilot light on the hot water heater? I didn't want to touch it, and honestly I don't really want to go down there right now."

"Of course." He returned in a few minutes and assured her that the tank was working fine and would take an hour or so to heat the water again.

"Let me know what the bill for the glass is. That shouldn't go on Mrs. Thomas' tab."

He nodded.

They stood awkwardly at the front door, and he said hesitantly, "Would you...would you like to continue our conversation at another time?"

"Are you asking me out?" She inquired shyly.

He smiled and said, "Yes, I guess I am."

She answered his smile with her own. "Yes, I'd like that very much."

"Maybe in a couple of days when you're feeling better?"

"Perfect. I'll see you then." She watched him go down the steps and get into his truck with an unfamiliar happiness bubbling inside. He waved as he made the turn and headed back up the street.

Chapter 22

IT BEGAN to rain late in the day. She made one foray out to the co-op and Dream Time, the new age store on Main Street, looking for the short list of things Sarah had given her. After that she slowly straightened up her house, pushing boxes against the wall in the living room and trying to tidy up. Towards evening, Marianne began to get keyed up again. She'd found the little stones Sarah had given her lying on the windowsill. Trusting that they'd absorbed all the sun they needed yesterday, she laid them on the floor around her bed and slipped the sachet of herbs under her pillow. Unsure of their actual efficacy, Marianne shrugged mentally. Every little bit helps.

Sarah arrived after 5:30, holding a small, squat cast iron pot in her arms. She still wore her work attire of crisp navy blue linen suit and white silk blouse though raindrops beaded her glasses. "Hey, how are you feeling?" She asked sympathetically.

"Come in out of the rain. I'm better but still sore."

Marianne let her in and followed her to the kitchen where the small bag of things she'd gotten sat on the counter. The dark metal bowl looked like it was nearly half an inch thick and blackened on the inside. Outside it was textured with a pattern of facets like it had been beaten with a hammer while still soft.

Sarah wiped her lenses down with a soft cloth from her pocket and settled them back on her face before placing in the bowl a bundle of white sage leaves tied with a bit of cotton string followed by a couple of reddish brown incense cones. Their faint dry fragrance drifted up.

"Alright, we need to invite Mr. and Mrs. Rutherford to join us. Where do you think they would be the most comfortable?"

Marianne looked quizzically at her. Sarah clarified, "Think of the Rutherfords as the people they used to be when they were alive. For some reason they are stuck here, and we are trying to convince them to move on. Where do you think they would be most comfortable talking to us?"

Marianne limped into the living room and gestured to the piano, its bench, and a nearby armchair. "Anne was a pianist, and George was very proud of her talent. She did a lot of concerts in here for their friends."

"Perfect." Sarah followed her with the bowl and a pair of hot mitts which she set on the coffee table.

"Okay. That's ready. Now we have to ground ourselves."

"What, like electricity?" Marianne looked confused.

"Kind of," Sarah said patiently. "Have you ever done meditation? Yoga? Tai chi?"

"I did a little yoga a couple of years ago but never seriously," Marianne said doubtfully.

"Well, grounding yourself is so you don't get lost. So your own spirit is firmly attached to your body, and you feel strong and confident. I always do this even for the little stuff because it's good practice and because you never know what you'll run into."

"Okay. How do I do it?"

Sarah slipped her low-heeled pumps off and stood barefoot on the hardwood floor, and Marianne slid her own sandals off and did the same. Taking Marianne's hand in her soft, warm one, Sarah closed her eyes and stood relaxed. Marianne closed her eyes and did her best to imitate the other woman.

Sarah's voice spoke calmly. "Imagine you are a tree. Your head and arms are your branches, your torso is the trunk and your legs and feet are roots." Her voice reminded Marianne of her old yoga instructor's calm, centered tone.

"Any particular kind of tree?"

"Nope. One you are familiar with, maybe a tree you know, if you like. If a tree doesn't work for you, try something else. Kelly always imagines herself as a mountain."

Marianne opened her eyes. "Kelly does this with you? She said she wasn't able to hear or feel anything to do with spirits."

"Maybe not but she's one of the most grounded, solid people I know, and she works with me sometimes when I need that."

"Oh." Marianne shut her eyes again, but her thoughts kept wandering back to what kind of work Sarah did that needed a mountain to ground her. She turned her attention back to being a tree, and she remembered her yoga breathing. She imagined each breath entering through her feet, swirling through her middle and up into her head, then coursing back down through her feet. Picturing herself as a tree taking up water and nutrients and growing down into the ground and up to the sky, she breathed in and out. She was elaborating on the kind of leaves she would have when the sharp sulfur of a kitchen match scented the air as Sarah lit the cedar cones. They smoldered, setting the dried sage alight and making a bright, pungent smoke that began trailing into the air.

Oscar materialized from somewhere and sauntered over to the couch, jumping up and sitting between them with his crooked tail wrapped around his feet. They sat on the cushions facing the empty piano bench and chair as if waiting for guests to arrive. Sarah spoke loudly and clearly, "Anne Elizabeth Eddy Rutherford and George William Rutherford, we ask you to join us here. We invite you to join us under the protection of sage and cedar. We know you are unhappy and ask you to come and tell us what is bothering you. If we can help you, we will. "

They sat in silence for a few minutes while the sharp smells slowly permeated the room. Marianne's thoughts drifted to memories of cooking and of the desert of the Southwest she'd once visited. She wondered if Anne would manifest herself or not and whether George would come at the same time. She gazed at the empty piano bench and chair, waiting for something to happen, feeling more anxious as the minutes passed. After a bit she stole a glance sideways at Sarah and saw she had her eyes closed, head slightly cocked as if she was listening hard for a very faint noise.

At last Sarah opened her eyes and smiled in the direction of the piano. "Thank you for coming, Mrs. Rutherford," she said cordially, as if welcoming a living person.

Marianne turned quickly, half expecting to see a physical person and saw nothing but an empty piano bench. The hairs on the back of her neck prickled eerily, but Oscar sat quietly, staring at the piano bench, his crooked tail gently bobbing up and down.

"I am Sarah, and this is my friend Marianne who lives here now. You've been trying to tell her something since she moved in, and I think you tried to tell the previous occupants something as well. We know you are unhappy and frightened. Yesterday was the anniversary of the terrible fire that took your brother's life. Please tell us what else is bothering you. We'd like to help you move on. Your family is waiting for you and wants you to join them."

Sarah gestured to Marianne to continue. Marianne closed her eyes briefly and imagined Anne Rutherford the way she'd sometimes pictured her. She could see a slender middle-aged woman with an anxious face, wearing dark, classically tailored clothes, radiating unhappiness. When she opened her eyes, the unoccupied seat across the room was jarring. So she closed her eyes again and rebuilt the image in her mind.

"Hi, Anne," Marianne began, pretending she was talking to a living, breathing woman who was just sitting quietly across the room. "I am an historian for a living, so I went to the library and found some newspaper articles about you.

"You used to live in a nearby town, Schukill, with your mother, father, and little brother, Samuel, when you were five. One summer, when your parents were away, something terrible happened." Marianne began to feel anxious and tense, but she pressed on with her story. "You were at home with the hired girl, Abigail, and your little brother. She was doing the ironing in the kitchen on the table and trying to look after you two as well. Somehow I think you and Sam were rambunctious children, Anne!" Marianne said with an understanding smile.

Suddenly, Marianne could clearly picture a sweaty, tired, and cross fourteen-year-old stuck inside on a stuffy, humid day with the family ironing next to a hot metal stove, a fire blazing within. What was worse, she also had to look after a couple of bored, restless children at the same time. Marianne wondered briefly if this was her own imagination or whether Anne was remembering and somehow beaming it across the space to her, and she plunged on regardless.

"It was so hot outside, and the kitchen, heated by the fire in the stove, was even hotter. You and your brother were playing. You both ran down into the basement where it was cool and were playing games down there, right? Maybe hide and seek?"

She remembered a fragment of the dream she'd had where a little girl had run down the hall laughing and holding a little toy or doll in her hand. "Did one of you have a little doll? Maybe you guys were teasing each other with it? Was the toy Samuel's?" The little kids she'd babysat had certainly teased each other. She began to feel more certain that had been the case. She lifted her head in the direction of the piano bench and thought she saw the dark haired woman nod her head slightly.

"It *was* his, wasn't it? You grabbed it and ran up the stairs, but he just stayed down there crying. You thought he'd run after you, but he didn't. When you ran through the kitchen, Abigail finally lost her temper with you and put down her hot iron and chased you outside. She only meant to put it down for a second, really. But she put it down on the laundry not the stove, didn't she?" The scene presented itself like a movie playing in her head, or like a memory of events that had transpired more than one hundred years ago. Having been in those shoes herself, Marianne could absolutely picture the irate fourteen-year-old chasing a five-year-old brat around the yard until her longer legs caught up with the little stinker. She'd grabbed her by the arm and swatted her behind with the flat of her hand until Anne cried. "Stay out of the way and stop teasing your brother! Play nicely!" Abigail had said angrily.

When she'd turned back to the house, there was a billow of smoke coming out of the back door. Marianne could sense Anne's desperation. "You both ran back to the house, but the dry laundry was on fire already, blocking the path between the back door and the cellar door. You looked for Samuel outside, but he hadn't come out. The fire blocked his path. You could hear him screaming and crying in the basement. Abigail panicked. She was only fourteen. She didn't have the presence of mind to throw the burning things out the door into the yard. The fire was too big, too fast.

"You both screamed until the neighbors came. They did their best to put out the fire. You told them your little brother was still trapped down in the basement. It was too hot for you to go inside and get him yourself. You were so scared," Marianne whispered.

She cleared her throat and resumed her narrative. "There was a man, a Mr. Kenny." Marianne saw him clearly in her mind's eye, wearing an old fashioned, collarless, button up shirt, denim overalls and heavy boots and with a handlebar mustache. Somehow in her mind's eye he resembled Ruari.

"He put a wet bandana over his nose and mouth and bravely made his way into the smoke and fire. Maybe he went through an outside trapdoor into the basement, so he didn't have to go through the burning house? After a few tense minutes while people did their best to put out the fire with buckets of water from the well in the yard, the man emerged covered in soot with burns in his shirt and pants, holding the small limp body of Samuel in his arms."

Tears running down her face, Marianne saw the memory through Anne's eyes. It was like watching a train wreck; she couldn't look away. The woman on the bench across the room twisted her hands silently. Marianne did the only thing she could and continued telling the story aloud. "Someone ran for the doctor to try and revive him, but he was too small to survive without today's technology to get clean air in his lungs and help him live. Mama and Papa came but they were too late, and Samuel died." She could picture Mrs. Eddy running up in a long linen skirt and shirtwaist, Mr. Eddy right behind her. Mrs. Eddy threw herself on the ground, clasping the little boy to her chest and cried and cried. Mr. Eddy held Anne to him.

"Anne," Marianne whispered, "I saw where they buried him in the cemetery by the road. I think you carried that day with you your whole life. You felt responsible that your baby brother died. I think you imagined over and over how Samuel must have felt as he was trapped in the basement until it became your own memory.

"But, Anne, you were only five. It wasn't your fault. It wasn't Abigail's fault. You didn't make the fire start on purpose. It was an accident. You did everything in your power to get your brother rescued. Sometimes bad things just happen, and they aren't your fault." Anne sat rigidly, hands clenched in her lap, tears running down her cheeks. Marianne opened her eyes, wiped her own wet cheeks, and sniffed her runny nose.

Sarah spoke soothingly in the miserable silence. Her voice was a balm. "Anne, we understand what happened. And it was a long time ago. It is time to let it go. It wasn't your fault. You need to forgive yourself. Your family, your mother, father and little brother are all waiting for you on the other side. They love you and forgive you and want you to be with them. Forgive yourself. It is time to move on. You don't need to stay any more."

Anne's spirit sat transfixed by her words. Sarah nodded encouragingly at Marianne as if this were all completely normal instead of completely bizarre. So, Marianne took a deep breath, closed her eyes again, and continued.

"Anne, the newspaper also said you'd gone to Julliard Music School when you were young. You must have been an amazing musician! I think you got married to George and gave up a career in performance to come back to Maple Hill to teach music. I got the feeling that you were a really good teacher, and your students loved you. I loved hearing you play the 'Pachelbel Canon.' Thank you for playing that night when I could hear it."

Marianne was on a roll as she continued, "George also was very proud of your talent as a musician. I heard that you played many times for your friends and his. But I also saw in a dream that he made you play when you were sick and didn't feel like playing. I know that he locked you in the basement if you stood up to him and refused. I think he knew you were afraid of the cellar because of what happened to little Sam, and he used that against you. That was vindictive of him. Husbands are supposed to be protectors of their wives not inflictors of punishment on them.

"Anne? You got married, like I did, for better or for worse, and that's why you stayed with him even when he was cruel. He was probably nice enough some of the time and made you feel like you deserved the treatment he gave you at others. But that's wrong. You never deserved to be made to feel ashamed, to be isolated from friends and family. No one does.

"You married each other in sickness and in health, and he stayed with you even when you came down with cancer. But, Anne, remember the next bit of your vows, 'til death do us part'? Anne, you and George died, and you are allowed to part. You don't have to stay here with him. He no longer has control over you unless you let him. The lock is off the basement door, and he can no longer hold you there. You are free to go. Your mother and father and little Samuel Jr. are waiting for you on the other side. They love you and want you to join them. Please go. You will be so much happier, and you deserve that happiness." She didn't know where the words came from, but she knew they were right.

In her mind's eye, Marianne watched Anne listening intently. Her sweet face framed by dark hair and heavy, narrow glasses slowly transformed with the realization that she was free. When Marianne finished Anne looked directly at her, nodded once and mouthed, "Thank you." Then she stood and turned and faded away. Marianne was no longer able to picture her clearly.

She and Sarah both sat for a few minutes letting the silence resolve into peace. Finally, Sarah said quietly, "When you were telling Anne the story of her life—by the way, that was brilliant and clearly just the right thing to do—how did you know about the toy?"

Marianne recounted her dream of the little girl running down the hall. Sarah looked thoughtful. "I have an idea. Come on." They stood up. "Do you have a flashlight?"

The sage and cedar had left woody ash on the bottom of the pot and mostly burned out. Sarah carried it into the kitchen and put it in the sink, while Marianne got a flashlight out of the drawer. "It's got new batteries in it, so it should work."

Sarah took it and headed for the upstairs. The little landing was dim and stuffy with the day's muggy gloom. Sarah headed for the small attic door. "Do you remember when I first came, and I told you there was something going on in the attic?"

Marianne nodded. Sarah continued, "When I was first here it seemed tied to the rest of Anne's unhappiness, but I didn't know why or how. Maybe this is it."

Mystified, Marianne watched as Sarah opened the door.

Inside, the attic was dusty, cobwebby and forbidding. Sarah switched on the overhead light, and it shone dimly on the joists.

Switching on the flashlight, she ducked in the door and walked, crouching warily under the roof beams with the nails of the shingles jutting like claws through the skip sheeting. Stepping carefully from joist to joist, Marianne followed her.

"Okay, Mrs. Rutherford," Sarah said conversationally. "If you are still here, is there something up here you need us to see now? Did you keep it all this time and hide it up here? Show us where it is."

Marianne's apprehension about being in the attic mounted, but she trusted Sarah.

"Here, can you hold this for me?" Sarah handed her the flashlight and unclasped her necklace. It was a small crystal pendant on a thin gold chain. She wound the excess chain in her hand and left enough for the pendant to swing freely.

"Mrs. Rutherford, please help me find the thing you are hiding. I think this is the last thing holding you here. How about, I'll ask you questions, and you tell me yes or no. Show me which way is yes." The crystal swung over her palm. Marianne couldn't tell which way and it looked like Sarah was making it swing. "Okay, which way is no? Thank you. All right. Is it behind me?"

Marianne watched in fascination as the little crystal swung in the flashlight beam. Sarah turned around and faced the little attic door. "Is it to my right?" By asking simple directional yes-no questions and divining an answer from the pendulum, Sarah led the way to the eaves of the house eight beams in from the door. The roof angled steeply downward there, and the two women balanced on the wood beams like a bizarre game of Twister. There was fluffy, dusty rock wool insulation filling the spaces between the beams, and both of them coughed in the disturbed dust. Finally, Sarah plunged her hand into the insulation and felt around. Marianne angled the flashlight as best she could.

"Aha!" Sarah withdrew her hand clutching a small brown-grey object. It was so dirty that at first Marianne couldn't see what it was. Sarah handed it to her with a smile.

It was a little rabbit dressed in very dirty, faded gingham pants and shirt and firmly stuffed with something stiff and fairly hard.

"Oh," Marianne breathed and coughed on the dust again.

"Thank you, Mrs. Rutherford," Sarah said, tucking the necklace into her pocket.

They crawled back to the center beam where they could stand up more or less and went back through the little attic door.

Sarah returned to the living room and put the little stuffed rabbit on the coffee table.

Sarah spoke formally and with great compassion. "Thank you, Mrs. Rutherford, for sharing yourself with us and trusting us with your secret. You were not to blame for your little brother's death. Please forgive yourself. George can no longer hold you here either. Your family is waiting for you on the other side with open arms. They miss you and want you to join them. Please, go in peace."

Marianne felt a weight of anxiety lift from her, one she had not realized she was carrying, and sighed. "One down, one to go," she murmured.

They refilled the iron pot with another white sage bundle and some cedar incense cones and sat on the sofa again. Sarah struck a match and lit the aromatics, waiting for the smoke to curl upwards again before she spoke. Oscar leaped onto the arm of the couch and sat erect, his tail curled neatly around his feet.

Sarah spoke firmly and cordially. "George William Rutherford, we ask you to come forth and make yourself known to us under the protection of sage and cedar. You are deeply unhappy here, and we wish to help you. Please tell us what concerns you so much."

They waited in silence in the early twilight as the rain beat against the windowpanes. Sarah called for him to make his wishes known again, but there was no answer.

Marianne began to feel apprehensive. George always turned up when she was doing something he didn't like, why wouldn't he show up and vent, given the opportunity? His absence was as ominous as a thunderstorm in the other room. Glancing at Sarah, Marianne watched her listening intently again as if for a very a faint sound with her head cocked and her eyes closed.

The silence lengthened and deepened as the room grew darker. The smudge burned itself down into white ash.

"Maybe I should get out my painting things and try to paint the living room or something?" Marianne suggested quietly.

Sarah opened her eyes and said softly, "Maybe." She cleared her throat and spoke more loudly. "Maybe we're only going to be able to help Anne today. George doesn't have to come if he doesn't want to. He is a strong spirit and probably doesn't like coming when called. After all, it's not as if I'm his mother," she added with a little smile.

Marianne really did not like the prospect of waiting for George to show up when he pleased. Sarah patted her on the knee and got up from the couch. Marianne rose after her, a little bewildered. Sarah had implied she was going to be with her until the releasing or banishing was done.

Sarah hugged her and said briskly, "I have to get home for dinner. Give me a call later, if you need to. You were amazing with Anne. Give yourself some credit. You'll be fine."

"But—" Marianne said in confusion.

"Call me later," Sarah said, squeezing her uninjured hand firmly and looking her in the eyes. Marianne thought she might be trying to tell her something, but it had gotten so dark inside, she missed it.

"Well, thank you for coming," she said awkwardly and led her to the door. Turning on the lights both inside and onto the front step, she opened the door and let her friend out.

Sarah waved as she walked down the rain-slicked walk to her car. Marianne closed the door, feeling a sense of abandonment. The room seemed very empty and gloomy in the twilight. She flipped the switch for living room light, wondering what to do next and feeling lost.

She heard a puma-sized growl and saw Oscar crouched on the sofa, his fur standing on end, tail lashing menacingly. Following his gaze, she saw a formless shadow filling the doorway to the hall. Her hair stood on end, and her heart beat like a trip hammer. She wanted nothing more than to run, but she was rooted to the spot. Suddenly, the overhead light burst with a shower of glass fragments, reducing the light. The air grew sharply colder until she could see her breath, and the mason jar of flowers on the top of the piano exploded. The outline of a man in a dark suit coalesced in the doorway, his bearded face in shadow. She drew breath and screamed.

Chapter 23

HER feet suddenly able to move, Marianne bolted for the front door, and ran headlong into something solid. George was suddenly there between her and the door, though she hadn't seen him move.

He reached out and grasped her bare arm tightly in his frigid grip. His voice hissed angrily in her ears, "Hello, Marianne. I don't come when called, like some pet dog. This is my house, and I am in charge here." His icy blue eyes, Geoffrey's eyes, bored into hers, and she cringed away from him. Her worst nightmare had come true.

He said coldly, with finely suppressed rage, "Now that my wife is gone, you will have to take her place. You two are very much alike, except that she played the piano brilliantly, and you have less ability than her meanest student. Nevertheless, you will learn. We will have concerts here as we did before. My friends and colleagues will come back and all will be well."

Marianne's horror mounted as she envisioned being made to practice piano for hours at a time with George standing over her, berating and belittling her, threatening to hurt her if she did not comply. She saw herself gradually turning inward, bound by his expectations of her, losing her friends and barely getting by. She became drab and meek and isolated in this house that became her prison.

The cold of his hands spread up her arms and began seeping into her chest. He pulled her inexorably past the fireplace into the hallway, toward the bedroom. A part of her wailed in despair. As a paralyzing fear crept through her something wild in her broke free. Before she could lose it, she yanked her arm out of his grasp and stepped back. Hot anger quenched her fear, and she said through gritted teeth, "I am not Anne. You treated her horribly, and you will not treat me that way."

His fury lashed out as he loomed over her. "You will do as I say, woman! You are nothing without me. You are not married. You have no place, no home, no life without a man, without me. Though you are worthless, my nephew was wrong to let you go. I'll grant that you are pretty. Perhaps I can mold you into something in time."

Although she quailed, she stared him down. "No. I won't. I am not yours, and you cannot keep me."

His open hand struck her face forcefully, and she reeled back, shocked that he could hit so hard. Her wild anger coalesced into fury, and she closed both her fists and swung hard at her attacker. Her right hand hit George as hard as she could in his stomach. She connected with something not all there. Without thinking, forgetting her stitches, her left hand swung at him. Her bandaged hand lit up with pain as it passed through his semi-solid torso and followed through until it hit something hard and unyielding. She yelped and pulled back, cradling her damaged hand.

"Enough!" Shouted a voice. Marianne turned to see Sarah standing in her navy blue suit, looking like a vengeful goddess, her spectacles reflecting the light momentarily like twin fires. "George William Rutherford, you will take the stand and give an account of yourself." Her voice was steely and commanding.

George halted mid step as he moved to take hold of Marianne again. His face contorted with derision as he snarled, "Who are you?"

"I am a *fully* vested member of Smith, Wolgust and Brown," she responded coolly. Then continuing without allowing him a moment to respond, she said in the clipped voice of one establishing facts, "Mr. Rutherford, you married Anne Elizabeth Eddy in 1924, is that correct?"

Reluctantly, he nodded.

"You took the traditional vows 'to have and to hold from this day forward, for better or for worse, for richer, for poorer, in sickness and in health, to love and to cherish; from this day forward until death do us part' is that correct?"

He nodded, seemingly unable to change the conversation.

"This is a binding social contract with legal ramifications, correct?"

Mystified, Marianne stood transfixed. The pain in her hand was killing her, and dimly she thought she might have broken some bones. She didn't want to move and disrupt whatever was happening, though.

George Rutherford answered curtly, "Yes, of course. She is my wife." He stated this with the same tone he would use to say 'my car,' 'my house,' 'my dog.'

"Then I argue that you have at best kept only a few of those obligations while violating the spirit of the others." Sarah paced the space between them, sounding as if she had a ream of legal briefs in front of her and a courtroom between them. "You recognized her talent and married her when she was in music school. Although you encouraged her to play and allowed her to teach the children of Maple Hill, you also demanded that she play many concerts for your friends, lodge brothers, and coworkers."

"Of course!" He said indignantly. "She came from a poor family, and I fed and clothed her. Her talent at the piano was the best thing about her. She would have been nothing without me. I gave her social standing and a good reputation in this town."

"And when she got sick?" Sarah shot back. "She suffered from cancer for several years before she died, and you still demanded that she play for you and your friends. You stayed married to her during her sickness, but I charge that you did little to care for her or protect her during that time or earlier."

"I took her to the best doctors possible!" He protested.

The avenging lawyer nailed him with her gaze. "You may have, but you did nothing to ease her suffering at home, reduce her stress level, or her obligation to play for you. You locked her in the basement when she disagreed with you or defied you in any way. You did that when you knew that she feared the basement above all because of what happened to her brother when she was a child. That is a direct violation of the 'to love and to cherish' clause of your marriage vows."

"How dare you judge me! She had an obligation to obey me as

our vows also stated," George roared back, outraged.

"I think God will judge you more harshly than I will, Mr. Rutherford. In any case, based on the fact that you reneged on your social contract numerous times and the fact that she died before you, you no longer have a hold on her. She is no longer 'yours' in any way." Sarah raised her hands before her, palms pressed together, and drew them down sharply, saying, "Death has parted you both. She has crossed over, and it is time that you crossed over as well."

George was nearly apoplectic, face darkening. "You cannot tell me what to do!"

"I can, and I will. This case is closed." Sarah's flat voice was relentless as judge, jury and executioner. "There was a reason you never made partner. You were so cold and hard, you were not deemed worthy. A family lawyer has to have a heart, Mr. Rutherford. It is time to go home to your natal family. Your mother, father, brother, and sister are waiting for you."

George opened his mouth to argue further but turned his head suddenly as if he heard something. Both women waited with bated breath.

"It is time to go, George," Sarah said softly.

Listening to something neither of them could hear, George's spirit turned away from them toward the front hall.

"Mother, no, please!" His voice, when it came, no longer held chilly disdain. Instead it sounded younger, pleading. "Not the basement. I was good!" The expression of growing horror and shame on his face was something Marianne would never forget. Then, he suddenly vanished like a blown light bulb.

They stood in the abrupt silence. Marianne finally whispered, "I don't think he wanted to go."

"No, I don't think he did," Sarah said quietly.

"What did he hear? I didn't hear anything—did you?"

Sarah's posture relaxed. "Nope, and I'm okay with that. Some things are better left unknown."

Marianne breathed out a sigh. "Is he really gone?"

"I think so." Sarah took a deep breath and let it out. "I can give you a few things to protect your house and make sure he doesn't come back, if you like."

Marianne nodded fervently. The motion jarred her hand, and she hissed with pain.

Sarah immediately helped her to sit on the sofa. "Are you okay?"

Marianne opened her hand gingerly and saw fresh blood seeping through the bandages. They unwrapped them carefully and saw she'd pulled the stitches in her palm, and her middle and ring fingers wouldn't open properly. "Damn. I was afraid of that. I think I broke them punching George."

Sarah exclaimed, "Holy cow, we need to get you to the doctor!"

Marianne nodded, cradling her hands gingerly. "I know. I'll go in a bit."

Sarah made a small impatient noise in the face of the other's stubbornness, but Marianne set her jaw. Sarah said, "I'm glad I came back when I did—although you were doing quite well without me." She smiled. "I'm sorry I had to leave like that."

"Yeah, what was that all about? I really thought you'd gone and left me alone with George," Marianne said distractedly as she fumbled to rewrap her hand.

Sarah reached up and unconsciously turned her crystal pendant between her thumb and forefinger. "I had to give him a reason to come out of hiding. He was more likely to come if he thought you were alone. I'm sorry. I would *never* really leave you in dire straits like that," she added fervently.

Marianne acknowledged her with a nod and said, "How did you know the legal angle would work on him? What did you mean 'you never made partner'?"

Sarah sat back and smiled slyly. "I did my research too. When you told me who was here, George's name sounded familiar. Turns out he used to be a lawyer who worked for Arnie Walgust's father in his day."

Marianne goggled. "That's your law firm! You're kidding!"

"I asked Arnie about it last week, and he told me that Rutherford was a good lawyer, tenacious and meticulous, but he was cold. Arnie's father never liked how he treated his wife, and even though he could see George was desperate to become partner, Arnie's father never offered it to him. They were a family firm, and they dealt with people in the community all the time. Arnie's father cared about the social side of things. I guess he felt George would not have treated his clients well."

"George must've been very frustrated."

Sarah nodded. "Too bad he took it out at home. By the way, I meant what I said earlier. You were awesome with Anne and were doing pretty well with George. Are you sure you've never talked to spirits before?"

Marianne shook her head emphatically. "No, not before living here! I didn't have a chance to tell you, but I talked to Anne the other day. She seemed to be watching as I was fixing up the office space, and so I talked to her."

Sarah was fascinated. "I have to say, it is so…unusual and refreshing to hear someone else talk about this kind of thing. Go ahead, sorry to interrupt."

Marianne said in some consternation, "Honestly, it's not something I'm used to doing at all. I took your advice and thought of her as standing there with me. At the time I thought the angry ghost might be Adam Sullivan. When I asked her if she knew who it was, some papers fell off the desk. I didn't know what to make of that. After that, she faded away."

She suddenly remembered her conversation with her grandmother. "Sarah, remember I told you about my Grandma Selene? She's the one I used to visit when I was a kid. I forgot to tell you she's been here, in this house, long ago, and she heard Anne play one of her concerts!" With growing excitement, she forgot her pain and gestured with her hands. "She said the whole Rutherford family was controlling, and that my ex, Geoffrey, was one of them!" Her reinjured hands were clumsy and one banged the back of the sofa, and she gasped in pain.

It was Sarah's turn to goggle. "What?"

Wincing, Marianne continued, "Geoffrey's grandmother was George's sister. She married into the Chubb family, and that's why I never put the two together. Geoffrey always acted like he owned the world. Grandma Selene said he was a late child and very spoiled. Which explains so much really," she finished, her hand throbbing painfully.

Sarah gently touched Marianne and said, "You look like you're in real pain. I wanted to clear your house and protect it before we leave today, but I think we need to take care of you first."

Marianne shook her head and said, "Just do it now. I'll go back to the Urgent Care Center when you're done. I want to know my house is safe and protected when I get back."

Sarah frowned reluctantly. "Okay then."

Marianne showed Sarah where her dustpan and broom were, and the lawyer swept up the glass shards in the living room. Marianne got a dishtowel and gingerly wiped up the remains of the spilled water and threw out the wilted flowers. Sadly, there was a big water stain on the corner of the piano lid and all down the side where the water had dripped.

When they were done, Sarah relit the iron pot with a new white sage bundle with cedar incense while Marianne took a couple of ibuprofen. Together they walked from room to room.

In each room Sarah declared, "Let all bad emanations and feelings be gone from this space. Let this be a place of happiness and light. With cedar and sage, so mote it be."

They went up into the attic through the little door a second time and wafted cedar and sage smoke into the area. Lastly, they walked through the basement touching all the walls and corners with smoke.

229

After all the drama, the cellar seemed very ordinary, just a little dark and shabby. Marianne was amazed both that she'd been so afraid of the basement, and that it seemed so unthreatening now.

When the third smudge had burned out, they adjourned to the kitchen.

Sarah regarded her with respect. "I've never seen a newbie do what you did with Mrs. Rutherford. You have a gift for communicating with people—living and dead—did you know that?"

Marianne was flustered and shrugged. "I never really thought about it. You and Kelly said to treat Mrs. Rutherford like a living person who was having trouble communicating. So, I tried to do that."

"That was quite a story you told. Did you make it up or were you seeing it as you were telling it?" Sarah rinsed the ash out of the pot as she talked.

Leaning against the counter, Marianne replied, "I read about some of it at the library for starters, but I'm not sure where my imagination left off and where I was reading Anne's memories. It's kind of a disturbing idea to think about reading a ghost's mind to "see" and "feel" events that happened more than a hundred years ago. But some of the things in telling the story just seemed right."

Sarah laid the pot in the sink and put her hand on Marianne's shoulder. "You're good at this. Under the right circumstances it's pretty safe to do. I can hear spirits in my head sometimes as words, sometimes just as feelings. And sometimes I get snatches of images that I know come from a spirit. Other times I just know when something feels right or wrong. Kelly was right. You are a brave woman."

"The Rutherfords scared the willies out of me plenty of times. But Anne scared me less when I thought of her as a person."

Sarah looked at her appraisingly. "I get scared too. But I don't have an option to not hear or feel a spirit if they really want to communicate with me. Are you sure you haven't ever dealt with spirits before?"

"No, I don't think so. I've always had a vivid imagination. My mom told me I had lots of imaginary playmates and made up elaborate stories with them. Geoffrey used to tell me I had too much imagination."

Sarah wrinkled her nose and said, "Figures."

Marianne nodded and handed her a dishtowel. "He had virtually no imagination at all by comparison."

Sarah wiped her bowl dry. "Well, you could probably do some training and become more aware of the spirit world if you wanted to. You should definitely make your home a protected safe space and learn to protect yourself. You're too sensitive to ignore it."

Marianne looked anxious. "I don't know. It was pretty scary when I didn't know what was going on. I'm not sure I want to open myself up more. I'm too tired to think about it right now. Would you show me how to protect myself, though?"

"Absolutely."

"And would you show me what you were doing with the little crystal thingie?"

"For a person who doesn't want to get involved, you're asking a lot of questions," Sarah said with a smile.

"Well, even if I'm not sure about jumping in further, I have enough experience now that I can't pretend it doesn't exist."

"Smart." Sarah approved. She tilted her head to one side and asked, "What are you going to do with the little rabbit?"

Marianne thought about it and then said, "I'll take it to the cemetery and put it on Samuel's grave."

"That sounds right," Sarah agreed.

The analgesic had dulled the throbbing in her hand, but she said, "I think I really need to go back to the Urgent Care place now."

"Let me give you a ride," Sarah offered.

Mercifully, it was a different duty doctor than the one they'd encountered before. He cleaned up the stitches and fixed her dislocated fingers. She and Sarah had concocted a reasonable story on the way over and, after receiving a stern warning to be more careful, Marianne was allowed to leave with some stronger pain meds if she needed them.

Although she was exhausted, she refused Sarah's offer of a place to stay. Instead she let Sarah warm some leftovers for her rather than try to do it all one-handed. After Sarah left, she sat on the couch and ate, filling the surprising hunger in her middle. Oscar sat pressed against her side, purring steadily as she watched TV, feeling like an invalid. She finally took herself to bed when she caught herself nodding off.

Chapter 24

MARIANNE awakened from the first deep sleep she'd had since she'd moved in. She rolled over and stretched lazily, flinching slightly at peak stretch when the healing cuts on her legs and arm twinged. Oscar immediately began nuzzling her face and urging her to get up and feed him. Smiling she petted him, her dark brown hair, frizzed in the humidity, surrounding her head like a cloud on the pillow. But her bandaged left hand ached where the stitches were, and her abused fingers refused to open all the way, reminding her of the drama of the past couple of days.

Scenes played and faded in her mind like images on her screensaver: Anne Rutherford's ghostly, anxious face transforming into a peaceful smile as she realized she was free; George's rage at his loss and the look of dawning horror and shame as he vanished; Sarah's steely prosecution of George's life as she made him realize he had no reason to stay any longer; the vivid images of Anne's childhood trauma and the loss of her little brother. She knew without a doubt that she and Oscar were the only people inhabiting the house now.

She wanted to thank her new friends for all their help and thought a housewarming party might be a good way. Her hand was going to prevent her from painting anything for a while. Well, they knew she had a house full of boxes and probably wouldn't care.

Her invitation list was fairly short with Sarah and Kelly at the top. She needed to do something special for them and had a few ideas. Ruari was next. He had asked her out—was it only yesterday? So much had happened; it seemed like ages ago. But her stomach flip-flopped pleasantly at the thought of seeing him for a social reason rather than as handyman for the rental company, and she grinned. The Cavarellis, John Irving, her mom, and Grandma Selene completed the guest list. She thought about food and drinks and toyed with a few dates before Oscar's insistence got her out of bed.

Before showering she put a can of cat food down and went around her house shutting windows against the Hudson Valley's late August humidity. The Cape Cod's internal brick and lathe and plaster construction held the coolness for much of the day in spite of the lack of central air conditioning.

After breakfast she called Kelly and Sarah and left messages inviting them to a housewarming party on Friday night. She dithered and delayed calling Ruari by phoning her Grandma Selene first.

"Oh, I'd love to come, dear!" She said with her slight British accent. "Tell me, are George and Anne still there?" Marianne recounted her confrontation with the ghosts, and Selene expressed great satisfaction with the expelling of George from the place. "Be sure you set up some barriers so he doesn't return out of habit, dear," she warned.

"Sarah mentioned that," Marianne said unhappily. "Is that possible?"

"Sometimes," Selene said ominously.

"She promised to help me do that."

"Well, if she doesn't get around to it, let me know and I'll help you as best I can."

"I had no idea that you knew anything about this kind of thing." Marianne still felt a little stunned by the apparent wholehearted understanding of her grandmother. "But I'm really glad you do!"

They had always gotten along, but Grandma had never revealed this side of her nature. It was nice to have an experienced ally in the psychic department who also knew her very well. She suspected Sarah would eventually become a close friend but it would take her a long time to know Marianne as well as her grandmother did. Suddenly, she wondered if her mother knew of Grandma Selene's talents. "Do you think I should tell Mom?"

"Mmm," Selene made a dubious noise. "I think she is aware of my conversations with spirits but prefers not to dwell on it too much. It makes her uncomfortable. You can try, but you'll have to choose your words and your timing."

Marianne agreed to think about it.

Marianne called her mother next and invited her to the Friday party.

"I've been worried about you! Of course I'd love to see your new place," she responded enthusiastically. "You'll have to come and pick me up, though, since someone has borrowed my car..."

"Of course, Mom! Can I come by around three? The party starts at six, and it'll take me about an hour round trip. Do you mind coming early to help set up? I'd love to have your help."

"I'll see you at three, then."

Marianne told her briefly about her injuries but assured her she was healing. She deflected questions about what caused them, promising to tell her the whole story on the car ride. After she'd hung up, she quickly dialed Ruari's number before she could chicken out.

"Marianne! How are you doing today?" He greeted her warmly, and she tingled pleasantly knowing she must be in his address book.

"I'm good—better than good really. Sarah and I were able to get my ghostly 'housemates' to move on yesterday, and I think they really did."

"That's great. How did you do that?" He sounded cautiously curious.

She grinned and teased, "I'll tell you over coffee some time."

"You're on." He sounded like he was smiling. "How does Friday after work sound?"

"Well, that's the other reason I wanted to call you. I'm having a housewarming party on Friday evening and called to invite you. It's a potluck. You can bring something to eat or drink, if you like."

"Okay, I'll be there! Maybe we can go for coffee on the weekend instead?"

"Sounds great, I look forward to it!"

Ruari closed his fist around his phone after she'd disconnected, feeling deeply happy. She was a little strange, but maybe that's what he needed to shake up his own life. His 'muse carving' was nearly complete except for the finish, and he knew where it was supposed to go now. He returned to his punch list of repairs for the day where it lay on the passenger seat of the truck and felt his life moving forward slowly for the first time in a long time.

Marianne pressed the hang up button and smiled delightedly. She figured she'd talk to the Cavarelli's in person and invite John Irving later that day since she planned to visit the cemetery anyway.

Retrieving the grubby little rabbit doll from her bedside table, she examined it carefully. The rough spun cotton fabric of the body had become a uniform gray-brown over time, and the brittle straw stuffing crunched under her fingers, trailing dust if she squeezed too hard. The rabbit's face, two eyes, a nose and mouth, had been sewn on with faded thread or floss, giving the animal an oriental look. The gingham trousers with shoulder straps went over a little shirt that must have once been white and was now the gray of rock wool insulation. Marianne could imagine little Sam Jr. getting it for a birthday or Easter and carrying it around with him everywhere. No wonder big sister Anne grabbed it to get her little brother to play with her. Marianne sighed. Teasing seemed to be a universal trait across time and cultures.

Taking it into the kitchen, she turned on the tap and spot cleaned the rabbit gently with a damp sponge as best she could. After dabbing at the dust and grime she recovered a clearer view of the expression on the face and the faded gingham looked a little brighter. She was afraid if she washed any harder it might begin to disintegrate in her hands, so she stopped. Laying it in the drainer to dry, she went on to her next project.

Now that she was going to have guests on Friday she assessed what she could do to make the place more lived in, less moved in. The dining room, kitchen and living room walls were beyond her both in time and with the limitations of her hand injury. But, she realized if she could paint the built-in bookcases on either side of the fireplace, she'd also be able to empty many of the remaining boxes.

She spent a bit of time dusting and cleaning the shelves one-handed, balancing on the ladder carefully. She got out the bright white semi-gloss paint and began working on painting from the top down. The little radio kept her company and Oscar slept on the couch as she worked. By noon she'd finished one side. As she stepped back to appraise her work, she realized that she'd worked uninterrupted all morning, and the radio had not been marred by static once. Anne and George seemed to be truly gone.

The little rabbit was dry now, and after a quick lunch, she wrapped it carefully in a clean dishtowel, got her purse, and bid Oscar a farewell. He lifted his head sleepily from his nap on the cushion and opened his mouth in a soundless meow before closing his eyes again.

She passed through town and out to the Maple Hill Community Cemetery. The day was hot with a deep blue sky above deep green trees. The world felt alive and full of movement all around her and she smiled contentedly. She had a flash of realization that a couple of weeks ago she had been surrounded by the concrete towers and asphalt roads of the city with preoccupied people hurrying everywhere, and the sounds and smells of traffic, construction, people, and the subway permeating her senses. In a way, Geoffrey's incomprehensible pursuit of her had forced her out of her old comfort zone and into this place. Being surrounded by greenery, blue sky, the sounds of birds, insects, and wind was an unexpected and wonderful tradeoff. In a strange way, she had to thank him.

The tan sedan "Flea" bumped over the uneven gravel and dirt road of the cemetery, and she pulled up to the little parking area near the old stone caretaker's shed. She parked, leaving a little veil of dust to drift away on the breeze. The doors of the shed were partially open leaving the interior in deep, chilly shade.

"Hello, Mr. Irving?" She called uncertainly.

There was movement in the back by the workbench, though she couldn't see clearly with her sun-mazed eyes.

"Mr. Irving? It's me, Marianne? I was here last week…" She peered into the gloom and saw a figure in overalls with his back to her. He looked stouter and perhaps shorter than she remembered John Irving being.

"Oh, I'm sorry. I'm looking for Mr. Irving. Is he here today?"

The man half-turned, his face still in shadow and said, *He's out in section five-c, up on the north side of the hill, trimming some branches and mowing.* His voice sounded a little odd in the confined space of the shed.

"Thank you. I don't know if I'll find him so would you please let him know I stopped by? My name is Marianne Singleton. Thanks." The figure raised his hand in acknowledgement without looking up and continued his work at the bench.

Back in the bright sunshine, she made her way back down the hill toward the grove of old trees that shaded the early twentieth century gravestones. She thought with a smile that walking along the curving gravel and dirt road was like going down a broad highway with the clusters of markers like towns or villages of houses. The green between the rows of headstones was like quieter roads and streets in each community. She imagined herself driving back down the years toward the early 1900s to visit the people in the village where the Eddys now lived. The cut grass smelled rich and green and heavy in the thick summer air. John Irving maintained the place beautifully, she thought, and it must be a ton of work. She wondered if the man in the shed helped out.

She oriented herself by the trees she'd noted before and arrived in the shade of the weathered and stained stones of the Eddy's "village." There she walked carefully along the grass above where the family and their neighbors were resting, peering at each stone looking for the right "address." She relocated Mr. and Mrs. Eddy and the tiny stone with "Samuel Eddy Jr." inscribed on it. The little rabbit wrapped in the dishtowel rested lightly in her hands. The sound of a passing car on the road a few yards away was curiously muffled, perhaps by the trees and hedges. It added to the impression that this part of the cemetery was a long way away from the twenty-first century. Instead the air here was dappled and heavy with the heat of summer and the lazy buzz of insects. She cleared her throat.

"Excuse me," she said aloud. "My name is Marianne Singleton. We don't know each other, but I met your sister, Anne, and she told me about what happened when you were both little. I'm so sorry that happened to you, Sam. She felt really bad all her life about that fire and blamed herself. She also kept the little rabbit toy you had. She kept it all these years, and I think she wanted you to have it back."

Marianne crouched down in front of the little stone and propped the rabbit up against it. "Anne was in my house until yesterday, and I think she really missed you. So, I hope she's with you now." She paused and then surprised herself by adding softly, "She became my friend, and I hope she's happy now."

She brushed her fingers over the weathered, streaked stone for a moment and then stood, clutching the folded dishtowel. She didn't have a sense of reply but felt like she'd done the right thing. After a few moments, she walked slowly back down the green avenue between the stone "house" fronts and felt like she was returning to the twenty-first century. Back on the crushed gravel road, she shaded her eyes and looked up the hill. She did some orienting and headed toward what she thought was the north side of the cemetery. As she reached the top of the hill, she heard the sounds of branches being cut and hauled.

John Irving, dressed in a long sleeved workman's plaid shirt and canvas pants and a big straw hat to protect him from the sun, stopped and looked at her. His golf cart with a small flatbed behind it was stacked with neatly cut branches.

"Hello!" She called as she approached.

His weathered face split in a broad smile, covered by a truly stellar snowy white mustache. Marianne smiled in return.

"You came back!" His unexpectedly deep voice said in a tone of welcome surprise, the loppers in his hands pausing in their work.

"Yes, I had to see someone."

"Oh?"

She explained her errand, and he nodded in understanding. Suddenly recalling the cemetery her father was buried in, she said in concern, "Toys and things aren't usually allowed to stay with headstones are they? Is there any way you can let the little rabbit stay with Samuel Jr.?"

He pushed the straw hat back up on his head a little and wiped away some sweat with a red bandana while he considered. "Well, I reckon that's a bit of a special case. It can stay a while," he assured her. "I think little Samuel will be right glad to have it back. He may or may not need to have it a long time, though. Don't worry, I'll let him tell me when it's time to move it."

"Thanks," she said in relief. The strangeness of the conversation would have struck her more forcefully a month ago. Now, it didn't seem so unusual at all.

"How did you find me?" He asked as he got a drink of water from a mason jar on the front seat.

"The fellow in the shed said you were up here. He named a section, but I don't have the layout memorized, so I just walked till I saw you working."

John gave her a frown. "Fellow in the shed? What did he look like?"

Marianne frowned and said, "I'm not sure. He seemed to be a little heavier than you and was wearing overalls. I didn't get a good look at his face. He was working on something at the bench."

John nodded as he replaced the lid. "That must've been Jesse Carleton. He was caretaker here before me. Sometimes he turns up to help with things. I'll have to be sure to thank him for telling you where I was."

"Oh, before I forget. I'm having a housewarming party on Friday night with some friends, and I wanted to invite you to come. It's a potluck, and I'll provide chicken and some basic drinks. Kelly and Sarah will be there, so you'll know someone else besides me. Jesse Carleton is welcome to come, too," she added generously.

John shifted the straw hat on his head, scratching his forehead, and smiled. "Well, thank you for the invitation. I'll have to see. It's nice of you to include Jesse, but I don't think he'll come. He sticks around here mostly, if you know what I mean."

Marianne had the feeling she was missing something important but didn't know what. She shook her head slightly and said, "Well, if he changes his mind, he's welcome."

John looked at her and said pleasantly with the air of a man mentioning discreetly the odd habit of an old friend, "I'll tell him but don't count on it. He passed away thirty some odd years ago and doesn't get out much."

Marianne's eyes widened in shock. "Oh! I'm sorry. I didn't know."

John smiled calmly. "It's okay. He'll be pleased to know you didn't know. Most people have forgotten about him, and he appreciates it when he's remembered."

Somewhat flustered Marianne made a little more small talk then let the caretaker get back to his work. As she walked back, she thought, I had no idea the man in the shed wasn't real. Not living, she corrected herself. He's perfectly real just not living. But he spoke to me! She protested. Did he, though? She realized she didn't have a clear memory of how his voice sounded, she just remembered "hearing" the information in her mind somehow. Well, I guess it makes sense that a former cemetery caretaker might turn up and continue working at his old job even after death.

She shook her head. Sarah Landsman and John Irving might have been conversing with the dead for their whole lives, but it still seemed weird to her. It was going to take some time to get used to this newfound ability.

241

When she returned to her car parked near the stone shed, she thought she'd have another look inside. The stone structure was chilly and dark compared to the bright sunshine, and she let the sunspots fade from her vision for a minute before entering.

"Hello? Mr. Carleton?" She said tentatively. "I found Mr. Irving and just wanted to thank you for telling me where to find him."

There didn't seem to be anyone there now. She stood inside the doorway and listened to the silence. She didn't hear anything in particular other than the thumping of her own heart. Mr. Carleton must have gone elsewhere. Or perhaps she couldn't see him now. The thought of him standing invisible right next to her made her neck prickle, but she refused to let her nervousness show. She turned to go back to her car and murmured, "Thanks again... have a nice afternoon." She thought she heard a faint, *thank you*, but could have imagined it.

Chapter 25

THE drive back to town was ahead of her, but on a whim she decided to visit Grandma Selene. Now that she knew the way, it seemed like no time at all before she was turning down the drive and pulling up to the big gray house.

After the heat of the cemetery and the ride in a car without air conditioning, she breathed deeply, inhaling the cooler air under the trees. It smelled of green leaves, the fragrance of some late summer blooms, and earth. The two-person, wicker chair swung slightly from the porch ceiling and Marianne noticed that there was a magazine on the cushions. The inner door was open as before to allow the cooler air in.

She got to the top of the steps just as Grandma Selene arrived at the front door.

"Marianne, I heard the car drive up! What a lovely surprise! Come in, come in before the mosquitoes find you and eat you alive."

Marianne entered allowing the screen door to bang closed behind her. She let herself be folded into her beloved grandmother's warm, firm embrace, feeling safe for the first time in a long while. Something tight inside her loosened and she sighed. Marianne stepped back and appreciated Selene's iron-gray bun held with a silver pin and her classically stylish attire.

"Grandma, you look wonderful! I was out driving and thought I'd swing by. Is this a good time?"

"Absolutely. Is everything still all right?" Selene inquired with concern.

"Yes. I slept without dreaming about anything, and I spent the morning painting and not a soul bothered me," Marianne replied.

"That's wonderful news!" She looked down as she ushered her granddaughter into the living room and exclaimed, "Oh, your hands! I didn't realize how badly you were hurt."

"I cut my hands and knees crawling out of the basement window. When we were dealing with George, he grabbed my arm, and I punched him without really thinking about it," she said ruefully. "I dislocated my fingers, hitting the wall behind him."

Grandma Selene fussed over her and said approvingly, "I'm sure George was very surprised that you fought back. Good for you!"

Marianne shook her head. "Sarah's the real hero from last night. I'm not sure George wouldn't have dragged me into his version of the past if she hadn't shown him he had no reason to stay and that he'd been a poor husband, at that."

"She sounds like quite a woman. I look forward to meeting her. Never you fear, my girl. You would have given old George what for on your own terms, if you'd had to." She hugged her granddaughter again and said, "I have some fresh iced tea if you want something to drink?"

Marianne nodded and watched her grandmother disappear into the kitchen at the back of the house.

The wide vertical wood paneling of the living room adorned with paintings and prints was warm and comfortingly familiar. Marianne breathed a deep sigh and relaxed a little more. She sat in the blue and cream couch by the fireplace and listened to the sounds of glassware and liquid.

Grandma Selene emerged carrying a pitcher with ice cubes clinking in amber liquid. "I'm trying to be good and not carry heavy things," she explained, "and you don't need to be lifting heavy trays either," she added firmly. "So we'll do this one at a time." Marianne lifted her bandaged hands apologetically. "Don't be ridiculous, my dear. Carry them with pride; they are battle wounds!"

Marianne made a gesture that encompassed embarrassment, automatic self-deprecation and appreciation. After a few minutes the glasses, sugar dish and plate of cookies rested on the coffee table by the sofa. They both sat and poured tea for each other and chose cookies from the plate. It helped restore some balance to her world.

Her grandmother raised her glass of tea in a silent toast, and Marianne suddenly felt her throat tighten unaccountably and couldn't stop the wave of tears as they filled her eyes and spilled down her cheeks. Hastily, she put her glass down as she started crying. She felt her face crumple and wished that she could do the cool, silent-tears thing, but she was a full-out sobber.

"Marianne! What's the matter, dear?" Selene said in some alarm.

"I don't know, I—just everything, I think," she gasped between sobs. She felt her grandmother get up and reseat herself more closely and put her arm around her shoulders. Marianne let herself cry for a few minutes then took some deep breaths and got herself under control. Selene gave her the time she needed.

"I'm sorry, Grandma. I didn't come here to do that. The last few days have just been overwhelming. I think I'm okay now."

"I think it's been more than just a few days, dear. The last year has been very trying to say the least." She handed her granddaughter a box of tissues.

"I'm okay about the divorce, but I'm so worried that Geoffrey'll come up here, and I'll have to move again." She blew her nose.

Selene said sharply, "No one's making you move again! This is your home and you have no reason to leave it. If he doesn't leave you alone, I'll be glad to have a conversation with him," she added fiercely.

Marianne smiled weakly and sniffed again. "Thanks, Grandma. Kelly and Sarah have been telling me the same thing. I think I have to stand up to him myself somehow."

"You will when the time comes, my dear, never fear. Singletons are strong people," she stated firmly.

They sipped their tea and nibbled on cookies for a spell before Marianne said, "Finding out that my dreaming is not only true, but that ghosts can talk to me in my dreams has also been pretty disturbing.

Does that happen to you?"

Selene sat back and considered. "Well, I talk to your grandfather periodically in my dreams, but I hadn't thought about it like that before. So, I suppose I can, but no one but your grandfather has ever... oh." She looked thoughtful before she spoke again. "When my mother died, I was very distraught. We had been very close, and I missed her very much. I finally dreamed of her, and she took me up into her lap and comforted me as she had when I was little. She assured me she was happy and in a good place, and that she loved me very much. It helped me a great deal. When your father died, I was very sad, but there was nothing I could do to change things. These things happen."

Marianne asked softly, "Did you ever see him, or dream about him?"

Grandma Selene shook her head.

Marianne sighed. "He died when I was so little that I never really knew him."

Selene leaned closer and put her arm around her granddaughter's shoulders comfortingly. "If I didn't hear from him, then I'm sure it was because he had crossed over. I know he missed you too." Marianne nodded, feeling melancholy. Selene took a deep breath and said, "So, I suppose it does happen to me but only with people who were close to me in life. I can imagine it would be very upsetting to have complete strangers invade your dreams."

"You're not kidding." Marianne told her about her dreams where George had shouted at her and pushed her around; his locking her in the cellar both waking and asleep; and finally his attempt to make Marianne substitute for Anne.

Selene was outraged and resorted to a few choice British swears that both shocked and amused Marianne who said hastily, "Don't worry. Sarah gave him what for and made him leave. He did not look very happy going to whatever place he was destined for. I don't know about heaven and hell, Grandma, but Anne was happy when she left, and George was frightened, so there must be some justice in the bigger scheme."

"I should think so!" Selene declared so forcefully, that Marianne could picture her arrival in the afterlife and giving whoever was in charge a strict talking to, if it didn't measure up to her expectations.

"Grandma, I'm starting to see ghosts everywhere." Marianne told her about her encounter with Jesse Carleton at the cemetery. "What am I going to do?"

Selene sat thoughtfully for a few minutes. "I suppose I could see spirits of the deceased if I really wanted to. I choose to see only those whom I loved in life. I think there aren't many who can hear ghosts, and they get desperate to be heard. If you want to hear and see them, you will, Marianne. But, forgive me dear, you are a very sweet and trusting soul, and they may overwhelm you with their needs. You are going to have to learn to be firm with yourself and with them and set your boundaries and stick to them. Geoffrey tended to railroad you with his wants and needs, and you are used to putting your own needs aside to accommodate him."

Marianne heard the truth of her words and said, "I have a hard time not feeling selfish if I don't put everyone else first before me."

Grandma Selene said resolutely, "Nonsense! It is not selfish to know what your limits are and to be clear when others are stepping over the line. If someone is pushing you and making you uncomfortable, you have every right to stand up and tell them so. It's all in how you say it," she added.

Marianne shook her head regretfully. "You are so much classier than I am, Grandma!"

Selene accepted the compliment with a smile and said, "Again I say nonsense! It takes some practice, but you can do it when you set your mind to it. Spend some time thinking about your own abilities and boundaries and practice every day knowing what you are willing to do and what you aren't, and you will find that you won't let yourself be pushed around when it comes to that."

Marianne nodded.

Grandma Selene changed the subject and said, "I look forward to coming to your housewarming on Friday. I want to meet Sarah and Kelly. They sound like good solid investments as friends. Who else will be there?"

Marianne gave her the rest of the guest list and did her best to make light of Ruari Allen, describing him as the handyman who worked for Gloria's Valley Homes and the person who'd come to fix things. She wanted her Grandma to meet him and see what she thought before spending more time with him. Selene made no comments, but her eyes twinkled suspiciously.

On the way back to Maple Hill, Marianne thought about her grandmother's advice and resolved to try.

It was later than she expected when she pulled into her drive, and she was tired and ready for dinner. Oscar met her at the door with a complaining meow, and she looked at the chaos of the living room. Her gut clenched a little as she thought about hosting a party here in four days' time and how much work still had to be done. At least there was a decent chance of reducing the number of boxes in the living room.

She was cleaning up after a simple dinner when her cell phone rang. She saw Kelly on the ID and picked up the phone with a smile.

"Hi, Kelly! How are you?"

"Hey, girl, I'm good, and you?" Kelly sounded energetic, and Marianne envied her briefly.

"I'm doing better." She told Kelly about her day and her visit both to the cemetery and to her grandmother. "How was your day?"

"Oh the usual," she said airily. "Haircuts, a couple of interesting color jobs, more haircuts. And you will never guess who my last client of the day was," she finished with a strong undercurrent of excitement and mischief.

Marianne shrugged, at a loss, "No idea. I'm new here, remember?" She took a wild guess, "Um, Sarah?"

Kelly laughed, "No! A certain local boy whom we both know…"

her voice trailed off.

Marianne was mystified and said with a shrug, "The guy who does the co-op announcing?"

"Ye gods, woman! Ruari was in here today! I've been wanting to give him a haircut all summer, every time I looked at him. He was in here today! I think the new girl in town has made an impression on him," she teased.

Marianne felt her face flush and was glad Kelly couldn't see her. "How can you know that?"

"Oh, I'm just guessing," she said loftily. "Anyway he looks a lot more respectable now. Besides, I got your message about the housewarming party this Friday. Did you invite a certain handyman?"

"Yeah, I did." Marianne realized her invitation had been made in the morning, so he could well have been reacting to that. Or, he could have just hit his limit on his long hair flopping in his face.

"Hah! I knew it!" Kelly crowed.

Marianne half laughed, half pleaded, "Please don't say anything to him! I don't want to scare him off. We've agreed to have coffee sometime this weekend."

"It's about time! I won't interfere, promise."

"Is Sarah around? I wouldn't mind talking to her, if she's available."

"Hold on. Hey, Lawgirl, Marianne's on the line." There were noises of the phone being transferred to other hands and Sarah's voice came on.

"Hey, Marianne, how are things on Violet Lane?" Sarah's voice was a deep pool of quiet water compared to Kelly's bubbliness.

"It's actually amazingly peaceful and quiet."

"Good. That's what I like to hear. I'll come by on the weekend and help you tailor the defenses we put up so you can screen your 'calls.' so to speak."

"That would be good since I think I'm starting to see more spirits." She described her visit to the cemetery to leave the little rabbit and see John Irving, as well as her unexpected meeting with Jesse Carleton.

"Wow," Sarah sounded impressed. "Yeah, I've met Mr. Carleton. He died before I started hanging out at the cemetery. But I met him soon after I met John. Mostly, he works in the shed, keeping the tools organized, and sometimes helping John remember all his appointments. I think he sometimes helps new arrivals get used to residing out there."

"Oh. I guess that would be very helpful." For a few seconds Marianne's imagination strayed to what that might mean. Then she told Sarah about visiting her grandmother and mentioned her advice to set her boundaries.

"She's not wrong about that. She sounds like an interesting person. I'd like to meet her."

"She'll be at the party on Friday, and I'll introduce you. I told her about our meeting with the Rutherfords yesterday, and she wanted to meet you, too."

"Excellent! Yeah, if you open yourself to seeing spirits who are still around and indicate to them that you are willing to listen to them, you may have more people knocking on your door than you want. We'll definitely have to put up some good barriers, so you can get some peace and quiet. We'll make them so you can let in the people you want to see and talk to and keep out the others. George, in particular, since he might be inclined to return to a familiar place."

Marianne shivered slightly. "I would like to keep him out for sure. I guess I wouldn't mind seeing Anne again, if she wanted to come by and play my piano, for instance."

"I think we can set up something like that. I'm pretty tired tonight, so I'm thinking of heading to bed. Is there anything else?"

Marianne felt guilty at the thought of draining her friend's energy yesterday. "I'm sorry," she said automatically. "No, that was it. Thank you again for coming yesterday and helping me with Anne and George. It has been so peaceful and nice here today. I didn't feel like anyone was looking over my shoulder when I was painting this morning."

"Good. I'll see you on Friday. Don't worry about me. Even though I'm a big, tough lawyer, being tired after facing down an angry guy, whether he's alive or dead, is part of the territory. Sleep well."

"G'night."

Marianne sat on the couch, stroking Oscar's orange and white fur as he lay next to her, and listened to the quiet stillness of her house. She closed her eyes and pictured the shelves painted with everything put away and hoped she could achieve that by Friday at noon. Beyond that, she was going to have to put some serious thought into making some money this fall. She'd nudge her history colleague, Gillian, tomorrow.

She slept with the windows open as usual to let the warm air of the house exchange with the cooler air from outside. Her dreams, processing events of the day, threw up jumbled images of trees, the cemetery, John Irving, her grandmother's house in Vandenberg. Eventually, they segued into her walking down a twilight cityscape with gridded streets and familiar shop fronts distorted by dreaming. She was trying to get home, but someone was following her. Whenever she turned to look, there was no one there, but the feeling persisted. She turned into a building to evade him and found herself walking down white corridors and through doors and up and down stairs, eventually ending up in a huge, industrial-looking basement encircled by pipes. She headed purposefully for a door across the room and heard footsteps behind her. She began to run, and the footsteps sped up. Just as she reached for the handle to wrench the door open, Geoffrey caught up with her and spun her around. He leered at her and said triumphantly, "I know where you live!" Marianne screamed silently and surfaced from her dream with a start.

She lay on her bed, her heart pounding with adrenaline for a few moments. Well, that was unambiguous, she thought. It's only a matter of time before Geoffrey finds me up here. The more she thought about it, the less likely it seemed he would take off work to drive up here. He was bent on pursuing her, but he'd so far done it on his own time, not company time. So, turning up on the weekend was more likely, and if the urgency of the dream was true, this weekend was a distinct possibility. She didn't know if he had her address, but she most likely knew she was in Maple Hill by now. Sarah was probably right that he would leave her alone if she stood up to him, but she didn't know what she could say or do that would work. Marianne lay awake for quite a long time fretting about her situation like a hamster running in a wheel before she fell asleep again.

Ruari worked late into the night finalizing the details of the face, hand, and hair of the "Sleeping Lady." The tiny tools cramped his hands repeatedly, and he had to stop and shake his fingers and palm out often. The thought of stopping never occurred to him. His eyes grew tired and gritty even with the better light he was using. It was a present from Erin who had dropped it by unceremoniously a couple of days ago. She'd been humming to herself, and Ruari had the impression she was happy about something. Maybe the job search was yielding fruit at last, but he refrained from asking her. She'd bitten his head off the last couple of times he'd inquired politely, so he waited for her to tell him in her own good time.

Living at home with their parents was wearing a little thin even for Erin. He'd hinted that she could come and sleep at his place if she needed to, but her eye-rolling expression was a clear enough answer. At least Erin knew she was welcome, he thought.

Marianne would be welcome too, he thought. He remembered her smile and the light in her beautiful amber eyes when she opened the door and saw it was him on the step. He'd gotten a haircut today, feeling self-conscious about his hair for the first time all summer. His tired fingers spasmed, and the tiny chisel slipped, leaving a straight gash when he'd meant it to be a curved one. I'm carving distracted, he thought and spent several minutes correcting the mistake.

His thoughts wandered again to watching Marianne's lovely curves as she led him to the kitchen, and the memory of the electric tingle when they'd shaken hands that one time caused him to slip again. This time the chisel pricked his palm below his thumb, and he hissed in pain.

"Okay, okay," he muttered to himself. "Pay attention, Ruari Allen, or you'll ruin all your fine work and end up in the emergency room to boot." He wiped his hand on his trousers, licked it till the bleeding stopped and continued with renewed focus.

Once the detail work was done, he began sanding the surfaces. The wood felt smooth and warm and curiously alive in his hands. The grain wove gently throughout the piece and echoed the curves of the curtains, the hair, and the tilt of the woman's face. He was pleased with how it looked. Only when he realized his sanding strokes were slowing and the pauses between them lengthening did he realize his fatigue was overwhelming. Setting the piece on the workbench, he brushed it off with a piece of clean flannel and placed the covering cloth over it.

He staggered toward his cot upstairs like a puppet with a drunken master and fell asleep almost before he'd undressed and pulled Nana's quilt over himself.

Chapter 26

MARIANNE woke the next morning feeling a little shaky and bearing a lingering shadow of apprehension from unsettled dreams. Losing herself in work was a good antidote. She managed to clean and paint the other set of shelves in the living room and got a load of laundry together.

Cautiously descending step by step, she made her way down into the cool, musty room below. Her knees still twinged but less painfully. Light illuminated most of the space, and she noted wryly, the lightbulb on the far side of the coal chute was working again. The new window Ruari had installed let in much more light than the old, age-frosted one had. She loaded her clothes into the washer all the while "listening" with senses other than her ears for any signs of ghostly presence but felt nothing. Oscar came down the stairs and prowled around looking for mice or other adventures. Satisfied that the basement was now just the room below the house, Marianne went back upstairs, leaving the door ajar for Oscar to return at his leisure.

Fixing herself a glass of iced tea and the last of her lunch makings, she went to her office and sat down to do some research. She checked her email and found nothing from Geoffrey, which wasn't nearly as reassuring as it should have been. She found an email proposal from Gillian, her NYU colleague, to co-teach a class called "The Victorian Age and it's Legacy in the Twenty-First Century" in January. Excitedly, she read it and spent some time responding with ideas of her own. The prospect of work in the near future helped push the disquiet to the rear of her mind. Mentally, she reviewed her savings and expenses and was confident that she could live well for a year. But, the settlement wouldn't last forever, and she needed a steady income.

After she sent her response to Gillian, she surfed the Internet for a while. It turned out to be quite a resource for ways and means to protect her house from spirits and other negative influences, and she made extensive notes. She was grateful she was right handed and glad her left was healing. After an hour there was a list of ingredients and other items compiled on a separate sheet, to which she added things for her painting project. The list was long enough that she might need the car to take it all home. A brief look in the fridge showed she was out of food as well, and she sighed and gave in to the need for a major shopping expedition.

Finding parking up on Main Street was not bad. Wednesdays seemed to have fewer tourists. She went to the hardware store first and got another container of wall patching material and replaced the dark brown trim paint George had tossed around. She wandered the tall, narrow aisles looking at the vast array of tools, fasteners, hardware, plumbing, and electrical supplies. There were a number of other customers, mostly men in work clothes and construction site boots, who all looked like they knew what they wanted. Down the electricals aisle, she saw a bearded man peering at a display of wire, fuses, boxes, and connectors. He glanced her way and did a double take. She smiled politely, nodding slightly, and moved on to the next row. She was walking down an aisle with dozens of gloves hanging by the wrists like limp hands when she heard a slight cough. Pausing, she turned. The bearded man was at the end of the aisle, staring at her hopefully.

Excuse me, miss. Could you help me find a twenty-amp fuse? He sounded polite and a little wistful.

"I'm sorry. I don't work here," she said automatically. Then she processed the curiously tinny sound to his voice and suspected that he might not be your ordinary helpless customer. She approached, noting his curiously weightless look. "Maybe I can help you. What are you looking for again?"

My wife sent me out for a twenty-amp fuse. It blew when the power went out just before dinner, but I haven't been able to find one. She's waiting for me, and dinner will be cold. He sounded sad and a little anxious.

Marianne said kindly, "Let me see if I can find out. Wait right here." As she walked to the front of the store, she thought, poor guy. I wonder how long he's been looking for that fuse? His wife must have waited for him for a long time. It must be awful to be in limbo like that. I wonder why he never made it home?

She caught the eye of the sandy haired young man who had helped her with paint and said, "Excuse me, could you tell me where the fuses are?"

He led her to the walkway adjoining the one where she'd seen the bearded specter and pointed to the fuses on their hook. Marianne thanked him, and he left. As soon as he was gone, she said softly, "Are you there?"

The bearded man appeared a few feet away, looking indistinct like a photo printed on a sheer curtain. "The fuses you are looking for are here." She indicated the place on the display.

He smiled and reached out for the little shrink-wrapped package. His hand passed through it, but he seemed unfazed. *Thank you*, he said faintly and was gone.

Marianne walked away feeling a bit unsettled. She wondered, was this going to keep happening? It's not as if the bearded gentleman was frightening in any way. It was just strange being privileged to see this entire other layer of existence overlapping the one in which she'd grown up. Maybe in time she'd get used to it?

At the counter she paid for the spackle and paint. The assistant asked if she'd found everything she was looking for, and she replied, "Yes, I just wanted to know where the fuses were if I ever need them."

He gave her an odd look, and she responded with an unconcerned smile. She hoped no one had witnessed her interchange with the ghostly man. If she wasn't careful, she thought, she was going to develop a reputation as a crazy person who talked to herself—and got replies.

Next she went to the co-op and did her food shopping and was able to pick up some of her protective ingredients as well. While she strolled through the aisles, she heard the telltale click of the PA mic and paused to listen.

A deep southern drawl said, "Dahnna, you have a cahll on line one. Dahnna, line one."

She smiled and made her way to the candles and herbals aisle. She

257

picked up several white beeswax candles with no scent, some more cedar incense cones and dried sage bundles, but there were no crystals or stones here. She planned her next stop at Dream Time, the New Age store down the street, and headed there after stashing her purchases in the car.

A little bell jingled as she entered Dream Time, and her olfactory senses were immediately assaulted by a variety of competing fragrances from patchouli to cinnamon, lavender, sage, and roses. A comfortable looking, middle-aged woman with thick brown hair beginning to gray at the temples looked up and smiled blandly at her.

"Let me know if I can help you find anything," she said and went back to working through a stack of receipts and papers.

There were cases of jewelry, books on spiritualism, meditation, witchcraft, dozens of tarot decks and instruction books, and a whole table of crystals and semiprecious stones in wooden bowls. She took out her list and selected some polished obsidian stones to put on her windowsills as spirit barriers and some rose quartz stones to help keep her spiritual energies clean. Then she lingered over the jewelry case, thinking of gifts for Sarah and Kelly who had done so much for her. She relished thinking of each woman and selected something that spoke to her of each one. Regretfully, she passed up all the other colorful stones, the deep blue lapis and brighter turquoise in their silver settings attracting her attention, as did the bright green malachite and amber-brown tiger eye.

She got her new things home as quickly as she could since the day was heating up, and the groceries wouldn't last much longer in a hot car. Oscar roused himself from a nap to join her in the kitchen, nibbling on a fresh can of kitty tuna while she ate chicken curry salad.

Marianne got out a bowl and poured the polished stones into it. The obsidian and pink quartz clicked together pleasantly as she placed the bowl in the sunlight on the windowsill to "charge" with solar energy.

The doorbell rang and, peeking through the side window, she could see Michael standing on the top step.

"Hi, Miss Singleton, how are you?" He said cheerfully and then leaned in conspiratorially, adding, "Do you still have the ghosts?" She let him in, and he looked around the room as if expecting to see them hovering somewhere.

She smiled and said, "As a matter of fact, no, I don't!"

His face fell a little, and he asked, "What happened? Did you get them to leave?"

She gave him a condensed version, editing out the more terrifying parts of George's apparition, and he listened raptly.

"Wish I could have seen it," he said a little wistfully.

"How were the tryouts?" Marianne changed the subject.

He gave her a broad grin and said triumphantly, "I got in!"

"Excellent!" She congratulated him. "This calls for some ice cream—that is if it won't ruin your dinner?"

He made a face in reply, and she amended, "I think your mom would kill me if I did, so just a small bowl then. We've got to celebrate!"

She dished out two bowls of minty chocolate goodness, and they adjourned to the living room. "I'm sorry I don't have a lot of places to sit right now. Maybe we'd better sit outside."

The stoop was in the shade of the house now, so the air was pleasantly warm but not scorching as they sat together eating their treat. Michael told her about the tryouts and some of the other guys on the team, including a girl who really wanted to play.

"I hope they let her in," Marianne said.

"The coach did let her in. Chris is Tim Payne's sister, and she's been playing with the boys since she could dribble. She's tougher than some of the guys on the team!" He said with admiration.

Marianne swallowed her bite and said, "I'm having a

259

housewarming party on Friday and wanted you and your family to come if you can. It's a potluck. I'll provide ham or chicken or something, and your family can bring a side dish or dessert. Do you think you can come?"

He said he'd mention it, but Marianne remembered that he was a twelve-year-old boy and wasn't necessarily trustworthy to relay all the details, so she resolved to stop by after dinner. They both heard the screen door bang next door and Michael's mother, Maria, hollered "Mikey!" in a voice straight out of a Brooklyn neighborhood.

He leapt up off the cement step as if he'd been suddenly electrified and said, "Gotta go!" and bolted down the sidewalk for home. Marianne smiled, thinking, "You can take the woman out of the city, but you can't take the city out of the woman," and took the dishes inside.

The first set of shelves seemed to be completely dry, so Marianne spent the next couple of hours unloading her books and knick-knacks one-handed and putting them away. She stood back to admire the effect. When she thought about how Mrs. Thomas was going to like her work so far, she remembered with a pang of guilt that she had not invited her to the party on Friday. Finding her cell phone and dialing her landlady suddenly became a priority.

Mrs. Thomas accepted the invitation and asked anxiously if the "neighbors" were bothering her. Marianne correctly interpreted this to mean Anne and George and told her that she had successfully asked them to move on, and the house was now ghost-free. Mrs. Thomas seemed relieved but perhaps a little sad as well. Marianne thought, that after a certain age, the loss of friends and acquaintances you'd known, even if they were reduced to lingering spirits, was still a loss.

Chapter 27

THE day of the party Marianne woke to a gray sky. She'd slept reasonably well, in spite of dreams that continued to have a theme of pursuit but without the intensity of a full-on nightmare. Perhaps, she thought, if she consciously understood the message, it was enough to quiet the messenger.

Oscar's customary whiskery greeting pulled her out of bed. She unwrapped the bandage on her left hand and carefully washed her wrist and palm. The black thread was stark against her red but healing skin. The middle and ring fingers were still a little sore, but she didn't think she'd need the braces anymore. She was looking forward to getting the stitches out since her skin was getting very itchy. It had been five days already since the phantasmal fire, she realized with surprise as she smeared salve on it.

Yesterday evening she'd finished filling the bookshelves and dumped the cardboard in the spare room upstairs and made sure the Cavarelli's had gotten the invitation. After making sure she had enough drinks in the fridge and that the house was as neat as it could be, she got into the "Flea" and backed out into the street. The drive to her mother's took a little less than an hour, and she arrived mid-afternoon.

Her mother was a taller version of herself. Marianne had inherited the short genes from her father's side of the family, and everyone else was taller. Her mother had the same dark, wavy hair now shot with gray but cut short so it curled attractively. She, too, was curvy and looked nice in her linen slacks and flowered blouse.

Marianne hugged her mom and stepped inside while she got her things together. Mom surprised her by asking her to carry the wrapped box in the front hall out to the car while she got a food offering from the kitchen. The box was bulky and rather on the heavy side. Marianne gingerly lugged it out and got it into the trunk, wondering what on earth her mom had gotten.

"What's in the box, Mom?" She asked as they settled themselves and headed back out.

"Oh, just a little something for your new place."

"You didn't have to do that!" Marianne protested.

"I know, but I wanted to. Now, tell me about the huge bandage on your wrist and all the scabs on your legs! I'm thinking you didn't tell me everything," she scolded her daughter.

Marianne knew her mother cared about her deeply and had always been supportive of her, but it had been a long time since they'd shared confidences. She wasn't sure how she would take news of her daughter moving into a haunted house. She decided to give it a try.

"Well, it's a little complicated," she temporized. "Grandma's friend's house turned out to be haunted by old acquaintances of hers. They were the first owners, and they returned to the house after they died."

Her mother made an incredulous noise and then said, "Haunted? How is that related to your injuries?"

Marianne sighed. "I did some research at the local library…" and she told the rest of the story, dreams and all, culminating in the anniversary of the fire and her own escape.

Her mother shook her head, trying to understand. "You're saying Anne thought there was a fire so she made you think there was a fire? And you broke a window to get out, and that's how you got cut?" Disbelief underscored her mother's voice.

Marianne nodded, her heart sinking. "That's about it."

Her mother frowned and said dubiously, "You've always had a vivid imagination. Are you sure it wasn't just that?"

"Yeah, I'm sure I wouldn't have crawled over broken glass just because of my imagination. It felt very real at the time." Marianne tried to keep the sarcasm out of her voice, but it was hard.

Her mother was silent as she watched the scenery go by for a few miles and then said, "I'm not sure what to think about that."

Marianne resigned herself to her mother's skepticism and said quietly, "I know it sounds incredible. I wouldn't have believed me either a few weeks ago."

"Well, however it happened, at least you're healing," her mother finished, trying to sound upbeat.

Marianne lapsed into silence, feeling disheartened, wondering if Sarah got this reaction often. Maybe it had been too long since she and her mom had shared personal things. Maybe it wasn't possible to get it back.

Some miles later her mother broke the silence. "So, who else is going to be at this party?"

Marianne let the subject go and gave her the guest list, explaining how she'd come to know each of them. She left out Sarah's ability to see ghosts and simply called her and Kelly new friends. Her mood lightened as the distance passed and they approached Maple Hill.

Ruari patiently worked his way through the punch list SueAnn Talmadge had given him that morning. He smiled gamely in the face of Mrs. Grumman's endless complaints about the water heater breaking yet again, even when she hinted it was because he hadn't fixed it properly the first two times. He patiently explained that the equipment was getting old, and he would submit a request to replace it.

Underneath he chafed to be done and show up at 25 Violet Lane. There were two more calls he had to make before finishing the list for the day. He still had to go home and shower and change his clothes and pick up his housewarming gift. On his lunch break he had picked up a bag of potato chips and dip that were now sitting on the front seat of the truck. Knowing it was a weak offering for a potluck, he hoped his other gift would make up for it.

Leaving her mom in the kitchen, Marianne changed her clothes to a long light blue skirt and long sleeved pale green blouse to hide her injuries and deflect questions. Then she and her mother finished laying out the table in the dining room with a pretty lavender cloth bordered with pansies, a jar of flowers from the yard in the middle, and lots of space for food offerings. The chicken was cut and ready to serve, and pitchers of lemonade, water and iced tea were out. Oscar had tried to help himself to the chicken by jumping up on the table twice, but the two women had scolded him loudly and chased him off. Offended, he retreated to the front window to wash himself and pointedly ignored them.

Grandma Selene had given her friend, Lily Thomas, a ride, and they were the first to arrive. Marianne met her landlady for the first time as Mrs. Thomas worked her way laboriously up the front stairs with a walker. She was hunched with osteoporosis, white haired, and had a sweet, slightly vague smile. Grandma Selene was right behind her in case she fell. Marianne was struck by how differently people aged and was secretly glad her own grandmother was so vigorous still. It would be such a shock to see her grandmother struggling like her friend was.

"Hi, Mrs. Thomas, it's so nice to meet you finally," Marianne greeted her at the door.

Lily Thomas peered up from her permanent stoop and smiled, "It's very nice to meet you, too. I brought a little something for the table." She fumbled in the canvas bag hanging from the front of her walker and handed Marianne a cellophane wrapped package of paper napkins with a sprig of flowers on them.

Marianne smiled and accepted them. "They're lovely and perfect. I'll put them on the table right away." Grandma Selene winked at her and nodded in approval.

"Hi, Grandma, I'm so glad you could come." She hugged her.

"Me too. Here is a little something for the table," and she handed Marianne a covered casserole dish that still felt warm. She greeted her daughter-in-law warmly with a peck on the cheek and then shepherded her friend toward a seat in the living room.

"No, no, I want to see the house first," Mrs. Thomas said firmly.

"Mrs. Thomas, I'd love to show you around. Let me put these things on the table, and I'll be right back." Marianne asked her mother to see to getting the new things out and turned to her landlady.

Mrs. Thomas and Grandma Selene were looking around at the now tidy but still pink living room.

"Oh, this brings back memories," Lily Thomas said with a fond smile. "I used to come here and hear Anne Rutherford play. She was so lovely and so talented. The piano was a Steinway baby grand right over there where you have your little upright. It was polished black and so elegant. She played so beautifully. You know she taught many children of Maple Hill how to play piano? A few of them went on to music school, too. It's a shame Anne never finished." She sighed. "George loved her in his own way, though he was pretty possessive of her. Do you still hear from them? I came and talked to them a few times in case they were still here."

Selene and Marianne exchanged glances. "Yes, Lily," Selene said gently, "It was Anne and George, and Marianne convinced them to move on."

Marianne noticed her mother hovering in the doorway to the hall. She had clearly overheard the exchange and wore a startled, unsettled look on her face.

"Oh? That's too bad." Mrs. Thomas sounded wistful. "I would have liked to hear her play one more time. I guess it's for the best, though."

"Mrs. Thomas, may I show you what I've done so far?" Marianne asked brightly, trying to shift the topic.

Lily Thomas turned her head to Marianne, looking sideways at her, birdlike. "That's right. You asked if you could paint. Yes, I'd like to see."

Marianne gave her the nickel tour and showed her the rooms she'd completed and told her about her plans to paint the rest of the house. Mrs. Thomas seemed to approve the color scheme when she talked about how much lighter and brighter the house seemed. The yard was another matter, though.

"It was a showcase yard with so many beautiful flowers and plants," Mrs. Thomas declared. "George would be saddened to see it looking so wretched now," she said with the bluntness of the aged. Grandma Selene rolled her eyes behind her friend's back and looked apologetically at Marianne who smiled and said, "Maybe you could show me some time what kind of plants they had, and I could perhaps work on replacing some of them."

Mrs. Thomas agreed and said she was tired now and wanted to sit. Marianne took their drink orders and left to fill them. Kelly and Sarah arrived soon after and introduced themselves to Marianne's mother at the door and went into the dining room to deposit a tabouli salad. Marianne finished pouring and greeted them with hugs and had a moment to murmur, "My mom's not cool with the ghost thing." Sarah nodded sympathetically, and Kelly shrugged slightly in understanding.

Marianne then introduced them to Grandma Selene and Mrs. Thomas. Within a few minutes, John Irving arrived, standing diffidently on the front stoop. His attire of loose canvas trousers and vertical striped shirt with a mandarin collar was nearly the same she'd seen him in at the cemetery, but clean. Marianne gave him a big smile and welcomed him in. He seemed shy with strangers and glad to see Sarah and Kelly.

"Mr. Carleton decided not to come, but he appreciated the invitation and said you could come see him sometime," he said with quiet dignity to Marianne. She was a little taken aback but nodded and thanked him. She carefully introduced her mother to him. Kelly got John Irving a beer and stood talking to him since Sarah and Selene were deep in conversation.

Finally, the Cavarellis rang the doorbell, and the noise level went up a couple of decibels as more people mingled with each other. Maria had made a huge green salad with pepperocini, olives, tomatoes, and what seemed like half a deli's worth of meat and cheese trimmings. The large bowl joined the platter of chicken and Grandma Selene's potatoes au gratin.

Marianne enjoyed her guests for a bit before she looked at her cell phone discreetly and realized it was forty minutes into the party, and Ruari wasn't there. Perhaps he'd changed his mind? She tried not to be disappointed and to tell herself that maybe he was late from work. Maybe something had come up, and Gloria's Valley Homes had kept him late. She talked distractedly with Michael about basketball practice. School started next week, and he was gloomy about the end of summer.

There was a distant drumming, whooshing sound and Marianne looked out the window to see it pouring rain. Still no Ruari. She was beginning to resign herself to his not coming when the doorbell rang. She excused herself from Michael and hastened to the door.

Ruari stood on the top step, his hair plastered down the sides of his head and his button up shirt splattered with rain across his shoulders. He held two packages in his hands, and she urged him inside quickly before he got any wetter.

He said apologetically, "I'm so sorry to be late. I had an emergency at work, and the temporary fix took longer than I expected. I brought potato chips and some French onion dip—if it's not too late?"

"No, no, that's fine." Marianne felt alight with happiness and said, "Come in the kitchen, and I'll find a bowl. Do you want a towel? The bathroom's across the hall and towels are in the little closet. Help yourself." He avoided the living room and disappeared through the dining room.

Marianne opened the bag of chips, poured them in a big wooden bowl, and put them and the dip in the living room on the table. The second package was a grocery sized brown bag with something heavy inside, wrapped in cloth. She opted to wait for him before opening it.

He returned to the kitchen a few minutes later, his hair tousled and definitely shorter than it had been. It looked good on him. A faint scent of Ivory soap accompanied him. She smiled and took in his large frame, tanned face, and blue gray eyes. She appreciated how the damp white cotton shirt, open at the throat and clinging to his muscular shoulders, set off his complexion perfectly. He smiled shyly, taking her in as well.

"I'm glad you made it! Um, would you like something to drink?" She offered, suddenly shy as if she'd been handed a lavish gift and didn't know what to do with it.

He accepted a glass of iced tea, and she introduced him to everyone there. Kelly gave her a wink as he turned away so that only Marianne could see it. Marianne grinned back at Kelly, blushing furiously. He shook hands with her mother, and immediately they fell into polite conversation.

Over the course of the party, Marianne received compliments on her painting and encouragement to finish. She was pleased that everyone seemed to be comfortable with each other. After Grandma Selene and Sarah's long conversation, they split up so Grandma could speak to Maria Cavarelli, and Sarah moved on to Marianne's mother. The two Johns seemed to know each other, and Marianne realized that John Irving probably knew many people in town through the cemetery. Michael and Kelly talked to each other for a while, and Marianne noticed that he hovered near the piano for a little, perhaps imagining the ghostly Anne playing. Ruari spoke in turn to John Cavarelli, Kelly, and Mrs. Thomas. Oscar surveyed the party from the foot of the stairs where he could watch unobtrusively.

At some point John Cavarelli cleared his throat and spoke over the voices in the living room. His big voice penetrated the entire first floor with little effort and everyone gathered.

"I'd like to be the first to officially welcome our new neighbor to Maple Hill!" He raised his glass and everyone said, "Hear, hear!"

After a drink from his beer he continued, "In the short time she's been here, she has made wonderful changes and improvements to this house. I hope she's here for a long time."

Marianne smiled and murmured, "Thank you." As she stood looking at the room full of people, she had an epiphany. She'd come home. Geoffrey had chased her out of her old life, hoping to leave her off balance and punish her for leaving him. Instead she'd come back to Maple Hill and discovered it was home. In three weeks through the activities of her invisible neighbors, she'd become friends with more people than she'd known over the last five years. And with that thought something inside her settled into place. She was divorced but in no way diminished. Instead, she had grown. Even though she had discovered some disquieting things about herself, she was not alone. She had friends, and that was worth a lot.

"This is a housewarming party, right?" John Cavarelli's strong voice continued. "Maria and I would like to give you a little something."

Maria, looking elegant in her casual work attire and glossy black hair, stepped forward with a wrapped package.

Marianne said with some embarrassment, "You didn't have to. It's wonderful just to have you all be here."

"Everyone needs a little something extra in a new house," Maria insisted and wrapped Marianne's hands around the box. It was unexpectedly heavy, and she thought for a moment it might be gardening tools. When she unwrapped it, it turned out to be a set of nesting glass bowls with sealing lids.

"You'll be glad you have them," Maria said with perfect confidence. Marianne hugged her and turned to accept the larger, more awkward box from her mother.

This turned out to be a small vacuum cleaner with brushes for hardwood floors. "Mom! Thank you." She hugged her mother as well.

"Don't mention it. Like Maria said, you'll be glad you have it!" Her mom quipped.

Everyone laughed.

"I brought you a little something, too," said Ruari quietly from the doorway. He had the brown grocery bag in his arms again, and she

269

stepped over to take it from him.

The contents of the bag were slightly heavier than the glassware. She set it down on the coffee table and knelt down to reach inside. Her fingers met soft cloth wrapped around something solid and oblong, and she carefully drew it out. Everyone was silent as she gently pulled the flannel away, revealing an exquisite carving. It was about twelve inches high and shaped like a seedpod made of beautiful reddish brown wood. One side was smooth, and the finish had highlighted the grain of the wood, giving it a depth beneath the surface. The other side had a woman's face, resting on her hand as it pushed aside the soft fold of a curtain. Her eyes were closed as in peaceful repose or meditation, and tendrils of hair fell across her brow and escaped across the other side of the curtains. The whole image was in perfect proportion and rendered so lifelike that it was easy to imagine the woman awakening and opening her eyes.

"Oh, Ruari, it's beautiful," Marianne breathed, overwhelmed. She looked up and saw his hopeful, vulnerable expression. "I love it!" She answered his unspoken question. "You said you were a carpenter. You didn't say you were an artist!"

He shrugged modestly. "I'm a carpenter, but I also make art pieces sometimes. This one just spoke to me. I'm glad you like her. She's called 'Sleeping Lady,'" he added shyly. For a moment it seemed like they were the only two in the room.

"It's amazing! Thank you." She stood up, and feeling like she'd set the precedent with the other two gifts, she reached up and hugged him briefly. He hugged her back awkwardly, saying, "You're welcome."

Suddenly aware of the other people watching her silently, Marianne stepped back and said loudly, "I think there's more food in the dining room and more beer and wine in the fridge. Please help yourselves!"

People began talking again and some moved to refill their plates. Marianne felt flustered and took refuge in urging people to eat more. Kelly slipped up to her and murmured throatily, "Wow, that's some housewarming gift. You really made an impression on Mr. Allen!"

270

"Yeah," Marianne said weakly. "I can't think about that right now, though."

"Have fun thinking about it later then," Kelly said with a look that would've made a saint blush and slipped away to find Sarah.

The party broke up soon after with the Cavarelli's departure. Mr. Cavarelli assured her she could keep the ladder as long as she needed it to finish the painting job. Michael said with school starting he would have to come on weekends after his homework was done to keep working on the lawn. Maria had put a healthy portion of the leftover salad into one of the new glass bowls and put it in the fridge.

John Irving said how much he'd enjoyed the party and invited her to come out to the cemetery to visit him again. "I will," she promised, thinking that the cemetery might be a little bit lonely.

Sarah and Kelly were ready to leave a few minutes later.

Sarah clasped Marianne's hands and said, "I really enjoyed meeting your grandmother. She's a very strong woman, and it was a gift to meet her."

"You're welcome," Marianne said sincerely. "I think she really enjoyed meeting you, too." Suddenly remembering the gifts she had for her two friends, she said, "Wait! I have something for you. I almost forgot." She dashed into her bedroom and brought back two little boxes.

"Oohh, presents!" Kelly said delightedly. "What's this for?" She and Sarah moved back to the sofa and sat down again.

"You recently rendered me a great service," Marianne said formally. "This is a token of my appreciation."

Kelly demurred but opened her box and took out a silver hairpiece. Three overlapping oak leaves molded in silver, shaped into a gentle arc lay on her palm with a silver pin to hold it in place. "Oh, wow! That's gorgeous! You got this in Dream Time didn't you? I've looked at this a bunch of times but couldn't find a reason to splurge." Kelly stood and gave her a quick hug and hastened to pull her thick blonde hair with its two lavender locks into a ponytail and slide the pin through the ends of the leaves. It looked as good as Marianne had thought it would.

Sarah opened her box and pulled aside the fluffy stuff inside. There was a polished rose quartz disc surrounded by swirls of silver hanging from a fine silver chain. "It's beautiful," Sarah said softly. Kelly helped her do up the clasp under her hair. It hung poised below her collarbone, framed by the vee of her shirt. "Marianne, you didn't need to—" she started.

"You guys totally saved my bacon," Marianne interrupted firmly. "Yes, I had to. I'm glad you like them."

"I promised I would help you shield your space this weekend. Let me know when it's a good time for you," Sarah remembered.

"I'll give you a call," Marianne promised. They left shortly after. The rain had let up, but it was still dripping under the trees.

Marianne turned back to see Ruari getting ready to leave.

"They must be really good friends of yours," he said, clearly having watched the presentation.

"They are," she said simply. She glanced back at the coffee table and the new sculpture that stood there. "Thank you again for 'Sleeping Lady.' It's really beautiful. I feel a little—" she started.

"I wondered if you wanted to get coffee tomorrow some time?" He blurted without letting her finish.

She blinked and paused before saying, "I would. What time?"

"How about ten at the co-op?"

"I'll meet you there," she agreed.

"Okay, then. See you there. Thanks for inviting me."

"I'm glad you could make it," she said, smiling, and saw him out the door.

Ruari walked out to his battered white truck and climbed in. Rain beaded the hood and windows, and he turned on the wipers as he pulled away from the curb. He'd asked her out, and she'd said yes, but he'd seen the hesitation in her face and wondered why. 'Sleeping Lady' had been a labor of love, completed over the last three weeks, and he was happy with how it had turned out. It certainly wasn't a vacuum cleaner or set of Tupperware. She said she'd liked it, so why the hesitation?

Marianne's body had felt very nice pressed against him when she'd thanked him, and he hoped that wouldn't be the last time. But she'd hugged Maria and her mother as well and maybe felt obligated to hug him as well.

He sighed and rested his head on the steering wheel for a moment at the stop sign. He hadn't gone out with a woman in quite a while and felt very rusty on reading the signals. Maybe coffee tomorrow would clear things up.

Heading back to his workshop/apartment, he pondered the last few hours. He'd enjoyed meeting the Cavarelli's, and John had sounded interested in a handcrafted entertainment center for the family. Maybe that would turn into a real commission. He'd seen John Irving from a distance before and wondered how Marianne had gotten to know him. Sarah and Kelly were familiar faces from high school and around town. He knew Mrs. Thomas slightly from having taken care of things at the house before. She was nice and a little dotty, the way old people sometimes were. Selene Singleton, Marianne's grandmother, however, was formidable, in spite of her age. She reminded him of his own Scottish grandmother who had been tough as nails all her life. Selene had a way of looking right into a person, past all the external nonsense that people put up to show others. He liked her. Marianne's mother seemed motherly and anxious about her daughter.

Well, one thing at a time. If his date with Marianne tomorrow was still confusing, he might have to ask Erin to interpret.

Marianne walked slowly back to the dining room, thinking about a date with the handsome Ruari. Her mother, grandmother, and landlady were industriously putting away leftovers and cleaning up. Mrs. Thomas sat comfortably in a chair with her walker to one side, chatting amiably with Grandma Selene as she put things into the new glass containers. Her mom had washed them and brought them out to be used right away.

"You'll have food for a couple of days, lovie," Grandma Selene said.

"Thanks for coming, everybody. I feel like I live here properly now," Marianne said.

"Of course you do! We'll be on our way soon. I think it stopped raining finally," Selene said.

Marianne nodded. "Mom, I don't have a spare bed yet, so I'm all set to drive you home again."

"Are you sure?"

"Yup. We can go any time you're ready."

They finished tidying up in the dining room and kitchen, and Grandma Selene and Lily Thomas took their leave.

In the car on the way back, Marianne's mother said, "You have nice friends. I hope you can settle there for a while."

"Me, too, Mom."

"Ruari Allen seems like a very nice young man," her mother ventured. "He is certainly a talented artist! I'm surprised he works as a handyman."

Marianne shrugged. "He's got to pay his bills, I'm sure." She paused and then said cautiously, "I'm having coffee with him tomorrow."

"That sounds lovely, dear," she said warmly. "Take it slow, but take it, as they say. Don't let Geoffrey be the last man in your life."

Marianne nodded and thought, you mean, like you let dad be the last man in your life? She'd never asked her mom about that before but felt that the moment was right. "Mom? Did you ever want to marry someone else after Dad died?"

Her mother was quiet for a bit. Then, staring out he window, she said, "I loved your father. He was a good man. We were married for eight years, and they were good years. I have had male friends since then, but none for whom I really wanted to 'keep house,' as it were. Losing your dad was hard. But I learned to be independent, and that was valuable. I didn't want to let go of that. It works for me." She turned to Marianne and said, "Be sure solitary independence is what you want. What works for you. It can be lonely," she admitted. "Will you listen to some advice from your old mum?"

Marianne nodded, keeping her eyes on the highway traffic.

Her mom turned to her and said, "Get to know Ruari. Take your time. You may have rushed things with Geoffrey—or you both may have just been too young. This time around, take your time."

Marianne nodded again. "Thanks, Mom."

The miles slipped by, and Marianne, encouraged by the mood, cleared her throat. "Mom? I've been thinking. I feel like we lost touch with each other over the last ten years or so. Geoffrey kind of consumed my life, and I let him." She paused, feeling vulnerable, "I miss you. I miss how we used to talk to each other. I know you don't believe my explanation about the house and the last few weeks, but, I don't care."

"Honey, I'm sorry. You seemed busy and happy, and I didn't want to intrude. I probably should have." She added diffidently, "I'd like to see more of you."

Unshed tears glittered on Marianne's eyelashes, and she said thickly, "Thanks, Mom. Me too."

By the time they pulled into her mom's driveway, it was deep twilight. Marianne got out and hugged her mom hard.

Mom leaned back and said, "Do you want to come inside for a

bit?"

Marianne shook her head. "I'm actually pretty tired. I think I'd like to go home. Call you soon?"

When she got back home, Oscar met her at the door meowing loudly. Her house seemed quite empty after the party, and it was dark outside, the evenings of summer getting shorter as the fall drew nearer. She opened a can of food for Oscar and got a fork and Maria's salad and went to sit in the living room. She sat cross-legged on the sofa and looked at 'Sleeping Lady' as she ate.

She was really happy that Ruari had come, but the sculpture was too much for a housewarming present. She wanted to get to know him better but didn't want to be intimate too soon. She remembered how warm and solid his body had been when she'd hugged him, and how pleasantly her insides had squirmed. Some part of her was putting on the brakes, though. Her relationship with Geoffrey had made her cautious, and her disastrous one-night-stand had certainly left her gun shy. She hoped Ruari would understand. Well, she'd been forthright with him up to now, and he'd come back. So, thus far it was a good strategy.

She finished the salad and snuggled with Oscar awhile, feeling happy and content, remembering her epiphany during the party. She felt like she had come home.

That night she dreamed of someone following her down twilight city streets. She was trying to get somewhere to meet people and do something important, but someone was following her. The surroundings turned into a blend of Maple Hill and city as she turned up the street where her house was. No matter how fast she walked, the footsteps were always behind her. She was nearly there, when the footsteps caught up with her. She turned and looked straight at her shadowy pursuer and said fiercely, "Okay, time to dance."

And she surfaced, her dream melting away like a snowflake on her glove. She never completely awoke and fell asleep again almost immediately.

Chapter 28

SATURDAY dawned with sunny skies and Oscar demanding breakfast. She showered and examined herself in the mirror carefully. Her legs were healing nicely but were still peppered with red welts. Her wrist continued to display black, poky stitches, but the edges of the slice were healing into a narrow red line and probably wouldn't scar much at all. Her wrist was itching, so she put more salve on it and lightly rebandaged the area to keep it clean. Luckily she was right handed, and she thought she might be able to sterilize a pair of scissors and tweezers and take the stitches out herself in a day or two. The bills for the Urgent Care Center were going to come in eventually and would probably be a shock.

She chose a pair of navy blue shorts hemmed above the knee and that hugged her figure nicely, along with a white and blue striped polo shirt. She brushed her hair and pulled it into a ponytail and regarded herself in the mirror. She didn't look particularly vulnerable (good). She also didn't think she looked particularly romantic (mostly good). She looked more like a fun person who was a sharp dresser (good for now). Friends, she thought, not lovers. Yet. She let the ponytail come down and used barrettes to pull her hair back from her face instead. That softened the camp counselor look. The scabbing on her legs looked like she'd taken a tumble in a gravel pit. Oh, well, Ruari already knew about her injuries, so no need to hide. Ankle socks and sneakers completed her outfit.

It was already 9:30 by the time she got her things together, and she decided to indulge in a pastry from the co-op for breakfast. She told Oscar she was going out and headed up the walk towards Main Street. The day was freshly washed after yesterday's rain, and everything sparkled. The sun was hot, but the air was cooler and less humid. It was a little preview for Fall. She smiled and hummed a little to herself.

Main Street was busy with traffic. There seemed to be a lot of extra people even for a weekend. She wondered what was going on when she realized it was Labor Day weekend. There must be a lot of people from the city up for a long weekend before school and September started. All the shops had their pennants and flags flying in the breeze with doors open and merchandise hanging invitingly from nearby sales racks. Marianne browsed a bit on her way trying to time her arrival.

Outside the co-op her phone jingled faintly from her purse, and she paused to extract it. Grandma Selene was named on the display.

"Hi, Grandma!" She said happily.

"Hello, dear, how are you?"

"I'm great! It was so nice to see you yesterday."

"Yes, me too. Listen, where are you?"

Marianne realized her grandmother sounded agitated and sobered immediately. "I'm in Maple Hill outside the co-op. Are you okay, Grandma?"

"Yes, dear, but I was out watering the flowers in front a while ago, and a car drove past the driveway very slowly. It might have been a tourist or someone looking for a different address, but it was silver. Doesn't Geoffrey drive a silver sedan of some kind?"

Her happiness burst like a soap bubble to be replaced by a creeping dread. "Yes, a Lexus. Do you think it was him?"

"I didn't get a good look at the driver, and I've been debating whether to call you or not. I don't want to worry you unnecessarily."

"No, that's okay. I'm meeting a friend soon, Ruari actually. Hopefully, it wasn't Geoffrey, and it's nothing to worry about." In spite of that, she reflexively scanned the street around her.

"I hope so too, dear. I'm sorry to bother you. Have a good time with your young man."

"Thanks. I'll call later." She pressed end and slipped the phone back into her pocketbook. Her carefree happiness had vanished in a wash of apprehension. Just then she saw Ruari walk up.

He was wearing a terra cotta colored T-shirt that said "Red Dirt Shirt" on it and a pair of blue shorts. His legs were strong and freckled. The new shorter haircut looked nice on him. His white teeth flashed in a smile when he saw her and sent a pleasant tingle through her in spite of her anxiety.

"Hey, how are you today?" He asked.

She put on her own smile, determined not to let Geoffrey's possible presence ruin her outing. "I'm fine. You?"

"Good. I haven't had breakfast yet, have you?"

She shook her head. "Me neither. I figured I'd check out the cinnamon rolls from the bakery here," she said.

"They're amazing!" He said enthusiastically.

They entered the cool space within and made their way to the bread racks and bakery bins. All the bread was out for the day and smelled so heavenly she impulsively bought a loaf of brioche. Then she got a huge cinnamon roll to eat now. Ruari selected a ham and cheese pastry, and they went to the drinks bar. She ordered a jasmine green tea and had them ice it. Ruari chose a large black coffee and doused it liberally with cream. After they paid they made their way outside and fortunately had to wait only a few moments for a table on the sidewalk to free up.

They settled themselves on the metal chairs and took a few bites of breakfast before talking. Marianne scanned the street and sidewalk surreptitiously.

"Thanks for having me at your party yesterday," Ruari said. "It was nice to meet your mom and grandmother. They seem really nice."

"They enjoyed meeting you too," Marianne confirmed as she took another wonderfully sweet, sticky bite. Food was helping to calm her nerves. "These are so good. I could become addicted to them!"

"Have you tried the other breakfast pastries?" Ruari answered.

"They're good too. I've had way too many of them myself."

They ate and talked of inconsequential things for a few more minutes before Marianne said, "The sculpture you gave me is really beautiful. Thank you. I…I wondered why you gave it to me?"

He finished chewing the last bite and said, "I work with wood and make furniture and practical things most of the time. Sometimes, though, I have the unexplained urge to make something like 'Sleeping Lady,' and I have to make it. If I don't, all my other work goes to hell until I work it out of my system. I didn't know you when I started 'Sleeping Lady.' I just worked on it. After I met you a couple of times, I just had a feeling it was supposed to go to you. I don't know why." He shrugged.

Marianne considered this and said slowly, "It's an unusual housewarming gift to give someone you hardly know, that's all. I was just wondering whether you expected anything of me?" She looked uncomfortable.

He said uncertainly, "Expected anything of you? No…" Then his brain caught up with her words. "Oh! I'm sorry. Uh, no, you're right, I don't know you very well. I don't—I'm not asking anything of you—I didn't mean anything by it! I just had a feeling it was supposed to go to you," he finished helplessly.

Her lips curled upward in relief. He looked sweet when he was confused. "That's okay then. I like you. I just don't want to rush things. That's all."

He smiled back apologetically. "I haven't gone out with anybody for a while, so I'm rusty on all the signals."

"Ruari," she said with the air of one laying her cards on the table, "I just got divorced after being married for fifteen years. Impulsively, I went out with one person for one night after that, and it was a complete disaster. I'm not in any hurry. I'd rather get to know you as a friend first."

He nodded in understanding. "Fair enough." They sipped their beverages in silence for a moment, letting things settle again. "You said you would tell me what happened to your ghostly roommates."

"Well, I didn't think I could manage it alone, so Sarah came over. You know she handles things like that?"

"Yeah. She has—"

"Marianne! What a wonderful surprise to see you here!" A garishly bright man's voice interrupted them.

Marianne stiffened in her seat. She'd forgotten to keep an eye on the street, and Geoffrey had snuck up on her like he had so many times in the last several months. Immediately she cringed, feeling guilty for no reason at all. Her carefully gained sense of independence and confidence evaporated in the flash powder flare of his voice. The bite of roll suddenly tasted like ashes in her mouth, and she choked a little swallowing it. She took a sip of tea to clear her throat and coughed as a little went down the wrong way.

By the time she turned to look at him, Geoffrey was grinning delightedly at her discomfort. He was dressed in a white polo shirt with crisp khaki slacks that set off his classic good looks and expensive tan. His designer sunglasses were resting jauntily atop his perfect haircut. He was alone for the moment, and Sandra was nowhere in sight.

"How unexpected to see you here!" he said again, coming closer to the table where they sat. "Who's your little friend?"

Marianne sat, paralyzed with fear and agony. He'd found her. There was nowhere left to hide. In spite of the warnings she'd received, she found herself falling back into old habits, and all she could reply was, "Um…"

Ruari rose to his feet and held out his hand and said guardedly, "Hi, nice to meet you." Geoffrey automatically clasped the proffered hand and did a double take when he realized the other man was taller than him. The momentary distraction allowed her to rally a little.

Geoffrey then invited himself to sit down in the unoccupied seat at their table. Ruari resumed his seat but remained watchful.

Marianne, hunched in her chair, said miserably, "Why are you here?"

He gave her an exaggerated look of hurt and said, "I'm just up here for a weekend in the country with Sandra. I'm upset that you never return my calls or emails anymore."

Marianne tried to pull herself together. "We're divorced, Geoffrey. I don't have to talk to you."

"Well, that's rude. I thought we could at least remain friends." He looked her over again, his gaze falling on her bandaged wrist. "What happened to you?" He said without much sympathy. "You always were such a klutz."

He was wallowing in her suffering, and she knew it. She looked in his eyes and was reminded forcefully of George Rutherford. His Uncle George who was now gone. Something in her stood up straighter, shaking off the habits of the last ten years with some effort. She heard her grandmother's voice again, "Singletons are strong people."

She lifted her head, ignored his question, and said more clearly, "Geoffrey, if you're looking for me, you found me. Is there something you want to say? If there is, just say it."

"Well, the little mouse has some backbone left," he said quietly, his eyes hardening. He leaned forward in his seat, putting his hands firmly on the table. "All right. The message is this," he glanced at Ruari before fixing his gaze on her again, "whatever you know about me, know this: you can't ever hide from me. I will always find you, so you'd better watch it."

The veiled threat was clear, but it took Marianne a moment to understand the reference. It dawned on her that he thought she would expose his bad behavior at work and perhaps take away all he had achieved. Sarah and Kelly had been right.

She took a chance and came out swinging. She took a deep breath, looked into his dark eyes and said, "You're right. I do know how you got your promotion, and it wasn't because you were the best candidate. I *could* call your boss and tell him everything, but I won't. You know why? Because we are divorced, and I don't give a damn what you do anymore."

A bitter look twisted his handsome face. "You little bitch. I should have gotten rid of you years ago," he snarled, hoping to hurt her again, but Marianne was past that.

Ruari made a noise and moved in his seat, but Marianne reached out and touched him on the arm, silently asking him to wait.

Just then, a buxom, beautiful blonde woman called brightly from the sidewalk, "Hi, Geoffy, there you are!" and approached the threesome. Sandra was dressed to show a lot of cleavage and long, elegant legs. "Oh, hi, Marianne! Fancy meeting you here!" Her big smile was a little guarded but seemed to be innocent of guile.

Geoffrey ignored Sandra and sneered, "Your boyfriend doesn't know what a little freak you are. When he finds out, he'll dump you, and you'll be sorry you ever left me."

"Geoff, honey? What's going on?" Sandra's smile faded and she looked confused.

"Nothing, baby," he said, his eyes still staring at Marianne, lip curled. "My ex here saw me passing by and called me over." Sandra put her hands possessively on his shoulders and looked defiantly at Marianne.

Something inside Marianne snapped. She surged to her feet, scraping her chair across the cement, and deliberately closed the distance between them, her gaze locked on his face. She was shorter than he was, but he was pinned to his chair by his new girlfriend. "Geoffrey," she said coldly and precisely, "we are done. I don't give a rat's ass what you do anymore. You can lie, cheat, and steal to your heart's content. We are divorced. Sandra is the woman in your life now and has been for over a year. If she isn't enough for you, that's between you and her. From now on leave me alone. Stop following me, texting me, emailing, and phoning me. If you don't, I can and will get a Restraining Order against you."

Geoffrey involuntarily leaned back in his chair, his sneer melting into uncertainty. She had never stood up to him like this before, and he was taken aback. "You wouldn't dare," he said.

Marianne, now vibrating with anger and adrenalin, looked at him as if he were a roach in the kitchen and said softly, "Try me. I would make sure it was delivered to your office." Her stare bored into him like a laser beam. "Geoffrey, go away and stay away from my town."

With a visible effort she turned to Sandra, softened her expression, and said pleasantly. "Sandra, just for the record: he's lying. He approached me. If you don't believe me, you can ask anyone here." She gestured to the crowd in general. Sandra stood openmouthed, shocked at being addressed, and Marianne continued almost gently, "Remember *this* man. This is the *real* Geoffrey. I hope he never aims this at you. I hope you are both happy together for a very long time. I really do."

Turning back to her ex, her eyes narrowed as she said with finality, "We. Are. Done. Walk away from here." And she stared at him, bristling with such steel in her expression that Sandra, looking alarmed, tugged at his arm. "Geoffy, let's go. She's crazy!"

Geoffrey pushed his chair back awkwardly, allowing Sandra to pull him away. Trying to restore some dignity, he fumbled his glasses down over his eyes and said, "This isn't over."

Marianne replied, "Yes it is."

With a final impotent glare over his shoulder he moved away, and the crowd parted to let them retreat. Someone started clapping and suddenly the whole crowd was clapping. Marianne's focus expanded and she realized she and Ruari were at the center of a crowd of fascinated onlookers who were applauding as if they'd seen a particularly good bit of street theater. Her face reddened in horrified embarrassment and she turned away. Abruptly she realized she was shaking and nearly fell into her seat again, placing her forehead on her palms. The clapping died away and people turned back to their own lives.

"Are you okay?" Ruari asked in concern. He'd been ready to intervene, but mostly, he just witnessed the confrontation. She hadn't needed anything from him. People who had been staring at the spectacle were starting to turn away again now that the show was over.

"I think so. I just need to sit for a few minutes." She closed her eyes and listened to the hammer of her heart in her ears. "I'm really sorry about that," she murmured apologetically. "That was my ex. Now you know why I'm divorced. I knew he was coming, but I didn't expect it to be today."

"Remind me never to make you mad," he said fervently.

She laughed shakily.

"Do you want—need to go home?" He inquired carefully, wondering if there were any residual daggers that might hit him.

She shook her head wearily. "No. I've tried very hard to keep my house a secret from him. I wouldn't put it past him to follow me home even now."

Ruari was silent for a few minutes, thinking furiously. "You said last week you like hiking. Would you like to take a walk somewhere outside of town? I know of a few nice places to walk."

Marianne considered. "That might be a good idea. It might help me unwind." She nodded. "A walk sounds nice. Where did you have in mind?"

"I know a bunch of places that are real hikes, but that might be more than you want just yet. Have you ever been to a place called Innisfree?"

She shook her head. "What's that?"

"It's an old estate in Millbrook that was landscaped into a Chinese cup garden in the first half of the twentieth century. It's mostly flat, very peaceful, and really beautiful."

She took a deep breath, released it, and opened her eyes. "That sounds nice. Is it far?"

"Maybe half an hour to forty minutes away. We could take a little more food and have a picnic?" He suggested tentatively.

"Okay." She was slowly recovering. "I've got the brioche. I could go back inside and get some cheese and fruit or something."

Still watching her with concern, he offered, "I'll go get my truck and meet you back here. Will you be okay alone? Do you think they'll come back?"

She shook her head. "I'll go inside. It would take more chutzpah than he's shown before to chase me in there. Besides, Sandra is with him, and maybe she'll be jealous enough to distract him." She giggled and then laughed with an edge of hysteria. "I never thought I'd say that," she gasped. She saw his slightly alarmed expression and waved her hand vaguely. "Go. I'll be here when you get back."

Ruari left with some misgivings. He walked quickly down the side streets to his workshop. He'd left his truck there, knowing how crowded the holiday weekend was likely to be. Wow, he had no idea Marianne could be so forceful. When he'd met her she'd seemed so vulnerable and fragile. Her ghost stories had indicated a strange side to her that he couldn't resolve comfortably. The day he'd seen her with all her injuries so fresh and the haunted look in her eyes, he'd just wanted to gather her into his arms and protect her.

Today, though, she'd confronted her ex husband and cut him coolly down to size. If he'd been in the other guy's shoes, he'd have slunk home with his tail between his legs and never bothered her again. He didn't know the other guy at all but hoped he'd leave Marianne alone after this. Ruari was impressed with her. Something had happened to bring out this unflinching backbone in her. If this is who she was, he kind of liked it. She had always been honest with him even when the honesty didn't leave her in the best light. Other women had been flirty and willing to like all of his likes just to impress him. He'd never been sure of their sincerity, though. Marianne was very different. Someone he was willing to take the time to get to know. He found he was looking forward to showing her one of his favorite places.

She met him on the sidewalk with a co-op paper bag full of

things, and he opened the door from inside. She climbed in and said with a weary smile, "Okay. Drive on."

They had a wonderful afternoon together eating as they overlooked the water by the parking lot first and then walking the trail around the lake. Marianne was completely charmed by the quiet tranquility of the gardens and finally relaxed. She told him the story of sending Anne and George on to their proper afterlives, and he was suitably intrigued. They talked about books and music and movies and found that one title led to another. She told him about her love of history and he, about his fascination with wood. It was a perfect antidote to the harsh scene earlier.

He brought her back late in the afternoon and walked her to her doorstep.

"Thank you for a really wonderful afternoon," she told him sincerely.

"Maybe we can do it again some time?" He asked.

"Minus the drama!" She clarified with a smile.

He laughed. "Definitely."

"When are you free again?" she asked. "I have some painting to do tomorrow, and I need to get back to my history colleague about the course curriculum."

"I work most days and am on call for emergencies at the rentals," he said.

She nodded. "Maybe next week some time, then?"

He agreed and made himself turn and head back to his truck. It had been a really peaceful afternoon. Their conversation had been relaxed, not weird, and that was refreshing. Part of him still wanted to feel her lips on his, but he now understood her need to take time before they got there. With any luck, there would be many more days like this one, and the kissing would come in time.

He turned back as he climbed into his truck and was gratified to see her still at the door waving to him.

Marianne closed the door behind her. They'd had such a lovely time together: relaxed, friendly, no expectations. A visceral part of her still tingled and trembled at the thought of getting naked with Ruari, but her mind was also gratified by their simple walk and conversation. They'd put little offerings out for each other; a book or movie they'd liked or hated and listened to each response. There were enough correlations and overlaps that there was room for more discussion. They'd filled two hours and a picnic with comfortable conversation.

Inevitably, her mind returned to the scene on the sidewalk that morning. Geoffrey showing up with Sandra was so like him. He'd come to intimidate and gloat, but she'd stood up and kicked his butt like Kelly had said. She still wasn't entirely sure where her moxie had come from. Perhaps she had to thank George and Anne for teaching her how to stand up for herself as well as for helping her meet people. Knowing she had friends who would watch her back helped too. She replayed her words, savoring the look of dismay and anger on Geoffrey's face, a smile spreading across her own lips. It had been very satisfying to tell him off. She didn't think Geoffrey would come after her again. Something told her that, like a playground bully, he'd been slugged hard enough that he would leave her be in the future.

Ruari had seemed okay in spite of her show down with her ex. She trusted that boded well for their future and reasoned, if he hadn't wanted to spend time with her, he wouldn't have invited her to Innisfree. She looked forward to seeing him again and hoped it would be soon.

All in all, her life had taken a turn for the better.

Acknowledgements

This is my first published story, and I have many thank yous! First, to my husband, Austin, who is my first, best reader and doesn't mind reading the same darn thing over and over. He has supported me from its inception three years ago and has always thought I should write. He is also has a good eye for consistency and the male perspective. To my editor, Jacqueline Beam: we are both new at this and let's hope we have many more collaborations. This novel wouldn't be half so good without you. Any mistakes still contained in its pages are solely my own! To Victorine who produced a wonderful cover unbelievably quickly. I hope to have many more collaborations with you. To my children who encouraged me to write and follow through to publication even though this story isn't "their cup of tea." I promise to write one that is more to your liking. To all the people who shared their experiences of the paranormal with me, you know who you are. To all my beta readers: Eric (who knew Marianne needed a new love in her life) and Betty (who knew there was something wrong with George from the beginning), Marta and Judy, Beth, Mom, Orion (who added punch), Kelton (who suggested multiple voices, thereby making the story deeper), and Kathy (who made some outstanding comments late in the process).

Writers are solitary by nature and need the input of living, breathing human beings. Being part of a supportive writer's group is incredibly rewarding and helpful. I am humbled to join you in the published world and encourage the rest of you to see your projects through to fruition. The Monday Night Writer's Group demanded more punch from the climaxes—thank you! Special kudos to Kayla: I wouldn't have gotten this far without your encouragement and guidance, you rock!

I did research in several places: the Starr Library in Rhinebeck, NY, the Wappingers Falls Rural Cemetery, NY (thank you Beth and Bill), Renaissance Woodwork in Pullman, WA (thank you Tom), Innisfree Gardens in Millbrook, NY, and, of course, the Internet. There were many websites that supplied information on spirits, haunted houses and dream communication.

Maple Hill Chronicles

"Dreams of Fire" introduces the fictional town of Maple Hill, New York which is nestled in the hills of the Hudson Valley. It is a composite of several places I've lived in or visited. I loved creating it and look forward to returning to Maple Hill in the future. There will be more stories with familiar faces and places as well as new ones, and I hope you'll seek them out! Ruari Allen will tell his story next in "Sylvan Dreams." Look for news about this and other upcoming stories at PalouseDigitalPress.com, Elizabeth R. Alix home page.

About the Author

Elizabeth R. Alix is a pen name. I grew up in the Hudson Valley and presently live in the Inland Northwest. Having come for graduate school in anthropology, I stayed for the bucolic countryside. I worked on the Ellis Island Museum project many years ago and have camped on remote, deserted islands in the chilly north while searching for traces of ancient Aleuts and other early newcomers to North America. I briefly contemplated becoming a forensic anthropologist but chose to write instead, so I don't have to leave beautiful eastern Washington. Otherwise, I am devoted to my family and have spent many hours being Taxi Mom. Now that my children are nearly grown and flown, I can sit down and spend more time writing. My husband takes care of our little farm and is incredibly supportive of my writing.

Sign up for Elizabeth R. Alix's newsletter at PalouseDigitalPress.com

Contact the author at PalouseDigitalPress.com

Made in the USA
Charleston, SC
30 October 2015